Book III
Beyond Those Hills Series

BEYOND THE DARKNESS

Vernal Lind

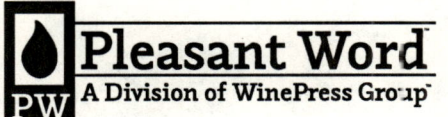

© 2010 by Vernal Lind. All rights reserved.

Pleasant Word (a division of WinePress Publishing, PO Box 428, Enumclaw, WA 98022) functions only as book publisher. As such, the ultimate design, content, editorial accuracy, and views expressed or implied in this work are those of the author.

No part of this publication may be reproduced, stored in a retrieval system, or transmitted in any way by any means—electronic, mechanical, photocopy, recording, or otherwise—without the prior permission of the copyright holder, except as provided by USA copyright law.

Unless otherwise noted, all Scriptures are taken from the *Holy Bible, New International Version®, NIV®*. Copyright © 1973, 1978, 1984 by Biblica, Inc.™ Used by permission of Zondervan. All rights reserved worldwide. WWW.ZONDERVAN.COM

Scripture references marked KJV are taken from the *King James Version* of the Bible.

Scripture references marked NASB are taken from the *New American Standard Bible*, © 1960, 1963, 1968, 1971, 1972, 1973, 1975, 1977 by The Lockman Foundation. Used by permission.

ISBN 13: 978-1-4141-1409-5
ISBN 10: 1-4141-1409-5
Library of Congress Catalog Card Number: 2009902132

BEYOND THE DARKNESS

Contents

Prologue 7

Chapter 1. 9
Chapter 2. 17
Chapter 3. 25
Chapter 4. 33
Chapter 5. 43
Chapter 6. 53
Chapter 7. 63
Chapter 8. 73
Chapter 9. 81
Chapter 10. 89
Chapter 11. 95
Chapter 12. 103
Chapter 13. 111
Chapter 14. 119
Chapter 15. 127
Chapter 16. 135

Chapter 17	145
Chapter 18	155
Chapter 19	167
Chapter 20	177
Chapter 21	187
Chapter 22	197
Chapter 23	207
Chapter 24	217
Chapter 25	225
Chapter 26	237
Chapter 27	247
Chapter 28	257
Chapter 29	267
Chapter 30	275
Chapter 31	285
Chapter 32	295
Chapter 33	303
Chapter 34	315
Chapter 35	325
Epilogue	331

Prologue

"And darkness covered the face of the deep."

The darkness tonight reminded Matthew Anderson of the darkness before the creation.

He switched off the last light in the barn after finishing the evening chores. The cattle were settling down for the night. The warmth of the barn caused him to pause a moment, and he stood by the barn door, completely enveloped in darkness. Fears of what lay ahead gripped him.

Matthew stepped outside into the crisp November air. Again darkness surrounded him. The yard light must have burned out. Clouds prevented any light from the sky to help guide his way back to the house. For a moment he shuddered, thinking of his sons in distant countries and a war that never seemed to end.

This Minnesota winter night reminded Matthew of his forty-four years—he was no longer young. His back ached from the lifting and bending of his chores. Standing alone outside the barn, he missed his sons. He wished all his children were safe at home.

As the present darkness surrounded him, he thought back to the morning of the New Year and the message his wife, Ellen, had read. He thought of the constant bombing in London and the dangers people faced. Those words Ellen had read from King George VI's Christmas message to British citizens had new meaning now, even in America: "I said to the

Beyond the Darkness

man who stood in the gate of the Year, 'Give me a light that I may tread safely into the unknown.' And he replied, `Go out into the darkness and put your hand into the hand of God. That shall be to you better than light and safer than any known way.'"

Matthew turned toward the house where light showed through the kitchen window, beckoning him. "Lord," he prayed, "lead me beyond this darkness."

Chapter 1

November–December, 1944

The minute Matthew entered the kitchen on that last Wednesday of November, he knew something was wrong. Ellen's face was lined with sadness and concern.

"I have some bad news," she announced.

"It's not about Johnie or James . . . ?" Then he remembered Joe, who was almost like a son. "Or Joe?"

"No, it's Glenn Robertson's boy, Tim. He's missing in action, presumed dead."

Matthew slowly took off his coat. "When did you find out?"

"Just now. Mabel called. Glenn wanted you to know. They received the telegram only an hour ago."

"I should go over right away, but I don't know what to say."

"No, I think they're coming to church to the special prayer meeting. Mabel said Glenn wanted to be among friends at a time like this."

"I'm not sure how I'd feel if something happened to Johnie or James or Joe." He stopped himself as he became aware of the presence of his five-year-old son.

"Hi, Daddy," Michael called out. "When I'm bigger I'll fight those Japs and Germans." He stood on his tiptoes, stretching to his full height.

"I'll be big and strong like Johnie. Then you won't have nothin' to worry about."

"Won't have *anything* to worry about," corrected Ellen.

Michael flexed his muscles. "I'll fight. It doesn't matter how I talk."

Ellen motioned for Michael to wash his hands. "Let's hope you won't have to fight."

Matthew slowly took off his jacket and boots. "I remember when Glenn's boy first drove the tractor. I happened to stop by that day. Tim wasn't more than six years old—about Michael's age."

Michael piped up. "Next summer I get to drive the tractor."

Always cautious, Matthew put his hand on his son's shoulder. "We'll see about that."

During supper Michael chatted on, asking questions about every conceivable subject. The constant questions wearied his father.

After supper, while Ellen washed dishes, Matthew read the daily paper. He thought the war should be ending soon, but it didn't look that way from the details of the news. Glancing up, he couldn't help noticing the letters on the dining room table, including one from their son James, stationed somewhere in England. At least James worked in a military office, making use of his skills as a typist and writer. Even so, he faced the dangers of terrible bombing raids in London. It was hard to picture him as a twenty-year-old army man.

Johnie wrote infrequently, so his letters were a real event. When Matthew thought of Johnie, he thought of the way he drove the tractor, loved animals, and enjoyed being in the outdoors. This son faced the greatest danger.

There was also a letter from Joe, now somewhere in the South Pacific. His last letter had arrived over a year ago, so they weren't certain whether he was dead or alive—or in some Japanese prison camp.

Matthew turned to the funnies for escape. "The Neighborly Neighbors" and "Modest Maidens" were up to their usual antics. Comics brought a welcome relief.

"It's time to go to church," Ellen said as she handed him his coat.

Matthew looked lovingly at his wife. She was older now, but in his eyes she was still that beautiful, petite country teacher he had married twenty-one years ago.

Chapter 1

Seated at the prayer service, Matthew felt Michael's head on his lap. It was good to have one child at home, safe within the confines of the family. But he knew children grew up and moved away. Margaret, just seventeen, was attending normal school and would soon be a country schoolteacher. Carol, sixteen and a junior in high school, stayed with Matthew's sister Victoria in town. Their absence, along with the boys far away at war, caused him to feel lonely at times. He missed his children.

Matthew put down the hymnbook as they finished singing, and Pastor Strand began to speak. The congregation had decided to depart from their usual Bible study and prayer service and instead spend time in meditation and longer prayer. Pastor Strand made some introductory comments about prayer and the need for all to pray.

Matthew's mind wandered. Sometimes God seemed far away. *Somehow, if Tim Robertson has died, God must have withdrawn*, Matthew thought. Desperately he wanted to feel God's presence, but at this moment, he did not.

Pastor Strand's tone changed abruptly, bringing Matthew's mind to the present. He began to realize what his pastor was saying: "I have been deep in prayer for some time. I have prayed about my place in this Oak Ridge country church and community—and about my place in the world. Not since I felt God's call to the ministry have I felt such a burden. I don't quite know how to say what I have to say."

He stopped and the silence fell over the congregation. Matthew could sense that every person was listening intently.

Strand continued, "I have felt first a burden and then a call. And after much prayer and discussion with my wife, I have acted. In about six weeks, I will leave to become a chaplain in the military. With the war continuing as it is, there is a desperate need for chaplains to counsel and conduct services. I hate the thought of leaving the communities of Oak Ridge township and Lake View village, but I realize this is my time . . ."

The pastor paused again, but this time several voices spoke up simultaneously. "We'll miss you." "We hate to see you leave us." "What will we do?"

". . . but it is now time to leave this beautiful community," he continued. "I ask you, of course, to pray for me. And to continue these special prayer times as well." Changing the subject, he went on, "During this Advent season, we look forward to Christ's coming. We look forward to the arrival of Jesus, the light of the world." He went on to present

Beyond the Darkness

examples of how the light of Christ enters and brightens lives and shows the way.

Matthew felt himself caught up in the imagery of Christ as light. He sensed God's presence, but at the same time God seemed far away. He couldn't explain why—except that tragedies such as the likely death of Glenn's son should not happen. Why would God permit a good boy like Tim Robertson to be killed in action?

Suddenly and without warning, the room went dark—no light whatsoever. This was another blackout, a drill in case the enemy should attack. These drills had become regular reminders of what happened often in Europe and England.

After a moment of silence, Strand picked up on the imagery of light and dark. "This black darkness that we now experience is the world without Christ. Without Christ's presence in our lives or in the world, everything is black. Blackness and darkness mean lack of direction, lack of hope. People wander, not knowing where to go or what to do."

Matthew thought of the darkness of death. He had looked around for Glenn Robertson, but his friend was not present. Death and blackness and darkness went together—unless God was in the picture.

He felt Michael move and awaken next to him. Then his young son cried out in fear as he found himself in darkness and a strange place. Ellen whispered to her son, "Michael, it's OK. You're in church. The lights are out; we've just had a blackout."

"I'm afraid," he cried.

Pastor Strand picked up on the young boy's words and used them as an example. "Yes, Michael, we are afraid. But we look forward to the light. We look to Jesus as our source to conquer the fears. Dear Michael, just as you looked to your mom and dad, we look to Christ."

As suddenly as the lights had gone out, they came back on. Several amused laughs could be heard because of the appropriate timing of the moment.

"Yes," Pastor Strand smiled, "the lights are back on. And that illustrates a point. We may find ourselves in darkness—in dark and frightening situations. And we do face darkness and uncertainty in the days ahead. But these lights came on. We can now see our way. In that same way, Christ will come to us, help us, and guide us."

Prayer time followed, but Matthew's mind moved elsewhere. What could he say to Glenn? Glenn had placed much hope in his son, knowing

Chapter 1

he would take over the farm. Now those hopes were dashed. How would Glenn go on living and working?

Matthew prayed silently a different kind of prayer, known only to him and God. "Lord, this isn't fair. Why did You take Glenn's son? If there was any young man who walked in Your ways, it was Tim. Lord, why do you let these things happen? Why is this awful war going on anyway? Can't You force people to stop fighting?" He tightened his fists as if he were about to fight the enemy. Deep within thought and prayer, he felt Ellen tug at his sleeve.

"It's time to go," she said.

Matthew knew this was the beginning of something. He must be ready to comfort his friend. He could not continue to question God. He needed to assure Glenn that God was ready to comfort him.

The images of the blackout were still vivid in Ellen's mind. She felt that darkness again as she thought of James and Johnie at unknown places in England and Europe. She gazed at the snow in the fields and walked up the steps to her mother-in-law's home. Elizabeth Anderson was a woman of prayer. The intense prayer of the community women must continue. Each woman usually prayed alone, but today they met together to feel the physical presence of one another as a community in prayer.

Ellen stood on the threshold and looked toward the new house that replaced the one she had lived in with Matthew as a young bride. "Lord, give me strength to face whatever I must face," she prayed silently. "I feel this emptiness because James and Johnie are far away. I miss Margaret, but I know she must continue her education to become a teacher. And I fear what Carol is facing in Lake View. Lord. Take care of my children. They need Your direction." She paused and looked toward the hills in the distance. "I will lift up mine eyes unto the hills from whence cometh my help," she quoted a beloved scripture. "Lord, I feel so weak and unbelieving. I fear that Matthew is at a breaking point. And I'm finding it hard to take care of little Michael, who becomes more active day by day . . ."

The door opened and Martha greeted her sister-in-law. "Ellen, why are you waiting out here? Is something wrong?"

Beyond the Darkness

Ellen followed Martha into the kitchen. "I guess my heart is heavy. I'm thinking of my own little family as well as the Robertsons. I don't know how I could face what Mabel is facing."

"Mabel has decided to come with my sister. Mary's started to drive, and she's bringing her over."

Ellen greeted her mother-in-law and two other ladies from the community.

"We have some serious praying to do," said Nora, one of their close neighbors. "And we need to console Mabel."

At that moment Mary and Mabel entered the kitchen. The women immediately expressed their sadness about Tim. These usually reserved Scandinavian women gave rare hugs of affection.

Soon the women were seated around the kitchen table. Somehow it seemed the best place for good conversation and for prayer. They decided to have their coffee after the time of prayer, but an awkward moment of silence followed.

Finally Ellen broke the silence. "I think we should pray for Mabel and what she's facing."

Mabel, one of those women who rarely spoke in a group, began to talk. "I don't know how to say this, but I have the strongest feeling. Timothy isn't dead. I know he isn't. He's missing and will be found."

Ellen held her breath. She knew that "presumed dead" meant just that. It was unlikely that Tim would return.

"I read just the other day about a soldier who was thought to be dead. Somehow the tags were mixed. He was actually alive," Mabel continued

"Let's hope that's true," said one of the other women.

"I have this inner feeling that my son is alive. I dreamed about Tim last night. He said, `Mother, I'll be home soon.' I believe that dream was a sign."

"Let's pray about him and the others," Ellen replied.

During the next half hour, the women prayed—about Tim Robertson and then James and Johnie and Joe, along with several others. Ellen found herself lost in the prayers. She felt herself transported to the battlefields of Europe, the remote areas of the South Pacific, and the dry regions of northern Africa. She experienced a new assurance that God was there with her boys. Suddenly, however, a disturbing thought entered her mind. Yes, God was there, but would her boys return? God hadn't promised an easy life. In this life she might have tribulation, Scripture taught.

Chapter 1

As the prayer time ended, Mabel announced, "I feel better. I wish Tim could be home for Christmas."

Ellen chose her words carefully. "Yes, we pray and hope for the best. But I'm afraid we must also be prepared the worst."

"I don't think we can ever be prepared for bad things," Martha responded. "When my husband died, I knew the time was coming. But I was not prepared."

Ellen regretted her comment. "You're right. God will answer our prayers." However, she feared the worst.

Time passed quickly as the women drank coffee and tried to focus on happier times. Soon it was late morning, and Mary and Mabel and the other women went home. That left Ellen to wait for Matthew's return.

"Why don't you stay for dinner," invited Elizabeth. "I've got some canned chicken, and we'll peel a few extra potatoes."

"And I brought a fresh-baked pie from the café," added Martha.

"I don't know what to say. Matthew doesn't usually stay this late when he visits Glenn—not unless something's wrong. I let Michael visit school and said we'd stop on the way home to see if he should stay the full day."

"Don't worry, Ellen," comforted Martha, "Mrs. Peterson will have everything under control. She can handle children of any age."

Martha began to peel potatoes. Ellen experienced peace and security as she visited with her sister-in-law and mother-in-law, but she kept remembering the blackout from the night before. That darkness seemed to signal more darkness to come.

Chapter 2

It was one of those friendships that seemed eternal. Matthew always knew Glenn was nearby. They had been together throughout their lives. In many ways Glenn was closer than a brother.

After leaving Ellen at his mother's for the women's prayer time, Matthew drove another mile down the road to Glenn's. In spite of their long friendship, he hardly knew what to say. What could you say to a father who had more than likely lost his son?

Matthew got out of his '35 Chevy, a car that should be replaced. The place seemed deserted. Glenn wasn't in the house having coffee. Neither was he anywhere outside. No noises anywhere around the house or yard announced his presence, so Matthew walked toward the barn. Maybe that was where Glenn did his thinking.

The cattle moved about in the barnyard. Warm December weather meant the cattle could remain outside. Matthew called out to his friend, but there was no answer. He opened the barn door and called out again. Still no answer.

The hayloft, he thought, *is a good place for thinking. I bet he's in some corner.* Matthew climbed the ladder as quietly as he could. As he stood up to survey the large amount of hay filling the loft, he thought he heard sobbing. He wondered if he should interrupt his friend in such a private moment.

Beyond the Darkness

He stood still, spellbound by what he saw. Glenn had always seemed brave, self-assured, and in control. A man always in charge. Now he appeared a broken man.

Finally Glenn looked up.

"I'm sorry," was all Matthew could say.

"I come up here when I need to think. I didn't realize you had come."

"I heard about Tim yesterday. Ellen said you were coming to church last night. I thought I would see you then."

"I thought we should come, but I couldn't face people. Matthew, my pal, I'm glad you stopped to see me. I need a friend more than ever."

"You've been there for me time and time again." Matthew sat down on a clump of hay.

Glenn looked down into the straw. "I think of the many times Tim came up here to pitch hay. He was a good worker. Of all my boys, he's the one who loved the farm."

"He and Johnie were a lot alike."

Glenn seemed to be searching for words. "I know we have to fight this war. Stop Hitler and the bloody mess. And also keep those Japs in check."

"Yes, but I hate war."

"My mind tells me the cause is just. I think of the "Star Spangled Banner," where it says, "Then conquer we must, for our cause it is just." But why must I sacrifice my son?"

Matthew hesitated, then asked, "Isn't there a chance that Tim could be alive?"

"I'm afraid that's unlikely."

The two men sat quietly for several minutes. Words were unnecessary.

Finally Glenn spoke. "My wife . . ." His voice trailed off.

"What's wrong with Mabel?"

"Mabel absolutely denies that Tim could have been killed. She's somehow determined that he's alive."

"There is that chance, isn't there?"

"I suppose." Glenn stood up, abruptly changing the subject. "Well, there's nothing like a good cup of coffee."

An hour later, Matthew and Glenn still sat at the kitchen table when the loud rings of the telephone interrupted thought and conversation.

Chapter 2

As Glenn answered the call, Matthew heard the words at the other end: "Your son, Tim Robertson, has been confirmed dead. He was burned beyond recognition in the helicopter crash. His remains are in a sealed casket. The casket should arrive in your train station within a week. We apologize for this delay in informing you."

Glenn stood speechless—too stunned to respond.

The speaker at the other end waited, then questioned. "Are you still there, Mr. Robertson?"

"Yes, I heard you."

"Did you understand the message?"

Glenn slowly repeated, "Yes, my son is dead. The casket will arrive next week."

"You have our deepest sympathies, Mr. Robertson. The army would like to deliver these messages in person, but we don't have the personnel."

"Yes, I understand."

The caller made some other comments about contact and arrangements, words Matthew couldn't quite hear. His friend didn't seem to hear either.

Glenn hung up the phone and looked at Matthew. "He's dead. My son is dead. There's no question about it." He moved away from the telephone, his face showing nothing for the moment. His dark blue eyes stared straight ahead. It seemed to Matthew that his friend had left for another world.

Saying "I'm sorry" seemed meaningless. "Sit down, Glenn. This news is too terrible for anyone."

Glenn sat down slowly across from Matthew. 'I'm afraid I knew this was coming. I believed he was dead, yet I felt there was hope. I wanted to believe my wife."

"Is there anything I can do?" asked Matthew.

Glenn began to talk. "Awhile ago, I did something men aren't supposed to do. I cried. I think you're the only person to see me crying except when I was a young boy. Now I feel empty. I'm like one of those rocks. I can't feel a thing."

"Ellen keeps telling me that it's good to express your feelings. She says death is harder for men because they can't or don't cry. I think she's right."

Glenn took out a handkerchief and wiped his forehead. "I wish I could cry now. Instead I feel angry."

Beyond the Darkness

"War is evil," replied Matthew. "But our country is fighting the evil in that part of the world. Tim is a hero. He lived as a hero and died even more so a hero."

Glenn doubled his fist. "But why did it have to be Tim? He was always the good kid. He loved people. He was much kinder to others than I'll ever be. He'd give the shirt off his back. And he seemed to love God more than any of the rest of us."

Matthew nodded. "Perhaps Tim was ready to die. Others are not."

"I can't see that." Glenn pounded his fist on the table. "Tim loved life. He had more zest for living and working than anyone I know."

Matthew decided words were both unwise and unnecessary. He let Glenn continue to talk about Tim and the unfairness of life. He was unaware of the car that drove up. Suddenly the kitchen door opened and Mabel greeted them. "Hello, Matthew. Hello Glenn."

Glenn stood up, walked toward his wife, and then stopped short. In that moment, Matthew wished he were miles away. How do you tell someone her son is dead?

Glenn moved over to the kitchen window and turned away from his wife. Matthew heard his muffled sobs.

"What's wrong?" questioned Mabel.

Matthew began slowly, "Glenn just had a call." He waited for Glenn to speak, but his friend only looked away. "Your son Tim was killed in action. His body is being sent home."

Mabel looked at both Matthew and her husband. "No, that's not true. We prayed for his safety and well-being. He isn't dead. He's alive."

Matthew turned to Glenn, not knowing what to say. An awkward silence followed.

Glenn turned abruptly. "Mabel, that's not true. Don't be so thick-headed. You've got to believe the truth. Tim is dead."

Tears came to Mabel's eyes. "No, I still don't believe you."

The next hour was one of the worst Matthew had ever experienced. He tried to comfort Glenn and Mabel, but the talk turned into an argument between husband and wife. Finally Mabel stormed off in anger to her bedroom, slamming the door.

Glenn turned to Matthew. "She'll have to believe the truth when the casket comes."

"I'm sorry." Matthew felt the hollowness of his words.

Glenn moved toward the door. "Well, I guess there's chores to do. Matthew, you've got work too."

Chapter 2

"Let me know if there's anything I can do." With those words Matthew left his friend to his grieving.

"I know something's wrong," said Ellen as she washed the last dish from their noon dinner. "Matthew never is this late."

"Would you like me to drive you over to Glenn's?" asked Martha.

Elizabeth straightened the dishes in the cupboard. "Oh, I wouldn't worry. I remember when Matthew and Glenn got together as kids. They'd lose track of time and could be away for hours."

At that moment a car drove up. Matthew had returned. As Ellen watched him get out of the car, she knew something was wrong. She dreaded hearing his first words.

The three women greeted Matthew as he opened the door, and he didn't waste words. "Glenn got a call. Tim's dead. The closed casket will be at the train station next week."

Ellen rushed toward her husband. "Oh, Matthew, how awful! And how's Mabel doing?"

Matthew gulped. "I'm afraid she won't believe he's gone. She's in a bad way."

Ellen knew how hard this situation must have been for her husband. "And you were there all the time?"

"I wanted to help, but I couldn't."

Martha interrupted. "Brother, have you had dinner yet?"

"I'm not hungry."

Ellen knew he needed to eat. "You have to eat, Matthew, whether you feel like it or not. If you don't, you'll be sick."

Martha opened the oven door and took out the chicken and potatoes and placed them on the table. "Matthew, sit down and eat."

Matthew sat and bowed his head. Then he began eating slowly and soon more eagerly, devouring most of what Martha had placed before him. The women hovered over Matthew. Ellen could see he was hungrier than he thought.

When tragedy happened, a community like Oak Ridge moved into action. Ellen, Martha, and Elizabeth talked about hotdishes and other good things they would take over to the Robertsons. The telephone lines were busy. News spread even faster with the party line.

Beyond the Darkness

Matthew put down the regional county newspaper, *River Falls Daily Journal*, that evening. The house seemed all too empty without the older children. In the kitchen Ellen was finishing the dishes, but Michael was strangely quiet after his big day visiting in school.

The memory of Glenn sobbing about Tim's death still haunted him. And then Mabel's stubborn determination that Tim was not really dead. It seemed unfair that parents should have to face the death of a son.

Ellen interrupted his thoughts. "This is one of those days we wouldn't want to repeat."

"I believe this is one of the saddest days of my life—next to Pa's death. Everything seems bleak and dark."

In the corner where he played with his blocks, Michael seemed to be nodding off. Usually he would be talking and letting his blocks crash down again and again. Ellen turned to her young son. "Michael, I think it's time for bed. You've had a pretty big day."

He disguised a yawn. "I'm a big boy now. The teacher says I'm ready for school."

Ellen sat down and took out her mending. "You will be next fall."

"We don't want you growing up too fast." Matthew folded the paper and put it aside.

"I can't wait to be big like Johnie and James. Then, I'll go off and help fight."

Matthew regretted the way war seemed exciting to young boys. "The war will be over by that time."

"Oh, shucks," Michael stated, then yawned.

Ellen put down her mending. "Michael, you go on upstairs and get into your pajamas," she insisted. "Then we'll come up and hear your prayers."

Michael left his blocks and climbed the stairs slowly.

Ellen turned to Matthew. "It won't be long until our little boy won't be little any more." She picked up her mending again. "Mrs. Peterson seems to think we should send Michael to school. She says he's as far along as the two children in first grade."

Matthew thought a moment before responding, "You know, Ellen, it might be easier for you. Michael's quite a handful. He needs to be kept busy, and school will do that."

"I've thought the same. We'll have to see about it."

Chapter 2

At that moment, Michael cried out, "I'm ready. Come up quick."
Matthew followed Ellen up the stairs to Michael's room.
Ellen reminded her son, "Fold your hands and bow your head."
Obediently Michael bowed his head and began the prayer Ellen had taught him and her other children. It was not the traditional prayer used by many of their community.

"Jesus, tender Shepherd, hear me; bless Thy little lamb tonight; through the darkness be Thou near me; keep me safe till morning light." Michael paused. "I don't remember." Ellen prompted him and he continued, "All this day Thy hand has led me, and I thank Thee for Thy care; Thou hast clothed me, warmed, and fed me. Listen to my evening prayer." He hesitated again and then went on, "Let my sins be all forgiven; bless the friends I love so well; take me, Lord, at last to heaven, happy there with Thee to dwell." Michael hurried into the last part. "God bless Daddy, Mommy, James, Johnie, Margaret, Carol, and Michael; and bless Grandma and Joe. Please bring James and Johnie and Joe home fast. And bless Rover and my cat Spotty. And bless my calf." He yawned. "And keep all the animals safe and warm."

Matthew waited.
"What do you say at the end?" prompted Ellen.
"I was thinking."
"You don't need a long prayer," said Ellen.
"I thought God would hear better if my prayer was longer."
Matthew couldn't help smiling.
Ellen added, "Amen."
"Isn't God pretty busy?"
"God is everywhere," answered Matthew. "He hears everything."
"Really?" Then Michael added, "I wish He didn't hear some things."

Matthew started to answer, but Ellen motioned him not to. Within a minute Michael was sound asleep.

"Oh, to sleep like a child." Matthew said, remembering his older boys. From the beginning, James was the studious one with long prayers. Johnie, usually more exhausted from physical exertion, kept his prayers short.

Ellen switched off the lights. The momentary darkness reminded Matthew of the blackout. The darkness of war and the absence of his sons and Joe filled his mind.

Chapter 3

Matthew walked slowly to the mailbox. He dreaded this afternoon. Today was Tim Robertson's funeral. Glenn had seemed to be the strong one, while his wife still didn't accept the fact that her son was dead—even with the casket.

Getting the mail was always a welcome break. The *River Falls Daily Journal* and sometimes a letter helped brighten the day. He opened the box. Headlines about the war greeted him, and Margaret's letter fell out.

Matthew hurried back to the house. "Ellen," he called out as he entered. "We have a letter."

The sewing machine stopped, and Ellen stepped into the kitchen. "I've been sewing dresses for Margaret and Carol. It just seems too quiet now that Michael's determined to go to school."

Matthew took off his jacket and handed Ellen the letter. The two sat down at the kitchen table, and Ellen began to read.

"Dear Mom and Dad,

"I'm counting the days until Christmas and Christmas vacation. My life is filled with both that which is happy and sad.

"I can't tell you how sad I am about Tim's death. I am sure his parents are devastated. Tim was always so kind to us younger kids. If someone picked on me or the other younger ones, he got after them. Then the bullying would stop.

Beyond the Darkness

"Life is strange, isn't it? There is all this joy and happiness and anticipation as Christmas approaches. On the other hand, I feel swamped with work to do. We have all kinds of tests and projects to finish before Christmas break.

"I look forward to being in the classroom. I am more confident than ever that I want to work with children. Perhaps I shall have a writer or senator or minister or important leader in my classroom."

Matthew smiled. "Or perhaps she'll have a lot of ordinary farmers like her old dad."

"No person is ordinary," objected Ellen. "You are a remarkable man. And each student in the classroom has some special purpose in life." She continued reading Margaret's letter aloud.

"There's something else I want to tell you. This is the first time a fellow has asked me out when I haven't been at home. He's a little older. He's twenty-three. He farms three miles out of River Falls. He's one of the nicest fellows I've ever met. In fact, he reminds me of Joe."

Matthew interrupted. "He's too old for her. She isn't even eighteen. She can't be serious."

"Look at Mary and Ed. Your sister's nine years younger than her husband. That happens all the time. Older men marry younger women."

"Well," Matthew said, "she's still too young."

Ellen looked down at the letter and read on.

" His name is Hank, and I want you to meet him some time soon.

"I keep on writing to James and Johnie and Joe. We haven't heard from Joe for so long. Sometimes I wonder if he's dead or alive. I feel such a hurt about that. Joe seems almost like a brother. In fact, he is a brother in many ways."

Ellen cleared her throat. "This time Margaret's wrong. She has not thought of Joe as a brother for years. She has a crush on him."

"Joe would make a good son-in-law."

"I better finish the letter." Ellen went on.

"There's a shortage of rural schoolteachers, so I should have no trouble getting a job. I'm excited about getting out there and teaching children.

Chapter 3

"But for now, I can't wait to taste your good cookies, Mother. Dad, I'll even help you out in the barn now that the boys are away. And please, don't put up the tree until I get home. Please buy a big one. We'll make this Christmas into a good one, even though James and Johnie are far away."

Ellen stopped reading. "Except for Michael, our children are grown. This house feels empty without them."

"I think of the boys when I'm out working. I keep hoping one day Johnie will take over the farm. That's what he always dreamed of doing."

Ellen began to prepare their noon dinner. Out of the refrigerator she pulled leftover potatoes and roast. She began to fry potatoes and heat the roast, along with some creamed peas, finding some comfort in the routine of life.

Matthew stared straight ahead at the casket. Several sprays of flowers covered the stark, plain, brown coffin. Except for the flowers, it appeared cold and impersonal. This ordinary soldier seemed like a pawn, something to be used to win a war.

At the moment it felt as if God had deserted this place. Matthew looked at the stained-glass windows, especially at the one picturing Christ holding a young lamb. He wanted to be that lamb or that child held in his Father's arms. Matthew felt nothing; his inner being resembled an unyielding stone. Why? Why did these terrible things happen?

Awareness of the music began to bring about a change in Matthew. The organist was playing with deep feeling. Suddenly and without warning, Matthew wanted to cry, but he held back. The most intense emotion filled his whole being. He loved Glenn almost as much as he loved his family.

Tim Robertson entered his mind—blond, blue-eyed, tall, and muscular. Tim and Johnie could have been taken for brothers. He pictured these two young boys playing hide-and-seek and getting into mischief. He remembered the time they tried to ride the young heifers in the barnyard.

Sunlight shone on the large picture in the front of the church, depicting three disciples looking up as Christ ascended into heaven. The light reminded Matthew of the Easter message outside the tomb: "He is not here. He is risen!"

Tears began to flow. Matthew was overwhelmed by a realization of something eternal. This life was not the end; it was a beginning, an introduction to eternity. Matthew's handkerchief disguised the presence of his tears.

As he looked down, Ellen placed her hand on his shoulder. The cold emptiness he had felt disappeared and an overwhelming love filled his whole being. He wanted to enfold Ellen in his arms. He looked ahead two rows to see Martha and Ma, and he wanted to tell them how much he loved them.

He experienced a new strength. He felt the urge to pray. He began praying silently for James and Johnie and Joe. "Lord, keep them safe in Your loving care."

All at once Matthew traveled back in time. Johnie was not even six, and he was tagging behind Matthew. Before he was six years old, he wanted to drive the tractor. And somehow he managed to do just that. He wasn't afraid to take chances.

For some reason Matthew never felt as close to James, who always preferred Ellen—families were that way it seemed. Where there were several children, one parent always preferred or was preferred by a particular child. James was entirely different from Johnie. While Johnie didn't like school and books, James always had his nose in a book.

And Joe seemed like a son as well. Joe, so very much alone and separated from his blood family, had helped on the farm when urgently needed. Matthew remembered the way Joe and Johnie had competed in throwing bundles and deciding who would drive the tractor. Those harvesting days were etched in his mind forever.

Then he thought of Tim and Johnie as they'd played in the school yard. It seemed they would carry on the friendship tradition of their fathers. But now all that was over. War destroyed what could have been a wonderful friendship.

The organist began playing the refrain of "It Is Well with My Soul." The family walked in and took their places—Glenn and Mabel, their other son and two daughters, then Grandma Robertson, who seemed devastated by the loss of her grandson.

During the next hour Matthew was only partly aware of what was going on. Pastor Strand delivered a sermon that sounded like other funeral eulogies. The hymns stirred memories of earlier times and places. But a

Chapter 3

deeper question penetrated Matthew's being: Why should a parent have to bury his or her child? That was not the natural order of things. Children were supposed to take care of their parents and be there to bury them.

As the service ended, Matthew thought of other times he had walked down these same steps. For a moment, darkness enveloped his spirit. He felt an overwhelming loss of the security he used to feel as he thought of family and community.

The family and part of the congregation walked down the hill and across the road to Oak Ridge Cemetery, where the burial service began. Pastor Strand intoned the words of Scripture: "From dust thou came, and to dust shalt thou return."

Why all this struggle? Matthew wondered. *Why work hard for these things that do not last?* Pastor Strand had expressed those thoughts, he remembered. "We must remember that which is eternal. Live today with eternity's values in mind." Could a man truly live with those values in mind?

The traditional funeral lunch followed. Somehow the crowd at this occasion was more subdued than at other funerals Matthew remembered. Maybe it was because of the youthfulness of the man just buried.

Matthew followed Ellen over to his friend. She extended her hand to Glenn and then embraced Mabel. "We're so sorry. Let us know if there's anything we can do."

Matthew awkwardly shook his friend's hand and then more awkwardly Mabel's. As they turned to leave, Mabel's plaintive cry startled Matthew. "They sent us a casket, but I know Tim's not dead. I know it."

"Now, Mabel," said Ellen.

Mabel kept repeating, "There's been some mistake."

Ellen moved to embrace her. "We'll pray for you and the family."

Mabel turned away. "I still don't believe he's gone."

That evening after Michael's prayers, Ellen and Matthew sat at the kitchen table. He seemed to have a hard time concentrating.

"I can't help thinking of James and Johnie," began Ellen. "I know I shouldn't worry, but I can't help myself. There's so much that can happen."

Beyond the Darkness

Matthew put down the paper. "At times I feel so cold and empty. It's almost as if part of me is dead."

"I know—" Ellen stopped in midsentence. "It's as if a part of me is over in England and Europe someplace. I have that gnawing pain. It won't go away until they're home."

"The emptiness keeps coming back."

"I'm afraid of what will happen to those boys. I know them so well. I fear for the chances they might take."

"Johnie's the one to take chances," Matthew responded.

"Yes, but James takes different kinds of chances. If there's something to learn. Or if there's a story, he may well follow that story to dangerous places."

Matthew couldn't help remembering. "Yes, there was the time James wanted to see what a blizzard was like. I found him in the haystack, but he could have frozen to death."

"James is unique. Do you remember when Jake and some other fellows bullied him? I'm just afraid some of the guys will make fun of him. Some fellows can be vicious."

Matthew saw the pain reflected in Ellen's face. "I guess a man has to learn to take care of himself. He has to stand up to bullies."

"But James is kind and sensitive. He isn't likely to do that," she said.

Matthew couldn't help remembering his own hurts when he felt he didn't quite measure up. "We must pray for him," he replied.

"You know, Matthew, we each have a son who is like us. I see so much my own personality in James. And I see your likes and personality in Johnie."

Matthew knew his wife was right. "Yes, Johnie loves the outdoors and the land and farming. That's what I love. But I fear Johnie takes many more chances than I would. In war that could be deadly."

Ellen stood up and went over to the refrigerator. "I think we need some hot milk or we'll be awake all night." Hot milk always seemed his wife's solution to a sleepless night.

Matthew thought of the many times they'd sat at this table through the years, talking over problems and trying to find solutions. This time the solutions seemed beyond their human capabilities.

Ellen brought out cups and poured the hot milk. "I guess our real responsibilities are right here. We have Carol. Of course, Margaret's practically on her own. And we have precious little Michael."

Chapter 3

"Michael's in such a hurry to grow up," Matthew stated. "He's ready for school, the way it looks." He thought a moment. "But I wonder about Carol and what she's doing."

"That reminds me," said Ellen, "Victoria wants to talk with us. I think it's something about Carol."

"Carol's a real charmer if she wants to be. But she can be a handful."

Ellen gave a quick laugh. "Your sister Victoria doesn't give in to charm. She's always the teacher and principal. And she can be suspicious of some students."

"Carol has met her match."

"We can't solve these problems, can we?" Ellen put down her cup. "Let's relax. We must place all our concerns in the hands of God."

In a symbolic gesture, Matthew folded his hands.

Chapter 4

Matthew and Ellen sat in front of Victoria's desk in the Lake View High School principal's office. Though Matthew had never been in high school, he felt as if the teacher had called him in for misbehaving. He felt even more awkward because this woman at the desk was his sister.

This was Thursday, the night of the Christmas concert. Victoria had called, asking Matthew and Ellen to come in early so they could talk.

"I suppose you're wondering why I asked you to come in," began Victoria. "It's rather an awkward situation because Carol is my niece."

"We know she's in good hands, staying at your place," said Ellen. "We knew she'd have to toe the mark."

Victoria didn't hesitate. "Well, she hasn't exactly toed the mark."

"Sis, you might as well let us know what the problem is," Matthew prompted.

"First, about the schoolwork and classes. Carol's grades have slipped from a B minus to D plus. She's not another Margaret, but she should be doing B work."

"We know that," he said.

"And teachers have reported that she falls asleep in class."

Ellen looked puzzled. "Why should that happen? She's certainly not studying that much at night."

Beyond the Darkness

Victoria's dark eyes flashed anger. "I just discovered something else. She spends a lot of time in her room. I guess I should have been suspicious of that. Anyhow, I found that she sneaked out after I was asleep. I caught her coming back at three in the morning."

"We've been suspecting there's some boyfriend," said Ellen. "Carol was not brought up to do things like that. We need to have a talk."

"I'm rather certain it's the banker's son, Jeff Grant. He's older and has a car. He had some kind of wound in the war, and he's home now."

Matthew's fatherly protectiveness found words. "I don't want my daughter going out with a man that much older. It's not right." At the same time he couldn't help thinking of Ed, who was almost ten years older than Mary.

"I just caught her last night—or rather this morning—so we haven't talked yet. When I left this morning, she was moving slowly. She did make it to school on time."

"We need to take care of this." Ellen gripped her purse. "We will confront Carol as soon as we can."

"Come to my place after the concert."

Matthew wondered aloud, "Shouldn't we take care of this ourselves? At home?"

Ellen hesitated. "You're right, Matthew. We'll come and get her right after school Friday. She'll be at home for the weekend."

"In the meantime," said Victoria, "I will have words with her about her grades and her curfew."

Matthew anticipated trouble. His stomach began to churn. He dreaded any kind of confrontation.

Ellen tried to enjoy the concert but couldn't. She kept thinking of Carol sneaking off to meet a man. Such conduct was far removed from any of the values they'd taught her.

She spotted Carol in the alto section of the choir. Carol had a strong voice that made her a valued member of any choir. Yet even from a distance, Carol appeared tired. Her escapades may have been going on for a long time.

Ellen kept wondering if she had done something wrong to drive Carol in this wayward direction. After all, Margaret always did everything

Chapter 4

right. Carol could never measure up to her big sister. Ellen tried never to compare the two, but had she inadvertently sent Carol the wrong message? And did that contribute to her bad decisions now?

The band played several numbers. Ellen did get caught up in the lively Christmas music until she remembered that Carol dropped out of band. Carol was never good at staying with something that demanded discipline and hard work.

The concert ended; the applause was polite and brief. The crowd was smaller because gas rationing meant less driving.

Ellen whispered to Matthew, "I'm going to catch Carol to let her know we'll pick her up right after school tomorrow." She hurried toward the front of the gymnasium, where the choir members milled around.

A sharp voice interrupted her search for Carol. "I want a word with you, Mrs. Anderson." The words were more of an order than a request.

Ellen recognized the voice of Mrs. Grant, one of the few people she would rather not see. She turned and politely responded, "Good evening."

"Something has come to my attention, and I'm very unhappy about it." Mrs. Grant, a full four inches taller than Ellen, blocked her way. "I do not appreciate your daughter seeing my son. I want you to put a stop to this."

Ellen couldn't quite believe her ears. "Mrs. Grant, your son is much older than my daughter. He bears that responsibility."

"Your daughter is chasing my son."

Ellen knew she was at a distinct disadvantage. She had little idea of the extent of her daughter's relationship with Jeff Grant. "I was just on the way to talk with Carol about my concerns," she told the woman.

Mrs. Grant continued to talk as she followed Ellen to the front of the room. Ellen looked around at the various choir members, but there was no Carol.

Seeing her niece Irene, Ellen hurried over to her. "Where's Carol? I need to see her."

Irene avoided her aunt's gaze. "I think she left already."

Ellen found herself becoming angry with her daughter. "Carol knew I wanted to see her. Do you know where she went?" She heard one of the other girls snicker. "I think you know," she pressed Irene.

Irene blushed and then spoke. "She's out with Jeff, I think. She's seeing a lot of him."

"Thank you." Ellen turned back and saw Mrs. Grant waiting.

Beyond the Darkness

The woman's voice heightened and sharpened. "Now, Mrs. Anderson, you can see how she keeps running after my son."

At this point Matthew joined Ellen and asked, "Did you find Carol?"

Mrs. Grant shook her finger at Matthew. "Mr. Anderson, your wife can see how your daughter runs out after my son. You need to put a stop to this."

Ellen thought fast. "We'll see what we can do about our daughter. But it's up to you to do something with your son."

"Where would your son take our daughter?" asked Matthew.

Mrs. Grant finally slowed down. "I suppose he has his car and they're driving around. Maybe parked."

By this time the gymnasium had cleared out. The janitors began to put away chairs. All the students and audience had left, but Ellen and Matthew continued their conversation with Mrs. Grant regarding their children's whereabouts. It turned out that Mrs. Grant had little idea.

Victoria appeared, interrupting their discussion. "It's time to lock up. What seems to be the problem?"

This time Mrs. Grant was silent.

"We're wondering where Carol might have gone," answered Ellen. "She's probably with Jeff Grant."

Victoria cleared her throat. "Carol has orders to be at my home fifteen minutes after the concert ends. She should be home now."

A few minutes later, Ellen, Matthew, and Victoria drove up to Victoria's house. Ellen felt a sense of relief as she saw a light in the upstairs bedroom. Carol was where she was supposed to be.

Victoria led the way into her house and upstairs. Just as they approached the bedroom door, the light turned off. Victoria knocked on the door and opened it, quickly turning on the light. "Carol, we have something to discuss."

She stepped in, followed by Ellen, while Matthew waited in the hallway.

Ellen saw that her daughter was pretending to be asleep. She felt anger rising within. She had taught Carol honesty, not deceitfulness.

Carol rubbed her eyes. "Why is everyone here?"

"You know full well," her mother answered. "We have much to discuss. You think about what you've been doing behind our backs. We happen to know."

Chapter 4

Carol sat up and defended herself. "If you weren't so tough on me, I wouldn't have sneaked out," she told her aunt. "You know what the kids say about you."

"Carol, you are not to speak to your aunt that way," commanded Ellen. "She's been kind enough to let you stay here so that you could go to high school."

"I don't care what you think. I'm sixteen. I love Jeff, and lots of girls get married at sixteen. I love him, and I don't care what you think."

Ellen was thankful that Matthew entered just then to stand beside her. She knew how he must feel in response to his daughter's words. "Yes, you're sixteen," she told Carol, "but Jeff is much older. In ten years that age difference might not matter. But right now he is far too old to be going out with a teenager."

Carol, flushed with anger, began crying. "You always think Margaret's perfect. She got to do everything she wanted."

"This situation has nothing to do with Margaret." Ellen walked over to the bed where Carol sat. "We're concerned about you."

"I bet. You don't want me to have any fun. You want me to settle down and marry some stupid farmer."

At this point Victoria spoke up. "Young lady, your father is a farmer. He is a smart man, and one of the finest I know. If you married a farmer like Matthew, you could not find a better man."

Carol turned to her father. "Dad, I didn't mean you were stupid."

Victoria continued her lecture. "Carol, you need to watch that tongue of yours. You use it far too much. You hurt people with your remarks. And yes, Carol, I know what the kids say. They've called me a big, bad, black witch. But they also know I'm right about discipline. And they know I'm fair."

Matthew moved away and went downstairs. Ellen knew he was hurt deeply by his daughter's words and actions.

Ellen's conversation with Carol continued, repeating the same points and arguments. Finally Ellen realized the discussion was useless.

Victoria moved to the bedroom door. "I think we've said enough for tonight. We'll settle this tomorrow."

"Yes," Ellen agreed. "Tomorrow afternoon, your father and I will pick you up at school. You will spend the weekend at home, going nowhere except to church. After that, we'll see if we can trust you."

Carol turned away, saying nothing.

Beyond the Darkness

All at once something within Ellen made her sit down on the bed and take Carol's hand. "I think we need to ask the Lord's help. Let's have our bedtime prayers."

"I'm too old for that," grumbled Carol.

Ellen began softly, "Our Father Who art in heaven—"

Quietly and tentatively, Carol joined in the prayer.

The next day, Friday, at precisely 3:30, Matthew stopped in front of Lake View High School. In minutes a mass of students made their exits. He strained to see Carol. She was supposed to look for the familiar Chevy and come out immediately.

He waited for what seemed an eternity, but Carol never appeared. Soon all the students had left except for some stragglers. One by one and in groups, the teachers began to exit.

Matthew knew something was wrong. He wished Ellen were with him. He got out of the car and hurried into the school to Victoria's office.

Victoria looked up from her record books. "I know what you're here about. I just discovered that Carol skipped class the last hour. I'm afraid to think what she's up to."

Matthew trembled inside, experiencing both anger and fear. "We didn't bring her up this way."

"Carol's always had a mind of her own. She's been a wayward child."

"Where can she be? What can we do?"

Victoria put aside her work. "Let's first check at my house. We'll see if she could be there—or if there's any indication of where she's gone."

A short while later, Matthew followed his sister into her house and up the stairs to Carol's room. Victoria quickly surveyed the situation and went to the closet.

"I can't see that she's taken anything." Victoria moved over to the dresser drawers and rummaged through several of them. "She's left most of her things here and in the closet. It doesn't seem she took off for a long time."

"That's a relief."

Chapter 4

"Matthew, I don't know if there's anything we can do now." Victoria led the way out of the room and downstairs. "And don't you have to get those cows milked?"

"Where could she have gone?"

Victoria moved over to the telephone. "I think we need to check with Mrs. Grant. Carol is undoubtedly with Jeff."

Victoria dialed central and in moments was talking with Mrs. Grant. Matthew listened intently but could tell nothing.

"I guess we don't know much," announced Victoria. "Jeff's car is gone, and Mrs. Grant has no idea where he is. She tried to hide that fact for a while, but I managed to get the truth."

"What can we do?"

"I suppose we could drive around town, but I suspect they're not in town." Victoria paused a minute, then added, "In fact, sometimes I hear more than I'm supposed to. I heard there's a dance in River Falls tonight. I have a feeling that's where they're headed."

"But what about Carol coming back? She knows she's supposed to be staying at home with us. She's forbidden from going anywhere."

Victoria reached for her coat and handed Matthew his. "Let's just drive around town to see if we can find out anything. Then I'll get a list of her friends, and Ellen and I can do some calling. Otherwise there's nothing we can do." She paused a moment. "I guess we could call the sheriff, but would that help?"

"No, let's see what we can do first," he answered.

The drive around town turned up no clue about where Carol might be. Matthew decided he might as well go home and do chores. That evening, Ellen tried calling Carol's friends, but those calls revealed nothing new.

Finally Matthew and Ellen retired for the night, but they slept restlessly until the telephone rang shortly after midnight. Ellen hurried into the kitchen to answer. Matthew followed, listening intently to the one side of the conversation. He could tell very little. Finally she hung up, and visibly shaken, turned to him. "There's been an accident," she sighed.

Matthew felt as if his heart had dropped through the floor. Remembering the fateful call about his brother's death, he managed to ask, "It's Carol, isn't it?"

"Carol's doing OK. She's in the River Falls hospital, being checked out."

"Should we go now?"

Beyond the Darkness

"Matthew, I can't leave Michael alone. You better go. You can pick up Carol and bring her home." She stopped, then said, "There's more. Jeff Grant was driving. He was intoxicated. I'm afraid Carol was drinking also. Jeff apparently turned in front of an oncoming car. He was hurt more seriously; he's still unconscious."

"What were they thinking of?" questioned Matthew.

"Carol hasn't been thinking clearly for some time."

Ellen picked out Matthew's clothes, and he quickly dressed and left for River Falls.

When Matthew arrived at the entrance of the hospital, he was surprised to see Sheriff Walker sitting with Carol.

He greeted his daughter with questions. "What happened? You could have been killed! You should have been safe at home."

"Good evening, Matthew." Sheriff Walker extended his hand. "I've been having a little talk with your daughter."

"I'm sorry, Mr. Walker. I guess I'm upset."

Matthew suddenly found Carol in his arms, clinging to him. "I'm sorry, Dad. I didn't think."

Matthew smelled the faint evidence of liquor on his daughter's breath. "What were you thinking?" She backed away. "But I'm glad you're OK. Your mother and I have been terribly worried."

Sheriff Walker began to explain. "Carol was with Jeff Grant. They'd both been drinking, but Jeff was pretty bad off. He's regained consciousness and should be all right in a few days. Some bruises and scratches."

Carol began crying, "The Grants blame me. Jeff's the one who gave me the beer, but he's been drinking that other stuff that I don't like."

"Carol," began Matthew, "you're sixteen. Drinking is not right. And it's illegal for a sixteen-year-old."

"Yes," added the sheriff, "it is even more serious business for a twenty-three-year-old to provide liquor to a minor. Jeff is in serious trouble."

"But I love Jeff. He's the most important person in my life."

Sheriff Walker looked down at Carol. "Young lady, it is time for you to go home with your father. Jeff will be all right—except he will face drunk-driving charges. He's in serious trouble."

"I want to stay with him."

"His parents are by his side. And they don't want you around."

Matthew wished Ellen were here. She would know what to say.

Carol turned to her father. "Can't I stay? Can't we stay?"

Chapter 4

Matthew found it hard to believe that his sweet little girl was a misbehaving young woman. "No," he said sternly. "You are coming home with me. Besides, in another hour I have chores to do."

Sheriff Walker's friendly approach disappeared as he sternly told Carol, "I'm letting you off easy. You've been drinking illegally. I could take you down to the jail and lock you up for the night. Do you want that?"

Carol looked away from both her father and Sheriff Walker. "No," she answered sullenly.

Matthew thanked the sheriff for taking care of Carol, and Walker once more faced Carol. "Look at me, young woman." She looked up reluctantly. "If you keep going out with this young man, you'll be in as much trouble as he is," he warned. "You're not that kind of person. You're not from that kind of family."

Carol was silent.

"Did you hear me? Don't you realize what's going on?"

"I'm not drunk." Carol began to walk toward the door. "I'll go."

In the those early hours of the morning, Matthew drove the thirty miles from River Falls to their Oak Ridge farm. Carol was soon sound asleep.

When he arrived home, Matthew got out of the car, walked around to the other side, opened the door, and scooped Carol in his arms. He remembered many earlier times when he had carried his little girl. "Dear Carol," he said to the sleeping girl in his arms, "please don't leave us this way. Please wait for the right young man to come along. I love you, darling. I don't want anything to happen to you."

The warmth of the kitchen light welcomed him as Ellen opened the door. He was home once more. Carol would be safe and secure within this home.

Chapter 5

Matthew finished milking cows early that December Friday. Christmas Eve was two days away, and his girls would be home for Christmas vacation. For two weeks the family would be at least partially complete.

Ellen had supper ready. Matthew ate quickly, cleaned up, and changed clothes. Ellen and Michael would ride along to Lake View and then on to River Falls. He looked forward to seeing the Christmas lights and decorations as they drove the streets of the city.

Matthew parked in front of Victoria's house. Ellen and Michael got out of the car and ran toward the door, where Victoria greeted them. "Carol's upstairs packing. She should be ready any minute."

"How's she been these past days?" whispered Ellen.

Victoria gave one of those looks that Matthew recognized as he joined them. "Well, she's been rather quiet. She's stuck here for the present. Jeff's doing OK, but he's in the hospital for now. And his parents have no intention of letting him use another car."

"I'm afraid Jeff Grant is not any good for Carol. I wish she could understand that."

"What's it mean to be not any good?" asked Michael.

"This is grown-up talk. Never you mind," answered Ellen.

"But I want to know. You said, Mommy, that I should ask questions."

Beyond the Darkness

Ellen smiled at her son's inquisitiveness. "I'll explain later."

"Michael, why don't you go into the dining room," said Victoria. "There are some blocks and Tinkertoys in the corner. You can play with them."

Michael followed his aunt's suggestion. Then Victoria continued her report on Carol. "I checked on her these past days. Her teachers say she's been doing somewhat better, but she's still not working up to her potential."

Ellen thanked her sister-in-law. "I hope her life will get back to normal after Christmas vacation."

Matthew wondered if his daughter's life would ever be "back to normal."

Carol appeared in the doorway with her suitcase. "Hello, Dad. Hello, Mom, I'm ready to go home." She walked over and gave her father a kiss on the cheek.

Their conversation, though somewhat strained, centered around Christmas and vacation and activities and going home. Finally Carol made her request. "I want to stop to see Jeff. I know he wants to see me."

Victoria didn't hesitate to respond. "Carol, my child, you know what the Grants said. They don't want you anywhere near Jeff. I'm afraid if you try to see Jeff, there'll be trouble."

"We'll see about that when we get to River Falls," said Ellen. "I think it's time to move along so that we can pick up Margaret."

Matthew realized his wife could take care of the situation. As he and his family drove to River Falls, light snowflakes fell, turning the countryside into a Currier and Ives winter wonderland. Matthew felt the warmth and love of family, but he had a gnawing concern about Carol.

Carol hurried into the River Falls Hospital. As Ellen watched her disappear through the doors, she wished they hadn't let Carol talk them into this stop at the hospital.

"I'm afraid that girl is headed for trouble. The more the Grants forbid the two to see each other, the more they will want to be together. I'm afraid we can't stop them," she told Matthew.

"You're right, dear."

Fortunately Michael had fallen asleep in the backseat.

Chapter 5

"Carol has always been contrary—wanting her own way. Margaret's always done the right thing. I know we've tried not to compare the two. Maybe we haven't succeeded."

Matthew quoted the familiar Scripture, "Train up a child in the way he ought to go, and when he is old, he will not depart from it."

"I hope and pray that will come true."

They pulled up in front of a large Victorian house, a house that had become home to a number of girls attending normal school.

The large three-story house appeared to be dark except for lights in the front hallway and the landlady's living room. She was probably saying good-bye to Margaret.

Matthew got out of the car and walked toward the front door. Ellen could see Margaret hurry out and greet her father with a hug. It would be hard for Matthew to see another man take his place in his daughter's life.

Matthew put her suitcase in the trunk. Margaret, with books and notebooks in her arms, gently moved Michael over so she could have space in the backseat. "Vacation's here, and I'm ready to come home."

Ellen turned around to grasp Margaret's hand. "We're ready to have you all to ourselves for two weeks."

"I never thought I'd miss you so much. And I miss my brothers more than ever."

"The house seems so empty," observed Ellen. "Four of our five children are away. But that's the way life is supposed to be."

Matthew began driving down the streets toward the hospital. "We have to pick up Carol. She insisted on seeing Jeff."

"She's serious about him, isn't she?"

"I'm afraid so."

Margaret cleared her throat. "Mom, Dad, he's not good for her. He's pretty wild. When he isn't seeing Margaret, he's gone out with another girl from my teacher training class. She dropped out a few weeks ago. She and Jeff went to all kinds of parties, and she didn't do her work."

"Did you hear much about the accident?" asked Ellen.

"Jeff was very drunk, that's what the man next door said. He's a police officer in town. He said it was a miracle that Jeff wasn't killed and that Carol was hurt only a little."

Ellen turned to her daughter in the backseat. "God spared our girl. She has to realize how close she came to death. I'm thankful God protected her."

Beyond the Darkness

Matthew stopped the car in front of the hospital. "Margaret, would you run in and get your sister?"

Margaret made a hasty exit. But when she did not appear with Carol a few minutes later, Ellen began to wonder, *Did Carol somehow manage to sneak away? Is Jeff well enough to disappear with her?* She felt certain that such a decision would destroy her young daughter's life. In spite of her concerns, Ellen said nothing. The couple sat in silence.

"What's keeping her?" asked Matthew finally. "The more I learn about Jeff, the less I trust him."

"He's supposed to be in the hospital a few more days."

Matthew repeated, "I don't trust him further than I could throw him."

It seemed an eternity, but finally the girls appeared. Ellen gave a sigh of relief even though she could hear them arguing. Her role as mother would be crucial these next weeks. As her daughters approached the car, she heard Carol's sharp words to Margaret. "It's none of your business what I do with my life. I'm soon seventeen."

Ellen and Matthew greeted their daughter, but Carol merely mumbled an answer and remained silent. On the drive home, Margaret made up for her sister's silence as she talked about her classes and about several of the girls in the training program. Ellen could see that Margaret was born to be a teacher and would follow in her footsteps.

As they approached the warmth of home, Ellen knew she had to talk with Carol. Somehow she had to prevent her daughter from making some serious mistakes.

Matthew loved Christmas Eve and all its rituals. This year, however, he felt a deep sadness. James was in military headquarters somewhere in England. Johnie's whereabouts could be on a remote battlefield. At this moment, as he dished out the feed for the cattle, Matthew heard echoes of James and Johnie talking during previous Christmases.

"I'll do that," Margaret interrupted his thoughts. "The boys aren't here, so I'll do their job."

"My dear, you don't need to."

"Yes, I want to, Dad. I know how much you miss the boys. And I do too."

Chapter 5

Matthew handed his daughter the pan for dishing out the oats. "Christmas Eve has a way of bringing back memories."

"I know. Next Christmas, I hope we can all be together."

"I pray for that." Matthew then added, "Give the cows an extra portion. After all, it is Christmas."

"James told me about this. The old legends say that the animals worship the Christ child on Christmas Eve. And you know, I think that's true. This barn seems so warm and safe when all the cattle are in their stalls."

Margaret went about doing her job. Matthew climbed into the hayloft and pitched down hay so there would be an adequate amount for that evening and the next day.

During all this time, he thought of James and Johnie and where they might be. Under his breath he prayed, "Lord, bring my boys safely home. I don't know what I would do if something happened to them."

Margaret finished dishing out the feed. Matthew let in the cattle as she closed the stanchions for several of the cows. Carol had usually done this work in the absence of the boys, but this time Margaret helped her father.

While the cattle ate, Matthew waited for a short time, as he always did, before milking. It was good to have the company of Margaret in the quiet of the barn.

"Dad, I can't wait until next September. I hear there's going to be a shortage of teachers. That means I'll have an easy time getting a teaching position."

"My dear, you'd never have trouble getting a teaching job. You're like your mother. She was a good teacher. And you're just like her."

"Dad, thank you. You couldn't have paid me a higher compliment."

Matthew wanted to preserve this moment in his mind. More words were hardly necessary. Father and daughter proceeded with their work—Matthew milked the cows as Margaret fed several young calves and then milked one of their older pet cows.

Matthew carried the cans of milk to the cooler tank. The brisk winter air outside the barn made his spirit come alive. In another hour the family, or at least part of the family, would gather for the traditional Scandinavian Christmas Eve supper.

Matthew switched off the lights in the barn. He and Margaret stood by the door, looking in at the cattle. Life was good. God had been good.

Beyond the Darkness

A little voice suddenly came through the darkness. "I want to help milk the cows." It was Michael.

"We're all done with milking," said Margaret. "You're too late."

He ran to his sister. "Margi, you stay here all the time."

She scooped her little brother into her arms. "No, Michael, that's not the way life works. It's time for me to learn to be a teacher."

"You stay here. You teach me."

Matthew and Margaret laughed.

The warmth of the house and the lights reflecting into the dark winter night invited Matthew and his children to the celebration of Christmas.

An hour later, Matthew sat at the head of the table in the large dining room. The old oak table had been extended to its limits, and two smaller tables had been brought in. The children sat at those tables so the whole large, extended family could be together at the same time. These would be special moments, because life's circumstances often separated families. Mary and Ed were present with Beth, home from college, and Irene, home from school in town. Ed talked from time to time about moving to California, but Matthew's sister and her family were still here this Christmas. Corrine and Warren and their girls were also part of this family gathering.

As Ellen and Victoria and Martha and Margaret brought in platters and bowls of all the Christmas delicacies, Matthew thought of those present. In a moment everyone was seated. Ellen looked to him to say the Christmas prayer. The room became quiet.

"Let us look to the Lord in prayer." Matthew paused and began quietly, "Thank You for this family gathered here. Thank You that we can all be together in this place where there is freedom and safety. We pray for those who are not with us. We pray especially for James and Johnie and Jake and Joe. Keep them safe in Your tender care. We pray that You would bring them safely home for another Christmas."

Matthew thought he heard some muffled crying as he finished, "And now we thank You for this feast we are about to have. Bless those who prepared it. Bless this food, and bless and guide our talk and fellowship.

Chapter 5

But most of all, thank You for the Christ of Christmas. May He guide us throughout our lives."

The lutefisk was passed, along with melted butter and cream sauce. This was followed by Swedish meatballs, potatoes, creamed peas, and homemade rolls. Matthew relished the delicious food. A quietness prevailed as the family ate the Christmas meal.

Soon, however, Michael interrupted the silence. "I don't like this stuff. It tastes awful." Laughter filled the room.

"You have to learn to like it," said Carol. "I didn't like it either when I was your age, but the lutefisk grows on you."

Ellen quietly moved Michael's lutefisk aside. "You eat the meatballs and potatoes. You like those."

"It smells," Michael added.

"Never mind."

Michael's outburst encouraged others to talk more. In minutes various conversations were going on around the large table.

Matthew couldn't help reflecting. While many others talked, Matthew thought about the future. The terrible war should soon be over. Would James and Johnie be home next year? After all, they hadn't heard anything from Johnie for weeks. On the other hand, Johnie never was much of a letter writer. Nephew Jake was training in Georgia. Would he be sent overseas? And Joe. There was the likelihood that he was in a Japanese prison camp.

World War II had indeed touched this family in many ways. Matthew felt dirty from the war. He wanted something to happen so that the country would be washed clean.

People began to eat more slowly. Many had seconds and thirds before they sat back and yawned from being well fed.

Then Ma spoke, and everyone seemed to pay attention.

"My dear ones, we need to stop for a moment. We're all together this Christmas—except for James and Johnie and Jake . . . and Joe," she added. "We miss those who are not here. We pray for their safe return."

She stopped. Everyone remained at attention.

Her voice had an edge to it. "I'm seventy-six years old, but I'm with you this year. I miss John so very much. Just a few years ago, he was with us for the last time. And P.J. was with us, and we had that special Christmas at his new home. I miss him too. But what I want to say is that we should sit back and just appreciate and love one another. We are family. We should never take one another for granted. Life changes fast. Suddenly people are gone—and we can never go back."

Matthew sensed that other changes were about to take place, changes he had no control over. Somehow, if the boys came back, he wanted everything to be the same. But he knew that would never happen. They could never return to what was before.

It was Margaret who broke the silence following Ma's remarks. "Grandma, you are more special than you realize. I have learned much from you. But you have shown me how life is always changing and that we must move with the times."

Elizabeth Anderson looked across the table to her granddaughter. "My dear Margaret, I wish I could stop this fast-moving world and get off. I'm old. I can no longer keep up with the changes."

Matthew felt acutely the sadness and uneasiness in his mother. "Ma, you don't have to keep up with the changes. You will always have your family. You will always have us."

"Yes, Matthew. You don't know how much that means to me."

Several others echoed the same sentiment.

"What I'm trying to say is that I've lived my life. I know that my time may be short. I'm not sure what purpose God has for me right now."

Then Martha spoke up. "Mother, it's your job to be here. To enjoy this family that you started. I have a purpose to help my three girls and their families. God has given each of us a purpose for being here."

Victoria had been silent for a while, but chimed in. "Mother, everyone here needs a parent. I need a mother, and you are that mother. Something within each of us desperately needs that mother or father."

Mary also had been quiet, listening. "When I was in the sanitarium," she added, "the thing I missed most was my family. First, I missed Ed and the kids. But Mother, I missed you so very much, and all the rest of you too."

Ellen had quietly gone to the kitchen. When she resumed her place at the head of the table, she suggested, "I think it's time for dessert. I'm afraid the kids might be getting restless."

"I'm sorry," said Ma. "And I've been going on and on."

Ellen was quick to reassure her. "You said exactly the right things. We need to show our love for one another and speak of it also. We must remember we are on this earth for only a season."

"I want dessert," called out Michael. "Why do we have to talk so much?"

Chapter 5

Corrine's three girls echoed their agreement.

The hours that followed blended in with many past Christmas celebrations. Several of the women went to the kitchen to wash dishes and put them away. The three girls and Michael, with the help of Margaret, prepared a small Christmas program.

As the family gathered in the living room, the children sat on the floor, looking up at the lights of the large Christmas tree. Matthew remembered the days before electricity when they lit candles. He looked around at each of the people gathered in that room. His sister Mary appeared more thin and tired than usual. Ed always seemed angry at something or someone; this year was no exception. Beth, now a college student, visited with Margaret. And Irene and Carol rekindled some of their childhood comradeship.

Victoria seemed more quiet than usual. Martha, involved more than ever with Ma as well as Corrine's children, actually appeared younger. And Warren and Corrine remained the concerned parents of their three little girls.

Matthew thought of his own children. He said a silent prayer for James and Johnie in their faraway places, and he added a prayer for Joe. He felt confidence in Margaret and what she would do. But Carol continued to be a worry to him. Little Michael was becoming more and more like Johnie, but Matthew hoped Michael would never have to confront what Johnie now faced.

The next moments became a silent tableau. The tradition continued for still another year. Ellen took out the old family Bible and read once more the familiar words, "In those days in Bethlehem of Judea . . ."

From oldest to youngest, everyone attentively listened. Michael found his way to Matthew's lap, and his father held him close.

"I love you, Daddy," Michael whispered.

"I love you too."

Matthew experienced an overwhelming sense of loving and being loved. In a world at war, he felt the peace that passed all understanding.

Chapter 6

"Mother Anderson!" exclaimed Ellen as she entered her mother-in-law's little house. "What happened?"

Elizabeth Anderson was struggling to get up from her easy chair. "I guess I slipped and turned my foot when I went to the outhouse."

"Here, I'll help you up."

"No!" came the stubborn reply. "I can get up by myself. It was stupid of me to be so careless. I'll be all right."

Ellen hesitated. "I'm not sure you should be here by yourself now that Martha's away for a short while."

"I'm perfectly capable of taking care of myself."

"We'll see about that."

Elizabeth limped over to the cupboard. "I made some raspberry muffins. I think the women will enjoy those."

"You shouldn't overdo. After all, we are here to pray for our boys."

"I may be old, but I can still cook and bake."

It seemed her mother-in-law was defending herself, but Ellen smiled, saying nothing.

At that moment several women arrived. Corrine also came down the hill from the big house. They all seemed ready to get down to serious prayer.

"Is Mabel Robertson coming?" asked Ellen. "I've noticed she doesn't seem to be herself."

Beyond the Darkness

"She can't seem to come to grips with the fact that Tim is gone. She keeps saying she knows he's alive," Corrine answered.

Elizabeth motioned for the women to sit down. "Nothing is more terrible than for a mother to lose a child. I know, because I've lost two. And it would be easy to want to deny the death of a child."

A woman who lived down the road added, "We must pray for Mabel, along with the boys."

Ellen remembered an article she had read. "I heard about a soldier who was declared dead. Six months later, it turned out he was still alive."

"Don't tell her that," said Corrine. "It would be unfair to give her false hope."

The women proceeded to talk about their other children, recipes, and concerns of the home. After a few moments of conversation, Ellen made sure there were enough chairs around the large kitchen table for their entire gathering. Soon the women were immersed in prayer.

As the last prayer was spoken, the door opened and Mabel Robertson appeared. "I'm sorry I'm late. I hope you prayed for Tim."

Awkward silence followed until Ellen broke the quiet. "I'll say a prayer for him and the others right now."

Corrine found a chair for Mabel, and as she sat down, Ellen reopened the prayers. "Dear heavenly Father, we thank You for the privilege of having sons. These sons have been blessings from You, dear Lord. We feel a sadness because we miss our boys. We lift up Tim to You. Keep him and the other boys safe from harm." Ellen went on to name each one and to add personal comments about their location.

Afterward Mabel thanked Ellen. "I just know that Tim will come home when this terrible war ends."

Ellen avoided her gaze. "It's time for coffee, and Mother Anderson's made raspberry muffins rather than cake. That's a real treat."

In a few moments the women were drinking coffee and devouring Elizabeth's tasty muffins. Ellen tried to steer the conversation away from the possibility of Tim's return.

When the women left, Ellen couldn't help thinking of her own sons and Joe. She had prayed and believed they would return. Though she had moments of doubt, she refused to admit those doubts to her mother-in-law or even to Matthew.

Matthew returned from town to pick up his wife. "I'm back," he announced, entering the house. "It's just about time for chores."

Chapter 6

Ellen pointed to her mother-in-law's foot. "I think we have a problem. Your mother fell on the way to the outhouse."

Matthew looked down at the obvious swelling. "Ma, we better get you to the doctor. We're taking you there right away."

"You have chores to think about," she objected.

"The chores can be late. Ellen, get Ma's coat." He helped his mother out of the chair, then turned and spoke sternly, "Ma, you lean on me and save that one leg. This could be serious."

Ellen found Elizabeth's coat. "I think it's time for you to leave this place for the winter. You can stay with us, just as you did several years back."

"But I have Corrine and Warren and the girls close by."

Without another word, Ellen went into Elizabeth's bedroom. "I'll take your good dress for church and two of your everyday dresses."

"Matthew, I need to get into the bedroom to get some other things," his mother requested.

Matthew helped his mother into her bedroom. Ellen could see how heavily she leaned against her son before she moved over to the bed and sat down.

"Ma, you have to stay off that ankle."

Elizabeth put her head down. "I think it's worse than I thought."

Ellen rummaged around for personal items while Elizabeth gave directions. Her mother-in-law seemed to agree to this new arrangement.

Their trip to town and the doctor's office revealed the expected news—Elizabeth's ankle was seriously sprained. Dr. Baker placed a secure bandage around it and ordered Elizabeth to stay off her feet for the next few weeks. Elizabeth quietly agreed to his orders.

Ellen knew she had her work cut out for her. She still had another week of vacation to deal with Carol and her attitude and problems. But now she needed to care for a mother-in-law who didn't want to be considered an invalid.

New Year's Eve 1944 arrived. Matthew thought aloud, "Nothing is certain. The boys are fighting a war. Will they ever come back? And life at home isn't the same." He felt keen disappointment that there would be no Watch Night service because attendance had dwindled during the past years. And tonight there would be no celebration at home because extended family members were busy or had moved away.

Matthew's family quietly finished New Year's Eve supper. He was glad Ma was with them, at least. Margaret and Carol, still home during their two-week Christmas vacation, seemed happy to help Ellen with the dishes. And there was little Michael, always constructing something with blocks or building windmills with his Tinkertoys.

While the family had been together for supper, Matthew knew it wouldn't last long this New Year's Eve. Margaret was planning to go out. Hank, the young farmer from River Falls, was coming to pick her up. Matthew liked the young man, though he wasn't sure he was good enough for his daughter. Matthew heard Hank's car drive up.

Margaret put on her coat and turned to her parents. "I should be home just after midnight. We'll see in the new year and then head home."

"Enjoy yourself," said Ellen.

Before Margaret could leave, Carol rushed into the kitchen with coat in hand. "Oh, some of us junior girls are getting together. I'm sure Hank won't mind if I ride along into town."

Matthew couldn't help seeing the harsh look Margaret gave her sister. "But I might mind," she replied to Carol.

"Oh, Margaret, I'm not going to steal your boyfriend. I don't even want to consider a farm boy as a boyfriend. There are men out there who don't have to go home and milk cows."

Ellen gave Carol a sharp look, then added, "There's nothing wrong with some good hard work. And remember your father."

Carol went over to her father and flippantly kissed him on the cheek. "You're a great dad!"

Matthew found he was becoming suspicious of his daughter. Every time Carol wanted something, she could be sweet and charming. Yet her mood could drastically change abruptly, and her actions continued to show disrespect toward her parents and her upbringing.

Margaret moved toward the door. "Have you ever heard of two's company, three's a crowd?" She then moved out, closing the door.

Carol opened the door and followed without another word.

Ellen looked up at her husband. "I'm afraid that girl is headed for trouble. I can't seem to get through to her."

Matthew was ready to go after her, but his wife stopped him. "It's no use," said Ellen. "We need to confront her in the morning."

Chapter 6

At that moment the telephone rang and Ellen answered. The conversation was brief.

"It was Mary," she said. "She wants us to come over. It seemed urgent. She hinted that she wanted to see you and me alone."

Matthew wondered what this meant. "Something must be up. Ed hasn't been the same lately. He hasn't been the same since Mary's bout with TB."

"This is a strange evening," continued Ellen "New Year's Eve is usually a family night. And we all used to go to church together."

Matthew thought of earlier times. "Yes, and everyone stuck around. All the families went to church. The young people had their games and fun. But that is no more."

"Times change," reminded Ellen. "Do you think we should leave your mother alone with her bad ankle? And what about Michael?"

"I don't think Ma will want to go out tonight."

"She's in her room. Let's go see what she says."

They found Elizabeth seated in a rocking chair with Michael in her lap. She had just ended the story of "King Midas."

"Ma, we thought we'd take a quick ride over to Mary and Ed's. Do you mind staying here alone with Michael for a few hours?"

"I'll be fine."

"Or," Matthew added, "you could go with."

"No, I don't get around well—not without a lot of help."

Michael snuggled up to his grandmother. "Tell me another story. Tell me about when you were a little girl."

The old lady smiled. "Yes, we'll have our own special time."

"I'll get your pajamas," said Ellen. "Then you won't have to move if you fall asleep."

Matthew helped his mother into bed, and Ellen got her young son into his pajamas. They left the two safely in bed with a grandmother relating stories of her youth. *This is life as it should be*, thought Matthew. *A little boy being touched by the life of his grandmother.* A sense of family history provided richness in a small boy's life.

As Matthew and Ellen drove the miles to Mary and Ed's, Matthew couldn't help thinking of Carol. "I'm afraid of what our girl might be doing," he admitted.

"There's not much we can do. We've tried to bring her up in the right way. Now it's time for her to make the decisions."

"I'm afraid she's been making some bad ones."

Beyond the Darkness

When they arrived to visit with Mary and Ed, Matthew's thoughts turned away from Carol. This time the two couples remained in the kitchen, a departure from the usual separation of men and women.

"Are any of the kids around?" asked Ellen.

"It seems so empty," replied Mary. "Beth went back to college. And, of course, Jake's probably being shipped out to Europe any time. Irene is with a group of girls, having a slumber party."

Ellen mentioned what had happened with Margaret and Carol at their house earlier. And as the two woman talked, Matthew couldn't help noticing the gray that had become increasingly evident in his sister Mary's dark hair. Deep lines in her forehead announced how hard her life had been.

As Mary spoke, a sadness accented her words. "Sometimes I wish we could go back to an earlier time . . . when our kids were little. Those were good times."

Matthew recalled how their seven children had played together. "And remember the scare we had when the three young girls were lost?" he recalled. "That was quite an experience!"

Mary laughed. "Yes, that was a stressful but memorable time. And you, Matthew, remembered the old house, the one place we hadn't looked—and we found the girls."

Ellen had that reflective look Matthew knew so well. "I remember the prayer meeting at church. I know that the Lord guided you to remember the place where the girls might be."

Ed grunted, "I sometimes wonder about that."

"Oh, Ed," scolded Mary.

For the next few moments the two couples reminisced of earlier times and the adventures of their children. The stories they remembered could fill several books.

Mary began to put on the coffee. "I suppose you're wondering what we wanted to talk about."

"I'll admit we're curious," Ellen replied.

Ed responded with force. "I'm ready to get away from this blasted Minnesota winter. These winters are more than any man should have to put up with."

"I can't imagine living anywhere else," said Matthew.

"But," continued Ed, "haven't you thought of living in a warmer climate, away from all this cold and snow and hard work?"

Matthew saw his brother-in-law's grim determination. "Hard work is a part of life. I can't imagine life any other way."

Chapter 6

Ed pounded his fist on the table. "I can! I don't think we have to put up with this kind of life."

Mary brought out a freshly baked cake and a bowl of Jell-O to the table. "A warmer climate will be better for my health."

"What are you saying?" asked Ellen.

Ed cleared his throat. "We've made a decision. This fall we're going to have a sale. We'll be selling the farm and moving to California."

"Do you have a job?" Matthew wondered aloud.

"My cousin has a construction business. He says business will be booming. And the war should be ending soon."

"We'll miss you," said Ellen. "What about the girls?"

"We hope they'll come with us. There are good colleges in California, some of the best."

"Irene will be a senior next fall. Don't you think she'll want to finish high school with her friends here?"

Ed's voice boomed out. "She'll be with her family. The high schools in California are probably better than anything here in Minnesota."

Matthew repeated his earlier remark, "I can't imagine myself living anywhere but here on the farm—or perhaps in Lake View when I'm too old to farm."

Mary reached over and touched her brother's hand. "Matthew, I'll miss you. We've been living close together all our lives."

Matthew began to realize the meaning of this change. "It's hard to imagine life without you close by."

As Mary served the evening lunch, talk returned to earlier memories. The four reminisced awhile, but then conversation again turned to the many changes coming to all their lives.

Ellen's expression told Matthew that she was deep in more serious thought. Finally she spoke. "Our children will face a whole different world. This terrible war has to end soon. What will come after?"

"I'm almost afraid to think of what the future holds," said Mary.

Mary's words reflected Matthew's unspoken thoughts.

An hour later, back at home, Matthew and Ellen sat at their kitchen table. Ma and little Michael were sound asleep in Ma's room.

"It's good," said Matthew, "that Michael gets to know his grandmother."

"We might as well wait up," added Ellen. "We won't rest until we know our girls are safely home."

Beyond the Darkness

Matthew sighed. "I wish the boys were safely home as well. And I include Joe with our sons."

"I'll never forget the way he came and took over the chores that winter you were so sick. He was only sixteen, but he did more work than any man would have done."

"He thinks of us as family. It's too bad his parents are so busy in the city. And without his grandparents, he doesn't have anyone."

Ellen brought out a letter she had been reading. "I've been looking at the last letter from James. He seems thoughtful and poetic. He writes, Christ stands at the door of the year, saying, "Come, place your hand in mine. Give me your burdens and cares. I am the way. I will lead you safely home.""

Matthew wondered exactly what James meant. "I wish James and Johnie were right here. I'd give anything if I could see them."

The hall clock chimed twelve times. "This is a brand new year," Ellen stated. She rose as she spotted car lights down the driveway. "The year of our Lord, 1945."

"And what will this year bring?" he wondered aloud.

All at once Matthew realized two cars had come down the driveway. Could it be possible both girls had returned at this early hour?

Within minutes first Carol, and then Margaret came through the back porch into the kitchen. Both girls looked serious.

"We thought you'd be a little bit later." Ellen went over to the refrigerator. "We thought you'd see in the new year at your parties."

"Hank was tired and he has to milk cows early," Margaret explained.

Carol, looking sullen, said nothing.

Ellen brought out a jar of milk and began pouring it into a pan. "I think it's time for some hot cocoa. That will be a good way to toast the new year."

Margaret smiled. "That's a great idea, Mother."

Carol's tears were evident. "I've never been so mortified. Jeff stopped at the juniors' party. He was with another girl. I had to get a ride home with one of the girls."

Matthew felt a sense of relief.

"I suppose you're happy now," she continued, "You said Jeff wasn't a good person."

Ellen began mixing cocoa and sugar into the heating milk. "Carol, I'm sorry you're having to experience this, but it's part of learning."

Chapter 6

Carol covered her face. "I guess you were right. I did some stupid things. But I don't understand why his parents were against me."

Matthew wanted to make his daughter listen. 'He's not good enough for you—even if he is the banker's son."

Carol wiped her tears. "I wish life could be simple the way it used to be. I wish James and Johnie were back home. Life was good then."

"Your dad and I were missing them too. I was reading part of James's letter," Ellen told her, and then repeated her son's quote.

"I wish Joe were back here too," said Margaret. "We aren't even sure if he's dead or alive—or maybe in a Japanese prison camp."

Ellen brought out cups and poured hot cocoa for everyone.

"Let's drink to a new year," said Carol.

Ellen held up her cup. "Let's drink to the future and to our family—especially to James and Johnie, and Joe as well. Let's pray for their safety and protection."

Matthew and Margaret and Carol lifted up their cups and drank of the rich hot chocolate.

"I'm thankful our girls are safe at home with us." Matthew savored the warmth of the milk and the warmth of family. Ma was safe in her bedroom, and little Michael was close beside her.

In those next moments, Matthew sensed the presence of others. He saw Johnie, ready and eager to go out and do chores or jump on the John Deere. He saw James, always going to his room to dream and write that great American novel. And Joe, always dependable, ready to help do the chores or join in the harvesting.

Somehow Matthew knew that wherever these three young men were, they were dreaming or thinking of home.

As they finished the cocoa, Ellen suggested, "Let's sing our song before we go to bed."

Matthew's rich tenor voice joined the others.

"Children of the Heavenly Father
Safely in His Bosom gather;
Nestling bird nor star in heaven,
Such a refuge e'er was given."

At the beginning of a new year, even if only for a moment, peace and love and security brought light to the Andersons' tired world that had been darkened by war and other conflicts.

Chapter 7

March 1945

"Dad, I'll help you with the chores." Margaret opened the barn door. She wanted to talk with her father. That's why she had come home for the weekend.

"Are you sure you want to get all dirty and smelly?"

"That doesn't matter. I want to be with you."

"I'm honored."

Margaret had always had a special relationship with her father. When she wanted a man's point of view, she would invariably go to her father. And now she had a decision to make—a decision that would affect her whole life.

Margaret walked over and picked up a pitchfork, but her father objected. "No, Margaret, I'll take care of pitching manure. You can put out the feed for the cattle. It's a little warm today, so we can leave them outside quite a bit longer."

"I think I know how much you feed them. I still remember from Christmas time."

Father and daughter went about doing their chores. Margaret felt a sense of continuity—of permanence in life. There was something wonderful about cattle—animals that gave of their milk for the good of people. She thought of her pet cow that had been her heifer project for 4-H.

Margaret recalled the dreams she'd had for many years. It seemed she always knew she would be a rural schoolteacher. She would teach for a few years, until a handsome young farmer came along. Then she would marry him and raise a family.

But last night's proposal came unexpectedly. Hank was a solid, good man. However, she thought of him only as a friend. He was like a substitute brother, now that James and Johnie were fighting in the war. She didn't feel ready for a proposal.

Margaret put feed in the mangers, and Matthew cleaned the gutters and spread fresh straw in the cattle stalls. Margaret, who had been deep in thought, realized her father had been watching her with what she interpreted as a look of adoration, pride, and love—all combined in the brief glance of a father. Could she ever find a man who would measure up to him?

"Honey," Matthew said, "I think there's something on your mind. I don't have the smarts of your mother, but I can listen."

Margaret felt tears spring to her eyes. Her father always seemed to think he didn't quite measure up. Yet he measured far above all the men or boys she had ever known. She walked over and threw her arms around him. "Oh, Dad. I wish I were a little girl again. Then I could let you hold me, and all the problems would go away."

"What's wrong? You're doing fine at school."

"I've had these dreams—of being a teacher. I want to make a difference in children's lives. It's something I felt God wanted me to do."

"Has something happened?"

"Yes and no."

Matthew pointed at the ladder to the hayloft. "When I want to think, I like to go up into the hayloft. I think that's what we should do."

Margaret felt the strong hands of her father boost her up the ladder. She loved the strength of those hands and arms. He followed close behind, and soon they were seated on a mound of hay.

"The world is changing so fast," she began, "I feel as if I can't keep up."

Her father waited and then spoke. "I think of your grandfather coming from Sweden. He learned a whole new language. He faced change again and again and again."

Chapter 7

"But I don't want things to change. At least I want James and Johnie home, and I want life to go on as before."

Margaret observed her father's mind in motion. Then he said, "My dear, when James and Johnie come home, they will be different people. They left as boys, but they will return as men. What they've been through will change them forever."

"I guess we have to move on." She paused briefly and then blurted out what had been on her mind. "Hank proposed last night. He wants me to marry him."

Matthew smiled. "Your mother suspected this, and I guess I did too."

"But I'm not ready to be married. He says I can teach a year and we can be married a year from now. But I don't really know. I want to be sure."

"Hank seems like a nice enough young man."

A picture of Hank flashed in her mind—average looking, light brown hair, average height, pale blue eyes, not especially muscular. The community would consider him a good, solid farmer. "Hank is a good person," she admitted. "I like him the way I like a friend. But I'm not sure I love him."

"Love is a strange thing," replied her father. "Love doesn't come all at once. I love your mother now more than I ever have. I can't think of life without her."

"Mother and you have something special. That's what I want in my marriage."

Her father momentarily seemed at a loss for words. "We didn't necessarily start out that way," he said slowly. "Your mother was a teacher. She could have married any number of young men. I think I loved her the minute I saw her. Sometimes I don't know what she saw in me. But I think the love I had for her then has grown through the years."

"You mean I could learn to love Hank more?"

"If you think you don't love him, then you know the answer."

"But I'm not absolutely sure. I think I'm falling for him."

Her father reached over and took her hand. "Darling, you are only eighteen. That's awfully young. You have time to decide."

Margaret changed the subject. "I wish James and Johnie were here right now." She stopped a moment. "And I wish Joe were alive and safe and back home."

Her father gave her one of those looks.

Beyond the Darkness

Margaret wasn't sure what to say next. "I miss Joe. And I care for him," she said softly.

"The women are praying for his safety."

The image of Joe remained etched in her mind. He was like a brother, only much more. "I read about those dreadful Japanese prison camps. I'm afraid Joe couldn't survive one of those. The Japs torture our boys."

"Men," began Matthew, "can survive much more than we think. Man has an intense will to live, and that desire can see him through almost anything."

Margaret didn't exactly feel comfort in her father's words. In her mind she kept seeing two young men, Hank and Joe. In that moment she realized she was not ready to make any decision.

Her father reached for his pocket watch. "Margaret, it's after twelve. Your mother has dinner ready. I bet she wonders what's happened."

Margaret stood up. "Dad, thanks for this talk. I know something for sure: I'm not ready to say yes."

The moment Matthew entered the kitchen, he knew something was wrong. Ellen's face told him this was serious.

"What's wrong, Mother?" Margaret asked.

Matthew saw Ellen seated at the table, wiping the tears from her eyes.

"I took a call from Western Union. There was a telegram."

Suddenly Matthew felt weak; his legs were about to buckle underneath him. His stomach felt that awful sensation that came with sudden fear.

Ellen continued, "The telegram said Johnie is missing in action. He was wounded and did not return with his company."

Matthew felt the worst emptiness he had ever experienced. Could it be that the son he loved most was dead? This was too much to bear. Margaret found her way into her father's arms. He held back the tears he wanted to shed. He had to be brave.

Ellen began to take the potatoes off the stove. "I'm a little late too. Dinner is ready." She went on about her business, as if resuming everyday tasks would stay any fear. "I know Johnie is alive. I believe that with my whole being. I know he will come home."

Matthew wanted to believe his wife.

Chapter 7

At that moment, little Michael entered. "My windmill won't come together right. It fell down." Michael had been playing with his Tinkertoys; he couldn't always get the parts to fit together.

"I'll help you after dinner," said Margaret.

"Why is everyone so sad?" asked Michael.

Ellen continued to place the food on the table as she searched for the right words. "Well, Michael, we had some news. Your big brother was hurt, and we're concerned about him."

The next minutes they tried to explain to a little boy that his big brother was injured, yet Matthew knew it was best not to let Michael know the seriousness of the situation. Besides, they all had to keep hoping. Hope made the difference.

Dinner did not include the usual lively conversation. Even Michael said little, perhaps realizing the seriousness of Johnie's situation.

Matthew needed to be alone after dinner. Instead of taking his usual nap, he went outside and walked toward the east pasture. There he found an oak tree that reminded him of the one he had often gone to as a child. This was one of those good places where he could think and pray through problems.

He knelt in a patch of melting snow. Somehow this body position helped him pray. "Dear Lord," he prayed aloud. "I need You now. Please keep my son Johnie safe. He's so full of life and love. He loves this land. He loves this place. Please bring him back to us safely."

In the next moments Matthew lost track of time. He kept seeing Johnie, first as a little boy climbing onto the old John Deere tractor. Then he grew quickly into a strong husky man, taller than Matthew himself. He felt the warmth of the love of his son.

Matthew wasn't sure how much time passed, but he became aware of a presence. It seemed he was not alone; Johnie was with him. He thought he heard a voice. "Dad, I'll be back home. I'll survive this war. I'll be back home with you and Mom."

During the next moments, time seemed to stand still.

Another voice echoed in his mind. "Lo, I am with you always." The words replayed in his mind. "I am with you." "I am with you."

Once more, that peace that defies all understanding was with him. Yes, there was darkness in this world, but he saw the light beyond.

Beyond the Darkness

Ellen spent a restless evening. She needed to shield little Michael from harsh reality. She comforted her mother-in-law. And she and Margaret talked of Margaret's work and her decision not to say yes to Hank.

Matthew surprised her. He was strangely calm during the night. He kept saying that he knew Johnie was alive. God had given him that assurance.

It was not quite seven in the morning when the phone jangled its three long rings. Ellen knew immediately something was wrong. Or could it be a message that Johnie wasn't missing in action?

Tensely, she took down the receiver. The voice at the other end was Victoria's.

"Ellen, I just got up, and Carol didn't come home last night. I think she sneaked out with Jeff again. I've been watching her closely."

"We'll be there as soon as Matthew finishes the chores."

Ellen set about preparing hot oatmeal for breakfast. Matthew came in shortly. After Ellen explained the situation, he commented, "Everything happens at once."

As Matthew took care of necessary outdoor chores, Ellen talked to Margaret and her mother-in-law about taking care of Michael. It was a good thing that Sunday worship services were now in the afternoon. With no regular minister since Pastor Strand left, a visiting pastor conducted their services.

When they arrived at Victoria's, Ellen noticed her sister-in-law was extremely upset. "I've never confronted such a young woman," Victoria exclaimed. "Carol cannot be trusted one bit. She lies and does anything she can to be with Jeff."

For a moment Ellen felt personally insulted. "I've tried everything to get through to Carol," she told Victoria. "I've prayed about it. I've tried countless mother-daughter talks. But nothing seems to make any difference."

"I'm sorry," Victoria apologized. "I know Carol could not have a better mother. Sometimes children stray from what they have been taught."

"We had some other news," said Matthew.

Ellen noticed how pale her husband was.

"You mean we have concerns other than Carol?" Victoria asked.

Ellen thought of the dreadful phone call from yesterday. "Western Union called," she said. "Johnie is missing in action. We're afraid of what this could mean."

Victoria went over and hugged her brother. "I'm so sorry."

Chapter 7

Matthew stood stiffly. "Yesterday I was sure everything was all right. Now I'm beginning to have doubts."

During the next minutes, Ellen, Matthew, and Victoria sat and talked, trying to make sense of everything. Drinking coffee seemed to make things better.

When the telephone rang, Victoria quickly answered. Ellen could tell little from the conversation until Victoria said, "You wait right there. We're coming to River Falls."

"What happened?" questioned Ellen and Matthew.

"Jeff's car broke down. They stayed overnight with one of his friends in River Falls." Victoria paused a moment. "The other day Carol was supposed to be with girlfriends, and instead she was with Jeff. That's how she lies. Anyhow, I said we'd go get Carol."

Ellen felt both relief and anger. "And we are going to have words with that young woman. She has some answering to do."

Victoria's black eyes flashed anger. "I'm the principal and teacher at Lake View High School. I cannot tolerate this conduct. I don't know that I can be responsible for Carol living here any longer."

"We understand," said Ellen.

Victoria rose to get her coat. "I'll drive. I can see that the two of you have bigger concerns."

An hour later, Victoria walked up the steps to a large Victorian home. Matthew and Ellen followed close behind. At the door, a young man appeared. Victoria briskly announced, "We have come to get Carol Anderson."

Jeff came to the door and mumbled, "She'll be right down."

Victoria took charge. "Young man, you know that Carol was forbidden to go out with you. And what were you doing in River Falls?"

Jeff stumbled over his words. "I'm sorry, ma'am. Carol and I care for each other. We want to be together."

"Carol is sixteen years old. Much too young for you." Victoria shook her finger at Jeff. "Young man, you could be in serious trouble."

Jeff backed away as Carol appeared in the doorway.

"Can Jeff have a ride back to Lake View? His car is in bad shape."

Victoria did not hesitate. "Absolutely not. Young woman, you are coming with us. You are underage, and you have some explaining to do."

"What if I won't?"

Ellen couldn't understand her daughter's attitude. "Carol, you are coming home with us," she demanded. "If we can't trust you to stay with your Aunt Victoria, you're coming home to the farm. Many girls either work at home or go out as hired girls. So there are no ifs, ands, or buts about this."

Jeff squirmed. He turned to Carol, "I think you'd better go."

Carol reluctantly followed her parents and aunt as the four walked to the car in awkward silence. As they drove down the street, Ellen turned to Carol. "We have other news—sad news—Johnie is missing in action."

Carol showed the first sign of feelings besides anger. "Oh, no! That could mean something much worse."

The news seemed to break the ice, making Carol more contrite.

Once they were on the road, Victoria began her lecture. "Carol, you will not be staying at my place if you continue your present actions. I do not allow that kind of questionable conduct. Besides, you were forbidden to go out of town."

"I'm sorry. But I care for Jeff. I love him."

Ellen knew well her daughter's determination. "When you're on your own," she told Carol, "when you're eighteen, then you can make your decisions. Right now you are living at your Aunt Victoria's or at our home. You do not have the right to disrupt our lives by staying out all night. You were brought up to know and act better than that."

"I haven't done anything wrong. Jeff and I are good friends."

Victoria raised her voice. "If you return to my place, you will obey my rules, or else you are out."

"And," continued Ellen, "if you are out of your aunt's home, you will work at home. Your father needs help, and so do I. Or you are welcome to find a job. Hired girls are in demand."

"I'll run away."

Victoria pulled the car over to the side of the road and turned to Carol in the backseat. "You do that, and you'll find that life out there isn't so easy. And your friend, Jeff, doesn't have a job of his own. His parents don't want him having anything to do with you. The Grants hold the purse strings. Jeff isn't going to give that up."

Carol covered her face, and all at once Ellen felt sorry for her daughter. "You're going to have to make changes," she sternly reminded Carol.

The lectures and conversation continued until they drove into Lake View. As they got out of the car in Victoria's yard, Ellen announced, "Carol, you're coming home with us for today. We'll drive you to school in the morning. At the end of the week on Friday, we will pick you up

Chapter 7

right after school. You're not going to have another chance to do what you've been doing."

"I'm in prison," Carol moaned. "What about my school activities?"

As they walked into Victoria's house, her aunt spoke authoritatively. "You are barred from school activities. Your grades are not good. As principal, I have that authority."

Carol said nothing. In fact, no one spoke another word as Carol went upstairs and got her overnight clothes and books. Ellen knew she had a serious task ahead.

It didn't take long for Margaret to realize the tension between Carol and her parents. Carol reluctantly went with the family to the afternoon church service at Oak Ridge Church, but it didn't seem the same without Pastor Strand. A pastor from the neighboring town preached that afternoon.

Later that afternoon, back at home, Margaret went with her father to the barn to help with chores. It was a good chance to talk again.

"I don't understand Carol," she told him.

Her father responded thoughtfully, "I don't either. She's become an entirely different person. She's not the girl I used to know."

Margaret remembered seeing Jeff with other girls. "Jeff cannot be trusted. He's out for a good time. I'm afraid he means trouble for Carol."

"You're right. I don't know what we can do."

"I'll try talking to her again. But she probably won't listen."

Father and daughter went about milking the cows, feeding them, and seeing that the milk cans were placed in the cooling tank. As they walked back to the house, Margaret spoke again. "I've made my decision. I'm telling Hank that I can't think about marriage to anyone for at least another year. I'm not old enough. I'm not ready. I don't want to make a serious mistake."

"You're a wise young woman."

Margaret's mind was filled with hopes and dreams, but fears as well. She was eager to begin teaching. She dreamed of the good she could do and a future that involved a family of her own. Yet she also feared for Johnie's life. At the same time, she couldn't stop thinking of Joe.

Chapter 8

Matthew had moments when he felt a heavy darkness within. At times he thought he would never again see Johnie. At the same time, Johnie's voice seemed to echo almost everywhere Matthew went.

He left the barn with all the cattle safely in their stalls, fed and taken care of for the night. The milk cans were in the tank, ready to be picked up by the milk truck tomorrow. Shadows of evening stole across the landscape. This time of evening encouraged Matthew to reflect and remember.

For a moment he saw a small six-year-old climb up on the John Deere, insisting he was old enough to drive. He remembered the home farm and the way he and Johnie went out in the pasture to find the cow and her newborn calf. Then there was that Sunday morning before Armistice Day when Johnie went out hunting, just wanting to enjoy the outdoors. That had been a turning point in his son's life. He wanted to believe that Johnie was alive and someplace safe now.

At least James was in a safer place. Stationed at an army base in England, James worked with military intelligence and communication at headquarters.

Then there was Joe. They'd had no word from him for over a year. If alive, he was probably in a Japanese prison camp. Could any human being survive such atrocities?

Beyond the Darkness

"Lord," he prayed aloud, "give me strength. Please let Johnie be alive. Bring him and Joe and James back home safely. Cause this terrible war to end quickly. Hitler and others must be brought to justice. They cannot be permitted to go on destroying people and plunging this world into the horror of war. Please bring peace to this troubled world."

Once more, the kitchen lights beckoned him. He thanked God for Ellen and for little Michael and for the way Ma was regaining her strength. In some aspects, life continued in the same manner. Many things changed, but much remained the same.

And there was Carol. She seemed to have settled down, or was she just playacting? For a week, Victoria had given good reports of their problem daughter.

Margaret would be away at school for several weeks and unable to come home. She spent long, hard hours of study, working on many projects she had to finish. This daughter was his pride and joy.

Ellen greeted him at the door. "I wondered what was keeping you. Supper's ready."

Ma and Michael were already seated at the table.

"Any news?" Matthew asked. He could see in Ellen's face that she had something to say.

"After supper," she said. "We'll talk then."

Supper was always the time for talking over general family concerns. Matthew sensed Ellen had something more to discuss, but obviously later. The kitchen grew quiet as they ate. Ma finally spoke up. "Matthew, I heard from Martha. She's coming back next month."

"I'm happy she's coming back. Life always seems better when she's here."

"I was thinking," continued Ma, "that I'd like to go back to my little house. I could live there with Martha."

Matthew looked across to Ellen. "But Martha often leaves to be with one of her girls. Do you want to stay there alone?"

"I'll always have Corrine and Warren close by. My ankle's healed and I'm feeling just fine. I like the idea of being in my own home."

"Gramma," interrupted Michael, "I want you here. Don't leave us."

Ma smiled. "I'll miss you, but I'll be nearby. You can come and visit me, and even stay overnight."

That assurance seemed to satisfy Michael.

"I want to get back to my quilting and sewing," continued Ma. "I miss my sewing machine and my knitting."

Chapter 8

"You've knitted here," said Ellen. "We'll bring all your quilting materials over here."

"It's not quite the same."

Matthew knew his mother's determination. "We'll take you back at the right time—when all the snow's gone," he promised.

After supper, Ellen and Ma did the dishes. Matthew read the *Daily Journal* and tuned to a radio mystery program. But he wasn't really listening. He was wondering what Ellen needed to talk about.

Ellen put Michael to bed and heard his prayers. Ma got out her book and went to her room to read after Ellen came downstairs. Now that they were alone, Ellen told Matthew the news. "Sheriff Walker called. He didn't want to talk too much over the phone. But he'll stop by tomorrow."

"What could he want?"

"It's about our nephew, Larry. They want to let him out of prison. Parole."

"I hope he's learned his lesson."

The next morning as Matthew was going into the house for morning coffee, Sheriff Walker drove up. Matthew motioned for him to come inside. They would visit over coffee.

Matthew trusted and admired this law officer and friend. The sheriff had come into their lives a number of times. When Margaret and his niece Irene were young and got lost, the sheriff had helped with the community search for the two girls. Then when P.J. was the cause of many problems for the Anderson family, Walker was there to help. And after that, when Larry managed to get into deeper trouble than P.J., Walker helped again.

Seated in the Andersons' kitchen, the sheriff first expressed his concern for Johnie. "There's a good chance that he's going to come back. Johnie's the kind of young man I'd like to have in my sheriff's department."

Ellen smiled. "I think Matthew would like him back here on the farm."

"He could do both."

The three of them settled down to conversation and coffee. Ma discreetly stayed behind in her room.

Eventually Walker changed the subject. "I guess I'd better get down to business about what I came for."

Beyond the Darkness

Ellen voiced the very thing that worried Matthew. "We're a little concerned about having Larry around here. We remember all too well the trouble he got into before."

"I may have good news, then," said Walker. "The prison wardens say he's been a model prisoner and that he's turned around his life. I hope it's true."

Matthew thought of P.J. as a play actor. Son Larry had those same abilities.

"Can we trust him again?" questioned Ellen.

"The wardens say he's had some kind of religious experience—that he's a whole different person."

Matthew hoped this was true. "I'm afraid when he was sent to the state prison, we lost contact with him. And I guess he wasn't much to write. Ma kept on writing him, and I did visit several times awhile back."

"He used to blame us for the trouble he was in," added Ellen.

"What I'm asking you to do, Matthew, is to check on Larry from time to time. In other words, Larry will have to report to you regularly. You'd be his parole officer."

Matthew swallowed hard. "I wonder if I'd be good at that."

The sheriff looked directly at him. "Matthew, you're one of the most honest men I've ever known. I don't know anyone I would trust more."

But Ellen objected, "Yes, sheriff, he is. But Matthew's so kind he doesn't want to hurt anyone, so Larry might take advantage of him. And where would he live? I think Rita's house has been rented out."

"I'm doing some other checking."

"Doesn't he need work?" asked Ellen. "We know he's no good as a farmer. When he farmed, his wife, Joan, did half the work with the cattle."

"Larry has another talent," said Walker. "He's good with machines. He can be a mechanic at the local gas station. Old Gus is in need of help."

"Matthew has to speak for himself, but I wonder if he is the best person to check on Larry. I have another idea if Matthew wants to back out."

Matthew knew his wife was right. "I'm afraid I'm too easygoing to do a good job. Larry would take advantage of me."

"Victoria would be the perfect person," suggested Ellen. "She's a great disciplinarian. As principal of Lake View High School, she knows how to get people to toe the mark."

Chapter 8

Sheriff Walker smiled. "I wonder why I didn't think of that. If anyone can do the job, it's Miss Victoria Anderson. Some of those misbehaving boys in school tremble at the thought of being hauled into her office."

Sheriff Walker and his friends visited awhile longer. Then he left.

Matthew went outside to do his late morning chores. He felt relieved that Larry would not be his responsibility, though he would do what he could to help. Victoria would make sure the letter of the law was fulfilled.

Sadness continued to fill Matthew's spirit. Thoughts of Johnie would not leave him. And when he wasn't thinking of Johnie, he began wondering about Carol.

The dirty melting snow of spring was similar to the darkness of the world around him. A world tired of war.

Ellen felt she had failed as a mother when it came to Carol. "Lord," she prayed, "what did I do wrong? I brought her up the same as the others. Yet she is rebellious. Please, Lord, show me what I can do."

Ellen closed her Bible. This was one of those rare times when she was alone in the house. Michael was at school, moving along in first grade. Matthew had gone to town and left his mother at the little house so she could check on her place.

Just as Ellen was about to turn on the radio to listen to "Ma Perkins" and "Pepper Young's Family," a car drove up. She wasn't expecting company. Perhaps it was a salesman. She bought goods only from the Watkins man. Other salesman she turned away quickly.

A woman walked toward the back door. Usually only family and friends used the back door, but recent snow hadn't been shoveled from the front of the house. It took only a moment to realize the visitor was Mrs. Jeffrey Grant II.

Ellen took off her apron and waited for the knock at the door. She was far from happy about a visit from Mrs. Grant. This could only mean trouble.

A loud authoritative knock revealed Mrs. Grant's impatience. Ellen opened the door.

"Good afternoon, Mrs. Anderson. I felt we needed to talk. May I come in?"

"Yes, certainly," she replied. "I'll take your coat."

Mrs. Grant took off her mink coat and carefully handed it to Ellen.

Ellen saw no way of making this visit easy. "Why don't I put on a fresh pot of coffee?" she offered.

"That would be fine. But please don't make it too strong."

Ellen filled the coffeepot with water and put it on the stove. She kept wondering exactly what Mrs. Grant wanted. No doubt, Carol was at the center of the woman's concern.

At first Mrs. Grant rambled on about Jeffrey and their plans for him to take over as bank president in the future. Ellen realized one thing so far: Mrs. Grant did not want Carol to be any part of that future. Mrs. Grant's approach this day was more friendly than at any previous time, however. The two talked about growing up and about family life. It turned out Mrs. Grant grew up on a farm and started her adult life as a rural schoolteacher, just as Ellen did. They had more in common than Ellen realized.

Ellen poured the coffee and brought out the cookies. As they continued their talk, Mrs. Grant warmed up to Ellen by saying, "Let's not be so formal. Call me Loretta."

"You must call me Ellen."

Loretta Grant went on, "You know there was something good about the country school. Each grade learned from those ahead of them and could review for those a grade behind. The problem was, there were often too many students for one teacher."

Ellen remembered her days as teacher. "I was seventeen when I started. I had thirty students in my first school. Several of the boys were older than I."

Loretta replied, "I had twenty-five for a short while. Then I went to a smaller school."

The two women began to reminisce about their experiences in the country and about their experiences in the classroom. But eventually Loretta Grant stiffened. Ellen knew it was time for the less pleasant part of the woman's visit.

"There's something we need to talk about." Loretta Grant's words seemed ominous.

Ellen waited for her to go on.

"I've been hearing some rumors about our children. I don't know exactly how to say what I have to say."

"Just say it."

Chapter 8

"Well, our kids have been seeing each other on the sly. And the story is that your daughter is pregnant with my son's child."

Ellen gasped. Underneath she had known this was a possibility. "I know nothing of this."

"The kids are too young."

"Your son isn't. He's twenty-three, isn't he? Carol is only sixteen. She'll be seventeen this year."

"We have an understanding for Jeff. There is a fine young woman from River Falls who is planning to marry my son. They are from the same kind of family as ours. She's the daughter of the bank president."

Underneath Ellen felt anger but held back and said nothing as Loretta continued, "These two would be such a perfect match. Ginny is almost twenty, just the right age for getting married."

"It's up to the children to decide about marriage," Ellen replied, "and Carol has more than a year before she can think of getting married."

"That brings me back to the purpose of my visit." Loretta Grant cleared her throat. "If there is a pregnancy, we feel Carol should go away for a while. There are places for unwed mothers. She should go there, give up the baby for adoption, and not disgrace her family and community."

Ellen felt anger rise within her. "Now, Mrs. Grant, we don't even know that Carol is pregnant. These are just rumors. Yes, we don't want Carol going out with your son either. He's too old for her. But there doesn't seem to be much we can do."

Loretta Grant sat up erectly in her chair. "We used to say that the girl or woman sets the standard. Boys will be boys. If the young girl acts properly, the boy will respect that. On the other hand, if the girl forgets that she is a lady, a young man will treat her as such."

Ellen tightened her first. "Your son is the adult. My daughter is still a child. Your son is the one who is more responsible. Carol is a minor. Jeff is an adult."

Loretta's voice quieted again. "But you won't let Carol ruin Jeffrey's chances of getting ahead in the world, will you?"

"Jeffrey will ruin his own chances. He's done some things that might have destroyed his future and even killed him."

"You have to understand, Mrs. Anderson, he went through a lot when he was in the army. Some people even call it shell shock. He can't be held responsible if he does some drinking."

Ellen stood up. "We'll do what we can to take care of Carol. If she is having a baby, we'll deal with that."

"But think of the disgrace to our families. The whole world doesn't have to know. Carol can go away quietly this summer. And no one has to know." Loretta Grant rose and towered above Ellen in an intimidating stance. "My husband and I will help with the expenses."

"If this is true, your son is the responsible one. He should help."

"Please don't be hard on Jeffrey."

Ellen picked up the mink coat and handed it to her visitor. "I don't think there's anything more to say."

Mrs. Grant's carefully modulated voice changed to a higher, demanding pitch. "Don't you forget who we are. The Grants have power and influence. We can make trouble for you if you don't take care of this situation."

Ellen moved toward Mrs. Grant. "My husband and I will do what is right. We don't care who you think you are."

"Just remember—"

"Yes, we will. And I believe the law is on our side. Your son is an adult. Our daughter is a minor. Perhaps we should talk to Sheriff Walker."

Mrs. Grant's tone changed suddenly. "Please don't. Please—that would only make things worse."

"I think it's time for you to leave." Ellen opened the door. Loretta Grant left without another word.

When Matthew returned late that afternoon, he knew something was wrong.

"It's Carol," Ellen said. Then she proceeded to tell him of Mrs. Grant's visit and the rumors she had been told.

Matthew still regarded Carol as a little girl. It was hard to imagine her as a mother. "She's our girl," he said, "and we love her no matter what she's done."

"And it's only rumor," replied Ellen.

"Problems seem to come in threes. There's Carol. Johnie is missing in action. And Larry's coming back from prison."

"That's superstition about problems in threes," remarked Ellen. "We have much to pray about."

Chapter 9

April 1945

Something must be wrong, Matthew thought as Victoria got out of her car that Tuesday evening. *Why would she pay a visit on a school night?*

"Hello, Matthew," she said. "The snow from the other day is melting fast."

The countryside had been blanketed with an unseasonable storm a few days before. But spring snow disappeared fast.

"Is something wrong?" questioned Matthew. "You don't usually drive out on a school night. Has Carol been up to something?"

Victoria's serious look changed to a smile. "No, I came about something else. However, I have to say there's good news. Carol has been doing much better. I think she's done a real turnaround."

Matthew gave a sigh of relief. "I'm relieved that the rumors aren't true."

Victoria did not hesitate. "I came to talk about Larry."

"Is he out of jail?"

"Yes, he's supposed to be coming at any time. He's heading for Joan's parents' home. It sounds as if she'll have him back."

"I don't know that he deserves it after the way he treated her, but," Matthew added, "our family doesn't believe in divorce."

Beyond the Darkness

"I've been working with Sheriff Walker. We have a job lined up for him with Old Gus at the gas station. So that means Larry can be pumping gas and working on cars."

"Where will he live?"

"Well, I talked with his mother. Rita says her house at the lake is rented out. That leaves one of the cabins for them to live in. Not much room."

"What is there for me to do?"

"I know you have many concerns, but Larry has looked up to you. I thought maybe you could be part of our welcoming group. I understand he's turned around completely, and we should let him know that we forgive him."

"I suppose I can visit him, but I'm not sure how he feels about giving up his claim to some of our land."

Victoria began to walk back to her car. "We may have to remind him of our rightful ownership. He has to know that his father did something terribly wrong. In fact, the court would have found P.J. guilty of fraud if Rita had not given in."

"I'll do what I can. Why don't you come in and stay for supper? I have chores to do, but then we'll have supper."

Victoria thought a moment. "I guess that would be all right. I'll call my house, and Carol can fend for herself."

Matthew quickly completed his chores. The cattle were good company, and the work helped him push the concerns about Johnie to the back of his mind. Life had a way of moving forward.

A few minutes later, Ellen was peeling potatoes for supper. She refused Victoria's offer to help. "You're tired. We can visit as I get things ready."

Victoria reviewed her discussion with Matthew.

"I'm concerned about Matthew," said Ellen. "Johnie missing in action has hit him hard. If Johnie doesn't return, I don't know what that will do to him."

"Johnie is, without question, Matthew's favorite."

"I have to admit he probably is." Ellen placed the pan of potatoes on the front burner. "We try to be fair with our children, but Johnie loves everything Matthew loves. That has to bring them closer. And James

Chapter 9

and Margaret's love of learning brings them closer to me. We just can't help it."

Victoria looked away. Ellen thought she saw tears in her eyes.

"Ellen, you make me realize what I've missed by not having a family. Sometimes I feel so very much alone."

Ellen realized how very fortunate she was. "You're always welcome here. You've been such a part of our lives all through the years."

"When I think of it, your family has been more than special. I've never felt as close to Mary and Ed. Ed is a good man but he has that violent temper."

"Yes, we used to have more to do with Mary and Ed. They seem to be drifting away from us as they think about moving to California."

Victoria got up from the kitchen table and walked over to the window. "Families do drift apart. I'm thankful Mother is with us. She helps keep the family together."

Ellen's thoughts moved elsewhere. She wanted to talk about Carol but wasn't sure what to say, so she remained quiet as Victoria set the table. Ellen took care of other meal preparations, welcoming the silence for a time. Then finally, she decided to speak. "At times I feel that I've failed Carol. When she was small, I was tired and not feeling well. I felt I took care of James, Johnie, and Margaret much better. Carol didn't get the same attention."

Victoria interrupted. "Ellen, I've watched you and the children all these years. No one could have been a better mother."

"Thank you."

"I've seen parents of all kinds. There are many good parents and some very poor parents. But as I look at all of them, I see few that do a job better than you and Matthew have done."

"But Carol, with all her lies and sneaking off. That isn't the way I brought up my children."

"Children make choices." Victoria paused the way a teacher pauses in the classroom. "I've had all kinds of experiences with parents and their children. Many times I am puzzled. There are no easy explanations."

"What are you saying?"

"I've seen some of the model parents whose children have gone in the wrong directions and turned out badly. And I've seen some alcoholic parents whose children turned out remarkably well. It's a puzzle."

Ellen kept thinking of Carol. "But what about training a child up in the way he ought to go? When he is old he will not depart from it."

Beyond the Darkness

"That is absolute truth." Victoria spoke with full authority. "Carol may make mistakes now, but she will come back to what you have taught her."

"I keep thinking, though," continued Ellen. "When Carol was young and impressionable, I was so tired. After all, I had four young children—not too far apart in ages. I just didn't have my usual energy. I felt discouraged and overwhelmed by motherhood and all the responsibilities of being a farm wife." At that moment Ellen wanted to sit down and cry.

"Don't be afraid to talk," Victoria urged. "It's good to talk through our concerns."

Ellen sat down. "I haven't had anyone to listen to me. Right now I just want to sit down and have a good cry."

Victoria reached across and took her sister-in-law's hand. "You go ahead."

Ellen found her tears flowing easily. She was not inclined to cry, but the tears seemed to have a cleansing effect. Victoria quietly held her hand. After a few moments Ellen wiped her eyes. "I feel better. Life doesn't seem so hopeless now."

Two distractions came. Michael burst into the room, wondering when they would eat supper. And the potatoes began to boil over.

The sound of Matthew stomping snow off his overshoes announced his arrival for supper. As Ellen joined Victoria and Matthew and Michael in the table prayer, she experienced its truth. "Come, Lord Jesus, be our guest, Let these gifts to us be blest. Amen."

She felt secure in God's presence with her family close by.

Matthew looked with satisfaction at the healthy cattle in the barnyard. The morning chores were done, and the cattle could be left outside. He looked to the fields and hills and realized that he could be in the fields soon.

Family had always been important to Matthew. Not just his wife and five children but also his brother and sisters and nieces and nephews, as well as his cousins and other extended family members. Next to his love for God was his love of family and this land he farmed. At this moment the awful war and other problems seemed very distant.

Chapter 9

As he turned toward the house, a car drove up. He recognized it as the one P.J. had driven several years ago. Larry got out of the car.

For a moment, Matthew thought of the little nephew he had played with, a boy who had seemed like a little brother. Then he looked at Larry with his dark hair and handsome features, duplicating the features of Larry's father, P.J.

Larry stood by the car as if he didn't know what to expect. "Uncle Matthew. I'm back."

Matthew stood for a moment, not knowing how he felt. Was this a man like P.J., controlling and dishonest? Then he hurried toward his nephew as the father had run to greet his prodigal son. Matthew extended his hand for a sturdy Anderson handshake, then opened his arms to his prodigal nephew. "Welcome home."

During the next minutes there was routine conversation about weather and farming and such things. At the same time Matthew sensed his nephew wanted to say much more. "Uncle Matthew," the younger man began tentatively, "I have something else to say."

Matthew waited.

"I'm sorry for all the trouble I caused you and everyone else. I was such an awful person. I have no right to expect anything from you."

"You're family," Matthew said. "Family is important."

"Please forgive me. I know it's a lot to ask, but I humbly ask your forgiveness."

Matthew hesitated, knowing P.J.'s history of broken promises, and again extended his hand. "Yes, my boy, I forgive you."

"There are some more things I'd like to say. I don't know where to begin."

"Why don't you come in? We'll have morning coffee."

"Let me say this to you before I see Ellen."

Matthew hoped and prayed that these words would be sincere, not just smooth talk in the tradition of P.J.

"I'm a changed man," Larry began. "When I was in prison, some men had a jail ministry. They came each week and visited many of us. Then we had a service and they preached." Larry looked away, seeming to grope for words before continuing. "Through their visits and preaching I began to see who I was. I was dreadfully self-centered. I thought only of myself and what I could get. I could see that if I continued in the same way, I would only destroy myself and others."

Matthew realized how serious his nephew was.

Beyond the Darkness

"I knew at one moment—a moment when I thought about taking my life—that Christ was the only answer. I came to Him in tears. I asked forgiveness for all the terrible things I had done. At that moment I felt a peace come over me that I still cannot completely understand."

Matthew could say nothing. Larry had said it all.

"I realize I must ask forgiveness from those I wronged. I've talked with Aunt Victoria. I need to go to other people as well. And I've come to you."

"My boy, I'm more than happy that you've made this change."

Matthew realized Larry was looking into his eyes.

"I need to ask a favor," Larry began. "I don't quite know how to ask. It's a different kind of favor."

"I'll see what I can do."

"I miss Dad. In his way he tried to be a good father. He gave me everything—except what I needed most. He had little time for me, and he tried to control everyone."

Matthew remembered some of the good in his brother. "Yes, but he had his good side. At times he was very generous."

"I thought maybe I should put this into words. Uncle Matthew, I need someone who's like a father to me. I can think of no better person than you."

Overwhelmed with the compliment, Matthew could say nothing.

Larry stumbled over his next words. "I'm sorry if I'm out of line."

"Oh, no, you're not. I feel honored that you would ask. I'll be your uncle; that's right next to being a father."

"Thanks, Uncle. I have those wonderful memories of you when you played with me as a kid."

"I remember." Matthew's mind took him back to those school days—especially that day he froze and could not pass the geography state board examination.

"Is something wrong?" Larry asked.

"I keep thinking about my limited education. I never finished eighth grade. Your dad and the others all finished high school, and Victoria and your father went on to college. Somehow I felt I wasn't good enough. I didn't quite measure up."

Larry placed his hand on his uncle's shoulder. "I've always felt you were every bit as good as the rest. In fact, you are one of those few thoroughly good people."

Matthew wasn't quite sure how to accept these high commendations. "I think it's time to go in for coffee."

Chapter 9

Larry smiled. "Coffee sounds good."

Ellen greeted her nephew warmly. He repeated some of what he had said to Matthew, and Ellen said she would forgive him for past mistakes.

Larry began to tell them of his plans. He was trying to fix up one of the old cabins for Joan's arrival next week. At this point Ellen mentioned a suggestion. "Margaret and Carol are coming home this weekend. Why don't we plan for a cleanup and fix-up day so that things will be ready for Joan."

"You'd do all that for me?"

Ellen's enthusiasm seemed to grow. "We need a distraction. We have all our concerns about Johnie, and we've had other things on our minds. This will be good for everyone."

Matthew took out his watch to check the time "I have a task that I better take care of—changing the oil on the tractor. Why don't you come with, Larry? We can talk."

"And," added Ellen, "stay for dinner. We're having chicken for a change."

Larry didn't hesitate. "I enjoy home-cooked meals more than I ever did before. That will be great."

"Have you seen Joan?" asked Ellen.

"Yes, I stayed there two nights. Her parents aren't too thrilled that I'm back. I guess I have to prove myself. But Joan was happy, and my little boy. He's quite a guy."

Matthew and Larry were soon outside in the shed, working on the oil change. Larry took over the work that Matthew didn't care to do. At the same time, Larry confided, "Joan's parents don't want us back together. Joan's coming back on a trial basis. I have to prove myself."

Matthew thought he saw fear in Larry's eyes.

"I can't blame Joan or her parents. I was acting pretty rotten three years ago. I even became violent."

"I can see you've changed," Matthew encouraged him. "Joan will realize that."

"I hope so."

As he talked with Larry, Matthew knew the change in his nephew was genuine. That was one less worry. Now he could only pray for Johnie's safety and for Carol's attitudes and choices.

Spring had a way of bringing hope.

Chapter 10

May 1945

The weeks that followed were perhaps the darkest in Matthew's life. There were times he could not see beyond that darkness. Johnie was missing in action, possibly dead. Joe had not been heard from in over a year. He could be in a Japanese prison camp, or he might never be found. Carol seemed to be acting better, but the problem had not yet been solved.

Spring had always brought new hope to Matthew, but this year that hope did not seem to come. The war was winding down and should soon end, but even that was eclipsed by no word from or about Johnie. Matthew worked from sunrise to well past sunset every day. The April snows had delayed some of the annual planting.

Matthew trudged toward the house after finishing the last of his spring planting. Sleep would be most welcome. He realized he was covered all over with layers of dust from the planting and disking and all the rest. He needed a hired man, but none were available during wartime.

It was May, but the fateful day of April 12 still cast a cloud over Matthew, as well as the whole nation. The death of President Roosevelt had come as a terrible shock, bringing even more darkness into his life. The president had been resting in Warm Springs after his many efforts to bring the war to an end. Roosevelt had been anticipating the end of

Beyond the Darkness

the war as he posed for a presidential portrait by Elizabeth Shumatoff. How quickly this man's life came to an end.

During the next weeks it seemed as if the entire nation remained under that dark cloud. In a sense, life was at a standstill.

"The planting is finally done," Matthew said aloud as he walked up the porch steps. "But what comes now? I don't feel ready to go on."

Slowly Matthew opened the porch door. He never thought life would be this difficult. He stood for a moment, not ready to go inside. Then he became aware of Ellen's movements in the kitchen and went in.

"Matthew, I'm worried. You've been working too hard," Ellen greeted him.

"The field work's done. It will be easier now."

"You can't go on this way. No human should work the long hours you've been working." Ellen placed the laundry tub near the stove. "I've heated water so you can take a bath."

"Thank you. I'm filthy from all this dust."

Matthew shed his dirty clothes and got into the tub. Slowly he soaped himself and then began to wash off the dirt. Somehow life seemed just a bit better. It was almost as if some of the darkness and dirt of the past had been washed away. He felt a glint of hope.

A half hour later, Matthew sat at the kitchen table with Ellen across from him. She poured a cup of hot milk, always a relaxing drink before bedtime. By this time, Michael was sound asleep. Their quiet conversation was soon interrupted by car lights reflected in the window. Ellen got up. "Who could be coming at this hour? It's well after nine."

After all the recent concerns, Matthew dreaded what might be coming. "I'm afraid to hear what's happened."

At that moment he recognized the familiar voice of Glenn Robertson. The voice didn't sound like one bearing bad news. "Have you heard the good news?" he called out as he entered the kitchen.

"What news?" questioned Matthew. "We haven't had time to listen to the radio or talk with anyone all day."

"The war's over!" shouted Glenn. "And I have even better news. You won't believe the news that came through today."

"What news?" Matthew and Ellen asked at once.

"Tim is alive!" Glenn kept repeating the same words again and again. "Tim is alive!"

"I'm so happy!" responded Matthew, even though he felt more acutely the absence of his own son.

Chapter 10

"That means Mabel was right all along. She knew that Tim was alive, and we didn't believe her," Ellen said.

Glenn continued to talk. "Somehow Tim lost his dog tag and it was found with the wrong body. He was taken prisoner and released some time back. He's being checked out in an army hospital. He'll be home in a month."

Ellen picked up the coffeepot and began filling it with water. "I think this calls for a fresh cup of coffee—even if it is late."

"If we were drinkers, we'd celebrate with something stronger," Glenn laughed. "We gave that up years ago, didn't we, Matthew?"

As the three drank coffee and visited, Matthew continued to feel a sadness, almost a kind of despair about Johnie. Late that night he prayed. "Lord, bring Johnie home safely. I can't bear to lose my son."

Matthew thought of the dark that came just before dawn. During that darkness the stars shone most brilliantly. On many a sleepless night, Matthew dressed and walked outside to look up at the heavens. "How magnificent are the heavens, the work of Thy Hands," he recited aloud on those nights.

Yet even in the midst of these dark days came rays of hope. A few days later, after hearing Glenn's good news, a letter came from James. In his way with words, James gave Matthew new hope.

Matthew reread the letter many times:

Mom and Dad,

Don't give up the hope that Johnie will return. Johnie is physically and mentally strong. When we were kids, he could manage any kind of physical feat. He could run and beat out all the rest of us. Johnie's strength was unbelievable.

That's why I'm saying that he's out there some place. He may be missing, but he's in our hearts and prayers. I have a purpose in life to fulfill. I'm convinced of that. Johnie has his purpose that he must fulfill.

The war is winding down. It's a matter of time. We mourn Roosevelt's death. Though I didn't agree with his politics, I know he was a great man. He inspired all of us during the time of war. We do have nothing to fear but fear itself.

Beyond the Darkness

As I wake from dreams, I often hear Johnie's voice. When we were little, we fought as brothers do. But during our years in high school, I learned to love and admire him. And he grew to love and admire me. Johnie is a protector of those who are weaker. Johnie is a worker who will do whatever needs to be done. He will live up to the name of John Anderson—your father and my grandfather.

Keep the faith, Mom and Dad. As our national anthem says, "Then conquer we must, for our cause it is just." I believe that. God has given me a dream to be a teacher and a writer, someone who will fight to make this world a better place. Only I will fight with teaching and words. Johnie will move forward in his way to make this world better.

Mom and Dad, you have given us this vision. We owe more to you than we can ever express. Be ready for us when we come home. You and the farm and the rest of the family are what we have fought for.

And we are winning. I love you more than I can ever say.

Your son, James

After reading those words many times, Matthew knew most of the letter by heart. He felt the presence of both his sons.

"You look pale, dear," said Ellen when Matthew came in for breakfast the next morning. "I think you should visit Dr. Baker."

"I keep thinking about Johnie. I'd give anything if he were home."

"We must keep praying. Tim Robertson is alive. We have to keep believing that Johnie will survive and return."

"I'm finding that harder each day."

Matthew knew Ellen was trying to cheer him up. It always amazed him how his wife could retain her composure and go on with life in the midst of terrible situations.

"Why don't you drive into town?" she suggested. "Maybe you could stop and see Glenn. And when you're in town, pick up some groceries, and see how Larry's doing at the station."

Matthew agreed an outing would do him good, so he changed clothes and drove by Glenn's to see what he was doing. Glenn decided to join Matthew and go to town for coffee. Soon the men were seated in the City Café. As the two men visited about farm business and world news and community affairs, Matthew felt the darkness lift.

Matthew knew Glenn had something else on his mind. "Glenn, there's something else you want to say. Why don't you just say it?"

"Well, this isn't public knowledge yet, but I've been checking some possibilities for Tim. We heard from him, and he's decided he wants to farm."

Chapter 10

"That should be a great help."

"But," Glenn continued, "he wants to be on his own—not part of my farming operation. I guess young men want to strike out on their own."

"That's best."

"Here's the deal. Ed and Mary are probably going to leave for California this fall. Tim could easily take over their farm. I talked to Ed yesterday, and he seems to be agreeable. That would take care of everything."

The last statement caught Matthew by surprise. "I know Mary and Ed talked about California. I was hoping it might just be talk."

"Ed is definitely serious. In fact, he said he has a job lined up with his cousin."

Matthew experienced keen disappointment. How strange that his friend and brother-in-law hadn't confided in him about their latest news. "I'm surprised Ed didn't say anything to me."

"Ed told me the other day. This has just happened."

Matthew thought back to the last few years. "Ed hasn't been the same since Mary had her bout with TB. And then he had his problems with Jake. Ed hasn't been himself."

"He's sick of these Minnesota winters. Says he can't take the cold and snow anymore."

Matthew looked away, avoiding his friend's gaze.

Glenn seemed to understand. "You're worried about Johnie. I'm sorry about that. I hope you have some good news soon."

Those words invited Matthew to speak openly. "I've depended on Johnie. I thought he would always be around. I'm afraid something terrible has happened to him."

"Our women have kept on praying. I'm becoming a believer in prayer."

"These days have been dark ones for me."

The two friends drank coffee and talked on for a while. Then they left to take care of their other errands.

Things must be quiet at Gus's station, thought Matthew. *I'll stop and see Larry.*

Beyond the Darkness

As he approached the entrance, he couldn't help overhearing the discussion. He didn't mean to eavesdrop, but he heard Joan speaking, practically in tears.

"Larry, we can't go on this way. The stove doesn't work right. We're so crowded in that cabin, we can hardly walk around. It's either too hot or too cold. The conditions are dreadful."

"I'm sorry. I don't know what to do."

"Larry, I can't go on this way. It's not good for Lowell either. I'm afraid I have to go back to my parents, if nothing else."

"Please, darling," Larry pleaded. "I'll try to work out something else."

At this point Joan noticed him. "Uncle Matthew, I didn't realize you were standing there."

He began to apologize. "I'm sorry. I couldn't help overhearing."

Larry extended his hand. "It's no use hiding the fact that we have a problem. The cabin is fine for a weekend or week, but it's not any good for a permanent living arrangement."

"What about your mother's big house? Why doesn't she let you live with her?" questioned Matthew. "There's lots of room for many people."

Joan's manner changed. "Rita's back now. She wants her friends to come and go in her big house. And I'm not sure I could stand living in the same house as she."

"Mom doesn't want us around," Larry added. "She says since I got religion, she doesn't want me near her or her friends."

Matthew spoke with conviction. "We have to do something about this. It may be time to talk with Rita. Your mother could help in other ways."

"Good luck," said Joan.

"I'll talk with Ellen. Why don't you come over for Sunday dinner? Then we'll see what we can do. There are other ways to solve the problem."

Matthew felt a warm affection for Joan. She reminded him of his own mother and sister Martha. They would need to call on the extended family for help.

As Matthew drove home, he looked to the familiar hills. The darkness of despair and fear faded. He knew there was light beyond the darkness.

Chapter 11

Ellen poured the morning coffee. "Isn't it about time to put in the garden? We usually do it right after you finish the spring planting."

Matthew sighed. "Yes, it's that time. The garden's plowed and disked, so it's ready. I guess we can do it today."

"We have to go on with our lives. The boys will be coming home before long."

A deep sadness enveloped Matthew's spirit. "It's hard to go on. I keep on missing the boys, and the girls aren't coming home this weekend."

"We have Michael."

Matthew thought of his youngest son. "I'm thankful for Michael. Sometimes when I watch him I have the strangest feeling that it's Johnie running around and getting into things."

"They're amazingly alike. Only I think Michael likes school better."

"I remember when Johnie wanted to quit school and stay home so he could help me farm. I wouldn't let him. I didn't want him to make the same mistake I did."

Matthew and Ellen drank their coffee and talked of James and Johnie. Matthew missed the sound of the typewriter coming from the boys' room. He missed Johnie rushing out to check on his calf. And the girls used to be around, always brightening his day.

"Well, dear, it's about time we get to work," he told his wife.

Beyond the Darkness

"Oh, Matthew, would you carry up the seed potatoes from the basement? I cut them up so they're all ready to go."

Matthew carried up the seed potatoes and brought them to the spot in the garden. Ellen followed close behind with packages of seed and onions. Michael ran behind, ready to help or get in the way.

Matthew set down the sack of potatoes. "Aren't we planting too many potatoes for just the three of us?"

Ellen reminded him, "Matthew, remember we take some to Victoria because Carol is staying there. And Margaret will be home some weekends. And Michael's a growing boy." She paused a moment. "And James and Johnie will be coming home."

"Yes, we'll be a full house. Especially at Thanksgiving and Christmas." Matthew recalled earlier times. "I remember all the years we planted our garden at the home place. When the kids were small, they couldn't wait to work in the soil."

Matthew and Ellen continued to reminisce as they worked. Even Michael tried to help. Matthew dug the holes and Ellen followed, putting in the potatoes. Ellen gave Michael some potatoes to plant, but. the boy probably slowed the process rather than helped.

Ellen looked up from their work and gazed at the house. "You know it was only three years ago that James and Johnie and the girls were all here. We were together."

Matthew tried to recall that day. Since the years had a way of blending together, he couldn't separate one year from the next. Somehow the past had a way of seeming perfect and idyllic. In reality, the problems of the past were sometimes forgotten.

As Matthew began digging holes in the sixth row, he commented, "We'll have enough potatoes for an army."

Ellen laughed. "Did you mean that? Do you realize some of the army friends of James and Johnie could be stopping by?"

Matthew smiled for the first time that day. "We'll be ready." He continued to mark the rows. The onions came next. Then he made small trenches for the seeds. As the sun rose high in the sky, they finished planting the vegetables.

"It looks as if we'll have a late dinner," said Ellen. "I'll get it going while you take care of clearing away the tools and other things."

Michael continued getting in the way, wanting to help his father. Matthew realized he was more patient with Michael than he had been

Chapter 11

with his older boys. Some people would have said he had mellowed with the years. The same thing had happened with Pa a generation ago.

History repeats itself. He found himself thinking of what Pa might have said had he faced the problems Matthew now faced. Pa was so accepting of the trials and problems of life.

As he entered the kitchen later, he smelled the aroma of roast pork mingled with the fragrance of other food. Then three long rings of the telephone broke into his thoughts.

Ellen answered and motioned for him to come close. She whispered, "It's a phone call from Western Union."

Sudden panic spread throughout Matthew's body. He felt a dizziness as if he were about to faint, but he listened intently to the man reading the message: "John Anderson has been wounded. He is being brought to the hospital in Norfolk, Virginia. He will arrive there next week."

Ellen thanked the man and hung up the phone. For a moment Matthew could say nothing. Then he shouted, "Johnie's alive! He is alive! Thank God!"

"Praise the Lord," echoed Ellen. "Our prayers have been answered."

Michael ran into the kitchen. "What's the noise?"

"Your brother's alive!" shouted Ellen. "He'll be coming home."

"When? Tomorrow?"

"Soon," said Matthew, "Johnie will be home soon."

Matthew was too excited to eat dinner. "I think we have to tell the family."

"There were rubberneckers on the line," Ellen said. "The word is probably out there already."

Matthew made a quick decision. "Let's drive over to see Ma and then Victoria and Mary and Ed."

"We have to call the girls first. After all, they're the closest."

With only part of their meal eaten, Ellen called long distance to River Falls. Matthew could hear Margaret's exclamations of joy. When she called Victoria, she shouted her happiness as well. Carol was away, working on a Saturday job, so they'd have to wait to tell her. After the calls, Matthew, Ellen, and Michael went on their drive to tell their good news.

Ma, first on their route, insisted that they come in for coffee and dessert. "I've just frosted a chocolate cake. We'll invite Corrine and Warren and the girls. We can all celebrate."

By this time, Matthew remembered he had eaten very little dinner. "I guess some dessert might taste good." Within minutes, they were all seated around Ma's table, talking excitedly about the good news. Michael could only talk about the tractor rides his big brother would take him on.

Ellen decided to call Mary and Ed, but Mary had already heard the news. As they finished their cake and coffee, Matthew announced that they should drive to Glenn's.

When they arrived, Glenn came out of the house. "I have great news!" shouted Matthew. "My boy's alive!"

Glenn's face lighted. "Now, we can both celebrate and share in our good news!" The two men shook hands in that strong hearty way that only good friends can do. Ellen hurried into the house to visit with Mabel. Michael quickly found one of the barnyard cats to pet.

Matthew and Glenn celebrated in their talk, sharing the way they had all their lives. Such friendship was beyond the ordinary.

The remainder of the day Matthew and Ellen spent in visiting and announcing and celebrating the news of Johnie's survival. Only late that night did Matthew began to wonder what condition his son was in.

For the most part Matthew experienced new strength and energy, though he worried about Johnie's condition. However, Johnie was strong and could take almost anything. He would soon come home.

Pastor Andrew, the new student pastor who would be with them for the coming year, announced the good news to the congregation on Sunday morning. The people all joined in singing:

> "Praise God from whom all blessings flow.
> Praise Him all creatures here below.
> Praise Him all ye heavenly host.
> Praise Father, Son, and Holy Ghost."

Matthew would long cherish these days. The night of despair had passed. Life might not be perfect, but there was new hope.

Sunday dinner was always a special time for the Anderson family. Ellen usually made pie or some new dessert along with a hearty meal. Sundays were relaxed because only necessary work was done. In fact, Ellen prepared the special touches on Saturday so that Sunday could truly be a day of rest.

Chapter 11

This Sunday the girls had not come home, but Larry and Joan and young Lowell were guests, along with Ma. Matthew couldn't help noticing all the changes that had taken place. Four years ago, Larry had been absent from his wife. He had mistreated her. Joan had done all the farmwork. Now Larry was trying hard to resume their life together.

After they ate the last of their fresh rhubarb pie, Michael and Lowell hurried outside to play with the newest baby kittens. The attention, for the moment, turned to Ma.

"I thought Aunt Martha was coming back to stay with you for a while," Matthew asked his mother.

"When is Aunt Martha coming back?" Larry asked quickly. "She's talked about coming back, but she's stayed away a long time."

Elizabeth hesitantly answered. "I'm not sure. Her daughters always seem to need her for one thing or another."

Matthew spoke his concerns. "Ma, do you really think you should be out there by yourself. You had a fall the other day, and that could have been bad."

"Corrine and Warren are nearby. They check on me all the time."

"Ma, you know you can come back and stay here."

"I want to be on my own as long as I can. I love my home. And besides, Glenn Robertson asked me about boarding the teacher next fall."

"Do you think you want to do all that cooking?" asked Ellen.

Matthew could hear the defensive edge in his mother's voice as she answered, "I have to cook for myself, and it's almost as easy to cook for another person too. And my grandchildren still like my cookies and cakes. I manage pretty well."

"Your cakes are great," said Joan.

The conversation turned to Joan and her family and her time during the last years. Matthew sensed concern and sadness as she spoke. "I'm afraid my dad wanted me to stay on his farm. I was a handy milkmaid. I did most of the chores."

"But," said Ma, "you had your hands full, taking care of your young one."

"Mother took care of him. I realize now they were taking advantage of me. I was a hard worker. That's why they didn't want me to come back to my husband."

"You belong with your husband," Ellen stated. "That's part of the marriage vows you spoke some years ago."

"I realize that now."

"And," said Larry, "we'll get a better place to live. I'm working on that."

"The cabin's pretty crowded, but we're doing better all the time. I'm glad we're not in the big house with Rita. We need to be a family."

Larry looked away. "I'm afraid Mother isn't happy with me. We do need to be alone as a family."

Matthew knew instantly what his mother was thinking. Elizabeth Anderson looked directly at her son. "That's what I think. You and Ellen and Michael need to be alone as a family too. That's why I must stay at my place."

"No, Grandma," Larry objected, "I didn't mean that. You're completely different."

Joan added, "Grandma Anderson, any family you would live with would be lucky to have you. If we had room, you could live with us."

"Ma," interrupted Matthew, "you took care of me as a child. When you need care, Ellen and I will take care of you."

"That is right," agreed Ellen.

"You are so kind. I don't know what I'd do without my family," Elizabeth said.

Matthew remembered something—and he knew Larry wanted to talk with him alone. "It's time for me to check that gate that was sagging. I didn't have time this morning before church."

Larry stood up. "I'll help you."

Joan smiled. "I think that's an excuse to get away from us ladies. And I think it's time we did dishes."

Matthew grabbed a hammer and nails, and the two men walked toward the barnyard and the sagging gate. Just as Matthew had sensed, Larry wanted to talk.

"I don't know if you knew, but Mother's back in the big house. And we have more of her business associates around."

"Those business associates better watch themselves. Sheriff Walker's keeping a close eye on everything that goes on there."

"Yes, he's checking on me too. And so is Aunt Victoria."

The two men worked together to fasten and tighten the loosened wire. After finishing the task, Larry began to confide in his uncle. "Mother wants me to do some work for her business again."

"Is that wise?"

"I can sure use the money. She keeps saying it's all honest and legitimate, but I'm not sure about her associates."

Chapter 11

Matthew shrugged his shoulders. "Then your answer is a simple no."

"It should be, and I've said no. But I do need money to take care of Joan and my boy. And Mother is determined that I do the work."

Uncle and nephew continued their talk. Matthew realized that Rita's business might very likely be questionable or even illegal. After all, it was P.J.'s business associates that got Larry into serious trouble in the first place.

"Larry, you have to make a choice. And I think your mother's business may just get you into trouble."

"I know you're right."

At that moment a black Cadillac came down the driveway. Matthew knew instantly this had to be Rita. Sure enough, Rita got out of the car. She wasted no words. "Larry, I need to talk with you immediately." She turned to Matthew. "Alone."

"I'll go inside," Matthew replied.

"No, Mother. Uncle Matthew will stay here. I'm not working for you. I have my job at the gas station, and that will have to take care of us."

"But," objected Rita, "you'll make more money doing bookkeeping for me and my business. You can't pass up this opportunity. And I need you to take care of some matters, right now."

"Mother, I have to say no."

Rita turned to Matthew. "You've been turning my own son against me. He's been impossible since he got all this religion. He forgets his duty to his mother."

"Mother, you don't even want me and Joan living in your house. You let me use the small cabin—a place that's hardly big enough for three people."

"Larry, I don't want you around talking religion to my friends and business associates. I do want you to take care of some business matters—some bookkeeping. After all, you worked toward a business degree from the university."

Larry repeated his refusal.

"But," continued Rita, "I need you to take care of the books and some basic reporting right now. I don't know how."

"I'll show you some basics, provided your business is honest."

Rita blushed. "The business is legitimate. And I don't need you talking to Victoria. She gives me a hard time."

Beyond the Darkness

Matthew withheld a laugh. If anyone could confront Rita, it was Victoria. And Victoria would be scrupulously honest and critical of any appearance of wrongdoing.

Rita continued her demands, and Larry repeated his refusals. Matthew wanted to help his nephew, but he held back, saying nothing. Finally Rita opened the door to the car and turned to her son. "Larry, you're going to be sorry you didn't accept my offer." She repeated her warning, "You'll be sorry."

The two men said nothing as Rita drove away. But Matthew noticed Larry's troubled face and motioned for his nephew to follow him over to the lilac bushes. He picked a sprig of lilacs and handed it to Larry. "Take a smell of these. This can make you forget all the problems of the world."

"After those years in prison, I've come to appreciate the beauty of flowers and the outdoors. These lilacs make me sense God's presence."

Matthew felt a renewed bond with his nephew, something reminiscent of the days when Larry was a child visiting the farm. "I find that I love these hills and fields more and more as I live my middle years."

Larry smelled the fragrant lilacs again. "I always thought I'd be living in the big city. I never thought I'd be satisfied to live in the country or in Lake View, but now I want to stay here the rest of my life."

"I used to dream of going beyond those hills, but I never will," Matthew responded. "I'll send my children far beyond. But they will always come back."

He looked at his nephew who had already lost some of his youthful appearance. He thought of his own children and how they had grown up. And once more, he thought of Johnie, who was alive. The fragrance of lilacs reminded Matthew of hope and life.

Chapter 12

June 1945

Matthew hurried to let the cattle out of the barn. He had finished milking, so he placed the milk cans in the cooler tank. He eagerly anticipated seeing Margaret graduate today from teachers' training. With the pride and love of a father, he thought of this beautiful young woman, her graciousness, and the wonderful future she had ahead of her.

Ellen had the laundry tub filled with water when Matthew returned to the house. He took off his clothes and began to wash away the dust of the day and smells of the barn. *Someday,* he thought, *we'll have running water and a bathtub. Then life will be easier.*

Matthew quickly dressed, putting on his white shirt, tie, and dress suit. On this occasion it was important to wear his Sunday best. As he finished dressing, Ellen got Michael ready in his nicest clothes—a dress shirt and trousers that he was quickly growing out of. In minutes the three of them were all seated in the front seat of their '35 Chevy.

"We don't have to pick up your mother," said Ellen. "Victoria decided to spend time with her this summer. She'll pick up Mary too, and drive them all to the graduation."

Matthew started the car. "Did you remember the letter from James?"

Beyond the Darkness

Ellen held it up.

Matthew did have a stop to make at Kay's Café. He wasn't sure he liked the idea of Carol working as a waitress. Some of the men who came through town might get the wrong idea. He wanted to protect his youngest daughter. As he approached the café, he voiced his opinion. "I'm not sure it's a good idea for Carol to be staying here this summer."

"I'm afraid there's not much we can do," Ellen replied.

Matthew parked the car. "She's supposed to meet us here."

"I'll go in and get her."

Carol came running out and announced. "I have to work tonight. It's a busy time, and Kay is short of help."

Ellen gave her a sharp look of disapproval. "Carol, this is a special night. It is your sister's graduation. You should be there."

"She won't even miss me."

Both parents objected, and Ellen ended by saying, "Kay can manage without you. The café doesn't look busy now. I'll go talk with her."

Carol's face reddened as she raised her voice. "No! No! I will not go. I am staying here. I can use the tips."

Matthew saw that stubborn determination in Carol's face. Getting her to change her mind would be impossible.

Ellen got back into the car. "OK, I'm sorry you feel this way."

Carol hurried away from her parents back into the café.

A half hour later, Matthew, Ellen, and Michael were seated in the school's gymnasium, now carefully decorated for the graduation ceremonies. Matthew looked across the aisle to see Victoria, Ma, and Mary. He was grateful so much of his family was here to support and celebrate Margaret's accomplishment, but still disappointed in Carol's decision not to come.

As the ceremony began, Matthew thought how this graduation was like so many others—not that he'd been to that many. He thought of James's graduation when James gave the commencement prayer as well as the valedictorian's address. His oldest son would go far. Johnie's graduation wasn't quite so eventful, for Johnie never took well to schoolwork. Matthew also remembered the graduations of other family members—nieces, nephews, and others. And now Margaret, an honor student, would be recognized today with a number of awards. His heart filled with pride.

Chapter 12

Matthew kept his eyes glued to the stage where the graduates sat. There were twenty-four young women and one young man, but he saw only Margaret. What a beautiful, intelligent daughter he had!

The program included the usual invocation, followed by several instrumental groups and two singing groups. Then Miss Stone took her place on the stage and began her introduction. "This group of twenty-five is one of the finest I have ever worked with. With young teachers such as these, our rural schools will do well as we move toward the middle of the twentieth century. I would like to introduce our number-one student; we might call her our valedictorian. This young woman will speak to and for the class. She has the highest academic average here, and her projects have been only the very best. She will be a model teacher. I introduce to you, Miss Margaret Anderson."

Matthew had not expected this. Margaret had not told him or Ellen about this honor.

Applause followed Miss Stone's comments. Matthew noticed that most of the other graduates applauded enthusiastically. He knew they had to recognize the kind of person his daughter was.

Margaret, dressed in a blue-flowered dress, moved forward. Seeing this young woman, a bit taller than Ellen and more beautiful now than ever before, brought out all Matthew's fatherly and manly instincts to honor and protect her. After several words of introduction, Margaret began her speech. "I am a farmer's daughter. My father has been a farmer from the time he was quite young. My mother grew up on a farm and became a teacher. My parents have taught me to love God, to love my family, to love my friends and community, and to love this land and this way of life."

She paused a moment and held up something. "I have a seed here. You can hardly see this seed from where you sit." Then she looked down and read from Scripture the parable of the mustard seed, echoing again emphatically, "If we have mustard seed faith. . . . As a teacher, I will plant seeds of knowledge and truth. I will water those seeds in any way I can. I will pray that those seeds will grow within my students. Perhaps someday one of these students will become a lawmaker or a leader who will help bring peace to this world. Perhaps a student will write that great American novel, a book that will point the way to a better life."

As Margaret continued her examples, Matthew's thoughts moved to the hills that he had looked to and loved all these years. Margaret was continuing his dream of going beyond those hills. She would go beyond and so would her students.

He could tell she was beginning to close the speech. "And at this time I must thank two special people who have planted the seeds within me. My mother Ellen Anderson, in many ways, has been my example. She planted seeds of learning—learning from life, from Scripture, from books, from working at home. I thank you, Mother. Your seeds have grown within me and now I will plant seeds in others. And my father, Matthew Anderson, planted other seeds. He planted seeds of honesty and integrity. He planted seeds of love for people and for the land. We are not wealthy in a material way. But you have made me the wealthiest girl in the world. Your seeds are growing in me, and I will plant them in my students. For this, I thank you, Dad.

"Let us now go forward as teachers in the classroom. Each one of us is placed on this earth for a purpose. We twenty-five are placed here for the purpose of planting the seeds of truth in the lives of young children. Thank you. And may the Lord bless you all."

The applause began, somewhat subdued at first. Then someone in front stood up. Soon everyone in the gymnasium was standing. Matthew felt his spirit soar as the audience honored his daughter.

As the ceremony ended, the graduates lined up so their friends and family could congratulate them. Matthew enfolded Margaret in his arms. He wished this moment could last forever. Concerns about Johnie and Joe faded far into the background.

An hour later, in Ma's little house, the family and a few friends gathered. Victoria had made a big cake, and she and Ma had a lunch ready for the family. Eating was a wonderful tradition to bring people together. Once the coffee was served along with some delicacies, people seemed to open up and talk and experience a kind of fellowship and goodwill.

Watching Larry from across the room, Matthew still couldn't quite believe the change that had come over his nephew. In many ways he was like the boy Matthew knew years ago. He had changed from the selfish person who thought only of himself to someone who seemed genuinely to care for others.

The festivities soon came to an end. Mary, Irene, and Ed, who had joined them later, returned home. Corrine and Warren took their three

Chapter 12

girls up the hill to their place. Ellen helped Ma in the kitchen, washing dishes. That left Larry and Matthew together for a time to talk.

"Uncle Matthew, you certainly can be proud of Margaret. She's turned into a beautiful young woman."

Matthew looked to the kitchen where Margaret and the other women were visiting and cleaning up. He leaned over and spoke quietly. "I don't think Margaret realizes how pretty she is. She's going to be very popular with the young men."

"I can see what you mean. Joan's dad didn't approve of me. And now I realize why. I hope I can show him that I'm a trustworthy husband."

"He will come to know you are trustworthy, but give him time."

"Something else happened, or is happening, so I have some good news."

"What?"

"Well," began Larry, "part of it isn't good news. Gus isn't in such good health. After all, he's almost eighty."

"He's been good to work for, hasn't he?"

"Gus has been like a grandfather to me—or an uncle. And he's alone. He has some nieces and nephews, but they aren't around much. His nephew had talked to Gus and then to me about Joan and me moving in with him."

"Would that be good?" questioned Matthew.

"Gus has the big, old family home—lots of room. He needs someone to cook for him and look after him a bit. And Joan really likes him."

"It might be a good thing. Your cabin is too small and crowded."

"I think the man is lonely. He's been ever so helpful to me. I think he needs a family, and he wants us to be his family."

"That could be a good thing all the way around." Matthew hesitated a moment, wondering if he should ask his next questions. Then he forged ahead. "How about your mother? Are you getting along with her? Is she causing trouble?"

Larry chuckled. "You have Mother figured out. She took off for the city after that last time when I refused to take care of her business books. She hasn't bothered me since. I think she's gotten the point."

"I'm sorry if I said something nasty about your mother."

"Not at all, Uncle Matthew. I know my mother is a first-rate trouble-maker. I was just like her when I lived only for myself."

Beyond the Darkness

Matthew once more thought of his own past. "That's the way God works. My anger toward your father would have killed me, but I learned to forgive. With that forgiveness came peace and freedom."

At that moment Ellen called out, "Matthew, it's getting late. I think it's time for us to go home."

"Yes, dear," he said, and then added to himself, "My cup runneth over."

Late that night, Margaret lay in bed, thinking of the day that was past. This was the end of a perfect—at least an almost perfect day. It would have been perfect if her brothers had been home for her celebration. Of course, Carol wasn't there, but that was Carol's way these days.

Margaret also missed Joe. Where was he? Probably in a prison camp. Or maybe he wasn't even alive. The uncertainty saddened her. Her feelings toward Joe were not always clear. At times she thought of him as another big brother—but other times she wanted him to take her in his arms and kiss her. Sometimes she even fantasized about walking down the aisle and meeting him at the altar of Oak Ridge Church.

She had saved her last letter from James. Most of his letters were written to the whole family, but this one was sent only to her. She tore open the envelope and began to read: "My dear sister Margaret." Those words of endearment said something about their bond as brother and sister. James understood what she wanted in life. She understood the urge within him that gave him the desire to write.

His words flowed smoothly. "This day is one of those highlights of your life. You have achieved a goal. Enjoy these moments of satisfaction. I have a feeling that you received awards for your outstanding performance as student and future teacher."

She put down the letter momentarily, remembering the many times James had encouraged her. Even if no one else thought she could do something, James knew she could. When she used to play with her dolls, she would be aware of James looking at her in that "big brother" sort of way. In some ways her dreams and James's were similar. She picked up the letter and continued:

Chapter 12

I know you have dreams about your future. You will follow in Mother's footsteps. In many ways you are like her. You have the heart of a loving person, a sister, a mother, a teacher. You will make a big difference in this world.

We have similar dreams. I want to be a high school teacher or maybe a college professor, but I feel compelled to write. I want to tell stories of the way life is and was. I want to inspire people to lead better lives. I want people to turn to the Lord for their strength and hope.

Though I've been assigned to army headquarters, I've still seen bloodshed. I've seen how war destroys men in spirit as well as physically. When I come home, I would like to point people to a better life. Education is the great hope for avoiding war and its devastation. I want to be a part of helping make the world a better place.

I wanted you, dear Margaret, to know how special you are. You have a unique place in my heart. You are making your corner of the world just a little better. Actually, much better.

I can't wait to come home and be greeted by your beautiful smile. All my love. Your brother, James.

For a long time Margaret held the letter as if it were a sacred document. Finally she turned off the light. She dreamed that night of the past day and of her life. Hundreds of people walked in and out of her dreams, but Joseph Nelson appeared again and again.

Matthew could see Ellen wasn't sleeping either. "I can't seem to stop thinking about all that has happened today."

"It's been a perfect day—almost perfect."

"Yes." He caught Ellen's last words. "If only Carol had come."

"I'm concerned about her. I'm afraid of what she's choosing to do. But we can't solve that problem now."

Matthew couldn't help thinking of the bigger picture outside their own lives as well. "We live in a world with so many problems. The war with Japan has to end soon."

"The outcome is in the Lord's hands."

He moved closer to Ellen, taking her in his arms. "I love you. With God's help, we can face tomorrow."

A few hours later Matthew greeted the June morning. He spoke aloud the words of James Russell Lowell, words he had memorized long ago:

Beyond the Darkness

"And what is so rare as a day in June?
Then, if ever come perfect days;
Then Heaven tries earth if it be in tune,
And over it softly her warm ear lays;
Whether we look or whether we listen,
We hear life murmur, or see it glisten;
Every clod feels a stir of might,
An instinct within it that reaches and towers,
And groping blindly above it for light,
Climbs to a soul in grass and flowers."

Matthew looked to the hills, once more feeling joy in the beauty around him. Life was good. God was good.

He knew, though, challenges lay ahead. There was still darkness to overcome.

Chapter 13

Matthew liked the idea of Margaret helping him with chores while she was home for the summer. She didn't come out every morning, but this morning she had. The two of them had finished all the milking and cleaning by seven o'clock. They'd fed the pigs, let the chickens out of their chicken house to eat in their pen, and sent the cows out to graze in the pasture. With these simplest of daily chores, life moved forward in a predictable manner. That's part of what Matthew liked about farming. He liked this aspect of his life. It was something you could count on—almost like counting on God to be ever present.

Matthew entered the house for breakfast just in time for the seven o'clock news. The bloody reports of the attack on Okinawa continued. Thousands of Japanese had been killed. At least this should mean that the war would soon end. Whenever he heard reports of the war in Japan, he thought of Joe. Five years ago, Joe would have been helping him with the chores. James and Johnie would have been around as well. Now all three were far away.

He wondered if life would ever return to the way it was before this terrible war. What would life be like for Johnie, who had been wounded? James, of course, would leave for college. And Joe, would he ever come back?

Beyond the Darkness

Matthew, Ellen, and Margaret ate breakfast in silence as the news continued. This radio news always had a sobering effect these days. As the broadcast ended, the telephone jangled its three long rings. Whenever the telephone rang at this time of the morning, Matthew suspected something was wrong.

Ellen answered, and from her words, Matthew knew the call was about Carol. She must be in some type of trouble again. Ellen hung up and explained, "It's Carol. She's supposed to be working at Kay's this morning, but she's not in her room. She left late Friday evening."

"Where did she go?"

Ellen went on. "She asked for Saturday off—said it was urgent. But she was supposed to work early this morning. She's not in the apartment. Kay is upset because that's part of her work agreement; she's supposed to work at certain times to pay for renting the apartment."

Margaret piped up. "It has to be Jeff. They've taken off. The last time Carol talked to me, she said she wanted to marry him."

"She's not of age," responded Ellen. "But Kay wasn't sure who Carol went with. She thought it was Jeff, but she wasn't certain."

"What should we do?" questioned Matthew.

Matthew could see Ellen's mind in motion before she spoke. "I hate the thought of talking to the Grants, but that's what we need to do. Margaret, will you stay here with Michael?"

"I'd be glad to do that, but I probably should be with you. I think I might have some ideas where they might go in River Falls."

Ellen went over to the telephone. "I'll call Grandma and Victoria and see if they'll take care of Michael for the day."

Matthew went out to open the gates to let the cattle into the east pasture. Then he cleaned up and changed clothes. Within the hour they were on their way to Lake View. When they arrived at the Grants' house, Margaret sat in the car while her parents walked to the front door and Ellen rang the doorbell. After several rings, Mrs. Grant appeared.

Before the woman could say anything, Ellen questioned her. "Could you tell us where your son is? We think he might be with our daughter."

"Jeffrey said he was spending the weekend in River Falls with friends. But I don't know that it's any of your business."

Ellen raised her voice. "It is our business because your son is more than likely with our daughter. And your son is over twenty-one, and our daughter is not quite seventeen."

Chapter 13

Mrs. Grant shrugged her shoulders. "Your daughter has a teenage crush on an older man. She's been chasing him ever since he came home from the army. She probably tagged along with him or went after him."

Matthew had heard enough. "Now, listen here—"

Ellen interrupted, "Tell us where your son might be. We wish to pick up our daughter."

Mrs. Grant reluctantly backed away. "I'll see if I can find an address." She left them for several minutes and then returned with a slip of paper containing an address. "Are you sure they went off together?"

"We are certain," Ellen said firmly. "Thank you. Matthew, let's be on our way."

As they were getting into the car, Mrs. Grant called out, "Let me know what you find out." Then she added, "Please . . ."

Matthew realized Mrs. Grant felt a motherly concern for her wayward son.

"We need to stop for gas," he said as they drove away from the house. "Do you think Larry could have seen anything around town on Friday? He sometimes works late."

Ellen and Margaret agreed.

At the garage, as Larry filled their gas, Ellen brought him up to date on what had happened.

"You know," Larry replied. "I remember something. Jeff came here on Friday night—early. I filled his gas. He was talking with a friend of his, saying something about another friend across the state lines."

"Where exactly did he say he was going?"

"Just across the state line. But then he was coming back to River Falls."

"Do you remember anything else?"

Larry finished pumping gas and put back the nozzle. "He was driving a dark blue Dodge. I think it was a '39 or '40 model. I'd recognize that car anywhere."

"Then we have something to go on!" exclaimed Margaret.

"We're heading for River Falls right now," said Matthew. He handed Larry the bills, and Larry hurried into the station and then returned with the change.

"Uncle Matthew. Gus can take over for the day. I'm driving my car to River Falls. I'll help in the search. That's the least I can do."

Beyond the Darkness

They spent the next few hours driving around River Falls. Matthew first checked the address Mrs. Grant had given them. The young woman answering the door said she had seen nothing of either Jeff or Carol during the past week. Margaret led them to other places, but there was no sign of Jeff's car, or of Jeff or Carol. While Matthew, Ellen, and Margaret checked various places, Larry drove around the city, looking for the dark blue Dodge. An hour later, they met at the courthouse. Since none of them had found any sign of Carol or Jeff, Matthew came up with another idea. "Why don't we check with Sheriff Walker and see if he has any ideas?"

As they walked down the marble corridors of the courthouse to find the sheriff, Larry became strangely silent. Matthew realized that the jail was in this vicinity, as was the courtroom where he had been sentenced. Matthew reached over and touched his nephew on the shoulder. "Larry, I admire you and the way you've changed."

"Thank you, but I couldn't have made the change without the Lord. And the fellows from the prison ministry saw me through some rough times."

The sheriff's office was empty except for Walker himself. He greeted Matthew warmly, then looked at the others. "To what do I owe this honor?" he asked. Troubled faces must have signaled a problem. "I can see something is wrong."

Matthew always appreciated Ellen and the way she could explain things. He was satisfied to let her do the talking, so she explained the situation once more.

"I don't know if there is much I can do except be on the lookout for the car," Sheriff Walker told them. "Of course, Jeff could be in serious trouble since he has a minor with him."

"We're not wanting to make trouble for Jeff," said Ellen. "We just want our girl back home safe and sound."

"I've noticed Jeff is headed for trouble," began the sheriff. "He spends a lot of time in bars, and my deputies have warned him about his driving."

"He's not good for our daughter," said Ellen, "but we can't seem to stop the two from being together."

"I understand," agreed Walker. "I have children of my own."

At that moment he phone rang, and Walker talked for several minutes before he turned to them. "I think we've found your missing people. That

Chapter 13

was a call from the highway patrol. He brought a stranded couple into Valley Center, a small town about twenty-five miles west of here. They ran out of gas and may be having car problems."

Ellen's words expressed Matthew's relief. "Thank God, they're safe."

The sheriff turned to Matthew, "You know these fellows coming back from the service often have deep problems," he remarked. "In World War I, we called it shell shock. Drinking seems to them to be a way out. We have to try to help them rather than judge them. If necessary, we may even have to lock them up for a night to keep the highways safe."

Matthew couldn't help remembering his cousin. "My cousin Pete was in the service during World War I. He turned to drinking some years after he came home. He couldn't forget the bloodshed of that war."

"War is awful. But we can be thankful we've taken care of Hitler and the Nazis. Soon we should have the Japs taken care of and this war will end."

Matthew thanked the sheriff. Within the hour they were in Valley Center. He wasn't quite sure what to expect. He found his anger directed at the young man for taking advantage of Carol.

As he drove down the street of this small town, Margaret spotted her sister. "Carol's there. She and Jeff are going into the restaurant."

Matthew drove ahead and parked, and Larry followed. As they pulled in, Ellen called out, "Carol, we're here. We were so worried."

Carol stopped just as she and Jeff were about to enter the Valley Center Café. Jeff stood beside her, avoiding everyone's gaze, especially Matthew's.

"Where have you been? We've been worried,' Ellen repeated.

Carol straightened herself, giving a defiant look. "What are you all doing here? And Larry too? How did you find us?"

"Never mind," said Ellen. "Kay missed you this morning. You can't have a job and not show up whenever you feel like it. We didn't bring you up that way."

Margaret chimed in, "What were you thinking?"

Carol walked over to her sister. "Come, Miss Goody Two-Shoes. I'm not about to be cooped up with books. I want to have some fun. I'm not interested in being a teacher or some stupid farmer's wife."

"That is enough, Carol," scolded her mother. "You have no business making derogatory remarks about your family."

Jeff mumbled some words and then added, "Carol, let's go in and have something to eat." Then he turned to Matthew. "Maybe you could loan us some money so we can have lunch."

By this time Matthew had collected his thoughts. "Young lady, it's time for us to go home. There is work to do—and you are coming with us."

Carol backed away. "That's what you think. Jeffrey and I are married. I'm staying with him. You can't make me come home."

The words stunned Matthew into silence. However, his wife did not keep quiet. "Young lady," replied Ellen, "you're too young. You cannot legally marry unless we sign for you. And that we will not do."

Jeff again grunted something under his breath.

"I passed for eighteen," Carol stated defiantly. "The justice of the peace married us. And that is final."

Ellen had no answer, but Matthew found his voice and began questioning the two. "How are you going to live? Where will you live? Jeff, do you have a job?"

What Jeff showed could best be described as a smirk. "I'll be working in my father's bank. Carol will be well taken care of."

Ellen pleaded with her daughter. "This isn't right. This isn't the way we do things in our family."

"I'm married. There's not a thing you can do about it."

Larry faced Jeff with another question. "If your car's broken down, what are you going to do? How will you get back to Lake View?"

Jeff turned to Carol. "Maybe you better go back with your folks. Your money from Kay's Café will come in handy. I'll wait for the car repairs. It might take a few days to get parts."

Carol reluctantly agreed, gave Jeff a kiss, and sullenly got into her father's car. The ride back to Lake View was far from pleasant. Most of the attempts at conversation were greeted with awkward silence.

Ellen felt she was in some kind of surrealistic world. Carol's elopement had been such a shock that she felt almost out of control. She wanted to talk with Carol one more time when they got back to Lake View. However, Carol got out of the car and abruptly hurried into Kay's Café. Ellen was certain that Carol had another one of her elaborate apologies for her boss.

Chapter 13

Ellen realized there was nothing else she could say. Matthew seemed to be under control, and Margaret acted as if nothing had happened. Ellen heard Matthew thank Larry for all of his help. She heard herself feebly add her thanks to her nephew.

As they drove to the home place, she heard the questions: "What's wrong, Mother?" "Ellen, what's on your mind? You don't seem to be yourself." For the moment she didn't have the energy to respond.

When they stopped at the home place, Margaret quickly got out of the car and ran to the big house where she could visit with Corrine. As she and Matthew entered Mother Anderson's house, Ellen felt relieved. Maybe now she could speak her feelings. Usually Ellen was the one to do the explaining, but this time Matthew did. He told Victoria and his mother in few details that Carol had run off, lied about her age, and married Jeffrey Grant. All the time he was talking—and even though Victoria and Elizabeth expressed their surprise and concern—Ellen wanted to go back in time and forget all that had just happened.

"I'm starved," Matthew announced finally, changing the subject abruptly. "I just realized we haven't eaten since morning. We've been so busy we forgot about eating. Ellen, I think we need to hurry home."

"Oh, no," Victoria said, "we have cold pork for sandwiches, and we can warm up some chicken vegetable soup."

Ellen objected, "You shouldn't go to this trouble."

"Nonsense," said Elizabeth. "You've had a trying day."

Only vaguely did Ellen hear the conversation that followed. It was as if she were in another world. She felt light-headed and dizzy. What was happening to her? Suddenly the room and the people were whirling about. She felt her head hit the table and heard voices of concern echo around her.

Victoria placed her hand on her sister-in-law's shoulder. "Ellen, here's some water. You're overtired. You've had a rough day."

Gradually, she felt herself returning to reality. Now, she wanted to cry out in hurtful anger.

"I'm OK," Ellen said, "I just felt light-headed."

Victoria brought out the hot soup and sandwiches. "Some food will help you feel better."

Ellen realized how hungry she was, yet her emotions over Carol were greater. "I feel like such a failure," she said aloud. She heard the objections but continued. "You're being kind. I realize that by the time Carol came along, I had spent all my mothering energy. I already had two boys and a girl. Margaret was, of course, the model young girl. She did everything right."

Ellen kept on despite further objections. "I'm afraid I favored Margaret. I didn't mean to. It's just that Carol was so exasperating." Ellen always kept her words and emotions under control. She sensed the surprise in Matthew, his mother, and Victoria at her outburst.

After her emotions were spent, her mother-in-law spoke quietly. "When I was young, I was a completely different person. About the time you were born, Matthew, I became a changed person. I made a new commitment to the Lord. Victoria, you and Martha came right along with me, but P.J. didn't. He always went in his own way. I used to blame myself for the way P.J. turned out."

Ellen objected, "You can't blame yourself."

"I realized that was fruitless. Every person must make his or her own decisions. It's easy to blame a parent or someone else. But each person is given the opportunity to change and lead a better life."

Ellen thought of the pain P.J. had caused Matthew and the whole family. "You're right, Mother Anderson. I'm sorry for the way I carried on."

"That's OK," said Victoria. "Everyone needs to let off steam. Ellen, it's just not like you to go on the way you did. You're always so much in control."

Ellen smiled for the first time. "Well, I feel better. Now, perhaps I can go back home and learn my role as a mother-in-law. I wasn't quite ready for this."

Chapter 14

July 1945

The last days of June gave way to July. Matthew worked with Warren and Glenn to take care of the haying. In a few weeks it would be time for harvesting. Margaret had turned into an excellent tractor driver, and that made life easier for Matthew. But he couldn't help thinking about Johnie. No further word came from the army hospital in Norfolk.

During the summer Matthew and Ellen made frequent trips to Lake View and Kay's Café. Over the past weeks, Mrs. Grant had been strangely silent. Carol said that her in-laws were off to the Wisconsin Dells for their summer vacation. Yet even when they were home, Mrs. Grant had stayed away from Carol and Jeffrey.

Matthew often thought about the path his younger daughter had chosen. On one particular morning, after the surprise about the elopement subsided, he was thinking out loud about how she'd been more herself lately. "Carol has been more the sweet girl she used to be. She has such a lively spirit. She could do more than waitress work at the café. I wish she hadn't married Jeff. He's not good for her, but we must make the best of the situation."

While things had calmed down somewhat, Matthew was still on his guard. It seemed to him that tragedies or difficult times often came in threes. That's what happened one day in July.

Beyond the Darkness

The mail arrived early that day. Michael had started doing small jobs around the house, and one was going to the mailbox to pick up the mail. This morning he announced a letter had arrived. Matthew's anticipation grew as Ellen declared, "It's from the hospital in Norfolk. It's from the hospital, but it's a personal letter." She opened the letter and began to read:

"Dear Mr. and Mrs. Anderson,

"I'm a nurse who works with the soldiers in this army hospital. I have been visiting your son. The doctor encouraged me to write this letter to explain some things. Johnie is in a psychiatric ward. He is so very sad and speaks barely at all. He keeps staring into space. The doctors say he has what people call 'shell shock.' That experience in a German prison camp must have been too much for him.

"I try to get him to talk, but he barely answers. I would encourage you to continue to write letters to him. Write about his family and about what is going on. If he doesn't read the letter himself, I will read it to him.

"The doctors discourage you from coming right now. They are very busy, and sometimes your son appears to be extremely disturbed. He becomes violent when he thinks he is back on the battlefield. Then no visitors are allowed.

"Again, the doctors say that this sort of injury takes time. The gunshot wound in his side is healing quite well. He is extremely thin. He doesn't seem to want to eat."

Matthew couldn't help commenting, "That's a far cry from his days here. He could eat endlessly and never put on a pound."

"I think he needs some good home cooking," added Ellen.

"I wish we could go to Norfolk, but that's so far. And gas is in short supply."

Ellen continued reading, "The doctors will do what they can for now. They will then send him to a veterans' hospital in Minnesota."

At this point, Michael began asking every question imaginable.

Matthew saw the concern on his small son's face. He was glad that Ellen had a way with answering a little boy's questions. "Michael, dear, your big brother has been hurt badly in the war. Remember when you sprained your ankle. It hurt badly."

Michael nodded.

"Well, Johnie's hurt was a much bigger one. His hurt will take a long time to heal."

Even Matthew felt comforted by Ellen's explanation.

Chapter 14

Matthew left the warmth of the kitchen for the outdoors. He still had work to be done; it was time to clean the grain bins. He hated this dusty job, so instead of starting immediately, he first stood outside the building and thought of how Johnie and he had done this task together. As he began cleaning, he prayed aloud, "Dear Lord, be with Johnie at this moment. He's hurting both in body and spirit. Make him well. Bring him back home safely. Lord, I know that I sound terribly selfish, but I need my son to come home. Please, Lord, please . . ."

As he prayed, he heard Ellen calling to him. "Victoria called. We're invited for noon dinner. Then, she wants you to go with her over to Rita's. There seems to be a problem."

What's Rita up to this time? Matthew wondered.

"You are so secretive," said Matthew as he and Victoria drove down the road to Rita's home. "What's this all about?"

"I want you with me when I confront Rita. I want you to witness what I say."

"Tell me what this is all about."

"Two things. First, it seems that Rita is in business again. I have a strong feeling she has some illegal business connections. Second, I am going to demand that she give Larry a better place to live."

"I agree," said Matthew, "but Larry and Joan are moving in with Gus. They won't need to move into the big house."

"Even so, Rita should do more to help Larry."

As they entered P.J.'s mansion, Matthew remembered the other times he had been here. The first time was that happy Christmas celebration when P.J. had been so kind. Then there were the other times when he and Ellen confronted P.J. about his illegal and questionable activities. And then even the time when P.J., in desperation, had asked Matthew to retrieve money and documents from the secret room.

His thoughts stopped abruptly when Rita answered the knock at the door. "I was not expecting you."

Victoria straightened herself to her full height. Those dark penetrating eyes made Rita step back. "We have some business to discuss," Victoria stated.

Rita, dressed in a stylish business suit, stepped back. "Come in, but I do have several other matters to attend to."

"We won't take long." Victoria said. Without waiting, she walked down the hall to the library/office. "It has come to the attention of your neighbors that you have much traffic in and out of this place. The neighbors are certain that you are once more involved in illegal activities."

Rita looked away. "My business is legal. And the details of my business are not any of their business."

Victoria cleared her throat. "Then perhaps the sheriff will need to keep an eye on you and everything going on."

"There's no need for that."

"Oh, yes there is. And I am living with Mother. I will keep a careful eye on everything going on here."

"I have guests in the cabins. And I have friends and business associates staying here at the house."

Matthew wanted to applaud his older sister's directness as she grunted and continued, "That brings me to another concern. Why did you give Larry the small cabin that hardly has room for his wife and child? He's your son. He deserves something better."

Rita stiffened. "I would help him more if he helped me, but he refuses. And he's gotten into religion, so I don't want him around me or my business associates or guests. He has a chance to keep the books, but he won't. And besides, he and Joan are going to be living in town."

"Yes, he would keep the books if he knew what you were doing was legal and honest. But I believe he has your business figured out right."

Rita's face reddened. Matthew could see both anger and embarrassment in her face as she reacted to her sister-in-law's accusations. "Victoria, you're putting yourself into other people's business. P.J. said you liked to control people, and he was right. Get your nose out of my business."

Matthew sensed increased anger in his sister's demeanor. He knew Victoria would not take such comments sitting down, and he was right.

"Your business becomes my business when late-night noises waken me," she stated. "Your business becomes my business when there has been a history of illegal business and activity in this place. It's time for me to talk with Sheriff Walker."

Victoria turned to walk away, but Rita countered, "Please don't. We can work this out."

"So far, Rita, it is not working out."

Chapter 14

Rita's tone of voice changed, becoming more conciliatory. "I'll see that the late activity quiets down. And I will see about helping Larry."

Victoria, followed by Matthew, walked outside then turned back to Rita. "I expect immediate action."

Speechless, Rita stood outside the front door and watched Matthew and Victoria drive away.

Coffee and a snack at Kay's Café had become a tradition that Matthew enjoyed. It was quiet in midafternoon. Carol had joined him, Ellen, and little Michael in the corner booth.

Their talk centered on small events as well as how Carol was meeting people and enjoying her work.

Matthew relaxed as Carol talked about some of the city people who had visited in town. "You'll never believe it," she said, "but this guy from the city gave me a two-dollar tip. That's the biggest tip I've ever gotten. Most people around here don't leave even a dime."

"You do have a nice way with people," said Ellen. "There are many jobs you could do."

Carol frowned. "I suppose you think I should have gone to college to be a teacher like Margaret. I don't want to be cooped up in a classroom."

"That's not what I meant."

Matthew knew it was time to change the subject. "We had something else we need to tell you about. It's Johnie."

Carol replied quickly, "Is something wrong?"

Ellen began to explain the contents of the nurse's letter, then added, "He'll be coming to a veterans' hospital in Minnesota, but we don't have any idea when he can come home."

Carol's whole attitude changed. "That's terrible. I can't imagine him being this way."

At that moment she looked up. Before the Anderson family stood Mrs. Jeffrey Grant II. She spoke sharply to Carol, "I wish to speak with you immediately." Her words were not a request but a command.

Carol stood up. "I don't think we have anything to talk about. Your son and I are married, even though you do not approve. That is final!"

Beyond the Darkness

Mrs. Grant, planting herself firmly close to the young woman, spoke with authority. "There is nothing final about this marriage."

Matthew saw Ellen's uneasiness as Michael stared at the woman. The boy's face displayed fear. He had never seen such a violent attitude in an adult. Ellen placed her hand on Michael's shoulder and directed him to a side door. "Why don't you go upstairs to Carol's apartment? There are some blocks you can play with 'til we're ready to go home."

After Michael obediently left, Carol backed away from her mother-in-law. "Your son wants nothing to do with you."

Mrs. Grant's tone became threatening. "We'll see about that. His father and I hold the purse strings."

"We'll make it on our own. We may just take off for California or the city."

Mrs. Grant shook her fist and turned to Matthew. "Are you going to permit this underage girl to talk this way? She is not old enough to be married. She lied about her age. That makes the marriage contract illegal."

Ellen moved over in the booth. "Mrs. Grant, there's nothing we can do about it. Carol may be young and underage, but we'll only make more trouble if we hold back."

Mrs. Grant turned her attention away from Ellen to Matthew. "Just you wait. I've already talked with the judge. We can have the marriage annulled. That is what should happen. We will have the marriage annulled."

The redness in Carol's face accented the auburn tint of her hair. "You can't stop me. Jeff and I will run away if you try to annul our marriage."

"Young woman," shouted Mrs. Grant, "what you need is a good spanking! Your parents should have given you one long ago. If they had, we wouldn't be having this talk now."

At this point Ellen stood and declared, "Mrs. Grant, you have no business passing judgment on my husband or me. Carol may not have done what we wished, but threats and spankings never solved a problem. You forget the part your son played. He is the one who is supposed to be older and wiser."

"Men sometimes give in to wild young girls who are willing to give themselves to them."

Chapter 14

Matthew wanted to take Carol in his arms and protect her from the woman's nastiness. Somehow he now saw Carol as a frightened little girl, very much wanting to appear brave and unafraid.

Carol cleared her throat. "I happen to have an announcement. I am expecting a baby. Mother, Mrs. Grant, you are about to become grandmothers."

Mrs. Grant gasped. She was at a loss for words.

"Oh, darling," said Ellen, "when will the baby come?"

"I'm not exactly sure."

Mrs. Grant recovered from her silence. "You tricked my son. Young girls can trick young men into marrying them, particularly if the young man's family has money and position."

"I don't care for your money or position," sputtered Carol. "You think you're so high and mighty, but you're not. I know where you came from, and you don't want people to know that you grew up on a poor farm."

Mrs. Grant backed away. "You'll regret this, young lady. You'll regret this." With those words, she made her exit.

Carol sat down in the booth, next to her father, and tears began to flow. Ellen reached across to her daughter. "Darling, we're your family. We will stand by you. And we will love our grandchild."

Through muffled sobs Carol thanked her mother.

Matthew hated to leave his daughter. Somehow he felt she should be safe at home with her family. But she had a husband. He was her new family.

That night, Matthew fell into bed, exhausted. Sleep would not come. The tense moments of the day kept replaying themselves. First the letter about Johnie in the psychiatric ward. Then his witness to Victoria's confrontation with Rita. And finally the anger of Mrs. Grant, followed by Carol's announcement that she was carrying a baby. Difficult situations did come in threes.

When sleep finally came, Matthew's usual dreams were replaced by a horrible nightmare. There seemed a never-ending darkness. Matthew stumbled through the brush in a swampy, wooded area. He recognized it as the area where the whole community had once searched for the two girls, Margaret and Irene.

The fear of that day returned, only this time he saw Johnie, who was lost. Matthew kept on running and stumbling. Johnie kept calling for help but disappeared every time Matthew was about to find him. Then

Beyond the Darkness

he heard a cry. Johnie's voice called clearly, "Help, Dad, help! I need your help." The words echoed again and again.

Then the woods turned into battlefields. Gunfire he associated with hunting became the gunfire of the war. He saw the wounded soldiers he had read about in the newspapers. And he saw Johnie lying there, wounded and bleeding. Matthew kept running, trying to reach his son. Every time he came close, Johnie disappeared. He seemed to be descending into an abyss.

A sharp crash of thunder awakened Matthew. He sat upright, aware that Ellen was closing the windows.

"You've been talking and thrashing about, Matthew. You must have had a nightmare."

"It's Johnie. He was calling for help."

Matthew heard the rain falling gently on the roof, and then his wife's voice. "Johnie will need us when he comes home. We'll be here. God is in control."

The gentle rain and Ellen's words soothed Matthew's spirit, and he slept.

Chapter 15

"I'm worried about you, Matthew." Ellen sensed her husband was deeply troubled. She continued to prepare Sunday morning breakfast. "Why don't you talk about it? That helps."

"There are too many problems. I don't know where to begin."

Ellen finished frying the eggs and brought them over to Matthew's plate. "Let's pray our simple prayer." The couple prayed together, "Come, Lord Jesus, be our guest. Let this food to us be blest. Amen." Silently they began to eat.

"It seems altogether too quiet around here," began Matthew finally. "Margaret's gone for the weekend. Michael hasn't come down. Carol's away. James should be home before Christmas, and we don't know when Johnie will be home. And Joe, is he alive?"

Ellen felt a need to be strong, but she didn't feel strong. "These are tough times. It's almost as if the darkness won't go away."

"I know the war is winding down. Those Japs have to surrender. But even so, I feel the war never seems to end. I want the boys safely home."

The two finished their eggs, bacon, and toast. Michael, wiping sleep from his eyes, stood in the doorway. Ellen realized this fan of Tom Mix just wanted his hot Ralston, so she began to cook his cereal.

Beyond the Darkness

The telephone rang and Matthew answered. After the call he turned to Ellen and explained, "Tim Robertson's back home. They want to celebrate at church with a potluck. Can you bring your chicken hotdish?"

Ellen hesitated, then answered, "Yes, but I'll have to work fast. We have just a little over an hour to get ready for Sunday school." Ellen moved into action. *At least there is something good to celebrate,* she thought. But the joy of Tim's return caused Ellen to think even more about the darkness of Johnie in the psychiatric ward.

Matthew left to finish his morning chores. Ellen scurried about, preparing her chicken hotdish Fortunately she had a plentiful supply of chicken she had canned last fall. And she had a full-sized chocolate cake she could take to the potlock. These special dinners usually turned into a real feast. As she worked, she prayed aloud, "Dear Lord, thank You for the returning soldiers. Thank You for Tim's return. But heal the scars, both physical and spiritual. Show me how I can help in this whole process. Please," she pleaded, "bring Johnie and the others back to us. Let us once more be a family."

Then she thought of Matthew and his brush with death a few years back. "Give Matthew health and strength," she added. "Give us the strength to face whatever we need to face. We cannot do this in our own strength."

Later, as Matthew drove them to church, she put her arm around little Michael, who sat between them. She reached to touch her husband's shoulder and said, "Darling, the Lord is giving us strength to face all our tomorrows."

A peace she could not understand flooded over her.

Matthew loved people; he enjoyed friendship and fellowship. But big crowds he did not enjoy. He had always been shy, and those big crowds took him back to the days of his youth when he was extremely shy.

He talked with Tim Robertson after the potluck. Some of the men began playing horseshoe. Usually Matthew would join in the game, but today he moved to the sidelines. Normally he would visit with Glenn at these events, but Glenn was more than occupied today with family and friends.

Chapter 15

After watching horseshoes awhile, Matthew decided to head down the hill and across the road to the cemetery. This was one of the places where he liked to come and think. He walked along, appreciating the green summer leaves of the trees along the way. Finally he stopped at his family's gravesites. "I miss you, Pa, even after five years." He looked down at the family tombstone, then moved over and stood where his sister Lucille was buried. At that moment he thought of her tender, quiet ways. Yet when he glanced at P.J.'s marker, his brother's dark image seemed to rise before him.

"It's as if a darkness has settled over me," he said out loud. "I don't understand it. Everything is changing. I find it hard to think of the future. Yet I have little Michael to take care of. I hope he will grow up in a better world."

"Lord," he began to pray, "I don't understand this darkness. I know there is hope. James will be coming home. We're hoping and praying that Johnie will be all right. Margaret is becoming a beautiful woman and will teach and help others. Even Carol seems to be settling down. And there will soon be a new grandchild."

Then he thought of Mary and Ed. Ed had been a friend—almost like a brother—through these years, but now they were moving to California.

Matthew knelt beside the tombstone. Somehow Pa seemed present, and his voice echoed in Matthew's mind, "Be strong, my son. Life is always filled with change."

The words of a familiar hymn came to mind. "Change and decay in all around I see. Help of the helpless, Lord, abide with me." Matthew indeed felt helpless. He wanted to cry the way a child would, but the tears would not come. Suddenly he became aware that he was not alone.

"Uncle Matthew." The voice was Larry's. "I saw you here. I've come to like this place also. It gives us some serious reminders."

"Hello, Larry. I'm afraid I'm feeling down in the dumps."

"It's Johnie, isn't it?"

"Yes," said Matthew. "And Joe—we don't know where he is or if he's alive. And there's Carol . . . and more."

"I wish I could help. You've stood by me when I needed encouragement."

"You are helping by being here." Matthew stood and turned to Larry, "Let's walk over to the far corner of the cemetery. When I was a kid, we used to play there."

Beyond the Darkness

Larry followed his uncle. "When we visited Grandpa and Grandma during the summer, I liked to run down and play here among the older tombstones."

Matthew smiled. "I guess kids aren't so different, are they? I liked to play here when I was a kid."

They walked on to the far corner where some of the large old tombstones stood. Some were leaning. Others stood as erect as they had years ago.

"Look at the dates," Larry observed. "Old Eli here died way back in August 1888. That's over fifty years ago."

"That's twelve years before I was born," said Matthew. "Time has a way of passing. Here it is 1945, and we're almost halfway through another century."

The two men, uncle and nephew, walked back and forth. Matthew felt a sense of past and present merging into one. They laughed at some of the old epitaphs and noted the seriousness of others. As the two men finally began to walk back toward the church, Larry made an announcement. "Uncle, I think I have some good news."

"God only knows, we need some good news."

"Actually, it's two bits of good news. Joan's expecting our second child. This time I'm ready to be a full-time father."

Matthew extended his hand to congratulate Larry.

"And the second good news is that we've moved into Gus's house. It's really a beautiful house. I'm doing repair work, and Joan is putting some great touches in arranging everything. And we just love having Gus there with us."

Matthew felt a sense of relief that Larry would be away from the influence of his mother. "That's great! I can't get over the changes that have taken place in your life."

Larry's expression became more serious. "Only the Lord could bring about the change in me. I was completely out of control. But Uncle Matthew, you were a part of that also. Your life was a witness to the way God works."

Matthew remembered only too well the pain Larry's father had caused. "I had to learn to forgive or I would have been destroyed," he replied.

"I'm afraid my father did some awful things, and I followed in his footsteps. I was headed in even a worse direction. I could have ended up in prison for life."

Chapter 15

"The past is gone. Though we wish we could, we cannot change what is behind. We can look only at the present and try to make the future better."

"How wise you are, uncle."

"I only wish I were."

On the way home, Matthew realized something. "Ma wasn't at church or at the potluck," he told Ellen. "I think we'd better swing by there to see if everything's all right. And Corrine and Warren and the kids weren't around either."

Ellen agreed, and Matthew took a different turn to head for the home place. Now that Corrine and Warren had taken over, the place seemed less and less like the home he had lived in for so many years. But Ma's little house nearby remained the same.

Victoria greeted them as they came up the steps. "I suppose you wondered about Ma. She had one of those spells this morning, so we didn't come to church."

"How is she now?" asked Ellen.

"Those spells come and go so quickly. When it was too late to go to church, she seemed perfectly fine. During those spells, she groans and seems short of breath. Then suddenly she's all right."

Ma's voice came through loud and clear from inside the house. "Don't talk about me as if I'm deaf. I'm perfectly all right. You come in and I'll make some coffee."

Victoria motioned to Matthew and whispered, "I need to talk with you."

Ellen and Michael went inside while Matthew followed Victoria, who led them toward the garden. He noticed the neat garden rows with scarcely a weed. "Have you been doing the garden work? This looks like one of the best gardens Ma has had in years."

"No, Matthew, you know I'm not much of a gardener. Mother has been out here. She spends more time out here than she ever has before. Notice all those extra flowers by the house. She weeds and waters them."

"She does well for seventy-six."

"Yes, but I'm worried. Now she has these spells. She becomes dizzy, and she's fallen several times."

"You know she can stay at our place. She stayed with us last winter and a few winters ago."

"And I've invited her to live with me in town, but she stubbornly refuses. Matthew, I don't think she should be alone here—even though Corrine and Warren are nearby."

"She can be terribly stubborn."

"Matthew, she should absolutely not be alone."

Matthew knew his sister could be equally stubborn. "You'll have to convince her to move to town with you or to move in with Ellen and me."

"I think she'll listen to you more than she'll listen to me."

"But you're college educated—a teacher and a principal. You know how to be in charge. I'm just a simple farmer."

"Matthew, you are far more than a simple farmer. You may not be college educated, but you love and understand people better than I do. You have a way with Mother and other people that I wish I had. As a principal, I get respect, but you have the love and respect of everyone."

Matthew stepped back in surprise. "That's the best compliment I've ever received."

"Somehow, dear brother, we never tell those we love most how good they are or how much we love them. Now that Dad is no longer alive, you are the most important man in my life."

"I'm honored."

The two stood side by side for a moment, then Victoria said again, "We have to do something about Mother."

Matthew stooped to pull one of the few weeds. "I have to think and pray about this. By fall we should have a solution."

"Coffee's ready!" Ma's clear voice made the announcement.

As Ma served lunch to her guests, she seemed anything but old and fragile. At the same time Matthew realized something needed to be done.

The last rays of sunlight shone across the fields, reflecting on the trees of the hills across the way. Matthew stood at the edge of the yard. He quoted aloud, "I will lift my eyes unto the hills from whence cometh my help." At this moment, however, God's help seemed as distant as some of those hills.

Chapter 15

Matthew tried to pray, but somehow couldn't. Concerns were overwhelming. Johnie, in a psychiatric hospital. James, still not home. Joe. Carol. Ma. The war, not yet over.

He missed the old oak tree at the home place. He always went there when he needed to think. The oak tree on this farm was not quite the same. Still, he needed to have some quiet time with the Lord, so he walked to the tree and decided to kneel. "Lord," he whispered, "I don't know what to do." He saw darkness beginning to cover the landscape. Clouds now covered the stars and the sliver of a moon. His spirit seemed filled with darkness.

Ellen's voice suddenly broke into his awareness as she quietly approached. "We'll make it through. God will strengthen us."

Matthew stood up. "I need that strength now. So many things have changed. Everything seems dark and hopeless."

Ellen took Matthew's arm. "Come, let me show you the words of an old hymn. When it's dark, we look to Christ, our light."

The warm lights of the kitchen welcomed him. They sat at the kitchen table, and Ellen began reading the words of John Henry Newman:

"Lead, kindly Light, amid the encircling gloom,
    Lead thou me on;
The night is dark, and I am far from home,
    Lead thou me on.
Keep thou my feet; I do not ask to see
The distant scene; one step enough for me.

"I was not ever thus, nor prayed that thou
    Should'st lead me on;
I loved to choose and see my path, but now
    Lead thou me on.
I loved the garish day; and spite of fears,
Pride ruled my will; remember not past years.

"So long thy power has blessed me, sure it still
    Will lead me on,
O'er moor and fen, o'er crag and torrent, till
    The night is gone,
And with the morn those angel faces smile,
Which I have loved long since, and lost awhile."

Beyond the Darkness

When Ellen finished reading the words, they both remained silent for several minutes. Then, Matthew spoke. "The Lord is indeed a kindly light."

"Yes," said Ellen, "we're traveling on some dark pathways."

Matthew remembered a verse. "The Lord is my light and my salvation. Whom then shall I fear?"

"And," added Ellen, "the Bible is filled with messages about not being afraid. Our Lord, our kindly light, will lead us. Be not afraid."

At that moment, Matthew felt a surge of hope. "I'm afraid we have some dark times ahead. There will be many uncertainties. But I know the war will end. And Johnie may go through some tough times, but he will return to us whole. Johnie will come home."

"Matthew, I love you."

Matthew reached for Ellen's hand. "I love you more than ever. We can face whatever tomorrow brings."

Chapter 16

August 1945

"Will this war ever be over?" questioned Ellen as she sat at her mother-in-law's kitchen table. "The boys are coming home, but will they be whole again? There are wounds much deeper than the physical hurt." During their visit, conversation had again turned to their concern over the safe return of James and healing for Johnie.

Elizabeth Anderson seemed to feel the same pain, but she spoke slowly, "The Lord will see us through. He is in the business of healing those wounds."

"Johnie is on my mind all the time. And I'm normally not a worrier. And when I'm not thinking of Johnie, there's Carol, and then there's Joe."

"The Lord will not let us be tested beyond our limits."

Ellen put aside her coffee cup. "And I'm supposed to be helping you. Matthew and I want to look after you. You deserve looking after."

Elizabeth cleared her throat. "I am not good at being looked after. I'm strong enough to help other people, and that's what I want to do. I pray to the Lord every day that I will not be a burden to anyone."

"Oh, you would be no burden, Mother Anderson."

"Fiddlesticks! I was in a bad way those two winters when I stayed with you. I'm stronger now."

"We're thankful for that." Ellen remembered again the way the Lord had seen her family through so many difficult times. Then her thoughts turned to how He had answered the petitions of the women's prayer group about Tim Robertson. "You know Tim is a testimony to prayer," she said aloud. "Coincidences aren't really coincidences. They are God at work."

"Yes, just at the time we were praying the hardest, Tim had his brush with death. And something stopped his plane from bursting into flames until he was out. Now we must keep on praying that all our boys from Lake View and Oak Ridge township will return to us whole."

"God answers prayer. But it's not always the way we think He should."

Matthew's knock interrupted their talk. "It's soon time for chores," he reminded Ellen.

"How about coffee first?" asked his mother.

"No thanks. I think Glenn and I must have had about five or six cups. That's too much coffee at one time."

Still, Matthew sat down, so Ellen knew there was something on his mind. "What's up?" she questioned.

"I don't know how much I should say." He looked at his mother.

Elizabeth's strength and determination had obviously returned. "If it concerns me, son, then you better say it."

"I think Glenn will talk to you. But he's on the school board, and they need a place for the new teacher to live. They were thinking of you, Ma. Maybe you could board the teacher?"

Elizabeth didn't hesitate. "Now, that depends. What kind of young woman is she? Some of these young women have terrible habits. They even smoke cigarettes. I won't have anyone like that."

"We'll do some checking. Her name is Ruth. Ruth Roberts, I believe."

Ellen recalled the name. "Is she from Prairie Center? There's a Roberts family over there."

"I think so."

"The Robertses are a good family."

Matthew added, "I believe Corrine would be willing to help out with the cooking."

"I am perfectly capable of making the meals and the lunches for school. It might be pleasant to have a young teacher in the house." Elizabeth smiled. "Ellen, that's the way you came into the family."

Chapter 16

Ellen remembered that first meeting. It hadn't taken long for her to love this farm and school. Within a few months she had known that Matthew was the man she would marry.

"I'm afraid it's time for chores," announced Matthew. "The cows won't wait."

"Thanks for being here," said Elizabeth. "I'm seventy-seven now, and I guess I need my family more than ever."

"We need each other," Ellen agreed.

"Mother, you have an invitation," announced Margaret as Matthew and Ellen returned home. "Mrs. Grant wants to see you."

Ellen groaned, "Whatever can she want now? I hope this doesn't mean trouble."

"Actually," said Margaret, "she was very nice. She's inviting you for tea and dessert later. She said it was time for the women to talk."

"That excludes me," said Matthew. "I can visit Larry at the station if he's still there, or go see him at home. Maybe I can catch Carol also."

"By the way, there's a letter," said Margaret. "It's from James. It's not for the whole family; it's for you two."

Ellen's heart began to beat fast as she wondered, *Does he have good news? Is he coming home soon?*

Margaret handed her the letter. Ellen read silently at first, and then she began to read aloud, "I believe I can get an early discharge for two reasons. First, I want to return to college. The winter quarter starts in early December. Second, I've asked to visit Johnie in Norfolk. I am requesting to take him to the veterans' hospital in Minnesota. I think the army will let me do this."

As Ellen finished this sentence, Margaret quickly commented, "I never dreamed I would ever miss my brothers as much as I do right now. I'd give anything to have them here."

Ellen looked to her husband and saw tears in his eyes. "It seems forever since our children were all together."

"We'll be together soon."

While Matthew and Margaret went to the barn to do the chores, Ellen tried to anticipate the return of her sons. But fear of Johnie's condition clouded the picture, as did thoughts about a meeting with Mrs. Grant.

Beyond the Darkness

Several hours later, Mrs. Grant ushered Ellen into her living room. Ellen felt apprehension as she considered some of their previous conversations. Mrs. Jeffrey Grant generally wanted her way, and that meant trouble.

"I want to thank you for coming here. I felt we needed to talk," Mrs. Grant stated.

Ellen searched for the right words in response. "We will be sharing a grandchild in a few months. And we are concerned about our own children as well."

Mrs. Grant's attitude appeared to be such a contrast to their previous encounters. Ellen wasn't sure the woman was sincere now. She offered Ellen one of her fancy sandwiches. "First, I do want to apologize for the way I've treated you. I haven't felt my son was ready for a serious girlfriend or for marriage. That's part of the reason I acted as I did."

Ellen smiled. "Mrs. Grant, on that we agree. Carol is far too young to be married, but there's nothing we can do."

"I've decided we need to try to help the kids. And they are kids—not really adults, though Jeffrey is twenty-three."

"What do you have in mind?"

"First of all, I don't think Carol should be working at the greasy spoon. I want her out of there."

"They need the money," objected Ellen. "They need to be on their own."

"Mr. Grant is taking care of that. Jeffrey will work at the bank. After all, he is next in line to be bank president."

"Is that what Jeffrey wants?"

"Whether he wants it or not, he needs a job. Mr. Grant is prepared to train him so he can follow in the steps of his father and grandfather."

Ellen started to object, but Mrs. Grant gave her no chance as she continued, "We are providing a nice little house at the edge of town. We own that house; in fact, it's the house Mr. Grant and I lived in when we were first married."

Why this change? Ellen kept wondering. *There must be something else going on.*

"Mr. Grant has always wanted his son to take over the bank at some point. Mr. Grant isn't so young anymore. He's not been in the best of health. We've had a dream that our son and then our grandson would take over the bank."

Chapter 16

"Our children need to make their own choices. We can't determine what they should do."

Mrs. Grant set down her teacup with determination. "Most children don't know what they want. They have to be guided and directed. They need a little push."

"Come now, Mrs. Grant," Ellen protested. "Think of our initial objections to Jeff and Carol's relationship. That only drove them closer together."

Mrs. Grant's tone changed. "I can see that now. That's why I think we have to work together to help our children."

"Yes, I agree, but they don't need us to push them."

In the next moment Ellen began to see a woman who was not the wealthy, well-dressed community leader. She saw a woman not quite so sure of herself, a woman frightened of the future, a woman definitely not in charge.

"My mother pushed me—maybe more than she should have," Mrs. Grant admitted. "As a child I tended to be very shy. I needed my mother to push me forward."

"*Encouragement* is what children need. James was shy, and I had to keep telling him he could do it. And Margaret also needed that extra encouragement when she was young."

"I can see your children have thrived under your guidance."

That was the first compliment Mrs. Grant had given her. "Thank you," Ellen said. "I'm afraid I wonder about Carol, though. She made me doubt all my abilities as a mother."

"Jeff has never been easy either. I guess my pushing him hasn't done much good." She turned to Ellen as if to start over. "I do wish you'd call me Loretta rather than Mrs. Grant."

"And you call me Ellen. However, I think most people call you Mrs. Grant. You do have a certain prominence in the community."

"It seems you do as well. I've noticed that most people call you Mrs. Anderson. All the other women seem to be called by their first names."

"That stems from the fact that I came here as a teacher. Teachers maintain a certain distance, and people did show me a great deal of respect."

"You deserve it." Loretta Grant looked away toward an old family picture on the fireplace mantle. "I came from a different background that I've hidden from people. My parents were very poor. My mother pushed me to get out of poverty, to earn a good living. My husband's parents did not approve of his marrying someone from the other side of the tracks. The more they disapproved, the more determined we were to marry. As a result, we simply eloped."

Ellen gasped in surprise. "Just like Jeff and Carol."

"I hadn't thought of it that way. Yes, I wanted my son to marry someone in a richer class of people. I now see that was wrong."

Ellen looked up at the hall clock. She was grateful for Loretta's seeming change of attitude, but she was also ready to leave. "I should probably walk down to the gas station to meet Matthew."

"Let me call Mr. Grant and have him drive you."

"It's only a few blocks. I'll walk."

Loretta extended her hand. "Thank you, Ellen, for coming. Let's try to help the kids furnish their new home."

"We'll talk to them and see what they want."

Loretta smiled. "I'll have to be careful. I can be too pushy."

Ellen left the Grant home, smiling. There had been a major breakthrough in this relationship. Now, if only Carol and Jeff's marriage would work out . . . and if Johnie would come home a whole person . . . and if Joe would somehow turn up alive . . .

. . . then the darkness would lift.

When Matthew arrived at Gus's Garage, he found Larry working with several boys. They were deep in conversation, not about cars but about matters of right and wrong.

Matthew stood for a while listening. When the boys saw Matthew, one of them quickly said, "Thanks, Larry, for letting us work on my car here. You understand guys like me."

Larry wiped off his greasy hands. "You're always welcome here. Come back."

The boys hurried off.

"That sounded like a serious conversation." Matthew extended his arm to shake hands, but Larry pointed to the dirt on his own hands. "I think I see what you're doing."

"Those boys remind me of myself a few years ago. Headed for trouble. Serious trouble. They need a focus. Something positive to do. And most of all, they need the Lord."

Chapter 16

Matthew couldn't help feeling proud of his nephew. "You've found your way. I'm more than happy that you're helping others."

Uncle and nephew began to discuss routine details of life as well as spiritual truths. Time passed quickly, and before long, Matthew took out his watch and checked the time. "It's time to pick up Ellen. We plan to stop at Carol's and then go home."

Larry suddenly looked serious. "Uncle Matthew, I need to talk about something—about being a father. My father never really acted like a father, so he was no a role model for me to be a good dad."

"No one said being a father is easy."

"I think of little Lowell. I want to raise him right. At the same time, I'm afraid of being hard on him, because I can see he's a lot like I was. I want to keep him from making my mistakes. But if I'm too hard on him, I can crush his spirit."

Matthew smiled. "Boys will be boys. They will make mistakes and learn from those mistakes. Being a father means doing a lot of listening."

"You're right. But I don't have a lot of patience."

"Patience takes time."

"Uncle Matthew . . ." Larry began and stopped. "You've become like a father to me. You don't know how much that means to me."

Matthew choked on his words. "I'm honored. Somehow I don't feel I deserve this much respect."

"You have my deepest love and respect."

Matthew extended his hand and then opened his arms. Uncle and nephew embraced, cementing a bond that would last throughout their lives.

Ellen entered and cleared her throat. "I hate to interrupt."

Matthew turned to his wife. "We were having a serious discussion."

"We've been talking," said Larry. "Uncle Matthew is filling the place of a dad for me. I need a father's advice."

"You chose a good man." Ellen moved forward and embraced Larry. "You have made such a great change in your life. I'm proud of you."

Larry kissed his aunt on the cheek. "I couldn't have done it without help from people like Uncle Matthew."

As Larry closed the station, Matthew and Ellen headed into town. Finding that Carol and Jeff were not home, Matthew decided to take the long way back so that he and his wife could enjoy the beauty of summer.

Beyond the Darkness

As the sun set that early August evening, they drove down the road to their farm, their home.

In the lane past the barn, Matthew saw two figures in the shadows. He turned to Ellen. "Who is that?"

"It's Margaret, for one."

Their daughter waved to them as Matthew drove up to the house and recognized the other person. "Tim Robertson must be visiting our Margaret."

"She's a very attractive young woman. Young men know that."

Matthew disagreed. "She more than attractive; she's beautiful. Glenn told me that Tim had his eye on our daughter. Come to think of it, this wouldn't be a bad arrangement."

"She's still awfully young."

Later Matthew and Ellen decided to enjoy the summer evening on their porch swing. They talked about the events of the day, and their three children, and Larry and Joe.

As the shadows deepened, Michael made an appearance on the porch. "I can't sleep. I had a bad dream."

"Remember, it's just a dream," comforted his mother.

"I'm afraid. Johnie was hurt. I want him to be right here."

"We're praying for your brother. He'll be home."

"I'm still scared."

Michael squeezed between his parents, giving each one a hug. "I don't like Tim."

"Why?"

"He's taking Margaret away from us. I want Margaret right here."

Matthew smiled. "He's not taking Margaret away. She'll always be your sister."

Ellen added, "Just like James and Johnie will always be your brothers. They may be far away, but they'll always come back home."

Michael yawned. "It's time to get back to bed," said Ellen. "It's past your bedtime."

"Margaret put me to bed early. I didn't want to go, but she made me."

Chapter 16

"How about some hot cocoa? Then we'll go up and you can say your prayers."

Ellen went in the house to prepare Michael's cocoa. For several minutes Matthew sat with his arm around his little son. For a brief moment it felt as if he had his arm around Johnie. If only Johnie were safe at home.

After the three drank their hot cocoa, soon Michael was nodding his head. Matthew went up the stairs with his wife and son, and she tucked their youngest into bed. Michael said his usual bedtime prayer but with some additions. "Please, God, make Johnie well and bring him home fast. You can do anything else You want, God, but please hurry up and bring James and Johnie home. Please, God, do this and I'll be a good boy. I'll learn my Sunday school lessons, and I won't pull the tails of the cats or the girls' pigtails. Thank you. Amen."

Matthew waited a moment and kissed his son. By that time Michael was sound asleep.

Chapter 17

As Matthew built a stack of wheat, he couldn't help remembering other years. He recalled especially the year when James and Johnie were much younger, and Joe had come home on leave. It had been threshing time. He had been working with Ed, whose son Jake was also there. The three boys competed in pitching bundles and tractor driving. What a memorable day that was!

And now James had been transferred to army headquarters in Germany. Johnie was in the hospital at Norfolk, Virginia. Jake was somewhere in Europe. And they weren't even sure Joe was alive.

It didn't seem right now that they had to depend on the girls to help. Ed was in the wagon, with Irene pitching the bundles to him, and Margaret worked on the stack. The girls were actually good at their jobs, yet he kept thinking this wasn't the way things should be. The girls were doing men's work.

Change was always present. Yet change seemed to be coming faster than ever now. In a few weeks Mary and Ed would have their auction sale and leave for California.

Somehow Matthew had always felt Ed would be around—both as a brother-in-law and a friend. In two months they would be separated by thousands of miles. No longer would these two families be within miles of each other.

Beyond the Darkness

Ed called out, "I think you better let Margaret get down. You'll have to build the peak of the stack by yourself."

Matthew motioned Margaret down. Then Ed pitched the bundles higher, and Matthew worked to build the top of the stack. He could hear Margaret and Irene laughing and talking about girl matters. No . . . Margaret was not a girl, he realized. Margaret was a woman.

After he placed the final bundle in place at the top of the stack, Matthew slid down. Across the field, he saw Ellen running toward them. They still had much work to do. *It's not time for lunch,* he thought. *Is something wrong? Why is she rushing over this way?*

Ed was ready to start the tractor, but Matthew shouted, "Wait!"

Ellen arrived, out of breath, and Matthew felt both panic and concern. "What's wrong?"

"The war's officially over!" she exclaimed. "The Japanese have surrendered unconditionally. The war is over! The news came on the radio."

"Thank God!" shouted Matthew.

"The news said that the atomic bombs brought an end to this terrible war. The destruction of those cities was dreadful, but I guess it saved thousands of other lives."

"It's about time those Japs gave up," grumbled Ed. "They should have surrendered months, even years ago."

Margaret, in her quieter way, added, "Now we can only hope that Joe is alive. We want Joe safely home."

Ellen continued enthusiastically. "I remember how we celebrated the Armistice of World War I. Everything else stopped."

"We should celebrate," agreed Margaret.

"Why don't we invite people over tomorrow night?" Ellen suggested. "Even though it's busy harvest time, we need to celebrate and give thanks."

As the next hours flew by, Matthew felt a new surge of hope. Johnie would come home. James and all the others would come home. Joe had to be alive. He belonged at Oak Ridge township and the family farm.

The last stacks of wheat were built. Threshing would come soon, and the harvest would be safely gathered in—as would Matthew's family.

Chapter 17

Several days later, Ellen announced, "Matthew, we need to take some kitchen things into town for Carol. I need some time alone with her."

"I'll find an excuse to go over to Larry's. I need to talk with my nephew."

Ellen still had the gnawing sensation that she had failed her younger daughter. The other children seemed to be turning out well, but Carol's rebellion had led her into this early and unwise marriage.

Ellen knew Carol would be home. She had called and made sure of that. Followed by Matthew, she entered the little house that Jeff's parents had given to their son and daughter-in-law. Ellen would describe this place as a cute honeymoon cottage, a nice place to begin family life.

Ellen motioned for Matthew to set down the box on the kitchen-dining room table. "We brought you a set of dishes. The dishes are old, but they look good," she told Carol.

"Thanks, Mom. I guess I didn't think of all the things I needed."

"That's what mothers are for."

Matthew excused himself. "You women need to talk. I'll stop at Larry's for a while. By the way, where's Jeff?"

"Oh, he's uptown, I guess."

Ellen wondered what that meant but said nothing. Matthew went on his way.

Carol motioned for her mother to sit down on the secondhand davenport. "I didn't realize there was so much to do in setting up a home."

"Are you still working at Kay's Café?"

"I've been working there during the busy dinner hour at noon. Kay's been good to me. We need the money, too."

Ellen wasn't sure how to approach the next matter. "Carol, have you been taking care of yourself? That's important for the baby."

"I'm young. I'm healthy."

"Have you been to the doctor? You need to go."

"I'll go later."

Ellen scrutinized her daughter. "You need to go now. You're showing. Dr. Baker can make sure everything's all right."

"I'll go."

"When is the baby coming? Apparently the baby is not coming early next year as you said before. What is the date?"

Carol blushed. "I think it'll be November or December."

Ellen wanted to cry out to her daughter. Obviously the baby was conceived before their marriage. Carol had ignored the values she had been taught. Did she have no regret for her actions?

"Carol, you know—" Ellen stopped abruptly, deciding she would say no more. Her daughter turned away and an awkward silence followed.

"I'm happy I'm married to Jeff," Carol finally said. "I love him more than I can say."

Ellen wanted to say more, but remained silent to let her daughter continue.

"I'm sorry I've disappointed you. I can't seem to do everything right the way Margaret does. I'm not her."

"I don't expect you to be Margaret. I do love you, my dear. And now I expect you to be a good wife and mother. I will help you all I can."

Carol mumbled a thank you.

"How about if we check the kitchen and put away some of these dishes and other things? Maybe I can see some of what you need."

During the next hour, mother and daughter worked in the kitchen, putting away and organizing. When Ellen left, she felt uneasy about Carol and the baby and Jeff.

"I need to make some extra money," said Margaret. "Irene and I are going to do shocking over toward River Falls."

Matthew had finished his morning oatmeal, and now he set down his coffee cup. "What do you mean? You shouldn't be doing that kind of work."

"The farmers are hard up. They're paying some men sixty-five cents an hour."

Matthew hesitated and wondered what to say. After a moment, he told his daughter, "I'm surprised they're paying that much. That's what they pay men for an hour of good hard work."

"We girls can work, too. They're paying us fifty cents an hour because we're not as strong as the men. But Irene and I will show them."

Matthew looked to Ellen and wondered what his wife thought about this.

Ellen shook her head. "I guess women have to fill the workplace when men are off fighting a war."

Chapter 17

"Tim is coming to pick us up in just a few minutes. He'll be at the farm; he's working there, too," Margaret stated.

"Are you sure you want to do this?" asked Matthew, though it sounded like his daughter's mind was made up.

"I need new clothes for teaching, and Irene wants new clothes for school in California."

"Did Ed agree? They're busy getting ready to move."

"He says they need the money. It's expensive to move."

"Well, there's nothing for me to say. Watch out for some of those men. Sometimes they get ideas when young girls are around," he cautioned.

"I'll be fine. Tim will be there most of the time to check that everything's OK."

Margaret gave her mother a hug, kissed her father on the cheek, and then hurried out as Tim's car drove up.

Ellen smiled at her husband. "The world is changing."

Matthew thought a moment about the truth of his wife's comment. "I think I have time to drive over and see Glenn. It's always good to talk with him." Perhaps a visit with his friend would give him the perspective he needed about all the changes happening around him.

"By all means, go, Matthew."

He changed out of his barn clothes and drove over to see Glenn Robertson—who always seemed to have the latest news. With Ed and Mary leaving for California, Matthew realized Glenn would become an even more important friend. It was hard to imagine not having his sister Mary nearby. He had so many memories of the two families being together.

Matthew found Glenn near the barn, checking the wheat stack. Threshing would soon begin. He wondered if Ed's grain was ready.

The two men had little need for greeting or the usual social amenities. They generally began talking about whatever was on the mind of one or the other. Matthew began with a question. "What do you think about having girls out in the field with men? It's one thing at home with family. But I don't see them going out as hired hands in the fields."

"I guess times are changing. Women have worked in ammunition and war plants all over the country," Glenn answered. "Still, I've always thought a woman's place is in the home, or beside her husband."

"Margaret and Irene went out shocking today. I don't think that's right."

Beyond the Darkness

Glenn smiled. "I think I know what that's all about. Tim is working at River Falls too. I think my son is getting sweet on your Margaret. That might make a perfect match."

"I notice he's been coming around lately."

"I have some other news. Tim has decided to farm. He's going to begin renting Ed's farm after they leave for California, with the idea of buying it within a year."

"I was wondering what Ed would do with his land. He's been determined to get out, but I know he wanted someone to buy or take over his Angus cattle. Is Tim going to take over his Angus, too?"

"I believe they're talking about that."

Matthew thought of the many young men and women leaving the farms, just another change in their lives these days. "I'm glad at least one of our young men is staying on the farm. Too many are leaving."

"Farming's tough, but it's a good life."

"I'm my own boss here," agreed Matthew. "I don't have someone looking over my shoulder and telling me what to do."

The two men walked toward the house.

Glenn stopped and started to say something, then hesitated.

"What's on your mind?" questioned Matthew.

"What would you think if my son married your daughter? Tim seems serious about finding a good woman and settling down."

Matthew found himself surprised at the prospect. "You . . . you have a good son," he stuttered, "but is my daughter ready for marriage? Isn't Tim rushing a bit?"

"I don't think so. When I began courting Mabel, I didn't need much time to know she was the one."

"I'm not sure Margaret is ready. She needs to teach a few years before she settles down. Marriage is for life. I took my time. I was twenty-three and Ellen was twenty-four."

"I was just twenty-one," Glenn countered, "but I was ready to be on my own. My pa wasn't the nice kind of guy that your pa was. I wanted to be on my own."

This was one of those rare times when Matthew and Glenn did not agree. Glenn seemed to want Tim to marry quickly, and Matthew felt his daughter needed to wait.

"Well, Glenn, it's up to the kids."

With those words, they changed the subject and talked of farming and weather and community problems. Matthew felt a sense of well-being,

Chapter 17

because even when the two disagreed, their friendship remained the same. And somehow he felt he would need this friendship even more as the winds of change in their world continued to blow.

Saturday night was the traditional time for farmers to drive into town to shop and visit. This particular Saturday—following the announcement of the end of the war—also called for a time of celebration.

As they finished their early supper, Margaret hurried upstairs to get ready to go to Lake View. Tim was once more picking her up. *Maybe this is more serious than I knew,* Matthew thought as he watched his daughter run up to her room.

Ellen had heated bathwater for him. Now the laundry tub was filled, ready for his Saturday night bath. This weekly ritual made Matthew feel good and clean. It was a preparation for Sunday. It was a time to slow down and remember what was most important.

When Matthew finished bathing and dressing, he greeted Ellen with a kiss on the cheek. He couldn't help noticing how pretty she looked in her flowered blue dress. The color brought out the blue in her eyes and seemed to display her gentle kindness.

"On the way to town, why don't you read James's letter?" Matthew asked his wife. "I think you gave me only a few highlights earlier today."

Soon Matthew, Ellen, and Michael were on their way to Lake View. Ellen began reading to herself at first. "He seems to have written this letter in a hurry, but he does say a little more than I told you this afternoon."

"I like to hear everything James has to—"

"I want James and Johnie home right away," interrupted Michael. "I want Johnie to help me drive tractor."

"You're too young to drive the tractor," said Matthew.

"Johnie drove when he was six. And I'm six."

"Johnie drove when he wasn't supposed to," Ellen reminded him. "He almost got into an accident. We don't want that to happen to you."

"I'm big for my age," pleaded Michael. "I wouldn't get into an accident."

Beyond the Darkness

Ellen ignored her young son and began to read aloud. "'Thank God this war is over—except for some formalities. The surrender should soon be official. I don't know that I trust those Japs. The government has to be absolutely sure.' I can't believe those Japanese would try anything now—not after that bombing," she commented.

Matthew thought of the devastation of the Japanese cities. "I'm afraid the atomic bomb could be used again. Sadly, it kills the innocent as well as the guilty."

Ellen continued reading. "'I am now almost certain that I should be discharged in October. That means I should be home by November. I plan to travel to Norfolk and hope to see that Johnie is sent to a hospital in Minnesota. By that time we should be able to see him. I believe that when he sees family, he will recover more rapidly. And when he comes home, he'll be the same old Johnie.

"'I have seen so much of what this war does to people. I am more determined than ever that I should be a part of making this world a better world. I know that I want to be a writer, but I want to influence youth. I plan to be a teacher, a high schoolteacher. Maybe I'll move on to college teaching after that. I want to help show young people a better way of life. I am convinced that God is guiding me and showing me what to do.'"

Ellen stopped reading, and Matthew slowed down as they approached Lake View. "I'm proud of our son. He will make a difference."

"I've always known James would do something special."

"Ellen, I used to dream of going beyond those hills, but James is going to do that instead."

"He has already." Ellen took up the letter again. "'I eagerly look forward to coming home. Mom, I can't wait to sit down to one of your delicious meals. And Dad, I can't wait until I'm in the barn, helping you. I always think of you and your kindness to the animals. I picture Christmas Eve and the way we give the cattle that extra portion.'"

Matthew managed to disguise his happiness as Ellen went on. "'And my dear sisters, Margaret and Carol. They are now beautiful young women. I know I will see them soon. And Michael, I can't wait to see how high I can lift him. I miss his mischievous laughter.'"

"What is mischiev—?" questioned Michael.

"We'll explain later," Ellen interrupted. "Your big brother misses you and can't wait to see you."

"I can't wait either."

Chapter 17

Matthew parked the car in town as Ellen finished the letter. "'I never realized how important family is until these last years. I love you more than I can say. I hope I can be a credit to the Anderson name and that you will be proud of me. Once more, I see all of us together, seated at the table saying our table prayer. May the Lord guide so that we all meet once more. All my love, James.'"

No one spoke for several moments. At that moment the strains of "Stars and Stripes Forever" could be heard, coming from the center of town.

"It's time to celebrate and enjoy the victory and the music," said Matthew.

A bigger than usual crowd stood on the street as the band played. A festive, celebratory mood was obvious; Matthew could almost feel it. A sense of relief about the war's end permeated the crowd. Neighborliness and friendly talk filled the streets.

Ellen went to the grocery story while Matthew and Michael visited the barbershop. The place was busy, but both father and son managed to have their haircuts. They needed to look good for Sunday morning and other events coming soon.

As the three of them walked down Lake View's main street, Matthew saw many of their neighbors. Glenn and Mabel and two of their younger children did their weekly business. Mary and Ed were walking about. Margaret and Tim were in line for a movie at the small theater. Even Victoria had walked uptown.

After they finished their town business, Matthew and Ellen carried groceries to the car. He felt a tap on his shoulder. "Hello, Dad. Hello, Mother." Carol stood before them, and her parents enthusiastically greeted her.

"Why don't you stop for coffee?" she offered. "You won't believe it, but I've learned to make cookies, and they're good."

Matthew, Ellen, and Michael stopped for a visit in Carol and Jeff's new home. This time Jeff was present, doing his best to be a gracious host.

I hope things work out for Carol, Matthew said to himself as they enjoyed coffee together. For the first time he felt hope for his daughter and her marriage.

That night Matthew went to bed with a sense of security. Somehow the insanity of war had ended. The future looked far brighter. He saw a light coming through the dark times.

Chapter 18

September 1945

September 1, 1945, marked the beginning of another major change in Matthew Anderson's life. Today was the auction sale of Mary and Ed's farm goods. Somehow, their decision to move to California seemed like a permanent separation. Mary had been close by all his life, and Ed had been part of the family for over twenty years.

Other changes were in the air as well. Margaret had left for her teaching job in a school north of Lake View. She would be on her own, no longer living under his roof. And Carol would soon present him with his first grandchild. He still had a hard time imagining himself as a grandfather. Then there was Ma. She was growing frailer. Would she be able to live on her own, even with a young teacher living there?

Concerns about Johnie crowded out the problems at home, however. Would he survive this thing called shell shock? Matthew had heard of Great War soldiers who were never normal again. Then there was James. In a few months, after returning home, he would attend college. His dreams would transport him far beyond the familiar hills of home.

Yesterday and early that morning, Matthew had helped Mary and Ed place all the sale items out on display for the auction. The familiar dining room table looked out of place on the lawn. There was also the bed that had come from the family home—it didn't feel right to sell it. It seemed the private life of his sister's family was suddenly on display.

Matthew often went to auction sales. Sometimes he went to see about buying some farm equipment, but mostly he visited with neighbors and friends and then enjoyed the lunch, usually provided by the Ladies' Aid. This time was different; it was much more personal.

A wall clock chimed ten times to announce 10:00 A.M.—the signal for the auction to begin. These events always started on time, for buyers were anxious to buy what they had their eyes on. As usual, Glenn Robertson was right up front with Ed, helping the auctioneer. Irene was nearby, running errands. Seated near the auctioneer was Mary, whose eyes and face looked drawn and tired.

The auctioneer began his fast-paced, "How much am I bid?" The bids began slowly, but soon came more quickly. Matthew watched and listened, but his attention was on his own thoughts until a voice interrupted them. "Hello, Uncle Matthew."

"Beth," responded Matthew, "it's good to see you. I figured you'd be coming home."

"I finished my job in the city yesterday. I wanted to be here."

She gave Matthew a hug, which reminded him of how close he had been to her and his other nieces and nephews. Now they were grown and moving away.

"This move to California will be a big change for you, won't it?"

"I'm not moving. Just last night I decided to stay in Minnesota at the university. I'm not interested in California."

"You'll be far from your mom and dad."

"Yes, Mom and Dad aren't too happy, but I have friends. I'll be OK."

Matthew looked down at Beth, who reminded him of his sister Lucille who'd died so long ago. "You'll always be welcome in our home when you have vacation."

"Thanks, Uncle Matthew." She moved closer to him and hugged him again. Then she disappeared in the crowd.

As he looked around, Matthew figured the whole neighborhood must have turned out for this event. Over on the sidelines he saw another familiar face, one that had been absent for many months. He found his way through the crowd to greet his sister. "Martha, how good to see you."

Chapter 18

Martha welcomed him warmly. "I had to come. I've been with the girls so long, but I'm afraid I have to go back later next week." She often stayed away for long periods of time visiting and helping her children.

Brother and sister stood a moment. Then Martha threw her arms around Matthew. "Oh, how I've missed you. Why does life have to get so complicated? Two of my girls seem to need me more than ever."

In the next minutes, with the auctioneer's voice shouting in the background, Matthew and Martha visited and caught up on family happenings. "The family's going to be spread out," said Matthew. "You're in Wisconsin. Mary will be in California. Ma and Victoria and I will be here."

"That's just the way things are."

"I miss the days when we were all close together. I miss having all my children under one roof."

"Children grow up and leave home. They have to live their own lives."

Matthew looked around to see if Warren was nearby. He saw him up front near the auctioneer. "I'm glad that Corrine and Warren are near. Their problems seem to be working out. Warren's become a good friend."

Martha sighed. "Yes, I miss them when I'm in Wisconsin. But Warren is restless. He talks about following Mary and Ed to California."

"I figured something was on his mind. He hasn't been himself lately."

"Corrine told me about it last night after I got settled."

Matthew and Martha began to walk away from the crowd. Matthew looked at the house and the outbuildings that had become a familiar place during the last twenty years. For a long time Matthew and Ellen and their children had come here once a week. But that had changed in the past few years. Many things were no longer the same.

They approached the house that Mary had come to as a young bride. Outside in the back porch sat their mother. "Ma, don't you want to walk over and see what's going on at the sale?" Matthew asked her.

His mother looked away. "I guess I'm feeling a little bit sad. I still hear quite well. I can hear what they are selling. It's as if memories are for sale. Mary and Ed are selling their past. They're leaving this life and their family behind."

"But these are just things," said Martha. "People are more important."

"I know—and people are leaving too. I'll miss Mary. I'm an old lady, now seventy-seven. I may never again see her in this life."

"Oh, Mother, they'll come back to visit."

"It won't be the same."

Matthew, more keenly than ever, realized the truth of his mother's words. He left her and Martha and walked along the edge of the crowd. He reminded himself that life had always been changing. This change was just one of many that were part of life.

He moved closer to the auctioneer, who continued to sell Ed and Mary's household furniture. He recognized the bed and dresser he and his brother and sisters had given them as a wedding gift. It seemed wrong to sell such a sentimental objects. Familiar pictures and other items were next on the auctioneer's list. Soon the farm machinery would be auctioned off.

Matthew left the crowd and the auctioneer and the noise. He walked away to the pasture. Most of the cattle had been sold already. A few would be auctioned off to the highest bidder. A few weeks ago, many cattle grazed in this spot that was now empty.

"Lord," Matthew prayed aloud, "help me through the days ahead. I've loved the security of the land and the family and neighbors. I miss Pa. I miss Mary and Ed, even though they haven't moved yet. I am reminded that You are my security."

Matthew felt a renewed strength as he returned to the crowds and noise of family and community. During these moments, he determined to enjoy his family and friends and neighbors. There was joy and happiness in the present.

Elizabeth Anderson had felt a need to stay in the background at the auction. The crowds made her tired and nervous. Maybe her years were catching up with her. The rest of the afternoon reminded her of a changing world and a changing family. That evening she fell exhausted into her bed.

Sunday morning, she heard Martha's voice by her bedroom door. "Mother, it's time to get up. We'll leave for church in another hour."

Elizabeth slowly sat up in bed. This was one of those days her bones reminded her of her age. "I guess I overslept. I never oversleep."

Chapter 18

"Yesterday was a hard day, Mother. But today is going to be busy as well."

Elizabeth dressed herself and then ate the oatmeal Martha had prepared. Tomorrow the new teacher would be coming to stay. But it was good to have her daughter here for at least a few days. This daughter always seemed to understand the problems she faced—maybe she understood too well. As Martha drove her mother to church, she kept telling Elizabeth, "You shouldn't be living out here all alone. Why don't you go and stay with Victoria?" Still the older woman stuck to her resolve to stay in her own home.

Oak Ridge Church was full this Sunday morning. Mary and Ed and their two girls were present. The congregation was invited to return in the afternoon for a farewell party and program. After all, Mary and Ed would be leaving Monday morning.

The Anderson family gathered at noon for their first farewell dinner at the home place. Victoria and Ellen had organized everything, using Corrine's kitchen. Afterward all Elizabeth could recall was a sumptuous Sunday dinner, very much in the Anderson family tradition.

Elizabeth went through that Sunday as if in a dream. She talked with many people, though sometimes she thought they didn't seem to hear. She had lived long enough to know how to do what was expected, but underneath it all, the people and activities exhausted her. Throughout the day, family members came and went through Elizabeth's consciousness. Eventually, she felt dizzy. *What's happening to me?* she wondered. *Something's not quite right, but I don't want to worry Mary or the rest. They have enough to think about.* She left the crowd and went to sit in a corner.

As she rested, Elizabeth became acutely aware of those family members who were no longer around. At moments it almost seemed they were present again. Her husband of more than fifty years, John, stood before her asking, "What's wrong? You need to be out there with the family—not sitting in a corner here." But John had died six years ago.

Lucille, her daughter who died years before, walked into her awareness. In many ways, like Martha, Lucille had showed unselfish concern for people. Even when her health was deteriorating, she always thought of others first. Elizabeth almost heard her saying, "Mother, I think you should lie down and rest."

Next to walk before her came her handsome oldest son, Paul John, always known as P.J. He was his usual charming self. She saw him visiting with people, but then he appeared in that hospital bed, tormented with pain. She would never forget the last time she saw him alive. Two of her children gone before her. Children should bury their parents, not the other way around.

Something, perhaps the sounds of activity, brought her briefly back to the present reality, but she retreated again to memory. Others were missing from this family circle. Would this circle ever be unbroken? In eternity, would they all gather together as a family?

She longed for her three grandsons. James should be home next month. Johnie—he was alive, but when would he come home and be himself? And Jake, he would be stationed in Germany indefinitely.

Other family members entered her memories. Martha's two other daughters, Rachel and Jane, had not been home in several years. They had been around for John's funeral and later for P.J.'s. *I suppose they'll come for my funeral,* she thought.

Almost without warning, Elizabeth slumped forward. Suddenly family members were hurrying around her. She knew people were there, but they were only shadows.

"Call Dr. Baker," Martha commanded.

She felt herself being led into her house and into her bedroom. For an indefinite period of time, darkness enveloped her. In her deep sleep, Elizabeth wasn't certain she'd return to the present. She couldn't distinguish what was reality and what took place within her mind. She saw herself as a young woman. John knelt before her as he proposed marriage. Her own sisters and brothers were once more alive and young. Her mother and father sat at the kitchen table. She felt an intense longing for her childhood family. She saw the family gatherings—aunts and uncles and cousins. How she missed these people from her past! They were all dead or had moved away—or at least they were old, some very old.

Did she ever really appreciate her mother and father and those other special family members? She seemed more grateful for them after they were gone. *Why can't people show love and appreciate others while they are alive?* she wondered in the darkness of her mind.

Then all at once, Elizabeth's memory moved forward to recent times. Matthew, always the strong and dependable one, walked into her awareness. He'd had a brush with death, and the sensation that he was leaving his family and farm behind him. But then he was called back, she remembered him telling her.

Chapter 18

"Lord," Elizabeth called out, "keep my family safe. Keep them safe for all eternity."

Victoria's familiar voice broke into her deep reverie, bringing her mind back to the present and awakening her. "Mother seems to be coming back. What's happened? What's been going on?"

Dr. Baker spoke quietly. "Mrs. Anderson, how are you feeling? Can you hear me?"

Surprised at her doctor's presence, Elizabeth looked directly him. "I felt dizzy. Then everything went blank."

"You've had some kind of spell. I'm not quite sure what it was."

"I've been seeing all kinds of people. I saw John and my mother and father—and other people who have been gone for years."

Dr. Baker brought out his stethoscope and listened to her heart. "Your heartbeat is a little slow," he reported, "but it sounds fine." He began to take her pulse. "Your pulse is OK."

Victoria's presence commanded attention. "Mother, you had us all worried."

"Are you feeling better, Mrs. Anderson?" the doctor asked.

"I just feel weak and tired."

Dr. Baker put his arm on her shoulder. "You've had too much excitement for one day. I think a good night's rest will help."

"But what happened? I get tired easily, but this was something different."

"It may have been a blood clot that passed through." The doctor looked serious as he continued. "I may as well warn you, Mrs. Anderson. One of those clots could stop in the brain, which could end your life. Or you could live for years."

"I'm ready. When the Lord sees fit, He'll call me home."

"I'll leave some medicine for you. This should help. Right now, lie down and rest. Otherwise you have the health and strength to live many more years."

Dr. Baker left the room.

"Mary and Ed want to say good-bye. I'll get them. Then you have a good rest." Victoria left the room.

Elizabeth sat up, and in moments Mary and Ed entered. Mary spoke. "Mother, we came to say good-bye. We hate to leave you when you're not feeling well."

"I'm feeling better now. Just a little tired."

Beyond the Darkness

Elizabeth realized Ed was at a loss for words, so Mary continued, "We've had hard times here on the farm. These winters are cold. We feel it's the right time to move. And Ed has a job with his cousin. We'll have a better life there."

"I'll miss you." Elizabeth wanted to say more but words wouldn't come. Another of her children was leaving, and her feelings were too deep to express.

"Good-bye, Mother Anderson," Ed finally said. "We hope to come back next summer." He reached out and shook her hand.

"Take good care of Mary."

Tears came to her daughter's eyes. "Mother, I'll miss you. We'll be back to see you." Mary kissed her on the cheek.

"Good-bye, my child. God go with you."

Mary hugged her. No more words were spoken. Elizabeth couldn't help wondering if she would see her daughter again in this life, or if she would join the others who lived only in her memories.

Matthew, Martha, and Victoria stood beside the bed. She felt a warmth and security of having these three children close by. But the reality was that God was her strength and security.

She smiled. "Good night, my children."

The following morning, Labor Day Monday, Elizabeth awakened early as she usually did. She put on her robe and walked into the kitchen. *I'll start the fire in the kitchen stove and have coffee ready for Martha,* she decided.

Her aches of the past day seemed to have disappeared. With new energy, she dressed and did the small household chores. An hour later, she sat at the table, eating oatmeal and drinking coffee. She could hear Martha stirring in the upstairs bedroom.

For Elizabeth, Monday was always wash day. She went into her bedroom and stripped her bed of its sheets and pillowcases. She checked the dresses and underclothes that needed washing. Martha came downstairs, carrying her sheets. "Mother, I'll take care of the washing. You need to rest."

Elizabeth objected, "I'm feeling fine. We need to be ready for the teacher. She'll be coming sometime today—later this afternoon."

"We'll work together with the washing. At least I can hang out the clothes—you used to complain about carrying all those clothes." Together mother and daughter washed the clothes and hung them on the lines outside. This routine had been part of Elizabeth's whole life.

Chapter 18

In the afternoon Martha began to move her clothes over to Corrine and Warren's. "The upstairs should be left for the teacher," she told her mother. "She should have some privacy. I'll stay with Corrine and Warren, but I'll be over to help."

In late afternoon Elizabeth heard a car drive up. She realized she must have dozed off. When she heard a knock at the porch door, she hurried to answer. A young woman with dark auburn hair stood before her. "I'm Ruth Roberts. I believe I'll be boarding with you during the next months."

"Yes," answered Elizabeth. "Come in. Welcome to your new home."

Ruth set down her suitcase and pointed toward the yard. "These are my parents. I think they're in a bit of a hurry to get back to the farm. It's time for chores, you know."

Elizabeth greeted Mr. and Mrs. Roberts and invited them for lunch, but they helped Ruth carry her things to the upstairs bedroom and then quickly excused themselves.

As Ruth worked upstairs, putting away clothes and other things, Elizabeth prepared a supper of sandwiches and pea soup. She was glad her children had talked her into buying a refrigerator. That modern convenience simplified many tasks.

When Ruth walked into the kitchen, Elizabeth had to look twice. "Miss Roberts, for a minute I thought you were the woman who became my daughter-in-law. Ellen came to my home over twenty years ago. Two years later, she married my son."

"I guess we all have our twin."

"Why don't you sit down? The soup's almost ready."

"I see you've made my favorite soup. It smells delicious."

Elizabeth dished up the soup and asked a blessing. She noticed that Ruth bowed reverently as the prayer was spoken.

"Mrs. Anderson, why don't you just call me Ruth? Miss Roberts seems so formal."

"If you wish, but I always regard schoolteachers as special. To me, they have a high position."

"I haven't even started teaching yet. I hope I can earn your respect, Mrs. Anderson."

"You don't have to call me Mrs. Anderson. My name is Elizabeth."

Ruth put down her spoon. "You know something, my grandmother just died this summer. I miss her terribly. Do you suppose I could call you Grandma? You're so much like her."

Almost immediately Elizabeth felt a love for this young woman. She knew Ruth Roberts would become like one of her own grandchildren. "I have grandchildren your age—some of them older, some much younger. I will be honored if you call me Grandma."

In the moments that followed, Elizabeth and Ruth shared stories of their lives. Elizabeth saw that this young teacher's life was similar to many of her grandchildren's. As the older woman turned out the lights and got into bed that night, she missed Mary and Ed, but Ruth Roberts would help fill that void.

Two days later, in the afternoon on the way home from Lake View, Matthew decided to check on his mother. As usual she put on coffee and brought out cookies. As Matthew set down his cup, he observed, "Mary and Ed should be well on their way to California."

"I miss them, but life goes on."

Matthew wondered about his mother's extra chores with a boarder in the house. "Are you sure you want to handle the extra work of boarding the teacher? You're not so young anymore."

Ma gave one of her grunts. "I'm not young, but I can still work. Besides, I think we'll be good friends. She asked if she could call me Grandma. And of course, I said yes."

"I guess you've boarded teachers before, so you know how it all works."

At that moment, the porch door opened and in walked a beautiful young woman. For a moment, Matthew thought a younger Ellen had entered the room. This petite young woman, wearing a light yellow dress, could have been taken for Ellen—except she had auburn hair.

"Good evening, Ruth. I'd like you to meet my son, Matthew Anderson."

Ruth extended her hand. "Hello, Mr. Anderson, I've heard all about you."

Chapter 18

Matthew shook her hand, thinking of Margaret at the same time. "I'm glad to meet you. My daughter is doing exactly what you're doing. This was her second day at school."

They talked only briefly before Matthew realized he was already late for chores. As he left for his own farm, Matthew began to realize some things were working out. Ma had new purpose in her life. Margaret was beginning a new venture in a new vocation. James would soon return home. Hope was becoming a part of life.

Good news also had come over the radio. The final agreements had been signed officially. The world was now at peace. Light and hope were overcoming the darkness.

Chapter 19

October 1945

Ellen checked the temperature on the old wood kitchen range. The heat was exactly right. She placed the loaves of bread in the oven. Nothing smelled better than bread baking. The aroma was comforting somehow.

This Saturday was different from the last few—Margaret was home. It was her first weekend back since she started teaching. There would be much to talk about.

The telephone rang its three long. When Ellen answered, it was Carol. "Jeff took off to go hunting. I'd like to come home, but I can't unless someone comes and gets me."

"I'll talk to your father. Maybe he can come in sometime this afternoon."

Ellen could sense anticipation in her younger daughter's voice as she responded, "I was so looking forward to some time at home."

"Are you taking care of yourself?"

Ellen heard a catch in Carol's voice. "I've been working the dinner and supper hours at the café." Then she added, "Jeff and his father aren't getting along very well."

Ellen tried to reassure her daughter, "I'm sure Dad will drive in to get you. Then maybe you can stay overnight."

Beyond the Darkness

"Like old times with Margaret there."

As Ellen hung up the phone, Margaret entered the kitchen. "Oh, the bread smells good. There's nothing like homemade bread to wake up to. Mother, did you make some cinnamon rolls too?"

Ellen pointed to the pan. "When the loaves are ready, I'll bake the cinnamon rolls."

"I can't wait."

"What would you like for breakfast?"

"Mother, I'll make my own. I'll have some toast, but I'll have one of those cinnamon rolls for forenoon lunch."

"It's almost forenoon lunch time now."

Ellen sliced some bread, and Margaret put the slices on the stove for toasting, then poured herself a cup of coffee. "Tim kept me out late last night," she told her mother.

Ellen wanted to ask more questions but didn't want to be nosy. "Did you have a good time?"

"I may as well tell you. It all happened so fast, but Tim asked me to marry him."

"Are you ready for marriage?"

As Margaret buttered her toast, she answered, "Absolutely not. I don't plan to think about marriage for another few years. And I don't know how I feel about Tim. I don't think I love him. He's a nice man, and I enjoy being with him, but I can't imagine spending the rest of my life with him."

"You need to be sure. You're making a big decision."

Mother and daughter spent the next moments in silence. There seemed to be a different kind of communication. Finally Margaret spoke. "Mother, I think Tim wants a housekeeper. Someone who will cook his meals and wash his clothes and be his companion."

"I think . . ." Ellen began, and then realized the wisdom of not giving her opinion, ". . . you have to decide what is right."

"When I think about that, I become annoyed and even a little angry. A wife does all of that, but she's much more."

Ellen let her daughter go on talking. Some minutes later, she took out the fresh loaves of bread and put in the cinnamon rolls. The aroma made her hungry.

"You know what, Mother," Margaret finally said, "I'd like a slice of hot bread with loads of butter. That will be better than any dessert."

Chapter 19

Ellen found a knife and cut two slices. Margaret buttered the bread and smacked her lips.

"I think I raised a very wise daughter," Ellen remarked.

"Mother, if I'm wise at all, it's because I have such a good mother."

Feeling great satisfaction, Matthew looked at the straw pile near the barn as well as those in the nearby fields. He had plowed most of the fields. He felt a pride in black fields, plowed dark earth ready for another year of crops. Those fields held promise and hope for the days ahead.

Matthew wanted to believe that the darkness of the war was lifting. He recalled the newspaper headline a few days earlier: "Seven Million Soldiers to Return Home." What a change seven million men would make in the country! But he couldn't help thinking about Johnie. The hospital had reported no improvement. Soldiers who had shell shock sometimes never recovered. God wasn't fair if He let that happen to his vibrant, strong son. On the other hand, "All things work together for good to them that love God."

Matthew believed that truth, yet he still worried about Johnie. At the same time, he continued to wonder about Joe. There had been no letter for over a year. Could he be alive in some Japanese prison camp?

Matthew saw the feed bin was empty. He carried two sacks over from the corner of the barn and emptied them into the bin. Then he proceeded to dish out feed for the cattle. Everything would be ready for milking time this evening. In the meantime, he could enjoy visiting with Margaret. Perhaps they would take a drive around the countryside and enjoy the fall scenery.

Matthew looked again to the hills. He never tired of their beauty. A few red maples stood out among the yellows of the ash and oak and other trees. "I will lift my eyes unto the hills from whence cometh my help. My help cometh from the Lord, who made heaven and earth," he quoted quietly.

"Dad! Dad!" Margaret's voice seemed urgent

He walked toward his daughter. "Yes, I'm here."

Margaret had been running. She was out of breath. "There's a letter here from Jeanette Nelson. It could be about Joe. It's addressed to you and Mom."

Beyond the Darkness

Matthew sensed Margaret's urgency. "Let's go inside so your mother can read it."

In minutes, Margaret handed Ellen the letter, trembling. "I'm afraid what that letter might contain. I hope nothing's happened to Joe. He's such a good person."

Ellen opened the letter and began to read. "'Dear Ellen and Matthew. I feel that I should inform you about Joe. He has seemed very close to you, closer than to his own parents. The army has given us information about him.'"

Matthew's heart beat fast as he saw Margaret's face turn pale. He tried to prepare himself for bad news. Then Ellen's serious expression began to change as she read further. "'We received notice from the army that Joseph has been released from a Japanese prison camp. He will be shipped to San Diego and then released. The army was sorry that they could not give us any specific dates at this time.'"

If Matthew had been a child, he would have jumped up and down. As it was, his face broke into a broad smile. Margaret did jump up and down. "Joe is alive! He is alive!" she shouted as tears of joy rolled down her face. "After all this time, we finally hear!"

"There's more," Ellen continued. "'I'm afraid Joe has not been inclined to communicate with us. After all, he can barely read and write—an embarrassment to both my husband and me. If he does communicate or come to you, please let us know. After all, he is our son and we do care about him. Even though he sometimes forgets we are his parents.'" Ellen stopped a moment, then finished, "'Sincerely, Jeanette Nelson, Joe's mother.'"

Margaret reached for the letter. "I'm glad she's not my mother."

"One of these days," said Matthew, "Joe may call, or he may come walking into our kitchen,"

"Joe has always seemed like an older son to me. Ever since he helped us out when you were so sick, Matthew," Ellen recalled. She walked over to the stove. "Dinner's almost ready. We can celebrate with cinnamon rolls for dessert."

An hour later, after their meal, Matthew was only too happy to drive into town to pick up Carol. First, though, he stopped at Gus's Garage. He

Chapter 19

needed little excuse to visit Larry. Even now, he found it hard to believe the change that had taken place in Larry's life.

Larry came out from under a car, his face and hands covered with grease. He smiled at his uncle. "It's time for a break."

"You hardly look like a good Swede."

Larry laughed. "I could pass for black, I think."

Matthew told Larry the details of the letter about Joe. Then he added, "I'm on the way to pick up Carol. Jeff went hunting."

Larry grunted. "I'm afraid he's doing more than hunting."

"He's drinking again, is he?"

Larry nodded. "Drink does terrible things to a fellow. It helped destroy my dad, and it could have destroyed me."

His nephew's words reminded Matthew of the many things that seemed wrong in life. But he desperately wanted to hold on to hope in the midst of it all, especially with the news that Joe was alive.

Larry motioned to his uncle. "Come, sit down." He took out a thermos and poured some coffee into a cup. "Coffee's the best way to go."

Matthew sipped from the old cup. "I get the feeling that something's wrong. Is everything OK with Gus?"

"It's just that Gus is getting older. He's home now, cleaning out his garden—taking in squash and potatoes and pumpkins. We'll be well supplied. And Joan can really cook up a storm with all the produce."

"Gus needed you at just the right time."

"I needed a job. We needed a place to stay. The Lord provided."

"Yes, God comes through at the right time. Sometimes in the nick of time."

A car pulled up in front of the garage. A tall man wearing a light suit got out. He took the cigar out of his mouth as he walked around toward the two men.

Larry politely greeted him, but the man merely commanded, "I want oil changed on the car. Clean the car on the inside and wash it. Do a wax job. And I'm in a hurry."

Larry looked back toward the car he was working on. "Sorry, it'll be an hour at least. I'm in the middle of a job."

"You can leave that. I'm a business associate of your mother's. She said you were a good mechanic and that you'd get the work done quickly."

"I'm sorry, I can't leave this job."

Beyond the Darkness

The man raised his voice. "Apparently, you don't remember me. I worked with your father, and I met you a few years back. I have important business to transact. I pay well. I need the work done now."

"I'm sorry. There's another gas station a block away. And you could always try River Falls."

"Your mother said you could take care of this."

"I'm not working for my mother. I'm working for Gus. This is his garage."

The man changed his tone. "I could take my business with your mother elsewhere. She depends on me and others. I suggest you take care of my car."

Larry looked at Matthew and then directly into the eyes of the man. "I'm afraid I know your business, and it is illegal or at least questionable. I want nothing to do with it. My mother is better off if she has nothing to do with you."

The man walked back to his car, then turned to Larry. "You'll be sorry." Without another word he got in and drove away.

"What's this all about?" asked Matthew.

"Mother's trying to get me back into her business. I don't know exactly what it is, but I know it's the same connections that were there before. I want nothing to do with that business."

"Your mother's a determined person."

Larry looked away, then spoke. "As a Christian, I'm supposed to honor my mother. How can I honor a woman who is doing evil?"

Matthew thought of his own mother, whom he admired and respected. "That's a hard question. I don't have that problem. Your grandmother is a godly woman. I have always held her in high regard."

"I pray for Mother. I pray that someday she may truly know the Lord."

"That's a good prayer."

Matthew and Larry talked on for another half hour. Then Matthew took out his pocket watch and realized he needed to move on and pick up Carol. When he met Carol at the door of the small cottage, he took a careful look at his daughter. She was obviously in the final months of pregnancy. He also noticed that she was limping and had a visible scar on her left cheek. "What happened?" he asked.

"I'm clumsy, I guess. It's part of being pregnant."

Matthew took her small suitcase. "You look pale, too. I think you need some of your mother's home-cooked chicken soup."

Chapter 19

"I'm hungry for Mom's cooking."

As they drove home, Matthew knew something was not right.

In many ways Ellen felt like a mother hen. She loved the idea of having her children under her wings. At the same time she knew that children, like chickens, grew and left the nest. She missed those days when all her children were safe nearby.

Sunday afternoons were special times in the lives of farm families. Ellen thought of the many family and community gatherings through the years, and the frequent Sunday afternoon drives. Her mother-in-law had also joined them this day for Sunday dinner.

"How about a drive into the hills to the south?" Matthew asked as Sunday dinner ended. "The fall colors are still beautiful."

"Can we climb the big hill?" asked Michael.

"Sure," his father replied.

"I'd love a drive," answered Margaret. "I'll dream of the beauty of those hills when I'm busy teaching my children."

Very quickly, Carol, Michael, and Elizabeth all agreed.

Ellen and Margaret washed and wiped dishes. Ellen excused Carol, who was feeling tired and uncomfortable. After some insistence, Carol sat down and rested, along with her grandmother, while they finished the cleaning.

Despite many changes, life had its continuity. As she walked toward the car, Ellen remembered going for rides with her father in a horse and buggy. Their family went for a ride and then visited neighbors or relatives. Now, years later, they were doing much the same, just in a different vehicle. A host of changes had taken place in their world since then—and more were on the horizon.

Michael hurried into the car, taking his place next to Matthew. Ellen saw that her mother-in-law was seated in the backseat. Margaret and Carol found their places, and Ellen took her traditional seat in the front. She experienced a feeling of security and well-being as Matthew drove south and east. Riding up and down the winding roads gave her the sense of a journey—even adventure. The maples and sumac shone their brilliant reds. The gold colors of the ash trees and poplars and other assorted trees became extensions of the autumn afternoon sunshine.

Beyond the Darkness

There were moments of silence, but the family also talked of many things. Despite their comfortable conversation, Ellen felt an underlying concern for Carol. She doubted the wisdom of her marrying the banker's son. Everything she saw pointed to problems for her youngest daughter. Yet Ellen still believed in and felt the security of family. As she looked around to the many hills outside the windows, she realized where her help lay. She would continue to trust in God.

This October Sunday was a clear, crisp day. After driving awhile, the family stopped for a walk up one of their beautiful hillsides. They climbed the hill, or the peak, as some people called it. Even Elizabeth Anderson, seventy-seven years old, climbed with the rest of the family.

Ellen never tired of this scene, and thought that perhaps her husband loved it even more. Yet her motherly instincts kicked in as she looked at Carol with concern and asked, "Do you suppose you should have exerted yourself this much?"

"I'm OK. I'll be glad when this baby comes. I know I don't want five children, Mother. One's enough right now."

"You'll feel differently after the baby comes," said her grandmother. "Children are a blessing from the Lord."

Carol isn't ready to be a mother, thought Ellen. *And Jeff is even less ready to be a father.*

Michael ran around, exploring the trails that led down the other side of the hill. A boy almost seven years old brings a whole new perspective to life.

He returned with a yellow daisy. "Here, Mom."

Ellen thanked him. "Why don't you try counting the lakes that you see? There are so many."

Michael looked around and began to count.

"I don't think you can count high enough," challenged Ellen.

"I can count to twenty."

"Can you count twenty lakes?"

Michael pointed and turned around. "There are hundreds."

Matthew smiled. "There aren't quite that many, but I think there are more than twenty."

Ellen stood quietly, watching her loved one. Once more this part of the family was together. *James should be home later this month,* she thought. *Someday the family circle will be complete again.* But the life she had known a few years ago would never be the same.

Chapter 19

She looked to the south and east toward Prairie Center, the home of her childhood. Memories of her own parents, sisters, and brothers flooded her mind. Family was important. She loved Matthew and her children more than she could say. She dreamed of the time they would all be together.

She walked over to Matthew, who took her hand. The warmth of love permeated her whole being. As they stood hand in hand, a cloud suddenly covered the sun, and the brightness disappeared. She would remember this pleasant day, but the shadow told her that dark days lay ahead.

CHAPTER 20

Matthew hurried down the driveway to the mailbox, hoping for a letter from James. He hadn't written in several weeks—that was totally unlike this son. Could something be wrong, or was it possible he would arrive any day?

He opened the mailbox, hoping to see that familiar handwriting. He unfolded the *Daily Journal* and a letter fell out. At least there was news from Margaret.

In minutes Matthew sat at the kitchen table, cup of coffee in hand. Ellen began reading. "I guess I'm writing because I have some decisions to make. And Tim seems determined. He wants an answer immediately."

Matthew couldn't help responding. "I know what that means. She's too young. She isn't ready."

"I think we know that. Let's see what else she has to say. `Tim is eager that we should get married. Well, Mom and Dad, I think maybe I love him, but I'm not sure. He's a wonderful man. But I love my teaching, and I want to go on teaching for a few years. I just don't feel ready to make this big decision.'

"'I have a pretty good idea what I want out of life. I'd like to marry a farmer and live on a farm and have children. I'd like to follow in your footsteps, Mother. You are the kind of woman I'd like to become. And Dad, I'd like to marry a man a lot like you . . .'"

Beyond the Darkness

Ellen stopped reading. "I don't think our daughter could have paid us a higher compliment."

"We couldn't ask for a finer daughter."

She continued, "'Tim is a good man. He's a good farmer, and I believe he would be a good husband and father. But I have so many questions. Most of all, I'm not ready.'

"'I'm praying every night that God will show me the right answer. But with Tim's insistence, I wish God would hurry up and give me the answer.'

"'Have you heard from James? I can't wait until he comes home. I could talk these things over with him. Both my brothers are good at looking after us girls. I wonder what James will think of Carol's husband. I'm not sure he'll be happy about that.'"

Ellen put down the letter and changed the subject. "I'm worried about Carol. She doesn't look good, and Jeff is not treating her right."

"I'm afraid something terrible will happen." Matthew felt his concern about Carol even more acutely.

A few minutes later, Matthew walked across the barnyard to check the fence. During calving season, cows had a way of getting out and finding new hiding spots. It was hard to find a mother cow in the pastures to the east or the west when they got loose. He stood at the fence line and once more looked to the hills as he prayed, "Lord, please bring James home quickly. Keep him safe. And heal Johnie; make him whole."

Even as he saw a car drive down the road, he hoped somehow that James would get out of that car. He felt certain his son would return any day now.

James Anderson hummed the tune, but the words kept going through his mind. He was going home. The steady rhythm of the train made him think of the rhythm of life as it used to be—before this dreadful war. The words of the song repeated themselves in his mind.

> 'Mid pleasures and palaces, though we may roam,
> Be it ever so humble, there's no place like home;
> A charm from the skies seems to hallow us there,
> Which seek thro' the world, is ne'er met with elsewhere.

Chapter 20

Home, home, sweet, sweet home,
There's no place like home. There's no place like home.

James had learned that song in a one-room school years ago. He was now twenty-one. For some time he had felt like an old man. The bloodshed of war did that to young men. Even though he had worked at headquarters, the horror of surrounding battle remained as a scar.

Another verse of the song came to mind, but he couldn't remember the words—something about "an exile from home." That's what he had been—an exile. What joy it was to come home. But what would he come home to? Mom and Dad would be there, of course, as well as little Michael. From their letters he knew Margaret would be off teaching north of Lake View. Carol was already married, but that situation did not seem good. And Johnie, now released to a psychiatric ward, was unresponsive. That trip to see his brother at the veteran's hospital still haunted him. Would his brother forever remain that way?

How much should he tell Mom and Dad? Could his father handle the terrible truth about Johnie? Or did Dad somehow already know that truth?

As the train moved along, his mind played strange tricks. In those moments, he found himself in that little country school again. He sat in that small desk, listening to a seventh-grade geography lesson and looking at the large wall map of England and Europe. He dreamed of those faraway places. Someday he would travel to those places, he had vowed back then. And he would write about this big, wonderful world. Little had he realized that he would see this big world as a soldier. Somehow the world did not seem so big or so wonderful now.

He still wanted to write—to tell stories of the world he had known back home. His buddies said he should write about the war. Right now, however, he did not want to write war stories. Instead he wanted to escape from this war, leaving all those painful memories behind. But could he really leave them in the past? Everything about the war colored his thinking. Most of all, he found himself grieving over Johnie and what the war had done to his brother. Nothing was grand or heroic about war. War meant fear and bloodshed and agony. War meant the death of the bravest and best of young men.

"I'd like to be another Thomas Wolfe," James said aloud, to the countryside passing by his window. "But I want to chronicle reality, and at the same time inspire and uplift my readers' spirits. I want to hold out hope that there is more to life, that people can do something to make a

Beyond the Darkness

better life." Saying it out loud made it seem more real somehow. He held on firmly to the hope of that dream.

A phrase from an old hymn ran through his mind: "Hope of earth and joy of heaven." He looked out the windows again as the prairie fields changed to rolling hills surrounded by pastures and fields. Then the numerous lakes became visible. This was home, the place he loved more than any other in the world. The memories of Johnie and the horrors of war began to fade.

James began to envision the old home place where he had lived his first fourteen years. The big house was destroyed by fire a few years ago, but a very similar house replaced it. The new house wasn't the same—it looked nearly identical on the outside but contained none of James's childhood memories.

He tried to remember each room of the old house. First, he remembered the room Johnie and he had shared. He pictured the old desk where he wrote his first stories. That special desk had been moved to the bigger house on the farm his father now owned. Every detail of this room came to mind—the window looking east, the stain on the ceiling where rain leaked through, the ceiling light fixture with a string, the bookcase he had built, and much more. In this room his mind had wandered through other countries and other worlds.

In his mind he tried to picture the other rooms. His sisters' room was becoming less distinct in his memory. The dining room, used mostly when they had company, was also a blur in his memory. But he remembered the kitchen . . . and the old table where the family sat for each meal. That table had a broken leaf for a long time, but it seemed more personal than the new table they bought when they settled in the new home.

He saw Johnie in his memories, always ready to run out and play with Rover or check on his calf. Johnie was a young boy in perpetual motion. Margaret, always the well-behaved girl, did everything she was supposed to. And Carol, quite the opposite, was more the tomboy, tagging along behind Johnie. Mom and Dad were always there. That is, except when Dad had that serious ulcer attack and almost died. James found himself saying out loud, "I don't think I realized how serious that attack was. I could have been without my father."

The train jostled to a stop, halting his memories. James looked out the window to see the familiar rusty-colored railroad station. He grabbed his duffle bag and hurried to the exit. He must have been the only passenger. He stepped onto the station platform and hurried toward the building.

Chapter 20

He had seen this place many times, but this was the first time he had ridden the train.

"Welcome home, young man," a voice boomed out to him. A large portly man towered above him and extended his hand. "Good to see you home, my boy."

"Hello, sir, I'm more than happy to be home."

"Don't call me 'sir.' I prefer Tom."

James always felt he should address his elders as Mr. or Mrs. He wasn't even sure of this man's name. He thought it was Thompson.

"I'd like to make a phone call."

"Right over here, James. I'm supposed to make people use the pay phone, but you're a local boy and a veteran. I'll let you use our phone."

Realizing the man recognized him, James thanked him, put down his duffel bag, and dialed the operator. These dial phones that townspeople had were different from the old crank phones in the country. He gave the operator the number.

He was glad Tom disappeared into the back room, because strong emotion overwhelmed him as he anticipated his mother's voice. The phone rang its three long. He waited, and finally he heard his mother say, "Hello."

For a moment he could not speak as tears filled his eyes. He choked out the words, "Mother, it's me. James. I'm back. I'm home."

A brief pause followed. His mother must be having the same reaction. "Thank God you're home! " she exclaimed. "Where are you?"

"The railroad station."

"I'll get your father. We'll be there to get you as fast as we can. I'm so glad this day has finally come."

James wanted to say more, but words wouldn't come. "I'll see you soon."

"We'll be there. I love you, son."

James put the receiver back. He had dreamed of this moment many times. Now it was here. He could think only of seeing Mom and Dad and Michael once more.

Beyond the Darkness

Matthew took pride in a field plowed just right. This was probably the last plowing for the year. Late October meant a hard ground freeze could come anytime.

Out of the corner of his eye, he saw a figure hurrying through the pasture out to the field. *Who could this be?* he wondered. He kept driving toward the edge of the field and soon realized it was Ellen. *What has happened? Is something wrong?* She never walked out here except on rare occasions, or to bring him lunch. His heart began to beat faster. He felt that old knot in his stomach. He came to the edge of the field and shifted to a higher, faster gear. The John Deere took him quickly to the gate where Ellen now stood. He jumped down and quickly asked, "Ellen, what's wrong?"

Out of breath, she spoke. "Nothing's wrong. It's James! He's home! He's waiting at the railroad station. I said we'd be there as fast as we could."

Without a word, Matthew helped Ellen onto the platform. He opened the gate and drove the tractor fast toward the house. He stopped close to the garage and helped Ellen down. Usually he would head for the house to change from his work clothes. Instead the two hurried toward the car. Ellen still wore her apron and had smudges of flour on her face.

Matthew sped down the road. They couldn't get to Lake View fast enough, arriving at the train station in record time.

There he stood on the station platform, waving to them as they drove up. James, who had left for army training as a boy, had lost his boyish look. His face and everything about him told Matthew his son was now a man.

Ellen ran ahead of him, but Matthew knew there was a special bond between mother and son. He was her firstborn, and there were many months that summer when they wondered when they'd see James again. James enfolded his mother in his arms.

"You're home, my son. You're home," Ellen kept repeating.

Matthew extended his hand for that firm Scandinavian handshake. He felt the strength of his son's hand. Then the handshake quickly changed to a warm embrace. Matthew felt the love and strength of his son fill his whole being.

James put his duffel bag in the backseat and helped his mother into the car. As Matthew drove them back home, the air was filled with questions and answers. All these were punctuated with "I'm home," or "We're so glad you're home."

Chapter 20

As James got out of the car at the house, he was silent. Then he spoke. "I've waited more than two years for this day. Now it is here. This is the life I fought for. This is what I wanted to save and protect."

"We're proud of you, son," said Ellen.

As they entered the house, three long rings greeted them. Ellen hurried to the phone.

Matthew momentarily experienced an awkward moment with his son. He wanted to express his love for him as well as the joy that he was home, but words would not come.

"I'm helping you with chores tonight, Dad. I bet there are lots of young calves to feed. That's what I always did growing up."

"Your mother comes out and helps feed the calves. Michael tries to, but he isn't quite old enough yet."

"I can't wait to see Michael. I bet he's grown. Why, he must be almost seven."

"He's another Johnie in just about every way. He's never still—always up to something."

Ellen called out from the porch steps, "That was Victoria. She heard you were home. Said you should have called the school and she would have brought you home. She insisted on picking up your grandmother. They're coming for supper."

"I can't wait for a home-cooked meal. That's something I've dreamed about."

"I'll see what I can do," Ellen replied.

James went to his room and changed into his old clothes, prepared to help his father with chores. As he returned to the kitchen, Matthew objected, "You shouldn't be out in the barn on your first night home. This is a special time, a time to celebrate."

"You have no idea how many times I've thought of being right here and doing this. I want the full experience of being back home."

Matthew silently prayed a prayer of thanksgiving.

Ellen reluctantly asked James the previously unspoken question, "What about Johnie? You were at the veteran's hospital. What about him?"

James seemed to hold back. "He's the same. He says very little. He recognizes people but doesn't want to talk. The doctors discourage anyone from coming."

Matthew felt as if a cloud had suddenly blackened the happy occasion. If only Johnie could be home safely too. He said another silent prayer,

Beyond the Darkness

"Please, Lord, bring Johnie back to us. At least he's alive. And thank You that Joe should be coming home soon."

The routine of the day continued with the nightly chores. It felt good to have James helping again. What was best of all was the companionship of father and son.

James had never felt he would enjoy the smells of cattle or other farm animals, but these pungent odors somehow brought peace to his spirit. This was part of being home. Dad asked him to feed the young calves after he had milked one of the older cows.

At that moment Michael made his appearance. He burst through the barn door, and for a moment stared at his brother. "You're finally home!" he shouted.

James set down the pail of milk, and Michael jumped up and threw himself into his big brother's arms. James held Michael close as he felt the warmth of a young boy's love. Somehow he wanted to protect this little boy from all the evils out there in the world.

"I hardly recognize you. You're twice as tall as you were."

"I want to be as big as Johnie. Then I'll go off and fight."

James objected, "No. Let's hope there aren't any more wars to contend with."

Michael stayed close beside his brother all through chores. He kept asking questions that James didn't want to answer or didn't know how to answer. With chores finally finished, James and his father and brother walked toward the house. The lights from the windows beckoned them. A cold breeze blew through the trees, nearly empty of leaves. The cold and dark of this late October evening made James shiver. But then the aroma of roast pork from the house told James his mother had prepared his favorite meal, including the baking powder biscuits.

Aunt Victoria greeted James as he entered. "Welcome home, my dear nephew." She extended her hand and grasped his. "You look tired."

James noticed the strands of gray in Aunt Victoria's otherwise black hair. She too had grown older. Though he recognized this woman as his stern, law-abiding high school principal, he realized she also was a woman of great compassion. He smiled because her warmest greeting was usually a handshake, but then her handshake changed into a hug.

Chapter 20

"James." The familiar voice of Grandma silenced any other talk. "James, my boy. I've prayed for this day, and it is here."

James stood for a moment. Grandma, so familiar and so much a part of their lives, was the same, except she looked smaller and older. He loved that white hair and wrinkled face. But now her eyes didn't look as bright, and the wrinkles had become more pronounced. He stooped down and gave her a kiss on the cheek. Her hands reached out and grasped his. She stood up and pulled him to her, hugging him.

Then James became aware of a figure standing in the shadows near the door to the dining room. "Hello brother."

"Carol." He had to look more closely. "I hardly recognized you. You've changed."

"Yes, there are two of me. I'm seven months pregnant. That does make a difference."

Their evening was predictable in many ways. There were questions. There was talk of changes in the community. Mary and Ed, now in California, had written a letter that arrived a few days earlier. The daily routine of country living once more became evident in the easy way the family shared conversation and exchanged familiar quips.

Several hours later, James lay awake in the bed Johnie and he had shared so many years. Michael was now beside him, sound asleep. James was tired, but his mind would not stop thinking about the many changes he'd observed in arriving home.

Carol. He couldn't help wondering about her and how tired she looked. And why was Jeff not with her? Jeff was part of the family. He had never cared much for Jeff, even when they were both students at Lake View High School. Somehow he felt Jeff had not changed for the better.

Mother. She always seemed strong, able to stand up to anything. But she too seemed older. How would she handle Johnie's condition?

Dad. He noticed his father placing his hand on his chest. Was there something wrong? He knew this might be a sign of heart trouble, one of those inherited tendencies.

He couldn't help thinking of the old days when Aunt Mary and Uncle Ed and his three cousins came over so often. Now they were far away. But all these family changes were part of growing up and growing older. Perhaps they just seemed more acute because of all the time James had been away.

Beyond the Darkness

Soon James's thoughts turned from his family to his own future. The halls of college filled his mind. He loved books and the ideas that filled them. His life would be one of learning. Yes, he wanted to write and he wanted to teach—but in some way his greatest desire was to help make the world a better place.

Quietly James got out of bed and walked over to the window. He pushed aside the curtain and looked out into the darkness. Then he looked above to the stars. "When I consider the work of Thy hands . . ." he whispered aloud. He surveyed the darkness below. Then he looked to the stars again. A surge of hope filled his spirit.

Chapter 21

November 1945

"We'll miss you, son." Matthew wanted to say more, but he never felt confident when it came to using words.

James finished eating the last of his eggs and bacon. "I like it here, but this is something I have to do. I've always known I would go away to college. I'm no farmer."

Ellen smiled. "From the beginning I knew you were meant to leave Oak Ridge township and Lake View and go many places. It was meant to be."

Matthew gazed out the window and wondered what lay beyond those hills for his son. "We're living in a changing world. Your world will be far different from mine."

"You've always worked hard, Dad. You haven't had time to do some of what you've always wanted to do."

Matthew thought of the dreams of his youth. "I used to think I could travel and see our great country. I thought I might travel to Sweden to see the place where Dad was born."

"I'd like to see the country of our forefathers. Maybe we could go there as a family one day," James added.

"You know," began Ellen, "I believe I have cousins in Sweden. I don't even know who some of them are. I'd like to go."

Beyond the Darkness

James's face brightened. "Someday when I write a book, and it becomes a best seller, I'll take you two on a trip. We'll see Sweden and the rest of the world."

At that moment, Michael ran into the room, still wiping the sleep from his eyes.

"How about some eggs, Michael? Or do you want your hot Ralston?"

"Ralston," Michael managed to say. He went over to his brother. "Why do you have to go? Could I come with you?"

"I'm afraid not. College is for big people. Anyway, I'll be back tomorrow. The winter quarter doesn't start until early December. I'm registering today."

Michael continued to bombard his big brother with "Why?" questions. James tried his best to answer them until he glanced up at the wall clock and noticed the time. "I've got to be on my way. I'm supposed to see my advisor at 11:30. I don't want to be late."

Matthew hated seeing his son leave, even for a day. Ever since James came back from the service, Matthew did not want to let go. It seemed he may have lost Johnie, but now at least he had James home safely. Letting go again was terribly hard.

James said his good-byes. Matthew watched his son drive the family car down the driveway, while Ellen made sure Michael was ready for school. Then Matthew watched little Michael walk across the field and pasture on his way to school. Even his young son seemed to be growing up quickly. Before long, he'd be letting go of Michael too.

Matthew went out to the barn to finish the morning chores. At midmorning he entered the kitchen just as the telephone rang its three long. Ellen answered, and he could tell from her side of the conversation that something was seriously wrong.

Ellen hung up and turned to him. "Matthew, that was Sheriff Walker. Larry's been arrested. He wasn't able to say much about the reason. He was driving a truck, and there were stolen goods."

"I can't believe Larry's fallen back into his old ways."

"The sheriff wanted us to come. I said we'd try our best, but James has the car. What can we do?"

Matthew thought a moment before replying, "I remembered something. Larry needed more money for new furniture and clothes for Lowell. Some of Rita's business associates wanted him to drive for them. The business was supposed to be honest and aboveboard."

Chapter 21

"Can we drive the Model A? I didn't think it was working."

"I'd hesitate to drive it to River Falls. The Model A isn't that dependable."

Ellen's thought of another solution. "We'll call Rita. She can drive us to River Falls or let us use her car. After all, it's her fault this happened."

"I don't know that we have much choice."

Ellen went to the phone and called central. Hopefully Rita would be home. Matthew listened to the one side of the conversation. "Larry's in trouble," said Ellen. "He's been arrested."

Matthew wished he could hear what Rita was saying.

"James took our car. We need to get to River Falls. Larry's appearing before the judge for a bail hearing."

Rita must have said something about being busy.

Ellen's anger was evident in the sharp edge of her voice and words as she responded, "He is your son, Rita. He was doing work for your business associates. As a mother, you have an obligation."

Rita said more at the other end, then Ellen hung up. "She'll be here in fifteen minutes."

"That woman!" Ellen felt like saying much more. "I don't know how I can put up with her all the way to River Falls."

"You'll manage," replied Matthew. "She's some mother. I'm afraid Larry would be in worse trouble if he were working with her."

Ellen and Matthew quickly changed clothes. They finished just in time as the black Cadillac drove up in the yard. She closed the porch door and followed her husband toward the car. "Let's be careful what we say." She should have known better than to say that. Matthew was less inclined to speak; he never spoke out of line.

Rita greeted them. "Matthew, why don't you drive? I had close call with an accident the other day. I'm still a bit shaken from that experience."

Ellen breathed a sigh of relief. She had never been comfortable around Rita. And Rita's driving made her even less comfortable. The conversation on the way to River Falls was restrained, and nothing unpleasant was said. Rita smoked one cigarette after another. Ellen tried to hold back her coughing, but the smoke was giving her a severe headache.

Beyond the Darkness

When they arrived in the courtroom, Ellen was surprised to see Victoria talking with Sheriff Walker. She and Matthew and Rita sat in the back just as the judge entered and the proceedings were about to begin. Ellen was unfamiliar with court proceedings except for what she had heard on the radio. Everyone rose as the judge took his place. Judge Mortenson then asked the district attorney to state the charges.

She couldn't see Larry's face, but she saw him bent over in his chair. How much of this could he take? And Matthew—what about his close relationship with his nephew? Along with everything else, Matthew's old stomach problems seemed to have returned, and he kept placing his hand over his heart. Stress did terrible things to people. She was concerned for both her husband and Larry at that moment.

The district attorney proceeded with his opening remarks. "Mr. Larry Anderson is charged with transporting stolen property from the Chicago area through the state of Minnesota. We recommend bail be set at $100,000. Anderson has a previous record, which must be considered, along with the fact that he could be a flight risk."

"Let me hear from Mr. Anderson's lawyer."

A small, sandy-haired man spoke. "We recommend Larry Anderson be released in the custody of Victoria Anderson. He is no flight risk. I ask you to hear from this woman, designated as his probation officer. She is a respected teacher and principal at Lake View High School."

Judge Mortenson nodded to Victoria, who stood and walked to the front of the courtroom. She addressed the judge and began her defense. "I come here as a probation officer, not as an aunt of Larry Anderson. I have kept a careful check on Larry. He has been doing excellent work at the gas station. In addition to that, he has maintained and supported his wife and son. A second child is on the way. Larry is no flight risk. He has become a strong citizen of our community, even helping some of our young people who might otherwise get into trouble. I recommend he be freed on his own recognizance and under my supervision." Victoria paused briefly for effect, then continued, "I also want to plead his case. Larry did not leave the state. The truck was driven by another driver from Illinois to Minnesota. Larry was hired to drive the truck west. He had nothing to do with the contents of that truck. In that respect he is completely innocent. On that basis, I recommend all charges be dropped."

The judge turned to Sheriff Walker. "Sheriff, what do you have to say about the charges? I'd like to hear from you."

Chapter 21

Sheriff Walker stood. "The deputy who arrested Larry Anderson did so because he received an anonymous call. The charge simply states that Larry was transporting stolen goods. That, of course, constitutes a crime."

The judge spoke once more. "I believe this situation requires more investigation. If these are stolen goods being transported across state lines, the matter should be checked by the FBI. For this reason, evidence is lacking, and I am dropping the charges against Mr. Anderson."

Mortenson again turned to Sheriff Walker. "I hope you will see to it that the proper authorities take care of the investigation."

"Yes, sir."

The judge stood and addressed Larry. "Young man, Larry Anderson, I don't want to see you in this courtroom again. Court adjourned." Then he left.

Ellen wanted to applaud. She knew Matthew felt the same way. The two of them hurried to the front of the courtroom to see Larry. Rita remained behind in the back.

"Uncle Matthew, thanks for coming. Aunt Ellen, thank you."

Victoria greeted her brother and sister-in-law, then turned to the sheriff. "Mr. Walker, I believe this arrest should not have taken place."

"I regret it happened. But my deputy had no choice. He found the stolen goods."

Victoria walked toward her sister-in-law, still in the back of the room. "Rita, this was your fault. We all know your business associates are dishonest."

"I had no idea the goods were stolen. I knew Larry needed some extra money. This was a fast way of making some money."

Sheriff Walker moved over and stood beside Victoria. "Mrs. Anderson, I believe you're the one we need to investigate."

"Oh, Mr. Walker, I know nothing. Nothing at all."

"I'll ask you to come down to my office. I need to get names of these business associates. The investigation will proceed from there."

For a moment Ellen felt sorry for Rita, yet she realized Victoria was not about to drop the matter. "Rita, you have been trouble from way back," Victoria declared. "I'm sorry to say it, but my dead brother wouldn't have pursued those criminal connections if it hadn't been for you. Any trouble that comes your way is trouble you deserve."

Ellen thought she saw tears in Rita's eyes.

"You've never really treated me like one of the family." Rita began to raise her voice. "I was a good wife to Paul John. I deserved more land than you gave me."

"You have more than you deserve." Victoria turned her back on Rita. "Larry, Matthew, Ellen, you come with me. I'll give you a ride home. Rita's going to be busy with the sheriff. It's time for us to celebrate."

Larry stood back a minute, then asked Rita, "Mother, why did you let this happen?" But she turned her back on her son.

Sheriff Walker extended his hand to Larry. "I'm sorry about the arrest—the embarrassment. I can see you're leading a good, productive life in Lake View. Keep up the good work."

"Thanks for understanding."

Sheriff Walker and Rita left for his office. Matthew, Ellen, and Larry followed Victoria to her car. "We're going out for lunch. The treat's on me," she announced.

"How could you get away on a school day?" questioned Matthew.

"When you're principal, there are certain privileges."

Ellen realized more than ever that this stern, straight-laced principal and sister-in-law had a heart of compassion. And this unfortunate incident had turned out right. She took Matthew's hand and sensed the relief he felt.

As they ate lunch at the City Café and Bakery, Larry was strangely silent. Matthew wondered what was on his mind. Victoria and Ellen were busy talking about Carol and her baby, and other family matters.

Larry finally spoke. "Where was Joan? I don't understand why she wasn't here."

Victoria was quick to answer. "Oh, I'm sorry. I found she was not feeling well this morning. That happens when a woman is expecting. Actually, I didn't even tell her exactly what had happened. I said your truck had been delayed. I figured she didn't need to worry."

"I suppose the whole world will know soon enough."

Victoria set down her coffee cup with force. "Absolutely not. Sheriff Walker assured me this would be kept quiet. It should not be in the papers. No one else needs to know. However, I think you should tell your wife. She deserves to know."

Chapter 21

"I don't keep any secrets from Joan. She's been loyal to me through all my problems. The Lord couldn't have given me a more wonderful, understanding wife."

"Now," said Victoria, "it's time for dessert. This café has the best pie—especially apple or pumpkin. Since it's almost Thanksgiving, I suspect pumpkin will be the best."

In moments the waitress came, and they ordered their pumpkin pie. Within minutes they were enjoying delicious homemade dessert. Later, as they finished their pie and prepared to leave, Larry reached his hand across to his aunt. "I don't know what would have happened without you. I can't thank you enough. And Uncle Matthew and Aunt Ellen, you've been a wonderful support. Thank you."

Victoria's aloofness returned. "That's what families are for. I'm here to help. And that's what being a teacher or principal is all about."

"Yes. Amen," agreed Ellen. "It's important to build strong families. Our children need us even when they're adults. We're encouraging James as he leaves for college."

Larry looked first at Ellen and then at Matthew. "I see your family. That's the kind of family I want. I look to you as examples."

"Speaking of family," said Ellen, "Thanksgiving is in just a few days. I'd like all of you to come for the day. We'll go to church first and then have our dinner. I'm ready for a full house."

There was no hesitancy on the part of Victoria or Larry to accept the invitation.

That evening as he finished evening chores, Matthew observed the cattle contentedly eating their hay. As he put the cans of milk and cream into the tank, he spoke aloud. "This is the life. God is good. Life is good."

"This is home." James drove up the driveway to the family home, returning from college registration. "This is the place I want to come back to. But I have places to go and things to do."

He got out of the family '35 Chevy and hurried into the house. Mom, Dad, and Michael were having supper. He was just in time.

"Welcome home, son." His mother pointed to the place set for him.

Beyond the Darkness

Michael ran to welcome him. "Are you registered and set for college?"

James began to relate all that had happened. "I saw my English professor and advisor. I'm enrolled in the English major program. I want to keep writing, but I'll train to be a teacher. Teachers can make a difference."

His father smiled. "Your mother has made a big difference. Especially to me."

His mother passed him the potatoes and gravy. "Teaching is important. It is a noble profession."

"What's noble anyway?" questioned Michael.

Ellen paused to think, then explained, "It means that teaching helps people to become better people. It teaches people how to live."

"I don't think I want to be a teacher. It's hard," Michael stated.

"Not everyone should teach. Only a few people are teachers," she said.

James went on to relate other details of his day at college. "I was going to stay off campus, but instead I have a job at the dormitory. Since I'm older, the dean was interested in me as a dormitory assistant and counselor. He interviewed me, and I have a job beginning with the winter quarter."

His parents proudly congratulated him.

Later that evening, as James listened to his little brother's prayers, he couldn't help noticing the special petition: "Please, God, make Johnie well and bring him home soon." He silently prayed the same thing.

James kissed his brother on the forehead and then switched on the lamp by his desk. He wanted to think and write and read. Soon he found himself immersed in the Thomas Wolfe novel, *You Can't Go Home Again*. He read for several hours, losing track of time. Eventually he began to write in his journal: "I'm home, but I'm not. Things have changed. My brother and sisters are away. Only little Michael remains at home. Mom and Dad are older. I have a place here, but I don't. I know I must move beyond this place—beyond these beautiful hills. I have a different purpose in my life."

He stopped writing and stared out the window, whispering a prayer, "Lord, show me exactly where I should go and what I should do."

Just then Michael stirred and awakened. "Come to bed. I'm scared."

Chapter 21

"I'm coming." James turned out the light, undressed in the dark, and got into his pajamas and into bed. His little brother cuddled close to him and quickly fell asleep.

As James felt the warmth of his little brother beside him, the words of a favorite family hymn played in his mind:

Children of the Heavenly Father,
Safely in His bosom gather,
Nestling bird nor star in heaven
Such a refuge ne'er was given.

James felt loved and safe and secure.

Chapter 22

James awakened abruptly from a deep sleep on Thanksgiving morning. He became aware of sunlight streaming through the window and felt someone watching him. He opened his eyes wide to see his little brother standing next to the bed.

In his six-year-old way, Michael began to chant. "Good morning, Mary Sunshine, why are you up so soon? You scared the little stars away, and shined away the moon." Then he giggled and began to tickle his big brother.

James sat up, and he soon had Michael in his arms, tickling him. The two brothers settled into a brotherly tussle, laughing all the time. A knock at the door interrupted them, and Aunt Victoria opened the door. "What are you two up to? Are you going to sleep away the day? It's Thanksgiving."

"I'm sorry," apologized James. "I guess we visited a long while, and then I was inspired to write."

Victoria turned to leave. "You deserve to rest. You've done so much for your country—and your family."

"I'll be down in a jiff."

"Your mother wondered if you'd go to pick up your grandmother and drive her to church. Corrine and Warren and the girls had other things to take care of."

James did a mock salute. "Aye, aye, Aunt Victoria. Yes, I'll be glad to."

"Be quick about it!" responded Victoria, laughing.

James gently pushed his brother aside. "You go downstairs. Let me get dressed."

The aroma of Thanksgiving delicacies greeted him as he came downstairs a few moments later. Dad, Mom, and Victoria were having midmorning coffee, and Michael was drinking his glass of milk.

"Sorry, Dad, I intended to be up in time for chores. I wanted to help."

His father smiled at him. "Son, I have to get used to doing the chores on my own. In another week you'll be off to college. And I wouldn't want it any other way."

The family settled into small talk about family and traditions. James wanted to preserve these people and their ways and their relationships forever in his mind. These were the small things he had been homesick for, what he fought to preserve. At this moment he felt this tender love for each member of his family and for his country.

His mother gave him a bowl of Ralston, Michael's favorite cereal, probably because Tom Mix advertised the product. "I gave you a smaller bowl because we want to keep our appetites for dinner."

James relished the company and talk until Aunt Victoria reminded him, "You need to allow some extra time to get to church since you're picking up your grandmother."

James drove the six miles to his grandmother's place, known as the home farm. He still experienced a sense of coming home, for he had spent the first fourteen years of his life at this place. Life had changed radically in the years that followed, though Grandma's little white house remained exactly the same.

He bounded up the porch steps, where Grandma's cheery voice welcomed him. "I haven't seen very much of you since you came home."

"Sorry about that, Grandma. I shall remedy the oversight before I leave for college. I've been busy."

"I know you have."

"I've had a lot going on. I had to get over to the college to register. And I've been helping Dad and doing other work to get ready for college."

"Yes, James, I shouldn't complain. I'm an old lady and not very interesting."

Chapter 22

"No, Grandma, quite the contrary. You're one of the most interesting women I know. I want to spend as much time with you as I can."

"Now you're flattering me." She stopped a moment as she began to put on her coat. "I'm old. Seventy-seven. I've had a full life. I don't know how much longer I'll be around. The Bible says eighty is a special blessing. Beyond that, the Bible is silent."

James guided his grandmother down the steps and into the car. He realized how frail she was now. As he started the car, James wanted to express his feelings. "Grandma, I want you to know how much you mean to me. You have been an important part of my life."

James sensed a catch in her voice. "Yes, my boy, I know."

"There's so much you can tell me about your life. There's so much you can teach me."

Grandma chuckled. "That's hardly the case. You're a college man, and I went through seventh grade. That's all."

"You've experienced life. You have lived history. I want to know about all the history you've been through. I want to write about that life."

"I have faith that you will do so, but I'll not be on this earth to see it."

"I want you to be around when I write this book. I wish Grandpa were around too, because I think of him so such." His thoughts recalled a sad time. "I remember the day Grandpa died. He was thirsty. I brought him that cup of cold water, and he gave a blessing to all of us. He said that I would go beyond these hills. He knew I was not meant to be a farmer."

"We both knew that, almost from the beginning."

"I look at my life. I look at Johnie and what he does well. I'm not good at tractor driving and taking care of cattle. I don't like to do the things he enjoys doing."

"The Lord created you that way. You should do what God calls you to do."

"Why is it that some people think I should be a minister? A minister has a great responsibility. I've never felt called to that. I feel that I can do more good as a teacher."

"Then that's what you should do. I feel in my heart that you will be a great teacher, and your writing will bring honor to your family."

James would long remember and cherish these moments with his grandmother. He made plans to visit her in the days ahead. He wanted to fill his journal with stories only she could tell

Beyond the Darkness

The two of them soon arrived at church, and when James entered, many people rushed to greet him. Some were friends home for Thanksgiving; others had not yet seen him since his return. The sense of community and extended family touched him.

He should have expected it, but found himself surprised to see Tim Robertson escorting Margaret to the pew in front of him and his grandmother. In minutes the rest of the family joined them. James looked around at the members of the congregation. During his absence, little children had become big kids. Some of the older members had aged noticeably. And his own grandmother, sitting beside him, had changed, grown frailer. But such was life—it had a way of moving forward. Children grew up. Older people grew still older, and some died. *How brief earthly life is*, he thought.

He wanted this service to be special, but there was nothing unique about it. They sang the usual hymns. The organist was the same woman who had been there forty years or more. Her playing was slowing down. James thought the student pastor looked too young to be a pastor. He seemed pleasant enough, but he didn't really say anything worthwhile. James missed Pastor Strand, who preached every Sunday during James's growing up years. Pastor Strand always had a way of bringing out important truths.

Change was inevitable, he knew, but why did certain things have to change? James kept wishing a few comfortable, familiar things would never change.

The student pastor's sermon went far too long. When the service finally ended, everyone hurried away—probably for the prospect of a delicious turkey dinner with all the trimmings.

His mother hurried off with Aunt Victoria, both women intent on having everything ready on time. His father, Grandma, and Michael rode home with James in the family car. Margaret and Tim Robertson followed.

Shortly after twelve, all the invited family members arrived. Larry, Joan, and young Lowell were the first to arrive. James couldn't get over the change in Larry. This cousin was an entirely different person—no longer the irresponsible party animal but a sensible family man. Soon after, Corrine and Warren came with their three girls, who were no longer so little. Finally, Carol arrived with a sullen Jeff Grant beside her. In minutes, they were all seated at either the much-extended dining room table, the kitchen table, or one of several card tables. Aunt Victoria said

Chapter 22

a few words and a prayer, and the Anderson family members began to devour their Thanksgiving dinner.

As he ate, James remembered past Thanksgivings. A few years back, Grandpa had been alive. He and Grandma had helped keep the family together. Back then, Aunt Martha had often been with them. And through the years, Aunt Mary and Uncle Ed, along with cousins Beth, Jake, and Irene, had been at the family gathering. For years the seven cousins had played and grown up together. But now Aunt Mary, Uncle Ed, and the cousins were far away.

James began to feel restless. Margaret was moving out to establish her own life. Carol would soon become a mother. It was time for him to move on as well. Hopefully Mom and Dad and others would always be here when he came home.

Despite all the change, some Thanksgiving traditions remained the same. The children—now consisting of Corrine and Warren's three daughters, along with Michael and cousin Larry's son Lowell—played outside. The ice on the lake and ponds was not yet strong enough to hold them, but they played other games in the snow. Watching them run and play, James couldn't help thinking back ten years. He would have been eleven, and the seven cousins would have been playing together. Now they had all gone their separate ways. They were no longer children. But that was life—it always marched on.

As the late afternoon shadows lengthened, Mother and Victoria made up a lunch for the family and guests. People ate extra pieces of pie and leftovers, though additional food was hardly needed.

Almost like the dismissal of a class, everyone left at once, leaving only Mom and Dad, Michael and Margaret, and himself. James kept thinking it was time for him to move on. He didn't really belong here anymore—at least not all the time. He was glad that in one week he would leave for college. In fact, he couldn't wait to pursue his studies.

Later, after the evening milking and other chores were finished, James stood outside the barn. He looked up at the stars and then toward the dark ridge of hills to the southeast. Those hills seemed to stand for the new life that would greet him in the mysterious realm of tomorrow.

Dad was probably making sure everything was all right with the cattle and young calves. James also knew that his father did a lot of thinking during those times, and that he worried about the well-being of each of his children.

Beyond the Darkness

The barn door opened, and his dad stepped out. "Son, is something bothering you?"

"I was just thinking. Those stars are awe-inspiring. I'm looking beyond. There are even more galaxies far beyond."

His father looked up at the same stars. "You thinking about leaving? It's time for you to move on, isn't it?"

James wanted to choose all the right words, just the way he would in the novel he was writing. "I feel restless, as if I should be out there doing something. I love everyone here. This is the most wonderful community a fellow could ever find. But I don't think I'm supposed to stay. I believe God wants me to move on."

"We'll miss you. But it is time for you to live your own life."

James thought of the heavy load of farmwork he'd leave to his father. "But Dad, there's so much for you to do. You need a hired man, and there are none of those around."

"Michael will be a big help in a few years. And then I hope Johnie will come home and take over the farm."

James sighed. "I hope so, too."

The two men stood in silence. James again looked up at the Milky Way, sensing the wonder of God and His creation.

"Look," said Matthew, "someone's coming down the driveway. I can't imagine who would be out walking this time of the evening."

James observed the features of the figure. He walked fast the way a young man would, but he had a slight limp. Suddenly his father turned and began to run toward the man. In that moment James realized a soldier had returned—a young man who had been like a brother to him. Joe was home!

James followed his father slowly down the driveway, giving the older man time to greet this returning soldier. Soon he saw the two men run toward each other. His father extended his arms and the two men embraced.

"Joe, my boy, you're home! Thank God," James heard his father exclaim.

"I was afraid this day would never come," Joe replied.

Chapter 22

Matthew was too overcome to talk, even though there was much he wanted to say. Still standing out in the yard, Joe kept asking questions about each member of the family, and James was quick to answer. Finally Matthew interrupted. "Let's go in the house, Joe. It's getting cold."

James picked up Joe's duffel bag and the three men walked toward the house. The lights reflected a warm welcome. James hurried ahead and called out to his mother as he entered the house, "Someone just came by. Our friend is home." Just then, Matthew and Joe walked into the kitchen behind him.

"Joseph, you're home!" greeted Ellen. "You should have been here for Thanksgiving dinner. That would have made our celebration complete."

"I took the bus to River Falls, but I was too late for either bus or train, so I hitched a ride to Lake View. I walked part of the way from town."

"You should have called," said James. "We would have driven in to get you."

"I didn't want to bother you. I would have interrupted your Thanksgiving."

"Have you eaten?" asked Ellen. "You look so thin."

Matthew observed Joe Nelson. He was no longer a teenager. The years in the army had been hard on the boy. Now a mature man of twenty-five, he appeared different, but Matthew could tell he was that same caring person.

"Well," said Joe, "I grabbed a sandwich along the way."

Ellen opened the refrigerator door. "We have turkey and gravy and a few potatoes and dressing. I'll put it together for a quick turkey hotdish. We might even have some pumpkin pie left."

"That sounds too good to be true."

Seated at the kitchen table, James and Joe exchanged comments about some of their wartime hardships. As Matthew listened, he realized the horrors of war—horrors he had thankfully missed.

Ellen quietly put together the hotdish. This time of the year she kept the wood fire burning all day in the kitchen stove to provide extra heat for the kitchen and the house. In a matter of minutes, the aroma of a turkey dinner filled the room. She placed a plate and silverware and the hotdish before her guest, who was more like a son to them. Joe bowed his head to pray, then took a healthy portion and began to eat. After a few moments, he stopped and looked down. His dark blue eyes had a faraway look.

"I thought of you all many times when I was in the prison camp. I dreamed of coming back."

Ellen looked down at the young man. "You've been in our prayers all these years. In fact, a group of us ladies have met and prayed for all of you servicemen every week."

"I'm beginning to understand the difference prayer makes."

Matthew couldn't help thinking of the miraculous results. "Joe, do you realize every man on that list has come through the war? Most communities lost someone—some lost many. Now we're praying for Johnie, that he will come home and be healed."

For a few moments Joe ate quietly, not saying a word. "I don't know if you can realize how cruel those Japs were to us prisoners. I don't even want to think about it or talk about it."

Ellen looked at her own son and then at Joe. "There's a time to forget. This is such a time."

But Matthew saw the fire in James's eyes. "Yes, it is a time to be healed from those atrocities," said his oldest son, "but it is a time to remember the evil. We must prevent this from ever happening again."

Joe finished the last of the first big helping and looked at what remained. "No one should have to go through being in prison."

"James," said Ellen, "you must write to help us avoid another war. You must show the horrors of this war."

James avoided his mother's gaze. "I want to do that. But I don't think I can write about war itself. It is too awful. Instead I can write about the way life should be."

Joe dished himself some more turkey. "I don't have much learning, but I think some of those books are unreal. They're a far cry from what life really is."

"Don't get me wrong," James responded, "I want to show what life is really like, to show how people can lead a good life and make good decisions to avoid evil. I want to show how all choices have consequences—both good and bad."

"I just need to forget the starvation and the brutal torture I went through," Joe admitted.

"We may not have a lot," said Ellen, "but we do have enough to eat. You are welcome here."

"Thank you, Mom." Joe turned to Matthew. "Thank you, Dad."

That was the first time he had called them by his adopted names since his return. Matthew recalled the many ways Joe had acted as a son

Chapter 22

in the past. He wanted this young man to stay now, to work with him as a son.

Ellen turned to leave. "I think I better check on Michael. He was playing hard, but it's his bedtime now."

"I know Margaret's teaching," said Joe, "but isn't she home for Thanksgiving?"

James gave Matthew a knowing glance before answering his friend. "She's out for this evening. Tim Robertson finished his chores at home and came back and got her."

Joe looked disappointed.

Ellen returned to the kitchen. "Michael's been playing so hard, he fell fast asleep. I put him into bed without undressing him."

"Michael was just a baby when I left for the service," Joe recalled.

Time passed quickly during the next hours as their conversation continued, hearing of Joe's experiences and catching up on family happenings.

"I hope you plan to stay here," Ellen finally told Joe.

Matthew smiled. "I need a hired man. James is leaving in a week. I can really use someone to help."

"I was hoping you could."

"You're family. You're always welcome here."

Joe looked away. "I've said it before, but I don't think I could have lived through that terrible war if I didn't have you to come back to."

Ellen went over to Joe and kissed him on the cheek. "We've been praying for you. I know that our prayers have been answered."

At that moment the door opened quietly, and Margaret entered. "I'm surprised you're all still up." Then she saw Joe. "Now I know why." She seemed suddenly reserved and quiet in spite of her surprise at Joe's return.

Joe stood up slowly. Matthew could see he was overwhelmed in Margaret's presence.

"Welcome home, Joe." She walked across the room and gave him a hug.

"Margaret, you've grown up. You're beautiful."

Matthew knew immediately that what took place between Margaret and Joe was not brotherly and sisterly affection.

Beyond the Darkness

James stayed up late into the night, writing in his journal. Joe's return reminded him of the many other soldiers returning home. New life was emerging for millions. He thought of the future. The dark shadows of war were fast disappearing. College days and writing and new people would fill his life. Hopefully Johnie would come back from the darkness of his life. Margaret was a beautiful young woman. Would she realize how much Joe cared for her? Would Joe realize how much Margaret cared for him? Or would she remain with Tim Robertson? And Carol would soon become a mother. What about Jeff? Would he continue down the pathway he seemed to be taking? And then little Michael, a duplicate of Johnie. What would this new world hold for his little brother?

Other family members also found their ways into his journal. Mary and Ed. What would their new life in California mean? Cousin Beth was continuing at the university. Where would Jake and his military service take him? And Irene would soon finish high school.

Grandma. It was wonderful to have her in his life. He underlined the words, *"I must spend time with Grandma and hear her story. I want to preserve her life in writing while I can get all those experiences."*

Victoria always seemed there—always the same. But she, too, was older. Martha, his dad's favorite, had been away for such a long time. He missed her.

Larry and Joan. What a transformation in Larry's life. *"I need to get to know my cousin better. There indeed is a story to tell,"* he wrote.

"The future is unknown," he continued in his journal. *"The development of the atomic and hydrogen bombs could mean destruction of the world. Nuclear war could usher in a dreadful future. Dear Lord, I don't know what this future will be, but I know You hold the future."*

Chapter 23

Ellen stood at the porch door and watched the snow swirl across the yard, covering almost everything in white silence. Late November snowstorms were sometimes ferocious. She worried because Matthew was late coming in from his morning chores. Matthew always seemed sad when the children left home, and now James had gone off to college.

Her thoughts and prayers then turned to another of her children. "Lord, help Carol in her time of trouble. Bless that young baby when it comes. Give our grandchild a good home." Ellen still felt she had somehow failed Carol—that she hadn't been the mother she should be. Of the older four, three had turned out well. Carol had been the wild one who broke all the rules. And now she was realizing the consequences.

Ellen looked out once more, hoping to see Matthew trudging through the snow toward the house. Instead, three long rings startled her. She wondered if something was wrong as she picked up the receiver and said hello. Carol's voice and tears greeted her. "Mother, I'm so afraid. The baby's coming, and I don't know where Jeff is. I need help, and there's a storm."

"Stay calm." Ellen tried to think fast. "I don't know if we can get out. But have you called Dr. Baker?"

"He's in River Falls at the hospital."

"And that's where you should be. Call Larry at the gas station. He'll see that you get to River Falls. Otherwise the operator will get you help."

Carol once more shouted into the phone. "Yes, Mother, I will. But I'm so scared."

"Stay calm," Ellen repeated. "I'll be praying for you. We'll try to come as soon as we can get out."

Ellen sat down at the kitchen table, bowed her head, and prayed for Carol. Many things hadn't been right for Carol. "Please, Lord, make things all right with this baby."

The door opened and she felt a cold draft from outside. Matthew had returned. He took off his mittens and began to shed his jacket. "This storm looks bad. I think I'd better take the horses and get Michael from school. It's dangerous out—"

"We have a problem," Ellen interrupted. "Carol's having contractions. She needs to get to the hospital."

"I don't think the roads are open. I'm afraid we can't make it to town."

Ellen explained what she told Carol to do, then added, "I'll call the garage and find out if Larry was able to take her to the hospital." She cranked the telephone, gave the operator the number, and soon had Gus on the phone. Afterward she turned to Matthew. "Larry took the truck. The roads to River Falls are bad, but he should be able to get through."

Ellen saw Matthew breathe a sigh of relief. "There's nothing else to do right now," she said. "I guess we might as well have coffee."

"I miss you, Pa," Matthew said aloud. As he did the afternoon chores, he felt both restless and alone, thinking of his daughter and his inability to get out to help her to the hospital. He was tired of always working alone. Farmers needed to work in partnership the way he and Pa did for so many years. Now James had gone off to college, and Joe had left to visit his parents for a few days. That meant he was once more alone with all the work.

He carefully cleaned the barn, throwing out the manure. This was the job he liked least. He hurried, knowing the cattle shouldn't be outside for too long. The snow had stopped coming down, but the temperature

Chapter 23

was dropping well below zero. He decided not to leave yet to get Michael from school. Maybe conditions would improve later.

Matthew finished cleaning the barn and proceeded to fill the mangers with feed. The cattle needed to get in out of the cold. They should be finished drinking water out of the tank. If the temperatures remained cold, he might even have to carry water into the barn so the cattle could keep warm. He heard his cows begin their loud laments, anxious to come in out of the cold. He opened the doors, and the cattle eagerly found their places. Today there was no delay.

Matthew fastened the stanchions securely and decided to go up to the hayloft and throw down hay. This was also one of his thinking places, so after he threw down some hay for the animals, he took a moment to sit. Carol used to love to play in this hayloft. In his memory he saw her there as a young child, petting the little kittens. Or jumping from the balcony into the area below. She always tested the limits—especially leaping from the highest point possible. That was her way in everything she did. Yet Carol seemed to have had more problems than the other three put together. *Why is that?* he wondered. *Did Ellen and I do something wrong?* Maybe he'd spoiled this child. She had a charming and disarming way about her. He had given in to her wishes when he shouldn't have. Yet he remembered other times when he had to discipline her. He never disciplined well. Ellen knew how to be firm.

The shadows in the hayloft indicated that afternoon would soon turn into evening. Matthew checked his pocket watch. It was time for afternoon coffee, so he headed down the ladder and out of the barn. He shivered as he walked toward the house. Snow had stopped, but the temperature could be turning dangerously cold. He'd have to use the horse and sleigh to get Michael from school.

"Joan called," Ellen announced as Matthew entered the warm kitchen. "The contractions stopped. I guess our grandchild isn't ready to come quite yet."

"I hope nothing goes wrong. Where's Jeff, I wonder?"

"No word on that. Larry's staying at the hospital. He said you were with Joan when he wasn't there for Lowell's birth. Now he's happy to be around when Jeff isn't, and when our roads are blocked."

"Thank God for Larry. A few years ago, I'd never think that I'd be able to say something like that."

Beyond the Darkness

After coffee Matthew hitched the horses and picked up Michael at school. At least he knew one of his children was safe and secure at home. The rest he had to leave in God's hands.

That night the cold increased. As Matthew stoked the furnace, the warmth of the house became a haven from the cold and darkness of the world outside.

———

It was morning the following day. Sleep had eluded Ellen most of the night, and she knew the same was true for Matthew. She was weary already and it wasn't yet nine o'clock.

Ellen took down the receiver, hoping she could get through to the hospital or to someone. She was anxious to know how Carol was doing. Had the contractions started again? Was there a new grandchild? She could tell immediately that the lines were down; silence greeted her.

She heard Matthew on the porch, stomping the snow off his boots. "I think we can make it into town," he called out as he entered the kitchen. "Is there any news yet?"

"The lines must be down. The phone's dead."

"I'll go out in a few minutes. If I drive through and make a track with the tractor, I think we can make it to the county road."

"I think we should go if possible."

Matthew fidgeted as they drank their midmorning coffee. He seemed impatient to get going. "I hope we don't get stuck along the way. There will be a real problem with the cattle if we're late."

"Maybe we shouldn't take any chances. I suppose Carol is in good hands even if we're not there."

"A farmer is his own boss," Matthew sighed. "I like that. But he's always tied down."

At that moment there was a knock and the door opened. "I visited my parents, and now I'm back for good," announced Joe. "I'm home. I'm ready to work."

"Welcome home, Joe," said Matthew, "but how did you get here?"

"I have a car. My folks gave me their old car. I can't believe it, but I have a car."

Chapter 23

Ellen explained their concerns about Carol, and without hesitation Joe said, "You go to River Falls. I'll take care of the chores. Don't worry about getting back late. The work will be done."

"You'll gather the eggs, will you?" asked Ellen. "And make sure Michael gets home from school all right. It's cold out there."

"I'll take my car and get him. You tell me anything else I need to do."

"You might have to hitch up the horses to get Michael. The road to the school isn't open. Everyone walks except when the weather's really bad." She moved over to the refrigerator. "There's roast beef here that you can heat up for dinner. And some cold potatoes that you could fry or heat up. Just take whatever you want."

"Don't worry, I won't go hungry."

A few hours later Matthew and Ellen entered the hospital and walked toward the waiting room, where Larry greeted them with good news. "You have a healthy grandson. Congratulations! Mrs. Grant just came, so I'll be leaving."

"You mean you stayed here all night?" Ellen's statement turned into a question.

"I didn't think Carol should be alone," Larry explained. "Jeff finally came this morning, but he left a few minutes ago."

Ellen felt anger toward her son-in-law. "I wonder what he had to say for himself."

"Not a thing."

Matthew shook his head. "I don't understand how a man could ignore his wife that way."

"I'm afraid I do understand," said Larry. "I was pretty messed up when my son was born. I forgot about my wife. There was the pressure of business, and I was drinking heavily."

"I'm sorry," replied Matthew, "I shouldn't have said that."

"You were right, Uncle Matthew. Jeff has those terrible memories of the war. He's drowning his memories in liquor. He's out of control."

Ellen felt an apprehension about her daughter's life, but she also was eager to check on Carol and the baby. "It's time to see our first grandchild."

"I need to be getting home to my wife." Larry turned to leave. "In a few months Joan and I will be having our second child."

"And you'll be there beside your wife this time," Ellen assured him.

Beyond the Darkness

As they headed for Carol's room, Ellen wasn't sure how she would feel about seeing Mrs. Grant. The woman had warmed up to the family at times, but mostly she was cold and distant. When they entered the room, Mrs. Grant greeted them before anyone could speak. "I think Carol is a little tired right now." Ellen seemed to sense that Mrs. Grant wanted to control even their visit to their own child and grandchild.

But Matthew moved around her and over to the bed beside his daughter. "Carol, we're here to see you and our grandson." Ellen saw the moistness in Matthew's eyes. He hesitated briefly, but then Carol lifted her little boy and placed him in Matthew's arms.

"I'm glad you're here, Dad."

Ellen felt somewhat rejected by Carol's lack of response to her. She wanted things to be right between her and her daughter. When she moved toward the bed and kissed her daughter on the cheek, Carol's attitude seemed to soften. "Mother, I'm glad you're here."

"What's his name?" Ellen asked.

Carol started to speak, but Mrs. Grant interrupted. "His name will be Jeffrey Allen Grant IV. The first male of each generation has been given that name. His father's name is Jeffrey Allen Grant III. Jeffrey Allen Grant IV has a great family name and tradition to carry on."

Carol straightened up in bed. Her voice became sharp. "I will give him the first name Jeffrey as you wish. But his middle name will be Andrew, for the Anderson name. And we will call him Andrew or Andy instead of Jeffrey, to avoid confusion."

Mrs. Grant cleared her throat. "My son has agreed to our choice of name. He will be called Jeffrey Allen."

Ellen wanted to speak against Carol's mother-in-law but held back to let her daughter answer. "I am the mother," Carol reminded Mrs. Grant. "I carried this baby for nine months. I have some say in the matter."

"By the way, where is his father?" asked Ellen. "I would think he should be here."

"Jeff was here earlier. He'll be back."

"I am the mother," repeated Carol. "I have the final say on his name."

"If you want help from the Grants, you'll honor our wishes."

Ellen felt anger rise within her, but Carol said nothing. When her daughter burst into tears, Ellen could no longer keep silent. "Look how you've upset my daughter. We will call the boy Andy or Andrew as my daughter wishes."

Chapter 23

Mrs. Grant backed away. Quietly she said, "We'll see," and walked away. "I'll be back later. I have some shopping to do."

At this point the baby began to whimper. Matthew returned his grandson to Carol, who wiped away her tears. "I hate that woman. She's a witch."

"Please don't hate her," Ellen softly chided. "You don't have to like her, but Christians can't hate someone—even the worst person."

"I'm not a good Christian. Sometimes I wonder if I'm a Christian at all."

Ellen wanted to say more, but at that point the nurse entered. "It's time for me to take the baby back to the nursery. And I think Carol needs some rest." The nurse picked up Carol's son. "He's a beautiful, healthy baby. You can be thankful for that."

"That's all I have to be thankful for," mumbled Carol.

Matthew remained silent throughout the entire discussion.

"Carol, dear," said Ellen, "I think you need to rest. Your father and I will go and have some dinner. We'll come back later."

Matthew found a small restaurant where they ordered the noon special. After dinner they walked around to several of the stores. As they admired the displays in the store windows, Matthew said, "I wish we had more money to buy things for Carol and the baby."

"We can give them our love. And we can always be there for them."

They returned to the hospital. Carol was awake, sitting up in her bed. She looked much happier. Jeff was present, standing beside her. He politely greeted them.

"You have a beautiful son," Ellen congratulated him.

Jeff looked down at his wife. "I guess I haven't been here when I should have been. I'm going to change. I need to be there for my son and my wife."

Ellen simply smiled, hoping Jeff would keep his promise.

Matthew stood closer to Carol on the other side of the bed. "Having a son is a big responsibility," he told Jeff.

"I realize that, sir. I've been having a rough time. I can't seem to forget the terrible killing during the war."

"I know," said Ellen. "Johnie is still in the veterans' hospital. He's suffering the aftereffects of war."

The conversation that followed seemed to soften the previous differences between Jeff and Matthew and Ellen.

"I think I'll go uptown for something to eat," said Jeff eventually. "I'm hungry."

At that point Mrs. Grant entered. She went over and kissed her son on the cheek. As he began to leave, she stopped him. "Where are you going? Shouldn't you stay here?"

"I'm hungry."

Ellen caught a whiff of something she knew to be liquor.

Mrs. Grant gave her son a sharp look. "Be sure you stay with food. That is all you need."

"Oh, Ma, lay off."

With those words Jeff left. The moments that followed were strained and awkward. Then Mrs. Grant handed Carol a small package. "I saw the cutest outfit at the department store. It'll look cute on Jeffrey Allen."

Carol grunted. "Thank you." She opened the package. "It is cute. I can't wait to start dressing my son." Then quietly she added, "Andrew."

Ellen could see there would be a contest of wills between Carol and her mother-in-law. Perhaps it was good that Carol could be stubborn. She might need that will and determination. Ellen was relieved when Mrs. Grant finally left.

Even with Matthew present, mother and daughter talked over some of the necessities for mother and child. Ellen remembered she still had diapers from Michael's early years, and baby clothes as well. She promised Carol to get them to her as soon as possible.

"Mother, I feel better now that we've talked. I guess I need your help more than ever."

Ellen never thought Carol would make such a statement. "Your father and I are here for you," she told her daughter. "We'll love being grandparents. We want to help make a good life for our grandson."

Tears came to Carol's eyes. She reached over to hug her mother. "I'm sorry I've been such ungrateful, disobedient child. I'm sorry."

"I love you, my daughter."

"I love you too, Mother. I haven't told you that for a long time."

"And I haven't told you."

Ellen gave a sigh of relief. There were problems to face, but those problems could be solved.

Chapter 23

Matthew eventually decided to leave his wife and daughter alone. He never felt comfortable when women were talking about matters only women understand. He walked back to the waiting area to sit down. Suddenly a sharp pain penetrated his chest and extended to his left arm. He felt a moment of panic as he remembered his dreadful ulcer attack. But this pain felt different. He placed his hand on his heart. "Lord, what is this?" he prayed. "I have to be strong for Carol and the rest of the children. And for Ma and Larry."

The pain disappeared as quickly as it had come.

Matthew thought back to his grandson, so small and very precious. A new generation had arrived. Little Jeffrey meant another great-grandchild for his mother, but it was Ellen's and his first grandchild.

Then he thought of Carol. She was too young to be a mother. This should have happened years later. But he would love his daughter and her young child as only a grandfather could.

His son-in-law's quick departure haunted him. Jeff had resolved to change, but his eyes were tired and bloodshot. Matthew was certain he'd smelled liquor on Jeff's breath. Would this young man be able to change? How could Carol face such a situation, especially with a new baby?

Matthew breathed deeply, grateful the pain was gone.

"Lord," he prayed, "guide and protect that young boy. And guide and protect Carol. Keep them both safe in Your loving care."

Chapter 24

December 1945

Matthew entered the kitchen, pale and out of breath. Joe followed, clearly concerned about the older man.

"What's wrong?" Ellen set down the pen she had been using to write a letter. "I'm worried about you. You haven't been yourself lately."

Matthew protested. "I'll be OK. I just finished emptying out the last sack of feed. I grabbed wrong and slipped—that's all."

"You should let me do the heavy lifting," Joe reminded him. "That's what I'm here for. I'm your hired man."

"Matthew, listen to this young man," Ellen chided.

Matthew sighed, "I guess I'm not as young as I used to be."

Ellen walked over to the stove. "The coffee's hot. I made some fresh cinnamon bread. It's still warm." She poured two cups and carried the bread to the table. Matthew and Joe sat down and began to drink their coffee and eat the fresh bread.

"I think it's time for you to visit Dr. Baker," Ellen advised her husband. "You need to have a checkup."

Matthew objected. "No. These aches and pains come and go when you're older. I'm not going to go around complaining about my ailments."

Beyond the Darkness

"I've seen you holding your hand over your heart. Is that where the pain is?"

"Probably muscle cramps and indigestion. My stomach has never been good. It comes from Ma and her family."

"As soon as Christmas is over, we're going to the doctor."

Joe agreed with Ellen. "You should go."

Matthew drank the last of his coffee. "It's time we went to town. We need to hook up the trailer for a supply of ground feed."

"I'm writing to Mary and Ed," Ellen said. "Is there anything you want me to tell them?"

"You're the letter writer. You'll think of everything."

"Oh, Matthew, here's my grocery list. I need to get to work on Christmas baking."

Matthew and Joe put on their coats and left for town. Ellen looked over what she had written and continued her letter:

Dear Mary and Ed,

It's my turn to write so I'd better work on this letter or you won't hear from us before Christmas. Each year, Christmas seems busier. There are the usual family events, and I'm in charge of the Sunday School Christmas program. That gets to be a bigger job every year, but I love doing it.

I need to bring you up to date on the family. So much has been happening I don't quite know where to begin. Perhaps I should take each person in order.

Since you're most concerned about your mother, I'll begin there. Elizabeth Anderson, I must say, is doing remarkably well. Boarding the teacher is just what she needed. She prepares meals for Ruth. As you know, Ruth is a redheaded young woman. I think she is a darling. She reminds me of myself when I started teaching. She'll make someone a fine wife. Back to your mother. She seems to have more energy and looks much stronger. She'll stay with us a few days during the Christmas holidays when Ruth is home with her parents.

I've been concerned about Matthew. I think he's been working too hard. I always think of the stomach problems he had. Right now I wonder if there isn't something else. Please don't worry; I plan to get him to see Dr. Baker, one way or another.

I don't think you've heard about our wonderful surprise. Joe Nelson walked in on us Thanksgiving evening. He hitched a ride partway out to the country and walked the last mile. Needless to say, he made the conclusion of Thanksgiving more special.

More good news. Joe is willing to stay on as hired man. Matthew desperately needed help with all the work in the barn, plus some of the outside work. God does work in mysterious ways. Joe came to our rescue

Chapter 24

before, and here he is again. He is thin and limps a little, but otherwise seems to have survived the war and prison camp.

James left for college the week after Thanksgiving. He has now gotten a car so he can get around. He has a job and is able to visit Johnie regularly. James will realize his dream of getting an education. We've had several letters from him.

I don't know what to say about Johnie. Matthew and I haven't seen him yet. I think James and the doctors have wanted to spare us. However, the doctors have now agreed that it might be a good thing for Johnie to see his parents. We plan to go to the veterans' hospital tomorrow. James will go with us to see him.

Margaret loves teaching. She is a born teacher. Right now, Tim Robertson is pushing her to accept his proposal of marriage. He's a nice fellow, but I don't think she's ready for marriage. She wants to teach awhile before she settles down. I think that's a good idea. I taught for several years first, and I think taking some time to work is a good idea.

And Carol. Well, the baby arrived after Thanksgiving. Jeffrey Andrew Grant arrived during a snowstorm, so Larry is the one who ended up taking Carol to the hospital. Jeffrey, who we call Andy, is a healthy baby boy, and Matthew and I love to spoil him. Right now, I'm afraid his father has problems. Jeffrey, the baby's father, seems to have a drinking problem. Drinking has never been a way of life for our family. I'm afraid there may be serious difficulties ahead.

And then there's little Michael. Although he's not so little now. He's growing like a weed. Does well in school. He's such a duplicate of Johnie that I find myself calling him Johnie sometimes. There's one difference: I think he's doing better in school than Johnie did. Johnie always wanted to be out doing things. He didn't want to settle down to books.

That covers our family.

Larry, Joan, and Lowell are doing so well. Larry has become a first-rate mechanic. That's what he loves to do. I'm afraid P.J. tried to push him into a life that was not good for Larry. His mother Rita has left the country for now. We never hear from her. It's hard telling what she's up to.

Victoria is busier than ever at school. We haven't seen her since Thanksgiving. Martha remains away. The other two girls seem to need her. Corrine, Warren, and their three girls are doing well.

I want to say how much Matthew and I miss you. Our families spent much time together for more than twenty years. I miss our sisterly visits.

Your letters tell me you are busy and happy. That is good. The warm weather does sound appealing. I'll think of how warm you are on these cold winter days.

Our love to you all,
Ellen

Beyond the Darkness

Ellen put down her pen, then reached for an envelope. *If I hurry, I'll get it off to California in today's mail.* She addressed the envelope, put on the stamp, and hurried to the mailbox.

She arrived at the end of the driveway just as the mail carrier arrived. He stopped and announced, "Mrs. Anderson, you're the champion today for letters. You received the most of anyone."

"And I have a letter to mail to California." Ellen handed him the letter.

"This should make it just in time for Christmas." Their white-haired mail carrier handed her the *Daily Journal* along with several letters. "By the way, how's Johnie doing? I've heard he's having a rough time."

"The doctors have discouraged Matthew and me from seeing him. But now they think he's better. We're going to see him tomorrow."

"Good luck. My brother came back from the Great War, but he was never right after that. He died just a year ago."

"We've been praying for Johnie."

"I better be on my way. I hope you have a good trip."

Ellen shivered as she walked down the driveway to the house. She feared what the carrier said could be true of Johnie.

In the warmth of the kitchen, she read letters from Mary and James and two of her school friends. Their letters brought optimism and hope.

The next day, Matthew and Ellen arrived at James's college to meet him before going on to visit Johnie. Matthew was only too happy to let James do the driving the last few miles to the veterans' hospital. Those pains once more penetrated his side. He took a deep breath to control the pain. The last thing he wanted was to worry Ellen and James. He didn't want them making a big fuss over him.

Matthew enjoyed sitting in the backseat, something he rarely did. James and Ellen were busy talking about books and teaching. He felt far removed from that world. Besides, he was better able to disguise his discomfort since he was not sitting next to them.

His pain eventually subsided as the three of them entered the veterans' hospital. The corridors seemed endless. Thankfully James knew where

Chapter 24

to go. He spoke to several nurses and the receptionist before leading them farther down a hallway. Then a doctor met them as they entered the restricted area of the hospital. The doctor, worn and tired looking, cautioned them. "Please don't expect too much. John has been improving, but he has periods when he appears to be conscious of no one. He becomes completely unresponsive."

James added, "I've told my parents about what they might expect. We're hoping that seeing them might mean a breakthrough."

The doctor repeated, "Don't expect too much. Recovery is often very slow."

"We brought some pictures," said Ellen. "We thought that might help remind him of the life he knew—and his family."

"That's a good idea," the doctor replied as he unlocked the door. "I'll leave the door open. We have to lock these doors because some patients become violent, and we don't know where they might go."

The doctor turned to James. "I think you know the situation. I'll leave you, but find me if you need help."

Matthew couldn't believe what he saw. He wanted to cry out to Johnie, but words escaped him. His son looked as if he'd aged more than ten years. He was no longer that boyish son, strong and muscular, with light blond hair and clear blue eyes. His hair was darker, his eyes had lost their glow, and an unkempt beard covered his once clean-shaven face. He looked weak and tired.

Johnie sat in the one lone chair beside the single bed. The walls were bare. In many ways the room looked like a prison. In a sense, it was.

James went over and stood beside his brother. "Johnie, it's me, James. And Mom and Dad are here."

Johnie looked up, showing only a small glint of recognition. "Hello Mother. Hello Dad." He stood up, extending his hand.

Ellen extended her hand to her son and then embraced him. "Son, how are you?"

Johnie didn't answer. He seemed unable to respond.

Matthew grasped Johnie's hand. It didn't seem like the muscular hand that once was strengthened by hard work on the farm.

"Things don't seem right." Johnie spoke the words slowly. "Sometimes I don't know where I am."

"When you get better, you can come home. We want you home," Matthew assured him.

Beyond the Darkness

"The doctors tell me I have hallucinations and become violent. But I don't remember anything afterward."

Ellen handed Johnie a neatly wrapped Christmas package. "Your grandmother made this for you. I hope it fits. You're much thinner than you used to be."

"I was never fat." Johnie tore open the package and held up the hand-knitted sweater. "Blue. That's my favorite color." He took out the sweater and put it on.

"It's a little big," noticed Ellen, "but when you get some good home cooking, you'll find it fits you better."

"How's Grandma?"

James quickly answered. "She's doing much better now. She's boarding the new teacher. I plan to have long visits with Grandma so she can tell me some stories."

Ellen handed him another package. "I sewed some pajamas for you. They always fit better than the ones you buy."

Johnie held up the pajamas. "They'll feel better than the rotten stuff they give us here."

In the next moments Johnie became silent. It seemed to Matthew that he'd drifted into another world. James and Ellen tried to pick up the conversation, talking about all the family happenings. Johnie was mostly quiet and seemed indifferent now, after his initial brief words.

After a while, a young nurse knocked and opened the door. "Why don't you come down to the dining hall and share a meal with us? We've arranged a special table so you can eat together."

The dining hall was heavy with cigarette smoke. Matthew noticed that many of the men smoked one cigarette after another. At least it appeared that Johnie had not picked up such a habit. Ellen and James tried to make conversation as they ate a meal that was hardly tasty. Johnie picked at his food, while Ellen reminded him that he needed to eat in order to gain his strength back.

An hour later they had to leave Johnie sitting in his nearly empty room. Matthew wanted to take his son in his arms and tell him everything would be all right. But he knew many things were not. He looked into Johnie's eyes before he left and thought he saw more than just blankness—there were tears. He shook his son's hand. The handshake changed into an embrace. "Johnie, we miss you so very much."

Johnie backed away. "I want to come home."

"When the doctors say you are ready, you can come home."

Chapter 24

Johnie looked down and away. In that moment he appeared to leave the world of human companionship and drift again into some unknown place.

As they left and walked down the corridor, Matthew heard voices of soldiers. Was it Johnie calling for someone to help? The soldier obviously was reliving a bloody battle of the war.

The three said nothing as they left the building and returned to the car.

James started the car, then turned to his parents. "He's getting better. There's hope. He'll be ready to come home soon."

Matthew wondered if this was possible.

James drove his parents around his college campus in town before they left for home. Normally Matthew would have enjoyed the different buildings and the company of his son. Today he mourned as if he had lost another precious son.

When the time came for them to say good-bye to James, Matthew felt a sadness, but he knew James needed to go on with life. And he would soon be home for Christmas.

Matthew began to drive back toward home, toward the security of the farm he had come to love. He thought of the hills of home and again breathed a prayer of God's promise of hope and help: *"I look to the hills from whence cometh my help. My help cometh from the Lord, who made heaven and earth."*

Yet at times that help seemed far away. The clouds and shadows of the late afternoon darkened. As Matthew drove closer to Lake View, he thought about all of his children. While some of them faced new adventures, others still had difficulty ahead. Matthew wondered if the darkness would ever fully lift.

When Matthew and Ellen drove into the yard, he once more appreciated the lights of home. Reflecting out from the living room window were the lights of their Christmas tree.

Yes, it was almost Christmas. He hoped the season would bring light to their dark world.

Chapter 25

Matthew loved all the traditions of his life—especially the traditions of Christmas. Life was ever changing, but some things remained the same. Children and relatives and friends found their way to the Anderson home at Christmas every year. Tomorrow James would come home from college. And Matthew would drive north of Lake View to pick up Margaret, who had finished her first four months as a teacher in a one-room school.

It was Friday night before Christmas. The traditional school program would take place at District 185. Michael, though only a second grader, had a major role in the recitations, plays, and singing. Ellen hurried into the school ahead of Matthew, and Michael ran ahead of Ellen, to get ready for his parts in the program. Somehow this school didn't carry all the memories of Matthew's home school. However, Johnie, Margaret, and Carol all finished the eighth grade in this place.

Matthew talked with several of the men milling about outside. Then at five minutes of eight, someone rang the school bell, an announcement that the program was about to begin. Matthew and the others entered the school, searching for their seats in the semidark room. Electricity had not yet come to this school. After all, school was held during the day when there was no need for electric lights. Gas lanterns had been brought in for this occasion, so dark shadows filled parts of the room.

Beyond the Darkness

At eight o'clock, a young teacher, Miss Lund, welcomed the parents and friends. Most of these teachers looked alike to Matthew. The only one who seemed unique was his own Ellen, who stood out from all the rest. Miss Lund did have the fresh look of youth. She would probably teach a year or two and then marry one of the local farmers—just as Ellen married him.

As the program began, Matthew's mind was elsewhere. He thought for a moment about his daughter, also a teacher. Margaret was not ready to marry Tim, nor did she seem that interested. Perhaps Tim Robertson could find the right wife in this young teacher. Then he would stop pressuring Margaret into a quick decision.

Matthew's thoughts continued to wander as various children recited their pieces in the Christmas program. He thought of how each of his four older children had progressed through the grades in school—how each had changed from young child to almost-grown-up eighth grader. Now the older four were all young adults.

Focusing back on the platform, for a moment Matthew thought he saw Johnie, but it was Michael reciting the piece. His words rang out clearly. "'Twas the night before Christmas and all through the house, not a creature was stirring, not even a mouse." Matthew could almost repeat the words along with his son.

He's the best of the whole group, thought Matthew. *He's quite a boy.*

As the rest of the program progressed, Matthew's mind turned to Johnie. When Michael appeared later in a short play as a little child waiting for Santa Claus, he envisioned Johnie in the same part. Years ago, Johnie had stolen the show in a part just like this. Michael hammed up the part in the same way. If you had seen the two at the same age, they would have been taken for twins.

Matthew sighed as he said to himself, *Oh, if Johnie were only home and completely healed.* He breathed a silent prayer, "Lord, it's just not fair. It's just not fair." Finally he forced his mind to the present and enjoyed the rest of the program. Afterward, the children and their teacher exchanged gifts. Two other fathers passed out apples, while Miss Lund distributed bags of candy to each of the children.

The tantalizing smell of fresh egg coffee permeated the room, mixing with the odor of gas lamps. The coffee aroma announced to Matthew that a delicious evening lunch was on the way, a tradition in rural communities.

Chapter 25

As soon as Michael had collected his presents and opened them, he ran to his father. "Didn't I do good? I'm a good reader."

Matthew hesitated. Ellen would know how to handle this better, but he assured his young son, "You did a good job, but you shouldn't brag about it."

Michael ran back to his friends, seemingly satisfied.

As he watched his son run off, Matthew suddenly felt a slight pain. For a moment dizziness overcame him. He had to get outside, away from the crowd.

He took Michael's presents and hurried outside to place them in the car. As the pain receded, he remembered all too well the serious ulcer he had experienced back in 1937. Those pains almost led him to an early death.

As the dizziness and pain left him, Matthew returned to his friends and neighbors. The visiting and eating lunch were much like what happened at every rural school Christmas program. With the pain gone, he enjoyed the conversation and friendship of his friends and neighbors around him.

It is easy to forget pain when a person finally feels well. Matthew relaxed that evening, and most things seemed right with the world. Joe was around to help with chores and the heavy outdoor work. The family would soon be almost complete for Christmas. Life was good.

Ellen enjoyed some quiet time the next morning. It was a lull before the busyness of the holiday once the family was all home. Michael was outside playing—probably with their dog Lassie. Joe was doing the morning chores. Matthew had left to pick up Margaret and bring her home.

She decided to make one more batch of cookies. Everyone seemed to enjoy those date-filled cookies, even though they weren't the fancy cookies often associated with Christmas. She mixed the ingredients and rolled out the cookie dough. In minutes she had put the first pan in the oven.

The door opened and James entered. "Mother, I'm home."

"I can't think of any words I'd rather hear."

"And I can't think of anything I'd rather say."

Beyond the Darkness

James set down his suitcase and stooped down to kiss his mother. "Those cookies smell mighty good."

"I'll let you taste some of the others. It'll be a while before these are ready."

"You're making my favorite, date-filled cookies."

In moments mother and son were seated at the table drinking coffee and visiting. As Ellen prepared to put the final pan of cookies in the oven, James changed the subject. "How's Dad? I thought he looked pale at Thanksgiving."

"I'm concerned." Ellen moved back to the table. "He's had pain, I think. But you know your father. He's not going to admit it. But I've seen him; he keeps his hand over his heart."

"I've noticed that too."

"After Christmas I'll get him to the doctor. I can be very persuasive."

"He's worried about Johnie. I know that for sure. He's not going to admit it, but Johnie is his favorite. If Johnie doesn't get better, that could destroy him."

"I'm afraid you're right."

Mother and son talked back and forth, sharing their concerns, until Ellen turned the conversation back to her son. "James, what about you? You haven't said much about college or your classes."

"I'm taking two courses that I absolutely love. One is a course in British literature—it's a survey. We're into the Renaissance period, and I can't get enough of the great literature of that time. Shakespeare, Donne, Spencer, and others. And then I'm studying early American literature—the beginnings."

"I loved the courses about great literature in my time. I never had a chance to take all the subjects I wanted to take."

"Do you ever wish you had gone through four years of college?"

Ellen was startled by James's question, but she answered, "Yes and no. I loved learning, but times were hard. We couldn't afford more schooling. Besides, if I had done that, what about your father? I couldn't have found a better man anywhere. He may not have much education, but he has an education of the heart."

"I'd never thought of it that way. Dad doesn't have much formal education, but he seems to understand and love people. You don't get that at college."

"That comes with living. Some people have the gift. Some don't."

Chapter 25

James looked up at the kitchen clock. Time was moving quickly toward noon. "Shouldn't Dad and Margaret be back by now?"

"I don't understand why they're late. They should have been here a while ago. It's time for me to peel potatoes and get dinner ready."

"I'll help you, Mother."

James soon settled into peeling potatoes. Ellen took the last of the cookies out of the oven and brought out a jar that she had canned earlier. "We'll have meatballs. I can warm them up fast."

"What about Tim and Margaret?" asked James.

"That remains to be seen. Margaret isn't ready for marriage, but she keeps going out with him."

"Underneath, I think she still has a schoolgirl crush on Joe."

Ellen smiled her agreement.

At that moment the door opened. "Hello, Mother, I'm home." Margaret, followed by her father, set down her many packages.

Ellen looked at the brightly wrapped gifts. "You shouldn't have spent all your hard-earned money on Christmas presents."

Margaret came over and kissed her mother on the cheek. "I wanted to. You and Dad have done so much for me."

In minutes Ellen had dinner ready. Michael came in from playing outside, followed by Joe, who had finished the morning chores. Once more they gathered for a meal. Looking around the table, Ellen experienced that warm, familiar feeling of Christmas. "I'm glad we're together as a family," she said. "This is going to be a good Christmas."

Matthew wanted to savor the moments. It was the morning of Christmas Eve, his favorite day of the year. James and Joe insisted on doing the barn cleaning and morning chores. Matthew wasn't an indoor person; he enjoyed being outdoors. So he took the added free time to savor the outdoor beauty of a winter morning. He sat on the porch and gazed again toward his favorite hills, breathing in the cold, fresh air. As he looked back toward the road, a familiar car drove up the driveway. He and his good friend always visited before important holidays. Maybe each wanted to get away from the busy activity in his own home.

Glenn greeted him. "Another Christmas. We're older, and not necessarily wiser."

"I guess we do feel some aches and pains of getting older. We've been around a long time."

As they walked over to the granary, they talked grain prices and other concerns about farming. Then their conversation moved to their children. "You've got a mighty fine daughter there," Glenn remarked. "Margaret will make some man a great wife."

Matthew sensed where Glenn's conversation was leading. He didn't want any difference to come between them on this subject like before. However, he did want to keep his daughter's best interests at heart, so he reminded Glenn, "Margaret's young. Not quite ready to settle down."

"My Tim seems determined to marry and settle down."

"Your son is a fine man. He'll be a good provider and make a great husband and father."

"Wouldn't it be great if our two families came together? We've been friends our whole lives. Then we'd be in the same family."

Matthew avoided his friend's gaze. "That would be good only if that's what both children want."

"I'll tell you something." Glenn leaned over and almost whispered the words, "Tim's bought a ring, and he's going to pop the question."

"Margaret's still awfully young. She won't be nineteen until March."

"Tim will be twenty-three next summer. I was twenty-one when I married."

Matthew had to think a moment. "I was twenty-three, but Ellen was a year older. I figured that was about the right time."

"Margaret's got a good head on her shoulders. She doesn't need to wait."

Matthew knew his friend would be disappointed if Margaret declined the proposal. Something within him said such a marriage would be practical, and it would definitely have financial advantages; yet he knew his daughter's uncertainty. Instead of further disagreement with Glenn, Matthew gently changed the subject. "I know Ellen has the coffeepot on. Why don't you eat with us? We're having soup. We want to be good and hungry this evening for lutefisk."

"That would be all right. The wife's still busy baking. She says she got a little behind. And the girls won't be home until tonight. They don't have vacation the way your schoolteacher daughter has."

"Education's the key to the future. I can see that more and more."

Chapter 25

In this area of thinking the two men also differed. "Some people have too much education," Glenn declared. "Look at the mess some of our educated people got us into."

Glenn and Matthew put aside their differing opinions and joined the others in the kitchen for soup, followed by some of Ellen's Christmas cookies. James, Joe, Margaret, and Michael were all present, and Ellen managed to skillfully direct the conversation away from Margaret during their meal, with Glenn at the table. As they ate, however, Matthew noticed that Margaret was quieter than the rest. She probably sensed that a serious question was coming her way.

As Matthew and Glenn got up to leave, Ellen announced to her husband, "Someone needs to drive into town. Victoria's having car trouble, and we need to pick up your mother."

James quickly volunteered, "I'll drive in and pick up Aunt Victoria and Grandma. It will give me a chance to visit with them."

Matthew followed Glenn to his car as his friend looked off toward the hills. "I can't help thinking of the hard times we've had since we were young," he told Matthew. "I hope life is better for our children."

"We have no way of knowing the future. The future's in God's hands."

"I wish I had your faith," Glenn admitted as he got into his car.

The hours that followed seemed to fly by as the Andersons prepared for Christmas activities. James drove his own car to pick up his aunt and grandmother. Matthew and Joe finished all the extra tasks around the farm so that Christmas Eve and Christmas Day would require as few chores as possible. James returned in time to help them with milking, and as the three worked side by side in the barn, Matthew spoke the words he had said for so many Christmases, "Give the cattle the extra portion of grain. It's Christmas for the cattle as well."

This Christmas Eve blended in with many others, with a few changes. The family gathered around the enlarged table as usual, but with noticeable absences: Mary and Ed were far away in California; Johnie was not back home; Martha was still with her girls in Wisconsin; Corrine and Warren remained home with sick children; and Larry and Joan had decided to spend Christmas with her parents.

Christmas 1945 brought two additions to the family as well. Jeffrey Grant III sat at the table, sullen and quiet. Matthew suspected he'd had a little bit to drink—a serious worry. And little Jeffrey Andrew Grant brought out the love and warmth of every family member. A little child had a way of bringing the family closer.

This year Victoria spoke the Christmas prayer. To Matthew the words echoed both truth and change. "Dear Lord," she began, "we come before You, thankful for our first Christmas without war. We thank You that once more there is peace on earth. We pray that You would bring Johnie safely back to the midst of his family. We thank You that we still have the privilege of having Mother with us. May we appreciate her and each other. Bless and guide each of us as we face a future that seems to wear a face we do not know. Thank You for this bountiful feast before us. Bless the food, and we thank You for the food, the fellowship we share, and all the other gifts bestowed upon us. We pray this in Jesus' name. Amen."

Later that evening, the family left for the Christmas Eve service at Oak Ridge Church. That, too, was another change. Pastor Young, who had arrived only a few weeks earlier, seemed to have new ideas. No longer would they get up in the middle of the night to attend a traditional Julotta early morning service. Instead, at ten o'clock on Christmas Eve, they were celebrating with a candle-lighting service.

"You know, this isn't such a bad idea," whispered Matthew to Glenn, who sat right behind him in the next pew. "We won't have to get up in the middle of the night."

During that Christmas Eve service, Matthew prayed a fervent prayer. "Lord, bring Johnie back, whole in body, mind, and spirit." The absence of his middle son at Christmas was particularly heavy on Matthew this year.

After returning home from church, and after the Anderson Christmas Eve traditions were complete, Matthew stood outside and looked up at the stars that crisp December evening. He thought of the star of Bethlehem that had shined more than 1900 years before. A star, larger than the rest, seemed to stand out tonight as well. This "Bethlehem star," as well as the one two thousand years before, shone through his spirit and brought hope to the darkness of his world.

Ellen sighed as she sat down in the corner of the kitchen near the pantry. The Christmas Day meal and dishes were all put away.

Chapter 25

Victoria moved over to a chair and sat down. "You're tired, aren't you?"

Ellen took off her apron. "I think it's too large a crew to have all at once. We lost some family members, but we've gained others."

"Ellen, I hope you realize how much the whole Anderson family appreciates you. It's you and Matthew who have kept this family together."

"You've helped me all the way along. I could never do all the Christmas meals without you coming and helping each year."

"I like to sit back and review the changes every Christmas," Victoria noted. "We're all a year older, of course."

Ellen laughed. "Sometimes with Michael, I feel I'm a lot older. He's so bright and active, and I'm much older than when I raised the other four."

"Why don't you bring me up to date on all that's happened? We were so busy yesterday that we didn't have much chance to talk."

"Well, your mother seems perkier than ever, but I notice she went off quietly to take a nap. Boarding the teacher was the right solution to her problem. She needed purpose. She needed someone to take care of."

"Ruth seems like such a fine, sensible young woman. I can't help thinking she'd be a perfect wife for James or Johnie."

"I don't think James has met her."

"How is he doing?"

Ellen couldn't help feeling a special pride about her oldest son. "He loves the courses he's taking at the college. He'll major in English. He wants to write, but he has decided to become a teacher."

Victoria looked away. "James is a bright boy, but he's introverted. I hope he can relate to his students on their level."

"Oh, he will. Have no fear of that."

"Any news about Johnie?"

"Right now it looks promising that the hospital will send him home. Then we'll see what happens."

"That would be a big help to Matthew. And what's this I hear about Margaret? Is she engaged?"

"Tim gave her a ring, but she's not wearing it," Ellen revealed.

Noise from the living room suddenly quieted. Slamming doors indicated that a number of the kids had decided to go outside, probably to skate.

Ellen walked over to the window. "Corrine is going out with the children. I'm so glad her girls recovered quickly so they could be here with the family today. I see James is outside too. He'll help make sure the kids don't get into anything."

"Margaret's walking with Joe," observed Victoria, peering out the window.

"I think she cares for him. When she was younger, she had a serious crush on him. We used to tease her about it."

"I'm not one to speak in these matters, but I think Margaret would probably have a more secure life with Tim. He's a good, solid farmer, and he'll get land from his father."

Ellen was suddenly a bit annoyed with her sister-in-law as she answered, "The choice will be Margaret's. I don't think she's ready at this time for marriage to anyone."

"She's still young," Victoria acquiesced. "What about Carol? I notice she isn't here today."

"Mrs. Grant is having their Christmas celebration. She insisted that Carol, Jeff, and the baby all be at their place."

"Carol can be wayward and stubborn," stated Victoria, "but Mrs. Grant is no match for anyone. I feel sorry for Carol with such a mother-in-law."

"I do too. But I'm afraid Carol got herself into this early marriage. She'll have to live with her decisions."

The two ceased their conversation briefly, and noted absolute quiet from the living room, which invited Ellen to do some checking. Victoria followed her, and there they saw Warren and Matthew at opposite ends of the davenport, sound asleep.

"The men are tired," said Victoria. "They're getting some much-needed rest."

"Just like other Christmases. Matthew and Ed would talk and then nod off. You and I always visited with Mary." Ellen paused. "I miss Mary. Her absence this year leaves an empty spot."

The two returned to the kitchen where Victoria poured herself a cup of coffee. "I can't help thinking of Father tonight—and P.J. as well. I miss them even with the passing of years."

"Holidays are like that. I think of the times many years ago when my family was home and together for Christmas. There are so many of us now, and we're spread all over the state and country. Thankfully we do get together every summer."

Chapter 25

"I always consider you an Anderson. I forget that you come from another family."

Ellen poured herself a cup of coffee and responded, "I've been an Anderson for more than twenty years. And you have become my family."

The two women sat for several moments in silence. Then Victoria said, "I'll have to admit that you and Matthew and your children are my family—more so than any of the other Andersons. I would do anything to help you."

Ellen reached over and tenderly touched Victoria's hand. "In the absence of my sisters, you have become my sister."

Victoria stood up, almost abruptly, and pointed out the window. "Look, there are Margaret and Joe coming up the driveway. It looks as if they've had a long walk."

Ellen peered out the window. "I hope Joe realizes that Margaret cares for him—and not like a brother." She noticed a car drive up. Tim Robertson got out of the car and walked over to Margaret and Joe. Victoria and Ellen stood silently at the window, wondering what words were being spoken. Joe moved away and began to walk toward the house as Tim took Margaret's arm and ushered her over to the car. She got in and they drove away.

Ellen felt she could see the sadness in Joe's face. "I feel so sorry for him. The poor boy is devastated."

She knew Joe needed the Anderson family more than ever.

Chapter 26

February 1946

Matthew wakened particularly early with butterflies in his stomach. Today they would drive to the veterans' hospital and pick up Johnie. He felt both fear and hope as he looked to the future—wondering how his son would adapt to being back home, but thrilled to know the last of his sons would be back safe from the many years affected by the war.

Life during January and early February had settled into a pattern. James was away at college and Margaret was teaching. Neither had come home since Christmas, and Margaret still had made no decision about marrying Tim. Michael brightened their lives every day with his antics and questions. Ma still got along very well with boarding the teacher. Ruth seemed to be good for her, and Ma for Ruth.

Matthew saw less of Corrine and Warren this winter. They were preoccupied with other things and busy with their younger friends. And Warren talked frequently about moving to a better climate in California, like Ed and Mary. On the other hand, Matthew's nephew Larry was becoming more of a friend.

Little Jeffrey Andrew Grant became a regular visitor at the farm. Matthew experienced new feelings as a grandfather. His grandson became known as Andy most of the time.

Beyond the Darkness

Matthew tried to relax about taking this trip to pick up Johnie. After all, Joe could easily take care of all the chores by himself. Matthew could never find a better hired man. On the other hand, Joe should begin to think about a farm of his own before long.

After lying in bed awhile, unable to get back to sleep, Matthew decided to get up. He tried to change his clothes without wakening Ellen, but she was stirring already. A voice at the door spoke softly. "Dad," said Joe, "Matthew, I'll take care of the chores by myself. You get ready for your trip."

Matthew liked it when Joe called him Dad.

Ellen got out of bed, rubbing her eyes. "I'll make a big breakfast. Scrambled eggs. Bacon. I'll warm up some cinnamon rolls."

"I'm hungry already," Joe spoke from the hallway, then hurried on his way.

Later Matthew relished hot coffee along with his hearty farm breakfast. Michael came downstairs and into the kitchen with his usual barrage of questions and requests. "I want Johnie in my room. He can sleep with me."

Ellen explained, "We'll see, Michael. Maybe later on. But you have to understand that Johnie has been sick. He's going to need a room by himself for a while."

"What about Grandma and Aunt Victoria when they come?"

"Don't worry. We'll find a place for them. Or maybe Johnie will be well by then and can be in your room."

"I want my brother home."

"We all do," agreed Matthew.

"Can't I go with you?" Michael whined.

"No," said his mother. "You belong in school."

Still Michael continued his questions and pleas, and finally Matthew tried to appease his young son. "Johnie might be with us here when you get home from school."

"Goodie." That answer seemed to satisfy Michael, and he left the kitchen to prepare for school.

Several hours later as Matthew drove on the state highway, the butterflies returned. Hope and anticipation eclipsed his fear this time. He would soon see his son.

Chapter 26

The piercing sounds of gunfire were everywhere—within, without, and all around. Johnie Anderson wanted to scream but couldn't. He rushed forward in battle. Suddenly he stood still, ready to fire into that unknown enemy. Something stopped him. He could not move; he stood paralyzed by fear. Other soldiers moved forward, but he remained immobile.

The nightmare seemed it would never end. The same battle repeating itself again and again, and he could not escape.

"John Anderson." The voice, sharp and irritating, startled him, but at least it shocked him out of his nightmare. He jumped up, not sure where he was. "Your parents are coming to take you home today. You need to get ready."

"Yes, sir," he managed to say.

"Your shaving things are on the table."

The nurse quickly made her exit. Some of these nurses and hospital workers were cold and distant and efficient. Others were kind and tried to understand.

Johnie thought back over the last week. A week ago, he awakened from a lengthy period of nightmarish horror and inactivity. It seemed to him he had been half dead for an eternity—and then suddenly he woke up. The doctors and others called his problem combat fatigue or shell shock. He had heard about that before he entered the service.

The past year was hazy and indistinct. He knew he had been in a German prison camp for several months. Then he was transferred to an army hospital in Norfolk, and after that he had come to this veterans' hospital. He wondered if he would ever be able to erase all the terrible memories.

Slowly he got out of bed—not really a bed, an uncomfortable hard cot. Sleeping in a real bed at home would feel like heaven.

He made his way down the hall to the bathroom. As he shaved, he observed himself in the mirror. His blond hair, now turning darker, was too long. He needed a good haircut. The veterans' hospital was understaffed so that such matters didn't get taken care of. Perhaps he could get a haircut before he arrived home. He was glad he had decided to shave his beard a few weeks ago. That made him look younger. He shaved carefully. Until just a few days ago, someone always watched him while he shaved. They must have been afraid he would cut his wrists. Some of the more violent soldiers had harmed others or tried to take their own lives.

Beyond the Darkness

Johnie straightened himself to his full six feet, one inch. He flexed his muscles. He knew he was weak. Would he ever regain the strength he used to enjoy? What would it be like to go back home to work on the farm? Would he still love the quiet of his old life?

His face was pale, but his eyes were still a dark blue. The girls used to flock to him. He used to enjoy the way they swooned over his good looks. He still had his looks, but now he felt like an old man.

Right now, he wondered about Mom and Dad. James, of course, had visited regularly from the college nearby. Johnie vaguely remembered Mom and Dad coming a couple months back. During that visit he was only half aware.

He dressed carefully. He hated these slacks the hospital had issued; they didn't fit. Wearing good ol' farmer overalls would feel ever so much better.

He was late for breakfast, but he hated the hot cereal that would be cold by now anyway. In another day he would be eating bacon and eggs and Mom's delicious cinnamon rolls.

Johnie waited in the large reception area for what seemed like hours. Finally he went to the reception desk. "I'm waiting for my parents. I thought they should be here by now." The receptionist crisply informed him that Mr. and Mrs. Anderson were talking with the doctor. That interview was part of his discharge procedure.

"I suppose they think I'm some kind of mental case," he told the woman.

"You have been through many hardships. Some of the soldiers won't make it. You are one of the fortunate ones."

At that moment Johnie hardly felt fortunate. In a sense, he wondered if he had any kind of feeling left at all. The numbness wouldn't go away, even though his mind was now clearer.

As he sat down in a nearby chair, his mind returned to the farm he loved. He thought about cleaning the barn with Dad, putting out the extra measure of feed on Christmas Eve, and hunting ducks in the backwoods slough. And Mother—she was always preparing meals and making certain that he studied. He lost himself in the memories until a voice called across the room, "Johnie. Welcome back!" It was the tender voice of his mother.

Dad spoke his name too, with deep emotion.

Johnie straightened himself, standing up tall, and then stooped to take his mother in his arms. Words would not come as tears filled his

Chapter 26

eyes. He held her in his arms for a moment and then moved toward his father, hesitating. After all, men did not embrace. But his father opened his arms, and soon Johnie was embracing Dad. "I'm back, Dad. I'm back. I thought I'd never make it home."

As he took a closer look at his parents, he realized they had changed. Mother was a little heavier, and her hair had more gray. As they walked away from the hospital, Dad seemed to walk more slowly. He was thinner. Could something be wrong? Or had Dad just been worried about him?

The hours that followed on the way home were filled with talk and laughter and tears. They ate their noon dinner at a restaurant a short distance from the veterans' home. Then Johnie insisted on buying new clothes, his first action to separate himself from the army. When he got into his new slacks and shirt, he felt like a different man. "I'm out of the army and the hospital. I'm away from war. I'm going home!" he exclaimed. "I thought this day would never come."

His father then invited Johnie to drive. Driving gave him a new sense of freedom and further distinguished his new life from his previous months in the vets' hospital. Late afternoon shadows greeted them as Johnie drove into Lake View. A strange excitement traveled through his body. This was his hometown. This was the place they came to shop every week. This was where he had attended high school for four years. The stores and restaurants looked strangely unfamiliar; yet nothing had really changed. He was home. But would he feel a part of this place? People were different; he was different.

Dad directed him to Carol's house at the edge of town. He couldn't believe his little sister was married, and that he was now an uncle.

Mother knocked on the door of Carol's small house. The door opened, and there stood his little sister. She greeted him with open arms.

"Oh, Johnie! I've missed you."

"Carol . . ." was all he could say.

He stepped back. His younger sister was a woman now, not the girl he had left almost three years ago.

She turned and went into the small bedroom, then came out, holding the baby. "Here's Jeffrey. We usually call him Andy or Andrew, his middle name. Meet Uncle Johnie."

She presented him with his nephew, and he awkwardly accepted the bundle. "I can't believe all that has happened while I've been away." He held Andy and looked into his eyes. "Life moves on, doesn't it?"

Beyond the Darkness

As they visited and caught up on the past year, Johnie felt awkward. His little sister was not the same person. It almost seemed he didn't know her anymore. Is that what happened to people when you were away? Would this place ever be home again?

An hour later, as they left Carol's home, Johnie felt terribly tired. Matthew drove so his son could relax.

"Your grandmother is eager to see you. That is, if you're not too tired," announced his mother. "I think she's been baking your favorite cookies."

Johnie felt new energy at the prospect of seeing his grandmother. "I expect I probably ate more of her cookies than any other grandchild. James may have been down there more, but I spent my time eating cookies."

As they drove up the familiar driveway, Johnie thought of the years he had grown up here before they moved to the new farm. The new house looked almost like the one he grew up in. But Grandma's little house was the same. Light spilled out from the windows, welcoming him. Johnie felt renewed as he hurried out of the car and up the steps. He knocked on the door and went in. And there she was. "Grandma."

She looked the same, though frailer. Those tired blue eyes still held a brightness, perhaps the light of welcome.

"Oh, my boy, my boy. I've been praying for you. Our small group of mothers and grandmothers has been praying for all our boys. And now you are all safely home."

Johnie stooped down and hugged his grandmother, kissing her on the cheek. "I can't believe I'm actually here."

"Supper's almost ready. I want you to stay."

Johnie looked to his mother.

"Are you sure it's not too much trouble?" she asked Grandma, then paused and walked over to the telephone. "I probably better call home and let them know. I had food ready for Joe to make for Michael and himself." It took Mother a few minutes to explain to Michael what was happening. Then she hung up the phone and told Johnie, "Your little brother can't wait to see you."

Grandma scurried about the kitchen, getting the food ready. "I prepared extra potatoes because I thought you might be coming, and I have a pork roast. So there's plenty."

At that moment a petite, attractive redhead entered the room. "Hello, you must be Johnie. I've heard so much about you. I'm Ruth."

Chapter 26

He hadn't expected this. Aside from some nurses, he hadn't seen a beautiful woman in a long time. "Glad to meet you," he replied. Ruth extended her hand, and he felt a pleasant warmth as they touched.

With some help from his mother, Grandma's supper was soon on the table. Johnie hadn't felt this hungry in a long time.

"Matthew," Grandma said as they were seated at the small table. "Would you ask the blessing?"

Dad prayed softly and slowly, "Thank You, dear Lord, for Johnie's safe return. We can't thank You enough for finally bringing him back to us. Thank You for Ma, who has prepared this food. And thank You for this wonderful fellowship and the bountiful food. In Jesus' name. Amen."

For a moment Johnie was overcome with a torrent of feelings. He stood. He hadn't experienced feelings for anyone or anything until just a few hours before. And now those feelings were out of control. Tears trickled down his cheeks.

"That's OK, Johnie," assured Grandma. "Tears bring healing."

Johnie hurried into his Grandma's bedroom, where he could let the tears flow. For a few moments time stood still. Then he quickly dried his face and returned to the table. "I'm sorry," he admitted to everyone. "I don't think I've ever done that before. Don't let the food get cold because of me."

In minutes everyone entered into the spirit of eating and good conversation. Ruth had a way of describing the antics of her schoolchildren. Soon they all were talking and reminiscing about school days.

As they finished the meal, Grandma brought out the coffee and cut large pieces of chocolate cake. "I know this chocolate cake is your favorite."

When those expressions of love were put into deeds, Johnie again felt overwhelmed with emotion. Somehow he felt unworthy. This time, however, he controlled himself and enjoyed the cake, as well as the company.

An hour later, Johnie yawned. "I think it's time to go," said his mother. "Michael will have his nose against the window, waiting for big brother."

And that's exactly the way it was. His father drove up the driveway. The kitchen window was partially frosted over, but a nose and face were visible even as they walked toward the porch door. Johnie was finally home.

Beyond the Darkness

The door opened and Michael ran out and flew into his brother's arms. The welcome home had been warm so far, but this was perhaps the warmest. "Hello, buddy, I'm home."

"Give me a horseback ride the way you used to."

"Your brother's had a hard day," said his mother. But Johnie wasn't about to let being tired interfere with this opportunity to please his little brother. He got down on his knees, and Michael grabbed on to his back and shoulders. Johnie hopped along, giving his brother a horseback ride. The five-year-old he had seen when he was last home on leave was now a much bigger seven-year-old. This is what it meant to be home.

After some hours of visiting Mom and Dad and Joe and playing with Michael, he finally was ready for bed.

"I want you to sleep with me," pleaded Michael. "Please, Johnie. Please."

Johnie thought a minute. "I can try. But I've been thrashing about nights and having nightmares. Maybe I shouldn't."

Mother looked at both sons. "The guest bedroom is ready also. You can sleep there if you like."

Michael again pleaded for his brother to sleep in his room. "I'll try it tonight," he agreed. "But if I can't sleep or become too restless, I'll simply go to the other bedroom."

A half hour later, he was in his old bed, the one he and James had shared for many years. Only now, little Michael was with him.

Michael snuggled against him and soon was sound asleep. Johnie felt his little brother's heart beating. He knew this little fellow believed in him and trusted him completely.

In moments Johnie experienced a great calm and peace. He was home. The war was over. He welcomed the deep sleep that quickly enveloped his whole being.

Ellen switched off the light and joined Matthew in bed. "It's been quite a day."

Matthew found it hard to put into words what he was feeling. The son who had been lost was now safely home. But Johnie had not been the prodigal. Johnie was the son who would take over the farm—but

Chapter 26

would he? Was he well enough? "He's home," was all Matthew could actually say.

"Johnie's come a long way, but coming back to civilian life won't be easy," Ellen said, as if she were reading her husband's thoughts. She moved over, turning to him and changing the subject. "Matthew, you've put off going to the doctor. Now it's time to go."

Matthew knew Ellen was right, yet he wasn't ready to agree. "I feel much better. I haven't had that pain in a long time. I think I was worried about Johnie—that's what it was."

"We'll see."

Matthew sensed at that moment that the days ahead would not be simple, and not just for him personally. Postwar changes were moving forward rapidly in their country and in their community. He was reminded again of a hymn. He started to hum and then began to sing, "Lead kindly Light, amid the encircling gloom, lead thou me on. The night is dark and I am far from home. Lead thou me on." He stopped, not remembering the next words.

"Johnie's home safe," said Ellen.

"God is good."

Chapter 27

Matthew ate the last of his dessert that Sunday noon. This February day had been filled with celebration, a thanksgiving for Johnie's return home. In the usual tradition, Oak Ridge Church arranged for a generous potluck dinner. Matthew was amazed at all the people who had come together. It was like one of those serial stories where all the characters came together as the story ended.

Pastor Young rose from his chair. "This is a day of celebration. I've just met Johnie Anderson, but I see in him a fine young man who sacrificed for his country. We want to thank him for that sacrifice. We want to honor him at this time."

The congregation and family members applauded. Then something out of the ordinary happened. As the applause continued, someone in the back stood. Then Matthew saw his friend Glenn stand. Soon everyone was standing and clapping louder and shouting out their happiness.

Matthew and Ellen stood to honor their son, as did Ma and little Michael. Johnie smiled through the tears that glazed his eyes.

"I think that calls for words from our honored guest," Pastor Young encouraged.

The audience sat down and Johnie rose, somewhat unsteadily. "I'm overwhelmed," he began, then paused as the audience quieted. "I don't think I'd be back here if it hadn't been for the Lord's protection and healing. I thank Him for all He's done." He stopped briefly as his voice caught in his throat. "And my family—Mom and Dad, James, Margaret, Carol, Grandma, and others . . . even little Michael. It was your prayers that brought me back. I thank you for those prayers. You never stopped hoping and praying." He cleared his throat. "Thank you."

As Johnie sat down, applause once more broke out in the church basement. Then Pastor Young stood again and added, "I think we need to hear from our hero's grandmother. I'm new here, but I believe she was instrumental in getting a prayer group together. And now all the boys in this church and community have returned home safely. Let's hear from Elizabeth Anderson."

Ma stood up. "I'm not a speaker, but I know God listens and answers prayer. His answers are not always what we want—and the answers may take time—but the Lord answered our prayers. I thank Him for bringing all our boys home, but I thank Him especially for bringing my Johnie back to us safely."

Ma sat down. The applause began quietly and then grew.

Pastor Young stood up once more. "I feel privileged to be a part of this praying church. I don't know of a better way to give thanks now than to sing the Doxology. That says it all. Let's all stand as we praise God."

Pastor Young's rich tenor voice started the song as the rest of the congregation joined in, raising their voices throughout the small basement:

"Praise God from whom all blessings flow.
Praise Him all creatures here below.
Praise Him above ye heavenly host.
Praise Father, Son, and Holy Ghost. Amen."

One of the ladies called out. "There's plenty of coffee, and you can have a second or third piece of pie."

Matthew bowed his head and whispered, "My cup runneth over."

James was glad to be home for this special dinner honoring his brother. Johnie had suffered; he deserved special recognition. He looked around the crowded, noisy church basement and spotted the petite, redheaded schoolteacher. He walked over to her, looked down, and

Chapter 27

said, "Hello, Ruth. It's good to see you again. I'd like to hear about your teaching. Do you suppose we could go upstairs and talk?"

"I would like that," Ruth replied. There was something rich and soothing about her alto voice.

As they walked up the stairway, James wanted to say the right words. He had been immediately fascinated with this young woman from the moment he met her. "I've heard so much about you," he began, "and wanted the opportunity to talk with you, but you've always been gone when I've been around. Grandma can't say enough good about you."

"I'm fortunate to be able to stay with such a wonderful woman. She has so much wisdom, and she reminds me of my own grandmother."

"I appreciate Grandma more now than I did when I was a kid."

"That's the way it is, James. I have heard much about you as well. You are her pride and joy."

James and Ruth soon lost track of time as they talked about teaching and college and the matters of a changing world. As they sat in a church pew, he looked around at the stained-glass windows and spoke what was constantly on his mind these days, his goals for the future. "I want to help make this world a better place," he commented. "Teachers can do that. I want to teach high school or college English. I think I can influence kids to look beyond and work toward a better community and nation and country."

"I feel the same way," Ruth responded, "but the work is often hard and slow." She hesitated a moment before confessing, "I sometimes feel I need more education. I love staying with your grandmother, and I love the school. But I also feel a desire to go back to school as a student. One year of teacher training doesn't seem like enough. I need more."

"You could come back to college this fall. Mine has a good program for elementary teachers."

"I'm thinking about that and other possibilities."

"I suppose I shouldn't encourage you to leave my grandmother."

"Oh, I always felt I would be here only a year or two." Ruth stopped and glanced at her watch. "But I think Victoria may want to leave. I came with her and your grandmother."

This opportunity was too good for James to pass up. "I'll take you home," he suggested. "Then we can talk some more."

Ruth quickly accepted his offer, so James said good-bye to family members and friends and eagerly drove his new friend to his grandmother's. They soon sat at Grandma's kitchen table, deep in conversation.

Beyond the Darkness

"Ruth, I think you should keep a diary or journal. I see your life is full of stories. And someday those stories should be told."

She smiled. "Yes, I keep a diary, but it's private. And my stories about the children are personal and private as well."

James knew he had found someone who understood a writer's mind-set. "In fiction, you can change the details when you tell the story."

"Yes, that's true."

James got up to leave. "I hate to go. You've been wonderful company, but I have to get back to college. I won't be around here very much this winter and spring, but maybe we could write. I'm good at writing and answering letters."

"I shall look forward to your first letter."

With those words a new friendship began. James left minutes later, experiencing a new excitement about his life and future.

The people who gathered that day seemed in no hurry to leave the celebration. Many visited with each other, and everyone wanted to talk with Johnie. He had not lost his magnetic appeal to the young women of the community. Several seemed to find reasons to pass his way.

Ellen sat down to relax next to her mother-in-law, but she also observed the crowd and watched her son. Elizabeth Anderson seemed to be noticing everything as well. Eventually Margaret spied the two women and walked over to tell them she had to leave for her school. "Mother, I need to get back, and Tim has offered to drive me. Then Dad and you won't have to."

"We don't mind," said Ellen.

"Tim is insisting."

"OK. Come home when you can."

Margaret kissed her mother and then her grandmother. "I should be home in a few weeks."

Ellen looked across the church basement. She couldn't help noticing Joe. He watched intently as Margaret and Tim left. Even at that distance, she noticed the saddest expression on Joe's face. She couldn't help thinking he belonged with Margaret. But her children had to make their own decisions.

Chapter 27

"Aunt Ellen." Larry's voice summoned her back to reality. "I have a big favor to ask of you."

"Go ahead."

He pointed to Joan, sitting uncomfortably near the stairway. "I'm afraid Joan's baby might come at any moment. I need to get her to the hospital. Could you take care of Lowell? He's outside, playing with Michael."

Ellen did not hesitate. "Don't waste a minute. We don't want your baby born in a church basement or on the road. Go!"

"Thanks a million!" Larry stooped to kiss his aunt. "You're an angel."

After Larry had left, Ellen turned to her mother-in-law. "This is one of those days when everything seems to be happening at once."

At that moment Victoria returned. "Mother, I think it's time for me to get you home. I need to get back home too. There's always schoolwork to do."

"I'm glad you could be here for this celebration," said Ellen. "It's been a special time for Johnie and all of us."

Victoria moved over and whispered in Ellen's ear. "I just saw Jeff go outside. He was a little wobbly. I'm afraid he's been drinking."

"I guess we all know about that. I don't know where that's going to end."

Victoria's dark sharp features showed more than ever. "I think Carol's made a big mistake. And now she has to live with it."

Ellen knew Victoria was right. "She and Jeff need our prayers."

Victoria abruptly helped her mother get up. As they left, she assured Ellen, "I'll do my part too—with prayer and in any other way I can."

At this point Ellen noticed that the women in the kitchen had finished washing dishes, and most of the people had left the church basement. She needed to find Matthew and the boys and leave for home. As Victoria and her mother exited the church basement, Carol entered. Ellen could tell immediately that her daughter was upset. "Where's Jeff?" she asked her mother. "I can't seem to find him."

"Is Andy OK?" Ellen asked, not yet wanting to repeat Victoria's suspicions.

"The baby is sound asleep. He's not like his father." Then she added, "I'm afraid Jeff's been drinking again."

Ellen was all too aware of this fact. "This can't keep going on. We have to do something," she cautioned.

Beyond the Darkness

Carol moved close to her mother. "I'm afraid. Sometimes I don't know what to do." Ellen wanted to take her daughter into her arms and say everything would be all right, but she knew that might not be the case.

Johnie felt tired but elated from the celebration. Many had left by midafternoon, but a number of friends still remained both inside and outside Oak Ridge Church. In every sense of the word, it had been a celebration of Johnie's return to life and living. Having been the center of things, he now felt tired, but he had thoroughly enjoyed the people and the entire event. He felt truly welcome back home.

As he walked down the steps of the church, Johnie glanced toward a car and saw Jeff standing beside it. He knew only a little about Jeff, and despite the fears his family had about the man, Johnie wanted to get to know him better. After all Jeff was his brother-in-law. He walked briskly toward the car and called out, "Hello, Jeff. I didn't get to talk with you before."

Jeff grunted a greeting. "Are sure you want to see me? You've got all these good friends around."

"You are my brother-in-law. And I know you've been through a lot—with your wounds from battle."

"People don't really care about that—about how you feel."

"Yes, people care. I know some of what you've been through. I've been through some dark times myself."

Jeff opened the car door and reached in, bring out a flask. "Here, have some. This is my friend."

"No, thank you. That's not your friend. I know a lot of soldiers got into the habit of drinking, but liquor is nobody's friend."

Jeff smirked. "Well, this is mine." He took a big swallow.

Johnie wanted to grab the flask out of Jeff's hands and empty it, but he momentarily refrained himself, wanting to try to reason with the young man. "Jeff, please don't do this to my sister. Drinking is not the answer."

"Your sister's not perfect, no angel. In fact, she's something of a devil. Otherwise, why do you think she'd give in to me so easily?"

Chapter 27

Johnie felt an anger he had not experienced since fighting down in the trenches. His fists tightened. "I know she's not perfect, but she's my sister. If you do anything to hurt her, you'll have me to deal with. I'm a lot bigger and stronger than you—and I'm sober."

"Come now, brother, don't get so serious on me. We need to relax and forget the war and the fighting."

"That bottle is not the answer. Liquor makes everything worse."

"Come now, try it."

"I've tried enough to know. I've seen too much of the drinking life and how it destroys men."

Jeff put down the flask and reached for his keys, but Johnie grabbed them. "You're not driving home." Jeff started to reach for his keys, but he stumbled back. Johnie opened the back door and pushed Jeff inside the car. He didn't resist. "I'm getting my sister," Johnie told him. "I'll drive you all home."

Johnie hurried toward the church. Beside the door stood Glenn Robertson. "Son, I have to admire you. Jeffrey Grant is a jerk. He deserved a good punch for the way he's been acting."

"I came mighty close."

Glenn reached over and patted him on the shoulder. "Son, you're a real hero in my book. Not just a war hero. You're a hero here at home."

"Funny, I'm afraid I don't feel much like a hero."

Matthew yawned and turned off the radio as the living room clock chimed nine times. The telephone rang its three long, and Ellen hurried into the kitchen to answer. Matthew listened intently; people did not use the telephone at this hour except for something urgent. Most farmers were getting ready for bed to rise before the dawn. He managed to hear Ellen repeat the words, "A girl."

Little Michael had been ready for bed at the usual eight o'clock hour, and Joe had said little that evening and quietly gone off to bed. That left Ellen, Johnie, and Matthew sitting and talking and listening to the radio.

Ellen returned to the living room. "That was Larry. He and Joan have a beautiful baby girl—seven pounds, two ounces. Her name is Elizabeth Joan."

Beyond the Darkness

Johnie smiled. "They named her after Grandma. That is great. Grandma will smile and say they shouldn't have."

"She can be a playmate for Jeffrey Andrew," added Ellen. "A whole new generation is coming along. This generation will remember nothing of the war."

Johnie stood and began to pace. "I hope they never have to go through another war like this one."

Matthew had his own fears about another war. "The next one could be far more deadly. We could destroy half the world."

Ellen rose. "Let's not talk about this. It's bedtime."

"You're right. Morning comes far too fast," agreed Matthew.

"Dad," announced Johnie, "you let Joe and me do the chores. I still remember how to milk cows."

"No, son," Matthew objected. "You need to get your rest. Remember what the doctor said about plenty of rest. That's part of your recovery."

"We'll see. One of these mornings, I'll be out there."

Johnie continued to pace instead of heading upstairs. Ellen watched her son and asked, "What's wrong, Johnie? You seem agitated."

Johnie hesitated then told his mother, "It's Carol. I'm concerned about her. Maybe it's more about Jeff."

"Yes," said Ellen, "we know he's been drinking."

Johnie doubled his fists. Matthew saw the pain and anger in his face. Johnie's whole body stiffened as if he were ready for battle. "When I saw Jeff half drunk and talking the way he did," Johnie confessed, "I wanted to punch him out. I had such terrible anger and hate. I was out of control."

Matthew understood the anger within his son. He had felt the same way. Yet his wife had a way of smoothing over a situation. She stepped over to her son and gently but firmly reminded him, "All we can do is to be here for Carol and the baby. We can help and encourage, but Jeff has to find the solution to his own problems."

Johnie almost shouted, "I know! And I understand the terrible things that go through Jeff's mind. I've got to help. I want to help."

"You can help. You can talk to him and help him understand." She took his hand and gently said, "But for now, you need to rest. It's late."

"As usual, you're right, Mother."

"Son, I know civilian life is not easy. We're here for you."

Chapter 27

"Thanks, Mother." Johnie stooped and kissed his mother, then reached over to touch his father's shoulder before turning away to head for bed.

Matthew watched Johnie walk up the stairs to his room. "I wish I could hold him and shelter him from these terrible problems."

"Only the Lord can shelter us," his wife reminded him.

Chapter 28

Matthew felt it in his bones. A winter snowstorm was coming. The animals displayed unusual restlessness in the barn. Something about the whole atmosphere announced a storm. He didn't mind storms once they came, but the time before meant tension in both people and animals.

Joe had been a godsend these past months. Even now, with Johnie back home, Joe was a dependable worker. He was always there for chores when Matthew needed to be away. And Johnie wasn't ready to assume many responsibilities around the farm. He was still recovering and needed rest.

Matthew enjoyed company but often needed time to be alone. Joe was working on a carpentry project in the granary, and Johnie was helping him, so this was a good time to check the conditions of the empty brooder houses and the stoves. In another six or eight weeks, it would be time to start raising the pullets.

Life on the farm had its rhythms. In a sense winter was the quiet, dormant time. But dormant times really were a quiet preparation for another season of growth and change. Matthew always looked forward to spring and new life.

Matthew did the necessary checking. He could see several floorboards needed replacing. He would go to the lumberyard later this week. The water fountains and feeding troughs must be cleaned. Last fall was such a busy time, he hadn't had time to finish those projects.

As Matthew returned and walked toward the house, a familiar car drove up. Instantly he realized Glenn had decided to stop by. They hadn't visited for several weeks. As the two found a spot to sit and talk, Matthew sensed Glenn had something on his mind. Difficult situations were not easy for either of these two friends to bring out in the open. So after some aimless talk, Matthew decided to be forthright. "Glenn, I get the feeling something's bothering you. What is it?"

Glenn began to hem and haw. "Well, you're right. It's about my Tim and your Margaret."

Matthew realized he should have known. "What's up? Tim seems to be visiting my daughter quite often."

Glenn looked away from his friend. "It's this way. Tim still wants to settle down. He has a chance to buy Ed and Mary's farm. He loves Margaret and he wants to get married soon and move to the farm."

"We've discussed this before. My daughter's awfully young. I don't think she's ready to get married. She wants to teach a few years."

Glenn stiffened and his voice became sharper. "That's the problem. Your daughter shouldn't be stringing Tim along if she isn't serious."

Those words hurt sensitive Matthew. "My daughter does not string a fellow along if she's not interested," he stated firmly.

"Matthew, I'd like you to talk to Margaret. Tim has proposed—wants her to keep the ring. She needs to accept his proposal."

"No, I'll say nothing. If Margaret wants to talk, I'll listen. But this choice is my daughter's to make. I'll have no part of forcing her to decide."

Glenn remained adamant. "I think you should talk with your daughter. As my friend you can do that much."

Matthew felt a sharp pain in his chest, one he hadn't felt for some time. He coughed before answering, "I'll think about it."

"Do more than think."

Matthew felt increasingly uncomfortable with the conversation, so he sought to change the subject. "How about coming in for a cup of coffee?"

Glenn turned away to walk toward his car. "No, thank you, not this time. I have work to do."

Chapter 28

With those words Glenn left. Matthew wondered if he might be losing the special closeness he and Glenn had. This was a friend he did not want to lose.

Ellen watched her husband when he didn't think she noticed. She knew she needed to get him to visit Dr. Baker. She'd seen him outside with Glenn when he placed his hand on his heart. Perhaps today she could manage to get Matthew into the doctor's office.

As the men finished their dessert after noon dinner, Ellen announced, "Matthew, it's time you have that checkup. I called Dr. Baker and he's expecting you."

Joe quickly responded, "Yes, Dad, I've noticed some things. You need that checkup."

Ellen was getting used to the way Joe called them "Mom and Dad." She liked having this young man treat them that way—a special kind of love and respect.

Johnie added his agreement. "Dad, you're not so young anymore. We want you around for a long time."

Matthew quickly changed the subject, making reference to the weather. "I think a storm's coming. The air is heavy. I expect it will start snowing any time now."

"We'll get you back before the storm gets bad," said Johnie. "You're not going to get out of a visit to Dr. Baker. We're going to town."

"And if you're really late," said Joe, "I'm here to take care of Michael and do the milking and other chores."

Ellen couldn't help thinking of how Joe had come to the rescue when Matthew went through his serious ulcer attack. He came to the family just when the Andersons needed him. And now, in return, he needed this family.

Ellen washed the dishes while Johnie and Matthew cleaned up and changed into clothes suitable for a trip to town. No self-respecting farmer would go to town in his barn clothes—unless he was doing farm business.

An hour later, Dr. Baker poked and probed his patient. Ellen sat nearby to be sure Matthew reported his pains and that she got the report as well. Matthew might be all too inclined to ignore what he didn't want to hear.

After what seemed an endless amount of probing and questions and comments, Dr. Baker told Matthew he could get back into his clothes and sit down.

"Matthew, I think we can help your situation. But you have to remember you're not as young as you used to be. By the way, how old are you?"

"My age goes with the year. It's 1946, so I'll be forty-six in May."

"First, your blood pressure is higher than it should be. I'll give you some medication that should help. Hopefully that will take care of some problems." Dr. Baker stopped and looked more serious. "However, I have noticed another problem that I haven't told you about."

Ellen's heart leapt up into her throat. She experienced momentary fear that something could happen to Matthew.

"Fire away, Doc. I might as well know the truth," Matthew said.

"So far as I can tell, you have a slight enlargement of the heart. Many people live for years with such a condition if they take care of themselves."

"I'll make sure he does," Ellen assured Dr. Baker. "He has a good hired man, and Johnie is home now."

"What does that mean, an enlarged heart?" asked Matthew.

Dr. Baker launched into a detailed medical explanation and then added, "Matthew, you are in good shape otherwise. You're thin, and that's not bad at all. You have good muscle tone. Your biggest enemy will be anything that upsets you. Stress can do terrible things to people. Many doctors don't realize the seriousness of stress."

"Things are going quite well, now that Johnie's safely home."

Dr. Baker chuckled. "That Johnie is your pride and joy. I suspect he'll take over the farm in a few years."

"I hope so."

"And," Dr. Baker added, "be careful about overdoing the lifting. Avoid some of the heavy lifting and let Joe help. Take more time and care when you do lift things. Slow down."

"I'll try."

Dr. Baker's tone became somewhat more demanding. "You better do more than try. You better do exactly what I am saying."

Ellen knew she might not have an easy task in front of her. "I'll work on that," she offered.

Chapter 28

"Now," said Dr. Baker, "I want to see you for regular checkups. I'll see you in a month to determine how the blood pressure medication is working. Otherwise I just want to remind you to slow down."

When they left the doctor's office, snowflakes were coming down with more frequency and force. Suddenly Johnie ran to meet his parents. "Something's happened. Get in the car. We need to go over to Carol's."

Ellen sensed the urgency in her son's words. They got into the old Chevy and Johnie turned to her and said, "Mother, we'll let you off at Carol's. She's pretty upset. Jeff's taken off, and he may be in trouble."

Ellen wanted to say that was nothing new, but she remained quiet as Johnie continued, "Jeff took off this morning. Carol is certain that he left for the Grant's lake cabin about ten miles east of here. His parents tried to drive there, but they had to turn around and come back because of the snow. Carol is frantic."

"What's the problem?" asked Matthew. "Other than a young man who can't control his drinking habits?"

"The cabin's closed for the winter. The roads may hardly be passable as you get into that area. There's a report from a farmer that a car went into a ditch near there. It was probably Jeff's. This weather is dangerous if you're not prepared."

Ellen looked to her husband. "And you, my dear, should not be out in a storm. You need to watch yourself."

"Tell me about the checkup," Johnie requested. "I'm afraid the problem with Jeff put that out of my mind."

Ellen explained the doctor's report with emphasis on Matthew's need to slow down and take life a bit easier. Her husband continued his objections as they drove toward Carol's house. As they stopped out in front, Johnie suggested, "Dad, maybe you should stay here. Larry's coming. We'll take his car."

Matthew objected. "No, I'm not some invalid. I'll go."

Ellen knew there was nothing she could do to stop her husband. "Darling, be careful." She turned to Johnie. "Don't let him overdo."

"Dad, you can stay in the car. Keep it running from time to time."

Just then Larry pulled up to next to their car and got out in a hurry. "Come on and get in. I think we're set! I've thrown in extra coveralls and coats. There are some heavy boots as well. We have to keep warm."

Ellen gave her husband a hug and cautioned Johnie, "Watch your father, and take care of yourself."

Beyond the Darkness

Matthew and Johnie got into Larry's '39 Ford and the men drove away. Ellen whispered a prayer for their safety and for finding Jeff, then hurried up the steps and into her daughter's small home. "Darling, I'm here."

Carol entered the small living room. "Oh, Mother, I don't know what to do." Her eyes were red from crying.

Then Ellen noticed something else. "What's happened? That bruise on your cheek?"

Carol covered her cheek and mumbled something.

"Tell me the truth, Carol. Something is terribly wrong."

Carol dried her tears. "We had a fight—a terrible fight. Jeff had been drinking. I don't think he knew what he was doing. He grabbed a hunting rifle, said he'd go to the cabin and hunt rabbits and live by himself."

"Oh no," comforted Ellen. "There's a storm out there—looks like a blizzard. It could be dangerous. The roads are filling with snow."

"Yes, I know, Mother. The roads aren't open to the cabins in that area."

Ellen gently placed her hand on her daughter's bruised cheek. "But how did this happen? You can't go on this way."

"I suppose it was my fault. I was being stubborn."

Ellen felt anger rising within her. "No husband hits his wife. You can't live like this."

"Mother, I love him so much, but he makes me terribly angry."

At that moment the baby decided to announce he was wet and hungry. "Carol, you sit down. I'll take care of changing Andy." As she moved to the other room with her grandson, Ellen realized the problem with Jeffrey was far bigger than she anticipated. "Lord," she whispered, "I'm afraid I failed my daughter. Please show me what to do now. Protect Matthew and the others and keep them from danger."

Outside, the wind and snow increased. This was a full-scale Minnesota blizzard, a storm that could destroy life.

A drive that would take fifteen or twenty minutes during good driving conditions took more than forty-five. Wind and snow increased in amount and force as Larry drove in the direction of the lake cabins. Johnie tensely looked ahead out the frosty windshield to warn his cousin if he got too close the edge of the road. Finally they reached the back road to the east

Chapter 28

lake cabins. The road had been opened to the last farmhouse, but even that road was becoming difficult to navigate.

"This looks bad," said Matthew from the backseat. "Are you sure this is where he went?"

Larry kept his eyes on the road as he answered, "Carol seemed certain of what Jeff would do. And this is the road to the Grant cabin. Also, a farmer reported a car in the ditch near here."

They reached the peak of a hill. The snow had blown clear, leaving an icy surface on the road. Johnie could see a car in the ditch below. "There it is!"

Larry guided his car to a stop and the three men quickly got out. Johnie hurried down to the ditch. "This is Jeff's car. I hope he's here." But when he opened the door, he called out, "He's not here. He must have decided to walk."

"I see tracks along the road!" shouted Larry. "They must be Jeff's."

The wind blew like sharp knives against Johnie's face, as he looked in the direction of the tracks still visible in the snow. "He won't last long out in this weather if he doesn't find some shelter."

"I see he's stayed along the road," shouted Larry above the noise of the storm. "Let's drive on and watch those tracks and see where they lead us."

As they drove, snowflakes blasted against the windshield. Johnie opened the side window so he could see the tracks. Soon the open area changed to woods. The road here had not been plowed. Someone had driven there recently, but those tire tracks were filling in quickly. Jeff's tracks disappeared and then reappeared farther down the road.

Johnie looked ahead on the road for more tracks, but everything looked white. Then a lull in the storm revealed a gigantic snowdrift.

"I don't think we can drive any further." Larry opened the door. "We'll go on foot."

Johnie got out and stepped into the deep snow "I see his tracks—just barely."

"Uncle Matthew, why don't you turn the car around? When we come back, we may need to hurry back to town."

Matthew hesitated but got into the driver's seat.

Johnie and Larry trudged on, stumbling along, following the tracks that now were barely visible. Then the tracks disappeared altogether. Johnie tried to shield himself against the driving wind. "We better find him quickly or he's done for. Unless he's found shelter."

Beyond the Darkness

"Look!" shouted Larry. "The tracks go into the woods!"

Larry went on ahead, picking up on Jeff's trail again. Johnie followed. In this heavily wooded area, the tracks were more readily visible. The storm had abated—at least for the moment.

"I think he's heading away from the lake and the cabins!" Larry's words became muffled in the wind.

"We should have called Sheriff Walker!" Johnie called to Larry as he came up beside his cousin. "I remember how helpful he was when my sisters were lost years ago."

"I called him. He and his deputies were involved in another search. He warned us to be careful. He'll come this way when he can."

At this point darkness was settling over the countryside. Johnie had to admit the landscape had a strange, almost ghostly kind of beauty.

Larry continued to lead the way, using his flashlight to pinpoint the barely visible tracks. "Jeff seems to have lost his sense of direction," he noted.

Just then Johnie spotted something dark just ahead, and both men ran to the spot. Larry reached down and picked up a rifle and leaned it against a tree. "At least he hasn't had an accident with his rifle."

Larry pointed his flashlight forward and turned it in several directions. Off to the side Johnie saw something else dark, and the vision stopped him in his tracks. Johnie stood statuelike, unable to move. Larry hurried on past him to the shadowy object. "It's Jeffrey." He leaned down.

Johnie's mind began to play tricks on him. He was in two places: in a cold wooded area not far from Lake View, and at the same time in the midst of danger on the battlefield.

"Johnie, we're too late. His body is cold. Jeff is dead."

For the first time since his return home, Johnie felt a hazy unreality creep over him. In that moment he was back in the trenches, facing the enemy. He looked down at the rifle, wanting to pick it up in self-defense. Then he took a second look and backed away in revulsion. For a moment he wanted to run as far and as fast as he could.

"Johnie, are you OK?" called Larry. "There isn't anything we can do." He turned back to face his cousin.

Johnie's mind quickly returned to the present harsh reality. "I'm sorry. For a split second I was back on the battlefield."

Larry placed his arm around Johnie's shoulder. "It's too late for Jeff. There's nothing we can do. Let's go back to the car."

Chapter 28

Johnie remembered his talk with Jeff. He wished he had been kinder to his brother-in-law. After all, both of them had experienced those awful horrors of war. But now it was too late.

As they moved back toward the road, Johnie heard the familiar sounds of a tractor, a John Deere tractor, no less. He should have known his father would not have been idle.

For the next hour Johnie had the sensation of being there but not really being present. His father had gone to the closest farm. The farmer had taken his tractor and sled and they went back to pick up Jeff's body. They left him outside the farmhouse, ready for the undertaker.

The hazy unreality of death persisted for Johnie during the next hours. He merely went through the motions of walking, moving, getting in the car.

Matthew experienced a new kind of strength as they all drove back to Lake View. He saw what the discovery of Jeff's death had done to Johnie. Johnie seemed to be all right, but his mind seemed far away again. Matthew knew he had to be strong for his son, for his daughter Carol, and for his entire family.

When they drove up to Carol's home, Matthew turned to his nephew and son. "I'll go in. I think I need to break the news."

"I'm afraid the Grants have to be told too," said Larry. "I'll drive over and tell them. It'll be a terrible shock. He's their only child."

Matthew felt a deep concern for his son. "Are you all right, Johnie?"

"I will be. I just need time to think things through. I want to stay out here for a few minutes. Then I'll come in."

Larry drove off. Matthew hesitated briefly and then walked up the steps to Carol's house. He was about to open the door when Ellen opened it and welcomed him in. "What's the news?" she asked.

Matthew stumbled over his next words. "Bad news. We found Jeff." He stopped, afraid to go on. After what seemed an eternity, he flatly stated, "He was frozen to death."

"Oh, no!" was all Ellen could say. Her stunned silence spoke volumes.

Beyond the Darkness

Carol, holding her baby, remained remarkably calm. At first she said nothing. Then she looked down at her baby and spoke to him. "Little Jeffrey Andrew, you and I are now alone. We have a world to face."

Matthew wanted to gather Carol in his arms the way he had when she was a child. He wanted to protect her once more from those harsh realities of life. Ellen placed her arm around her daughter. "Come, Carol. You and Andy come home with us. You need family. We need to be together."

"Mother, Dad," she sobbed, "I don't know how I can go on. But I'm going to have to make it on my own."

Carol held Andy close to her heart. The baby was sound asleep.

Matthew repeated Ellen's words, "You come home with us."

"I suppose that's all I can do right now."

Matthew held his little grandson as Ellen and Carol packed some necessities. For a moment he wondered about Johnie. Was he all right? The darkness of night and the blizzard were outward indications of the turmoil of his son's spirit after the horrible ordeal.

Johnie came into the house just before Matthew felt he needed to search for him. Finally the blizzard abated enough so that the family could return home to the farm.

Several hours later as Matthew got into bed, he told Ellen, "It's a miracle we made it back. I can't believe Jeff is gone . . . but now Carol and Andy are safe. Johnie is home. And Michael and Joe have been here all the time."

"Yes, we're warm and safe from the storm."

Chapter 29

March 1946

The days that followed were as numbing as the blizzard and cold. Jeffrey Grant's death left family and friends with many regrets. Regrets that such a young life should come to a tragic end. Regrets from some individuals that they had not understood or done more to help Jeff after he came home from the war. Regrets that life did not always seem fair. Yet regrets and sorrow eventually gave way to life. Life and the seasons kept moving forward.

Several weeks passed. Following the February blizzard, cold weather kept people indoors as much as possible. Carol and young Andy stayed at the Anderson home. Ellen rather enjoyed having a baby to fuss over. March moved along, and with it came the spring thaws and the arrival of a new farm season.

One afternoon late in March, Ellen found herself annoyed with the problems of the radio heroine on "The Right to Happiness." This soap opera heroine never found happiness. *Things are rarely that bad in real life,* Ellen thought, so she turned off the radio and returned to her mending. A woman's work was truly never done.

"I've made a decision," announced Carol as she entered the kitchen. "I can't stay here forever. I have to make a life for myself."

"I understand. But you have your baby to think of."

"That's what I've thought about. Yesterday when I went into town, I went to Kay's Café and talked with Kay. I can get that upstairs apartment and work at the café. I'll keep my baby right there with me."

"Are you sure that's a good idea?"

"I can look after Andy at the same time. When I went there yesterday, the customers just loved him."

Ellen wanted to say more but she knew Carol. When this daughter was determined, she did exactly what she wanted to do. "Your father and I will always be here to help when we're needed," Ellen told her.

"I know that, and I couldn't have made it through this ordeal without you."

"What about Mrs. Grant? How is she doing?"

"I've seen very little of her since the funeral. I think she hates me. She blames me for taking her son away from her."

"I'm sorry she feels that way. But doesn't she want to see her grandson?"

"I guess not. She says he reminds her too much of her loss."

"That will change." Ellen knew that in time Mrs. Grant might even respond the opposite way—by using her grandson as a substitute for her lost son.

Ellen hesitated to ask Carol more questions, but finally inquired, "Do you think you want to work in a restaurant for the next years when little Andy is growing up? Is that what you want?"

"No, I've been doing some thinking."

Ellen waited for her daughter to go on. She noticed in Carol's face a new maturity that accompanied the sadness. With her once-more-petite figure, brilliant blue eyes, and long hair with its reddish tint, Carol had become a beautiful young woman. The boys had always been interested, but would a young man be interested in an instant family?

"You know, Mother, I'm pretty good at typing. And I can work really fast with numbers. I think I could learn to be a secretary and bookkeeper."

During the next minutes, Ellen saw evidence of that new maturity in Carol—a maturity she'd thought would never come. In other ways though, Carol needed her mother more than ever.

Chapter 29

Matthew sat down on the feed bin. In spite of a sudden spring snowstorm the night before, the weather had warmed up enough for the cattle to remain outside. That meant less work cleaning the barn. Freshly fallen spring snow seemed to energize him, but it was now time for an afternoon cup of coffee.

Joe stood nearby, and Matthew sensed the young man wanted to talk, so he walked over and stood next to him before heading into the house. After some comfortable silence, he told Matthew, "You know, I've been doing a lot of thinking. It's time for me to get on with my life."

"You can stay here as long as you want. I'll build up my herd of milking cattle and add more beef cattle as well. There'll always be plenty of work." But Matthew noticed a faraway look in the young man's eyes. The time in the Japanese prison camp had taken its toll. Joe needed more time for healing. This young man, so very much alone, needed family. Yet perhaps he also needed new purpose, to have his own family.

Joe went on in his quiet, unassuming way. "I'm twenty-five. I should think about being on my own—with a farm of my own. Johnie will soon be ready to take responsibility for this place. Plus, the manager at the elevator in River Falls says there's a job for me."

Matthew had always assumed Johnie wanted to remain on the family farm. Yet during these last weeks Johnie had often seemed distant. His mind was elsewhere.

"I can use you right here, Joe. I've depended on you through all the problems of the past weeks. But I don't want to take advantage of you."

"Oh, you would never do that, Mr. Anderson . . . I mean, Dad."

"As long as Ellen and I are alive, you'll have a place here to come back to."

"That means a lot to me. I'll see you through spring work at least."

Matthew reached down for his pocket watch and checked the time. "I believe we're late for afternoon coffee. Ellen probably wonders what's happened."

During coffee time, Matthew became aware more than ever of the changes on the horizon for his family. Though Joe said nothing more about leaving, the young man's restlessness was evident. Joe needed to find a life for himself. He needed to continue to adjust to civilian life.

Carol began to talk about her plans as they all sat in the kitchen. As he listened, Matthew couldn't help wondering whether she could handle these new responsibilities life had handed her. After all, she should be graduating from high school in the spring. *She's too young to handle the problems of being a widow and single mother,* he thought as he watched her leave the room to go check on her son.

As he sipped coffee, Matthew also thought of Johnie, who had not joined the family for their afternoon break. Johnie was a big help with farmwork, but he often took long walks or went away on short trips. Matthew knew his favorite son needed to sort out his life. He prayed that Johnie would somehow come out of these trials a stronger person.

Returning from school, Michael suddenly burst into the kitchen, interrupting Matthew's thoughts. "Daddy, why don't we have a milking machine? Jack's dad has a machine."

Ellen looked to Matthew to answer this question.

"Son, milking machines cost money. Right now, we don't have that money."

"Why?"

"It just happens we don't have the money."

"Our farm's nicer than theirs."

Ellen interjected, "We have other expenses."

"Someday," said Matthew, "we'll have a milking machine. And you can help. There's still work even when you have machines."

"I can't wait." Michael gulped down his glass of milk and ate his cookie, then ran up to his room to change clothes.

"He's growing so fast," commented Ellen. "Before we know it, he'll be in high school."

"Sometimes I wish time would stand still," Matthew replied.

"I think of that line from the hymn. 'Time and change are busy ever.'"

Matthew couldn't help thinking of their changing farm life. He looked tenderly at his wife. "I think of the hard work a farmer does. It's not an easy life. A farmer takes many chances and gambles on the weather. I can't do anything else because I don't know anything else. But I wonder if I want this life for my children."

Ellen's eyes spoke a tender understanding. "It's been a good life for us."

"Yes, but what about for our children in the future? I know James will have a different life. But Johnie, what about him? I know he loves this place."

Chapter 29

"I think we always want an easier life for our children. We don't want them to have to face the problems we faced. But in this life there will always be problems."

Matthew's eyes became moist. "I think of the hurt Johnie has been through. It's hard for him right now to get back to normal civilian life."

"The Lord will see us through . . . and Johnie."

And once more it was time for milking cows. The routines of life never ended, always moving forward. For Matthew, his farm chores put life into perspective. It was reality.

Johnie lost track of time. He had been walking along the township road and then across fields and up and down hills. Even in winter and early spring, this area was beautiful. The hills, lakes, and fields held many memories. He had gone far beyond those hills, but this was home. This was the place he loved. Perhaps he would spend the rest of his life right here.

He approached Oak Ridge Church. Suddenly his mind again was filled with images of the battlefield. Gunfire from all sides. Men in trenches. Men nearby gasping for breath. The screams of men in pain. Death and dying all around.

"Why, Lord?" he said aloud. "Why did You allow this to happen? Why the death of the innocent? Young soldiers. Innocent women and children. Why? Why?"

He stood on the steps of the church, looking at the beautiful landscape all around him, covered with patches of white from the sudden spring storm. There was something so pure and white about freshly fallen snow. Could you find a more perfect place on this earth? This must be where he should be.

Then his mind took a sudden turn. He saw himself just a few weeks earlier. He had stood in the woods blanketed in darkness with heavy snow falling, staring at Jeff's frozen body. When he had seen that body, he too froze in time and place. He could not move. The truth was too terrible to face.

In some ways Jeff had been through the same war experiences as Johnie, and yet Jeff's terrible remembrances had driven him to despair and drinking. Perhaps that same experience had driven him to take advantage of a young girl. Carol may not have been perfect, but she wasn't ready to be a wife and mother.

"How can I face this turmoil?" Johnie said aloud as he opened the church door, moved through the entry, and walked into the sanctuary. Though the large room was cold, Johnie felt a warmth and serenity. The familiar place helped him recall a host of childhood memories.

Immediately the large picture in the front of the sanctuary seemed to come to life. The three disciples looking up as Christ began his ascension into heaven brought Johnie an unusual sense of peace. He became one of those men, witnessing Christ rise up in front of their very eyes. Johnie felt a real presence that he could not explain.

He moved forward slowly, not wanting to lose that sense of reverence and awe. He found himself before the altar, where he knelt. The words below the picture flashed before him—those Swedish words that he knew as "Holy, Holy, Holy." He sensed Christ was present with him in this small country church.

Time stood still awhile, until a heaviness descended over Johnie. The evil and darkness of the war, the killing, the physical injuries, the mental and spiritual injuries, the disruption and destruction of lives—all pressed down upon him. The burden was too much to bear. In that next moment he found himself sobbing uncontrollably. As the tears freely flowed out of him, he felt the tension disappear and his body relax. A spiritual and emotional healing was taking place.

With the heaviness lifted, Johnie felt a new and sudden freedom. He stood and looked around the familiar church building. The shadows of afternoon lengthened, and the sunset rays reflected in a stained-glass window. There stood Christ, the Good Shepherd, holding the lost sheep. Yet it was not the Christ in the picture, but His presence that came down and touched him. Johnie saw himself as that lost sheep that had been found. He sat down in the back pew, suspended in time. He had no idea how long he remained there.

Eventually the sense of reverence and God's presence faded. He looked at his watch. "It's time to go home. They'll be worried about me," he said aloud.

He stood for several more moments at the back of the sanctuary, looking at the windows and their pictures and the picture at the front of the church. "Lord, where do I go from here? What about my future?"

Chapter 29

The voice he heard was not audible, but it came as clearly as if the words were shouted: *"Lo, I am with you always. I will show you the way."*

He closed the door and went out into the darkness of a March evening. A phrase seemed to repeat itself in his thoughts and in his heart: "Wait on the Lord."

"Should I take the car and look for Johnie?" asked Joe. "He's been gone a long time."

Matthew looked across the table at his wife. He was usually the one to worry about the kids. "Maybe you should," he answered Joe, "but I know he wanted to be alone—to have time to think."

They had finished supper. Ellen had made blueberry pie, one of Johnie's favorites. A large piece remained on the pie plate. Michael had disappeared into his room to play with his Tinkertoys. He was constructing a large windmill.

Joe left to find Johnie, leaving Matthew and Ellen alone. "There's something I didn't tell you," began Matthew. "When I was in town this morning, I stopped at the doctor's office. My blood pressure is much better. The medicine is working."

"Thank God."

"I guess I may need to be around for a while. Michael's only seven. I still have a job to do as father."

"Aren't you the one who said a man always needs a father? You've missed your father so very much."

"A mother is no less important. I'm so thankful that we still have Ma."

Ellen hesitated. Matthew knew she had something important to say, and he also realized he needed to tell his wife about Joe's possible future plans. But he waited for his wife to continue.

"Matthew," began Ellen, "Carol talked with me today. She's made a decision."

"I figured so."

"She says she needs a place of her own. She's moving back to town and she'll work at the café. But I'm not sure it's the best thing for her."

"Carol has a way of making up her own mind."

Ellen began to clear the table. "As a mother, I know I have to let go. Sometimes I've felt I failed Carol. But I have to let her go out on her own. She is a mother now."

Matthew decided it was his turn to tell Ellen about Joe. "Joe's restless. He's talking about leaving too—going out on his own. He said something about an elevator job in River Falls."

"I'm not surprised."

Matthew and Ellen sat for a while longer and talked quietly about many things. Soon Johnie entered the kitchen, followed by Joe. "I'm sorry if I worried you," Johnie told his parents. "I took a long walk—as far as the church."

"That's three miles. You did a lot of walking."

"And a lot of thinking. I feel better now."

Ellen warmed the food and Johnie ate with gusto, thoroughly enjoying his piece of blueberry pie.

Late that night, Matthew and Ellen talked of the many changes that were coming for their children. "Many things change," he observed, "but Jesus Christ is the same yesterday and today and forever."

"How right you are, Matthew."

"And Johnie is truly back with us."

Matthew welcomed the peace and sleep that healed the hurts and cares of the day.

Chapter 30

May 1946

Matthew knew this day would come—Joe was leaving for his job in River Falls. Spring work was finished, and Johnie would be around to help. There was no reason for Joe to stay.

Matthew strolled along the edge of the yard with its border of lilacs. Those lilacs had just begun to bloom. The fragrance was like none other. He should be happy, but he felt a heaviness and darkness. He could not get beyond the dark thoughts this afternoon. Joe would be alone in River Falls—completely alone. Matthew remembered the autumn he'd left home to work in the Dakotas. The threshing crew included a group of rowdies he had nothing in common with. He had felt complete emptiness and loneliness. Now Joe might face that same loneliness.

He was concerned about Johnie as well. His son still seemed to have many mood swings. One moment he seemed happy to be working in the great outdoors. At other times he was deeply discouraged—even despondent. In the past Johnie spoke out when anything was wrong. These days the young man was completely different—quieter, more pensive.

Matthew began to walk toward the house. Joe walked slowly down the steps carrying his duffel bag along with his suit and dress shirt. He was packed and ready to go. "I guess I'll be on my way," he said.

Beyond the Darkness

Matthew wanted to take this young man in his arms and yell out that he should stay. Instead he told Joe, "We'll miss you. Remember, you're family. And we're only thirty miles from River Falls."

"I know that, Dad. I don't think I could have made it this far if hadn't been for you and the family. I'll be back to visit."

Ellen appeared on the porch steps. "There will always be a chair at the table and a bed to sleep in."

"Thanks."

Matthew sensed that Joe wanted to say more, so she asked, "Are you sure you want to go? You have a place here."

"It's something I have to do."

Ellen walked down the steps into the yard to hug Joe. "You know how much we love you."

He turned away. "Yes . . ." Then he groped for his next words. "I suppose Margaret will be getting married any time now."

"She's not wearing an engagement ring," Ellen quickly replied.

"Tim said it was a matter of time."

Ellen smiled. "What Tim says and what Margaret says might not be the same. And Margaret has the last word."

"Margaret will make some man a wonderful wife." Joe blushed even as he said the words.

"You know you are very special to her. She had a crush on you before she was a teenager."

"I don't suppose she'd ever marry a dumb farmer like me—"

Both Matthew and Ellen began to interrupt him. Ellen let Matthew go on. "You're no dumb farmer. You're the best young farmer I know. You're a smart farmer. And don't be too sure about Tim and Margaret."

Once more Joe blushed. "I'd better be going."

"Remember," Ellen called to him. "She's not engaged."

Joe mumbled a good-bye, placed his duffel bag and clothes in the backseat, and drove away.

"He's too shy," said Ellen. "He lacks confidence."

Matthew knew exactly how Joe felt. This smart and pretty lady named Ellen still amazed him. She had seen something in him that no one else had.

Chapter 30

The last students had left the brick school. Margaret gathered their state board examinations and slid them into a large envelope to mail them. All the books were put away. The final records were complete. She would be back in September, but even so she wanted everything to be done right. The last teacher had left a mess.

As Margaret looked across the room, her thoughts turned to her own future, knowing she wanted to return to teach in this school the next fall, and knowing she was sure about something else as well. "I have made my decision," she said aloud to her empty classroom. "I will not marry Timothy Robertson. I cannot see spending the rest of my life with him. Besides, I don't love him."

She began to plan what she should do. She knew she should not lead Tim to believe she might change her mind. She had given back the ring, but he still seemed to hold out hope. At least that's what he was telling other people.

Margaret walked through the orderly, quiet room. The desks stood in neat rows, though the board members and others would come and do a thorough cleaning before school started in the fall. The water fountain was empty. The cloakroom and entry were empty of any leftover student possessions.

The place seemed ghostly, almost as if the students were still present. All at once she had an overwhelming desire to leave. This school year was over. Three months of summer lay before her, though one of those months she'd be in college classes in River Falls. She liked the idea that the state teachers' colleges came out and offered classes close by. She wanted to be a lifetime learner.

That evening Margaret made a phone call home with a request. It was, of course, her mother, who answered the phone. "Mother, could you and Dad come and get me tomorrow morning?"

Her mother appeared surprised. "I thought you usually had other transportation."

"I'll tell you about it tomorrow."

The following morning Margaret said her good-bye to Mrs. Cullen, who had been like a second mother during the past year. But Margaret was leaving only for the summer so the parting was temporary. She would return to board here in September.

When Mom and Dad came, Mrs. Cullen did the neighborly thing. She invited them in for coffee and her famous rolls with thick "yummy frosting." They visited awhile, and then as Margaret gathered her things to leave, Mrs. Cullen asked, "I thought your young gentleman friend would be coming to pick you up. Couldn't he come?"

Margaret realized she might as well tell all three at the same time. "I've made it clear to Tim that I want to teach another year. Another thing—I'm not in love with Tim Robertson. I have no ring, and I do not intend to marry him—not now or next year."

"That's definite enough," said her mother.

"Oh," said the kindly Mrs. Cullen, "there are several fine young men in this community who would make good husbands. I'll introduce you when you come back."

"Don't worry about that. I'm not ready for any serious relationship right now."

As they drove the twenty miles home, Margaret had questions for her parents. She needed to catch up on all the family news. Michael was growing up fast and spending time with Johnie. James would be coming home for a short break. Carol was busy with little Andy and her job at the café.

"By the way," added her father, "Joe left us yesterday. He's working in River Falls. He'll be at the elevator and feed store."

"Oh," she replied with disappointment and surprise. "He won't be around at home, then. But perhaps I'll see him in River Falls when I go for my class."

At the moment all Margaret could think about was a week at home. She could walk through the hills and valleys. She could play with Michael and perhaps spend a day with her nephew. The week to come would be glorious.

The Oak Ridge Church towered high above any trees or buildings in the area. Johnie had felt drawn back to the church again, and now he climbed the rickety stairway to the top of the steeple tower. Before him the bell stood, silent. He looked below and around. He could see the whole countryside with its lakes and fields, hills and valleys. During those awful days in Germany, he had dreamed of this place. He'd wanted to be home more than anything. But now, during this past week, Johnie experienced more restlessness. Though he loved the land of his home farm, he began to realize there might be other things he should be doing.

Chapter 30

Several miles in one direction he saw the old home place, the place where he had spent his first twelve or thirteen years of life. There he had known all the dreams and imaginations of childhood. Now his cousin Corrine and her husband lived there. And Grandma still lived in her little house next door.

Warren had been talking recently of taking a job in California, following Ed and Mary's family out west. Johnie wondered if this was a sign that he should consider farming the home place. He used to dream about living there and raising a family the way Dad had and Grandpa before him. There was something secure about living off the land. Grandpa used to say, "If you take care of the land, the land will take care of you."

As Johnie gazed at the home place and the surrounding beauty, he saw again that God did indeed reveal Himself in creation. He had always felt God's closeness in the outdoors. But this past week God had seemed distant.

Johnie walked around on the ledge, looking in all directions. If someone saw him, they might think he was about to jump. When he was going through his dark periods of depression and his nightmares, at times he had wished God would take him. Life was too awful to face. Now he needed a fresh sense of God's presence, like he'd felt in the church a few weeks back.

"God, where are You?" he spoke out loud. "I wish you'd take away this restlessness and wondering. I need to know where I'm going. Do I stay and farm with Dad? I always thought I wanted to run the farm."

From somewhere below a voice called out. "Watch out up there. Some of the boards on the ledge are loose. Watch out!"

Johnie looked below his feet and saw the loose boards. "I'm OK!" he yelled out. "I'm on my way down." He took one last look around the countryside. He was ready to return to the earth and ground level. When he came to the last step, Pastor Young met him. "Hello John Anderson. I've been wanting to talk with you."

"Pastor, I wasn't expecting you."

"Often I come out here to work on my sermon. I love this place."

The two men talked of routine matters until Johnie changed the subject. "Pastor, I've always wanted to be a farmer. But now I'm finding myself restless. I can't help feeling God may have something else for me."

Pastor Young waited for Johnie to continue.

Beyond the Darkness

"I've had some dark times when I didn't care whether I lived or died. I've seen how some people are destroyed by war and other circumstances. I've found the Lord—or the Lord found me. And I feel I may be beginning to find the answers for my future, but there's still uncertainty."

The pastor continued to listen, but this time Johnie began asking questions. "How do you ever know God's will? Do you think He has a specific task for me? If so, how do I know for certain what it is?"

Pastor Young smiled. Johnie couldn't help noticing that the pastor was only a few years older than he. He had keen blue eyes, youthful looks, and dark handsome features, which seemed to endear him to everyone. It could have been possible to take the two for brothers.

"How did you know you were supposed to be a pastor?" Johnie asked him.

"Everything in my life led me this way. I had some of the same feelings you have. I kept on asking questions. I read Scripture. I went to Bible camps. I talked with people."

"But how did you know?"

"I think I was at a Bible camp. Some of the kids there were so stupid and silly. They didn't seem to know where they were headed. I felt the Lord was calling me to help—to point them to Christ, the only one who could save them."

"I've seen the awfulness of war. I know Christ was the one who got me through. The prayers of my mother and grandmother must have insured that we came home. All of the men they prayed for came home. We were in some of the worst fighting in the war."

Pastor Young extended his hand. "Johnie, I wonder if the Lord isn't calling you to be a minister. I think you've got what it takes."

At that moment it was as if a light turned on. Johnie knew in an instant that he had a special mission in life. He said nothing, but the light flooded his inward being.

"Would you like me to pray?" asked the pastor. Johnie nodded, and the two men knelt on the floor. Pastor Young prayed, but Johnie heard little of the actual words. He sensed the presence that he had missed these past weeks. The words could not have been more definite if they had been audible: "Johnie. Johnie."

The pastor finished his prayer and stood up. "I should be getting home."

"I need to be alone to think," replied Johnie.

"Feel free to come to me if you need to talk."

Chapter 30

After the pastor left, Johnie found himself overcome with emotion. "Lord, I need You. I need Your guidance. I'm here, Lord. If it's what You want, send me. I am Yours."

Johnie didn't know how long he knelt there, but his future was becoming clear. God had become real in his life and was leading him in a definite direction—something entirely different than he'd ever dreamed. He kept remembering the words: "Lo, I am with you always, even unto the end of the world."

Matthew turned off the radio that evening and said to Ellen, "It's nine. I guess it's time for bed."

"I wonder where Johnie is. He's seemed depressed lately, but when he came back this evening, he seemed happier."

"Here I am, Mother." Johnie entered and took a seat across the room. "I need to talk."

Matthew looked up in surprise.

"We're glad to," said Ellen. "You've been quiet these last weeks. We've been wondering what you've been thinking."

"I'm sorry. I've had a lot on my mind."

Matthew and Ellen both looked into the face of their son. Matthew sensed an earnestness he had not seen before.

"I've been praying a lot." He stopped and looked aside as if he wasn't sure what to say next. "I've felt something I didn't quite understand." Johnie paused, then told them, "Now I think I do. I feel the Lord is calling me to be a minister."

Matthew couldn't hide his surprise. "Oh, my!" he gasped.

"I've been through the awfulness of war. It's almost as if I got a glimpse of hell. I've seen what war and sin do to people. It is a destroyer. I've seen how some people have lost all hope. And I realize I can bring God's hope to them."

Ellen reached over and grasped her son's hands. "I'm so proud of what you're saying. You've come a long way."

"I've seen what Christ has done in people's lives. I know what Larry was like before he went to prison. I see now how he has become a new person. And some of my fellow soldiers went into battle and gave their lives to save others. They went into battle knowing they had a hope beyond this earth." Tears came to his eyes. "And then I think of poor Jeff. He had lost hope, so he turned to drink. And that liquor destroyed him. He's dead because he lost hope and put his faith in something completely false."

Matthew couldn't help remembering his own encounter with the living God as he listened to his son speak so confidently about hope and his future.

"I've been walking and doing a lot of thinking," Johnie continued. "I can see in my life how the Lord has worked—even when I was unaware of it. He saved me from death countless times. I remember being a teenager out hunting on a Sunday morning and feeling His presence there. That was the moment I first truly believed in Him."

Matthew began to speak slowly. "I remember a time . . ." He turned to Ellen and clasped her hand.

"Tell your story," she encouraged him.

"Son, I had encounters as well. As a boy, some friends and I were swimming. We swam out farther than we realized. A sudden storm came up and I was going down—so was my friend. Then it was almost as if a hand came down and pulled me up. I made it to shore. God was very much present. I knew I believed."

"People need to hear." Johnie's eyes lighted with determination. "People forget about what's most important."

"Matthew has another story," Ellen reminded her husband.

"Do you remember when I had my ulcer attack and almost died?"

"I'll never forget it," Johnie replied. "I was angry at God when I thought you might die."

"I was on the verge of death. For some moments I stopped breathing. During those moments I saw many things. First I saw the farm and all the beauty of the countryside. Each member of the family came before me. I wanted to leave. Then I became aware of Jesus, like the Jesus in the picture where he stands at the door and knocks. He became very real. He stood there and kept motioning for me to come back."

"I had forgotten about that," said Johnie.

"It was then that Christ became more real than ever for me. That winter my life changed completely. No, I'd have to say Christ changed my life at that point."

"Thanks for telling me, Dad."

Chapter 30

Ellen stood and moved over to the refrigerator in the kitchen. "I think it's time to celebrate with hot cocoa. We'll be proud to have a pastor in the family. Pastor John Anderson."

"I've got a long way to go—college and seminary. But Dad, I'll be back summers to help on the farm. And I'll come home weekends to work with you."

"I'll miss you, son," began Matthew, "but you have an important mission. And I'll help you all I can."

Some minutes later, father, mother, and son sat enjoying their hot cocoa.

Matthew thought of the darkness of the past—it was lifting. And as he thought of the hills that he often looked to, he realized Johnie would be going far beyond those hills.

Chapter 31

June 1946

Margaret wanted everything to be just right. Her small River Falls apartment was cramped, but she could make a dinner. The beef roast was in the oven, and the potatoes were cooking. She reread the letter she had written. She did not want Tim Robertson to entertain any hopes that she would marry him.

> Dear Tim,
>
> I've enjoyed my time with you. You are a wonderful man. You will make some young woman a wonderful husband. You are a good farmer and will be a good husband and father and provider.
>
> I must clearly say that I will not marry you. Right now, I plan to return to teaching. I am not ready for marriage. That could change, however.
>
> But what I want to make clear is this. I will not marry you. I hope we can be friends in the years to come, but I don't feel the way a wife should toward a husband or a husband-to-be. Please accept my apologies if you thought I was leading you on.
>
> I want to wish you all the best for your life. God bless you. I remain your friend,
>
> Margaret Anderson

Beyond the Darkness

She folded the letter, placing it inside the envelope. She sealed the envelope and put the letter aside. She would mail it tomorrow.

Footsteps on the stairway brought her back to the present. She opened the door just as Joe was ready to knock. He held a bouquet of daisies and other wildflowers. "I knew you liked these."

"Where could you get my favorite wildflowers? They're beautiful."

"I took a drive out in the country. They weren't too hard to find."

Margaret accepted the flowers and realized she had no vase. So she found a glass, filled it with water, and placed the flowers inside. She put them in the center of the table she had set. A few moments of awkward quiet followed, and she noticed that Joe seemed suddenly bashful now that he was alone with her. Margaret thought of the crush she'd had on this young man for so many years. She used to dream of him during her high school years. He had been her knight in shining armor.

As she finished her final dinner preparations, she glanced at him, noticed his dark tan and the rugged physical features of a man. He was no longer the boy she'd had a crush on. Joe kept watching her, too. She felt he was no longer looking at her as he would a younger sister.

"How's school going?" Joe asked, finally breaking the silence.

"Oh, fine. There's quite a bit of busywork, but I'm keeping up."

"Well, I won't stay too late."

"Tomorrow's Friday. I have all my assignments done. So I thought you might even ask me to go for a ride."

Joe smiled broadly. "Yes, Margaret, let's do that. I miss living in the country. A drive will be nice."

Margaret served the meal. They said their table grace, and Joe began to eat the home-cooked meal he obviously enjoyed. They began to talk about how they missed country living, and the time flew fly by. Margaret served her rhubarb pie for dessert, and Joe began work on his second piece. "I don't think I've eaten this much since I came back from the service," he admitted.

"You do look thin. I'm surprised Mother didn't fatten you up."

"She tried. But my appetite has only recently come back."

They finished their pie and another cup of coffee, then Margaret stood to clear the table. "I'll do the dishes later. Let's go for that ride."

Soon they were riding in the country, enjoying the beauty that was June in Minnesota. The road wound along the river and brought them to the dam and North Country Mill.

Chapter 31

"I've never been here!" exclaimed Margaret. "This is absolutely beautiful. Let's walk down by the river."

Joe stopped the car. "I come here often when I have time. I get tired of the city. This is such a beautiful, quiet spot."

Soon Joe and Margaret were running down to the river's edge, simply enjoying the fresh air and beauty of their surroundings. Words were hardly necessary, but they talked of many things . . . and of nothing in particular.

"I haven't had this much fun in a long time," Margaret announced after a time. "I'm glad you're here in River Falls."

"I'm happy—only because you're here." He stopped a minute and looked down at her. "Margaret, I thought of you many times when I was in that prison camp. I treasured those letters you wrote. I still have most of them."

Margaret felt a warmth grow within her. "There wasn't a day I didn't think about you, and I prayed for you."

Joe's next words came out like a raging river. "I wish I weren't just a dumb farmer without even an eighth-grade education. If I'd had high school like Tim, or college, I'd be good enough for a girl like you . . . Oh . . . I make stupid mistakes when I try to say something."

Margaret took Joe's hand and looked up into his dark blue eyes. "I love . . . like you just the way you are. You're kind and honest and good."

"I know I have no right . . . but Margaret Anderson, I love you. I've loved you for a long time. And I want you to—"

Margaret felt tears welling up in her eyes. "Joseph Nelson," she interrupted, "I love you. I loved you long ago, but I thought you'd never notice."

"Will you marry me?" he shouted. "I have so little to offer you. But you're more precious to me than anything in this world. When I left your dad's farm, I thought I had lost you forever. I couldn't stand the idea of you marrying Tim."

"I never loved Tim. When I went out with him, I kept thinking about you. And yes, Joe, I will marry you. You're the only man I've ever really wanted to marry." A warmth she had never felt before filled her whole being. She looked up, and her lips met his. First they kissed tentatively, then with great passion. Margaret felt herself overflowing with love. This was life at its best.

Beyond the Darkness

The week that followed had Margaret planning and replanning her whole life.

"We're having company tonight for the weekend," announced Ellen early the next Friday evening.

"Who?" asked Matthew.

"Not really company. It's family. Joe is coming, and he's bringing Margaret home from River Falls."

Sometimes life moved too fast for Matthew. He was having a hard time realizing the changes that would come with Johnie's departure for college. Margaret would spend a few weeks at home this summer, but then she would leave as well.

This was one of those rare evenings when Matthew and Ellen were alone. Johnie had taken a short-term job to earn some extra money for college in the fall. Michael was spending the night at a neighbor's. Carol and baby Andy would not come out to the farm until Sunday. James might come home on Saturday, but that was not certain.

Matthew and Ellen finished their last cups of coffee after supper. He reached for Ellen's plate. "I'll help with the dishes."

"This is just like when we were first married."

"It seems so empty without any of the kids around," Matthew mused. "Makes me realize how important they are."

"Michael will be around for quite a few more years. I'm so glad we had this afterthought. I never dreamed I could have another child."

"Michael is a wonderful gift."

Ellen washed the dishes and Matthew dried them. He knew that words were not necessary to communicate their feelings. After cleaning up, Matthew sat down in his chair to read the *Daily Journal*. Ellen brought out her knitting and continued to work on a sweater for James. They didn't hear a car drive up, but all at once a voice called out, "Mom, Dad, we're home."

Matthew sensed an excitement in Margaret's voice. Both parents got up to greet their daughter, who rushed into her father's arms. Joe stood back, extending his hand to Ellen. Then, Margaret received her mother's embrace.

Chapter 31

Margaret held up her hand, displaying a small ring on her third finger. "I have some news. Joe and I are engaged."

Ellen extended her hand to Joe and then opened her arms to hug him. "Congratulations! You've been a son to us for years. Now you're making it official."

Margaret returned to Matthew's arms. He wanted to say the right thing but words would not come. "Margaret, Joe's the best," he finally blurted out. He wanted to say how much he loved her, but no words could express how he felt.

"Have you decided when?" asked Ellen.

"I'm teaching another year, and Joe's going to work and save money. We want to buy our own farm."

Joe shyly interjected, "I wanted to buy Margaret a nicer, more expensive ring, but she wouldn't let me. She said we needed to save for our farm."

Matthew cleared his throat. He wasn't sure how much he should say yet about Johnie's decision. It could affect Joe and Margaret's future as well. But before he could speak, Ellen interjected, "We do have some other news that might make a difference in your plans."

"What?" asked Margaret.

Ellen looked to Matthew to answer. "Johnie's not going to be taking over the farm."

Both Joe and Margaret gave exclamations of surprise.

Ellen finished the explanation. "Johnie's going into the ministry. He's felt God's call in this direction."

"My brother—a minister? Especially Johnie. I could see James as a minister, but not Johnie."

"He's changed. He understands problems and people. I believe God is calling him to be a minister," Ellen added.

Matthew held back for a moment, but he felt he had to share another bit of information, another possibility. "Here's something else that might make a difference. Warren is making plans to move to California. After all, Ed has a job there, and Warren's brother is out there as well. Both of Corrine's sisters plan to move there as well."

Margaret looked to Joe. "Then maybe we could buy the home place. That would be perfect."

That evening, Matthew listened to Margaret and Joe share their hopes and dreams. And their hopes and dreams became his as well.

Beyond the Darkness

The winds of change often blow hard and fast. That became evident on Sunday afternoon when the family gathered at Matthew's home—including Larry, Joan, and their children, as well as Warren, Corrine, and the three girls. Victoria and Ma were present, and all of Matthew and Ellen's children except James.

Matthew kept wondering why James had stayed away so long this time. He had always loved the farm, even though farming was not his life. It was uncharacteristic for James not even to write letters.

The children and some adults were playing a softball game in the pasture just beyond the barn. Others were visiting in small groups.

Victoria nudged Matthew. "There are several things I'd like to talk with you about."

"Is something wrong?"

"No." Victoria smiled. "I think some things are working out right. First, it's about Carol."

"After all the problems, I figured you might not want anything to do with her. She gave you a lot of grief."

"Oh, I know that. But I'm a teacher as well as an aunt. I'm in the business of helping young men and women become better people. I try to help them find their way into an adult world."

"You've helped many young people, Victoria."

"Carol hasn't said anything to you, but she's been working with the commercial teacher on shorthand and improving her typing. And she finished a bookkeeping course in a matter of weeks."

"Carol's not stupid. She just has to want to do something."

"There's more," continued Victoria. "There's a business school in River Falls that offers a six-month course. The instructors work their students very hard, and they get good jobs."

"I know Carol is determined to support herself and little Andy," Matthew replied.

"That is admirable. She can't be a waitress forever; there's no money in that. And she is capable of getting ahead in the work world."

"If money is the issue, we'll try to help."

"Matthew, I know money is sometimes tight for you. I'm paying the commercial teacher to tutor Carol. And I'd like to help with tuition and other costs for living in River Falls."

"We can provide meat and milk and some of her other essentials."

Chapter 31

"We're family," said Victoria. "I'm determined to help any way I can. Your children seem almost like my own."

"Thanks, Victoria. This means so much to Ellen and me."

"There's something else," Victoria began. "It's about Warren."

"He's serious about leaving the farm. I know that." Then Matthew realized the other possibility even as Victoria spoke again.

"Right now, things might seem complicated," she continued. "When Warren bought the farm, I financed the loan. Warren wants to work with me so that I buy what he has paid. That means I would own the home farm—except for Mother's little house. Corrine and Warren would like to move this fall if they can make all the arrangements."

"What are you saying?"

"I'd like to work with someone in the family so they could have the family farm. I'd give them very good terms."

"You mean Joe could work out a deal and buy the home farm and live there?"

"Yes, unless you want to, or someone else in your family."

"This is almost too good to be true!" exclaimed Matthew.

Margaret looked up at the kitchen clock as the family finished Sunday night supper. Most of their visitors had left. Johnie was outside with Michael, playing the role of big brother. Carol and baby Andy had returned to town. Only Aunt Victoria and Grandma remained.

"It's about time for Joe and me to get back to River Falls," Margaret announced. "It's been a full weekend."

Aunt Victoria spoke. "Before you go, I have something for you two to think about." She turned to Joe. "I have a business proposition."

Joe looked puzzled. "What?"

"You probably know that Corrine and Warren are quite serious about going to California. Well, I financed the farm, and they would like me to buy back their part. That means the home place is available at a good price."

Margaret didn't hesitate a moment but threw her arms around her normally reserved aunt. "Oh, Aunt Victoria, that's perfect!"

"You mean Margaret and I can buy the farm?"

Margaret quickly interjected, "I've been saving a little money every month, and I'll be teaching one more year."

"And," added Joe, "I've been saving my pay from the service."

"There's nothing I'd like better than to have you two own the home place."

Joe, usually so quiet, spoke up again. "I'm grateful to you, Aunt Victoria. I'm grateful to all of you. You're giving me everything I ever wanted."

Margaret reached over and clasped his hand. "I'm glad you finally realized I didn't want to be your little sister."

Grandma's face broke out into a broad smile. "You told me that years ago—when we had one of our talks. I couldn't ask for a better grandson."

Joe blushed. "Thank you."

Victoria interrupted. "I have one concern."

"Oh, Victoria," said Ellen. "You've taken care of so much now. You can't organize and take care of everything. Things will work out."

"I'm worried about you, Joe. You're so thin. If you're not getting married for a year, you need a housekeeper and cook when you move into the home place."

"He'll be our regular guest," said Ellen.

Margaret hadn't thought of Joe being out on the farm all by himself. That somehow didn't seem right. She looked over and saw Grandmother's eyes twinkle as she said, "I have the solution. I'm still a good cook. I'll take care of the man who will marry my granddaughter. That I can do."

"Won't that be too much for you?" asked Ellen.

"Mother, you're not so young anymore," Matthew added.

"Things worked out great when I boarded the teacher. But Ruth has left. And I don't know if the new teacher will want to board at my place."

As Margaret listened to them work out the details to take care of her fiancé, she realized something significant about family and caring. "This should work out perfectly," she agreed. "Joe needs someone to cook for him. And Grandma needs someone to check up on her. She shouldn't be alone."

Victoria sat up straight and looked at each member of the family. "I see what family is all about. God put families together to nurture and care for one another. We need each other. We need to reach out. Especially do

Chapter 31

we need to help young people getting started in life." She looked to her mother. "And we must look after those who are no longer young."

Elizabeth Anderson bowed her head. "I thank the good Lord for each of you. I want to take care of myself, but I'm no longer as strong as I was. I do need some help."

Ellen refilled their coffee, and Victoria raised her cup. "Aye. Aye. Let's drink to family and caring and looking after one another."

"To our family," repeated Ellen.

Margaret smiled and took Joe's hand. "God's in His heaven. All's right with the world."

CHAPTER 32

October 1946

"Matthew," said Ellen, "you need to take the day off. You've been working awfully hard."

Matthew set down his cup of morning coffee. "OK, I'll take you to church for your quilting. Then I'll stop and see Glenn."

"By the way, your mother said to come by for your noon meal. I'll be eating at church. One of the ladies is bringing a large hotdish, and I'm taking some of my rolls."

Though Matthew enjoyed plowing the fields more than almost any other farm job, he began to anticipate visits with his friends more and more these days. His world had been changing so fast, he found it hard to keep up with everything. And it seemed there would be more changes in the months ahead, especially in his own family.

Matthew drove Ellen over to Oak Ridge Church, then headed to Glenn's. For the first time in his forty-six years, there had been a strained relationship between the two. Glenn had thought Margaret was leading Tim on when she didn't intend to marry him. Matthew had known Margaret was not ready to marry Tim. Now Matthew wanted to make things right with his friend. He drove up the familiar driveway and saw that Glenn was working in the machine shed. His friend saw him and called out, "I'm out here."

Matthew walked over to the shed. "How's everything with you, my friend?"

"I'll be OK if I can get this tractor working right. I just got done putting in new spark plugs. I think I really need a new tractor."

"I need one too."

Glenn put down his tools. "I guess we haven't talked in a long time."

"I'm sorry . . ." began Matthew, and hesitated. "I'm sorry about Margaret and Tim. You would have been a good father-in-law to my daughter."

"Yes, you would be a good father-in-law to my son. But it wasn't meant to be." Glenn cleared his throat.

Matthew knew Glenn wanted to say more but was hesitating, so he searched for the right words. "I don't think Margaret realized that going out with Tim only encouraged him to think he had a chance. I'm sorry about that."

"No need for that, Matthew. I guess we've forgotten what it's like to be young. Anyhow, Tim came home with a new friend. He just popped the question to Virginia. She lives a few miles over toward Prairie Center. We've met her once. She seems like a nice young woman."

"Congratulations! Then you will be a father-in-law."

"At least I'll have one son living nearby. The other boys are getting good jobs in the city. And my youngest girl is going to business school next fall."

Matthew sat down on a wood stump nearby. "Well, we're still working our land, but farming's a tough life. Hard work. Long hours."

"We're our own bosses, at least. I couldn't stand the thought of someone ordering me around."

"Will Tim stay on Mary and Ed's farm? Or will he move back here?"

"It looks as if Mary and Ed want to sell. Tim's working with them about the terms of buying. Besides, I've got quite a few years left in the farming business."

"I do too. I'm forty-six, and so are you. But I do want to scale down my work as Michael grows up and is able to help more. Maybe he'll take over the farm."

"What about the home place, Matthew? Wouldn't you like to move back to the farm where you grew up?"

Chapter 32

Matthew realized his friend understood him rather well. "I've thought of that. There are many good memories, but I can't forget when P.J. told me that the home farm was his. I found I was better off with my new place."

"You had a tough time back then."

"I almost died. My anger toward P.J. almost killed me. But the Lord brought me back."

"I'm glad. I like knowing I have a friend around. But you're right; we are getting older. And as satisfying a life as it is, farming doesn't get any easier. I've been having lots of back pain lately," said Glenn. "I guess all the hard work and lifting through the years is catching up with me."

"Maybe it's time for you to slow down."

"Slowing down isn't in my nature. But how has your health been? You've always had those stomach problems."

"I've been to the doctor several times. My stomach's better, but now it turns out I have some heart problems. He gave me blood pressure pills, and I'm much better. I figure when my time comes, the Lord will take me."

"I wish I had your faith."

The two men talked for another hour until Matthew checked his pocket watch and realized he needed to drive to his mother's. The two friends parted ways on much friendlier terms now that things were settled for both Tim and Margaret. Matthew was grateful to have his friendship back on comfortable standing.

As he drove down the driveway of the home place, the blowing autumn leaves reminded him of the changing seasons and times. Only a few leaves remained. The willow out back still had its full array of leaves—gold and green. The willow reminded him of Ma, who remained strong even after many of her contemporaries had passed away.

Matthew immediately noticed the barn had a new coat of paint. Joe was a hard worker. The home place had always been taken care of, but Joe seemed to have brought a fresh neatness to the place.

Ma greeted him as he hurried into the kitchen. "I was afraid you were going to be late. Everything's ready."

"Hello, Dad," Joe welcomed him.

Matthew realized how hungry he was. Once more he would be treated to a good meal, cooked lovingly by his mother. The three sat and quietly prayed their table prayer, "Come, Lord Jesus, be our guest. Let these gifts to us be blest. Amen." The prayer, though brief, really brought everything into perspective.

As they ate, Matthew and his future son-in-law talked of farmwork and the business of farming. Farm prices had come back strong now that the war was over. After a piece of Ma's raspberry pie, Joe hurried out. He was eager to get back to work, doing the last of the fall plowing.

Matthew sat silently and sipped on a second cup of coffee.

"Son, what's wrong? What's bothering you?" his mother asked.

"You know, Ma, I guess it's all these changes. They're coming too fast for me."

"How's Johnie doing? You're not worried about him, are you?"

"No, Johnie seems to be taking well to college and Bible classes. Ellen and I are amazed at the way he's become such a student."

"He's a bright young man. Now he has purpose." Ma's gaze seemed to see through him the way she did when he was a child. "How about Carol?"

"She's busy. I think she's doing well at the business college. A young woman with two little children is taking care of Andy. What Carol's doing now is an answer to prayer."

"I won't ask about Margaret because I know everything's fine. What else is on your mind? Is it your health? Or it couldn't be James, could it?"

"Ma, you always did have a way of knowing." Matthew laughed. "I'm feeling much better these days. I'm cutting down on the number of cows now that Johnie's away. I rented out the east pasture."

"What's wrong, then?"

Matthew hesitated, then finally confessed his silent concern. "It's James. He hasn't been home for several months. We used to hear from him all the time. He was our letter writer. Ellen writes him regularly, but we're not hearing from him. We don't want to be nosy parents, but we're starting to wonder if everything is OK."

"I'm not worried. I have faith that James is all right. He's probably very busy."

"You know, Ma, families drift apart. I hate to see that."

His mother took his hand and clasped it. "My dear son, children must live their own lives. A mother or father has them only for a short while."

"I miss Martha. I don't know why she has to be away so much. Why couldn't she come back here?"

Chapter 32

"Her girls always seem to need her, and she needs to be close to them."

"And Mary and Ed. We were friends—visited every week. Now they're thousands of miles away. I miss my sisters."

Ma looked away at an old family picture. "I miss both my girls as well. And I think of Lucille, who died so many years ago. And Paul John. P.J. was wealthy and successful, yet he's my biggest disappointment. But I loved all of you. And I still do."

Matthew thought a moment. "I think of people moving far away from these beautiful hills. I wonder if they will really find a better life. I don't think you can find a better life than the one right here."

"The Bible tells us to be satisfied with our lot in life. I think of the hymn's words, 'Content whatever lot I see, since by His hand He leadeth me.' Son, we're content and happy, no matter how far apart our family may be. We have peace with the Lord."

"Thanks, Ma. You seem to know what to say."

Mother and son were silent in the minutes that followed. A communication took place that surpassed the spoken word. Eventually Matthew took out his pocket watch and said, "Well, Ma, I better go. I have one more stop. I thought I'd visit Larry for a few minutes." He left his mother's house satisfied in mind, body, and spirit—after a good meal and thoughtful conversation.

Matthew found Larry during one of those quiet moments at the gas station. He had finished working on the last car, and no one drove up to get gas. Larry took out his thermos of coffee and offered his uncle a cup. The offer seemed to signal a longer visit. "Uncle Matthew," Larry began, "I've been thinking."

Matthew waited for his nephew to go on.

"I wonder if I should stay around here. There are so many opportunities in the city. Should I be moving on?"

Matthew waited only a moment. "Larry, you've become an important part of this community. People have seen the way you've changed. You love working on cars. You're helping to keep some of these young boys on the straight and narrow."

"I keep thinking I could be doing more."

"That has to be your decision. And Joan is a part of it."

"Joan loves life here in a small town. I don't know what she saw in me a few years back. I was a thoughtless jerk back then. Now I'm just thoughtless part of the time."

"Don't be too hard on yourself."

"I look at James and Johnie. James going to college to be a teacher. Johnie taking college and Bible courses to be a minister. And Margaret—a wonderful teacher. Shouldn't I be doing something more?"

Matthew thought back to a Bible study a few weeks ago. "God didn't mean for all of us to be teachers or pastors. We have different purposes. I'm a simple farmer. I'm part of a family and a church and a community—"

Larry interrupted, "Uncle Matthew, you have been such an example to me and many others. Like Grandpa, you are the real strength of this family and community. You're in exactly the right place."

"I'd argue with you about that strength. It's the Lord helping—and Ellen—and all kinds of others."

Larry put down his cup, stood up, and pointed to the gas pumps. "Gus wants to sell. He's willing practically to give me this station. In fact, he will if Joan and I take care of him."

Matthew's response was immediate. "I think you should accept his offer."

Larry looked at him in shock. "Uncle Matthew, you surprise me. You usually say one should pray and wait for the Lord to answer."

"I think God's leading is clear in this case."

Larry smiled and extended his hand. "I think that's what I wanted to hear. It's time for me to buy this station and build it into something bigger and better. Maybe I can help this community in some way. I think God has plans for me right here."

Matthew grasped his nephew's hand. "Let's celebrate. How about a piece of pie at Kay's Café?"

Late that evening Matthew went upstairs with Ellen to hear Michael say his prayers. As usual, Michael was filled with questions before he could settle into his nightly prayer. "Am I really an uncle?" he started out.

"Yes, dear," replied Ellen. "Any time your brothers or sisters have a child, you will be an uncle."

"Don't uncles have to be older? Like Uncle Ed? Or even like Cousin Larry?"

She smiled down at her son. "Uncles can be any age. But you are younger because you were born long after your brothers and sisters."

"Why am I so much younger?"

Matthew felt relieved when Ellen answered that one. "It just happens that way," she said. "God gave us your older brothers and sisters first. Then you came along as a special gift."

Chapter 32

Michael looked puzzled and then yawned.

"It's time for your prayers."

Michael prayed his usual petition and then came to his list of people to bless: "God bless Daddy, Mommy, Grandma, James, Johnie, Margaret, Carol and little Andy, and Michael. Bless cousin Lowell and all my friends. And bless Joe. And bless . . ." He added names of friends and then pet calves and cats and dogs.

Matthew chuckled. "I think it's time to finish your prayer."

Finally Michael said his amen, but then sat up with a last question. "When Johnie gets to be a minister, will I have to call him Pastor?"

This time Ellen laughed. "No, my dear, Johnie may become a pastor, but he will always be your brother."

"Then he'll always be Johnie."

"Yes, he'll always be Johnie to you."

Matthew thought to himself, *And these children will always be my children. I thank God for each one.*

Except for his concern about James, everything seemed right with the world.

Chapter 33

December 1946

Matthew loved tradition. Somehow it connected the past and the present—and still pointed to the future. Part of their family Christmas tradition was the delicious cooking and baking Ellen did each year. The star and "S" cookies that she made for the holidays delighted his taste buds. He sat at the kitchen table, sampling some of her freshly baked cookies, while Ellen stirred dough and put another pan of cookies into the oven. Matthew sipped his third cup of coffee and savored the taste of another cookie. He thought of the Oak Ridge school program where Michael would again recite, sing, and act in a short play later that evening.

Then he thought of James. Matthew didn't want to call it worry, but that's what it was. James had remained absent and silent. Then came a note a few days ago: "I'll be home the morning of Christmas Eve. Sorry about the absence and not writing. I'll explain everything when I come home. I'm OK. Love to all, James."

What did this sketchy note mean? Why was the young son who always communicated so well not communicating at all? He'd sometimes written letters twice a week, but now, nothing.

Matthew left the warmth of the kitchen to do the chores. As he milked the cows that evening, he tried to get his mind off James. Instead he looked forward to the school Christmas program and anticipated the gathering of the whole family for this special season. He stopped a moment in the barn and breathed deeply of the aromas surrounding him. He rather enjoyed the smell of cattle and the sounds of their cud chewing and breathing. There was something "earthy" and "real" about farm life. Cows had a way of calling a person back to reality. If you milked cows, you could never feel too high and mighty.

After he finished the milking, he filled the two feed bins—one with oats and the other with ground feed. He was thankful to have enough extra feed to give the cows their Christmas meal again this year.

These cattle made him think of a stable in Bethlehem. The smells and sounds were earthy. Jesus seemed present tonight as Matthew did his daily work. Remembrances of many Christmases flooded his memory—the times he and Pa had done the chores; the years when James and Johnie were growing up and helping, and during that brief time after the war. Now he was alone, except when Ellen came out and helped—as did Michael help every once in a while.

Several hours later, Matthew sat near the back of the Oak Ridge school. In many ways this schoolhouse was like the one he had attended. He had moments when he missed that home school, where his four older children had attended most of their years.

Electricity still had not come to this school, though another year had passed. A few gas lamps cast shadows around the room during the evening hours. However, the school did have a new oil-burning stove, which gave off more warmth and added an oily smell to the atmosphere as parents and family members gathered there. The stove helped with the heat, but the room still had a few drafty places. Matthew tried to find a place to sit to avoid the cold dampness as the program started.

Matthew appreciated the predictability of this annual Christmas event. As usual, it began with the teacher, Miss Brandt, welcoming parents and friends. Then the sixteen students of Oak Ridge sang "Joy to the World." Michael, almost eight years old now, sang lustily.

Matthew tended to focus his interest on Michael throughout the evening. His young son performed his piece loud and clear. And he was chosen to be in the first play. Like Johnie had, Michael hammed up his lines, adding something extra to an otherwise dull play.

That evening, Matthew and Ellen talked long into the night. It was a night of anticipation. The older children would be coming home. Their family would be complete again, for a time.

Chapter 33

The next Saturday morning, Matthew hurried to finish all the necessary chores and get back to the house. He wanted to be free when the children came home.

Johnie arrived during midmorning coffee. He entered the kitchen with his duffel bag and an armload of books, which he tossed into an empty chair. "I've never studied so hard in all my life!" he exclaimed to his parents and younger brother. "And it's paying off. I'm getting good grades—almost as good as James's."

Ellen poured another cup of coffee. "Welcome home, son."

Johnie turned to his father. "I'm ready to change into my barn clothes and get out and do some good hard work."

"I got most of the work done already. We could leave cleaning the chicken coop until Monday."

"I'm ready to do it today. I want to get away from these books for a while."

"You haven't changed a bit." Ellen brought out more cookies. "Have another one of your favorite sugar cookies."

"May I have another?" asked Michael.

"No, you've had your limit. Besides, Johnie's older, and he hasn't had my cookies for some time."

"Just wait till I get big."

Matthew looked closely at his young son. He was big for his age. All too soon he would grow into a young man.

Johnie grabbed several cookies and hurried off to change into his barn clothes. Michael followed in exact imitation of his older brother.

Matthew put aside his cup and told Ellen, "I guess I've had enough coffee. Might as well go out and get ready for an unpleasant job. I hate cleaning the chicken coop."

Just as he spoke, two cars came up the driveway. "I think Margaret and Carol are here," announced Ellen.

In a minute Margaret rushed in, dropping several packages and a suitcase. "I'm home, Mother. Dad." She gave Matthew a kiss on the cheek.

Close behind came Carol, carrying her precious bundle. "Merry Christmas."

Ellen hurried over to accept that bundle. 'How's Andy? You're growing so fast, I can't believe how big you're getting."

Joe quietly entered, carrying another suitcase and several packages. But everyone focused his or her attention on little Andy. Soon Johnie returned from upstairs, dressed in work clothes, and he hurried over to see the baby. Even Michael, close behind, ran over to greet his little nephew. A baby did something to a family. Perhaps it helped them forget the harsh memories of the past. A baby had a way of bringing people together in a gentler, kinder way.

Ellen moved over to Matthew with the baby. "I think Grandpa wants to hold you."

At first awkwardly and then with more confidence, Matthew accepted his grandson. Andy cooed and looked up into his grandfather's eyes. Matthew saw the vivid blue in those eyes and saw himself in the precious grandson.

The softness and gentleness of love filled that kitchen. Matthew wished the moment could last forever.

An hour later, Ellen was alone in the kitchen. The men were outside, cleaning the chicken coop and doing other work. Margaret and Carol were in their room, unpacking. Baby Andy was sleeping in the kitchen under the care of his grandmother, who felt happy to be alone with her grandson for these precious moments. Ellen finished peeling potatoes and putting them on the stove.

"Mother." The familiar voice startled her.

"James, how wonderful! You came earlier than we expected."

There stood her oldest son. She looked up at him a second time, startled. "James, you're pale. You're so thin. What happened?" As he put down his suitcase, Ellen rushed forward to embrace her son.

"I've been sick. It's a long story. That's why you haven't heard from me."

Ellen pulled out a chair. "Sit down, son. Tell me what happened. Are you all right now? You don't look well."

James obeyed his mother and sat down at the kitchen table. "I just got out of the hospital. They let me out today."

"What happened?"

"I've been working very hard, putting in long hours—both my job and my studies. Then somehow I got a cold and the flu."

Ellen couldn't help thinking of the flu epidemic of 1918.

"Then I got pneumonia."

"Who looked after you? Why didn't you call us? You should have come home."

Chapter 33

"I didn't want to worry you, and I had lots of help. I was in the hospital awhile. Then the guys at the dorm helped me out. And Ruth was a great help."

"You mean Ruth, the girl who taught at the school last year?"

"Yes, we're good friends."

Ellen suspected there might be something more to it, but that was a subject for a different time. "When did this happen?" she asked James.

"The last month and a half. But . . ." His voice broke off.

Ellen waited tensely, realizing this was more serious than he'd told her so far.

"Two weeks ago, I kept having this pain in my side. It turned out to be my appendix. It ruptured, and I was very bad off for a while. In fact, the doctor feared I wasn't going to make it."

Tears came quickly to Ellen. "Why didn't you let us know? We would have been there."

"When I first got sick, I didn't want to worry you. Then when the appendix ruptured, it happened so fast that there was no time. In fact I remember very little about that whole week."

Ellen kept asking more questions, and James answered as best he could. Then she realized he was getting tired. "I'm sorry, son. I'm wearing you out."

About that time Margaret and Carol's return to the kitchen interrupted their talk. Then Matthew, Johnie, and Michael entered from the barn. The confusion and noise of another welcome filled the kitchen.

All at once, the attention focused on James. "You look terrible." "What happened to you?" "Why haven't we heard from you?"

"I've been terribly sick." James explained again—interrupted by questions and concerns.

In the midst of all the discussion, the potatoes suddenly boiled over. Margaret hurried to take care of the situation.

"It looks as if dinner is ready," announced Ellen.

"It's been a long time since we've all been together," said Margaret.

"We have much to be thankful for," said Johnie, "including James's recovery. Let's sing our thanks." In his deep rich bass voice, Johnie led the family in the Doxology:

"Praise God from whom all blessings flow.
Praise Him all creatures here below.
Praise Him above ye heavenly host.
Praise Father, Son, and Holy Ghost. Amen."

Beyond the Darkness

These moments in the Anderson kitchen were as worshipful as any church service.

After dinner James and Johnie disappeared to their room. Something was secretive about their manner. Ellen couldn't help thinking they were up to something—but after all, it was Christmas.

Christmas Eve arrived with all the splendor of the season. Light snow fell on the wintry landscape. The world looked clean and fresh. The darkness of war and the problems of past years were fading.

Matthew stood outside a moment, gazing at the warmth of the light streaming from the windows of his home. He breathed a silent prayer of thanks that his whole family was back together. All five children home at the same time. The four older children were all moving forward in their adult lives. And this was his first Christmas with a grandchild.

Suddenly Matthew remembered something. *Was the west barn door latched?* He hurried back to the barn, turned on the light, and went over to the door. Sure enough, it had been latched. The cattle seemed surprised but went on chewing their cuds, looking contented. *Perhaps*, he thought, *animals feel a closeness to the Christ Child on Christmas Eve. Maybe that's why Pa always gave them that extra portion of feed every year.* Matthew had carried on the tradition, and now both James and Johnie did the same without a second thought.

Matthew turned out the light and hurried to the house. He loved these few moments alone, but soon Ellen would start to wonder where he was.

Christmas 1946 was different in several ways. Ed and Mary and their children were far away. It was also the first time in several years that all his children were home. And this year, a grandson and a future son-in-law were part of the family.

Victoria had come early to help Ellen. Ma, of course, was in her usual spot. More than ever, Matthew enjoyed the lutefisk and Swedish meatballs and all that went with their traditional Christmas dinner. This year they added raspberry sauce to put on the rice pudding.

This Christmas Eve dinner began like all the others, except for a few moments after they first sat down, when the entire family seemed uncharacteristically quiet—almost meditative. Perhaps each was lost in

Chapter 33

his or her thoughts. But this didn't last long. Soon everyone was laughing and talking. Afterward the women did the dishes, but Johnie insisted on helping clean the table.

Then came the tradition that began the first Christmas after Ellen and Matthew were married. Ellen sat beside the Christmas tree and read the Christmas story, while he listened from across the room, looking at his wife. She was beautiful in a mature way. Her hair was almost completely gray, and she was not quite as slim as she once was. But her blue eyes sparkled as she read the story.

At her feet sat Michael, probably more interested in the presents under the tree. Carol sat next to Ellen, holding little Andy. Joe tenderly reached over and took Margaret's hand. James sat next to Ma, but he still looked very tired. Johnie sat cross-legged on the floor. Ma still had energy, but she was looking frailer these days. And Victoria sat straight and poised in a chair next to James; she maintained a certain strength and dignity at all times. These were the people who meant the most to Matthew. There were many gifts under the tree, but Matthew's wealth was not material. *My wealth is invested in these people I love*, he realized, as Ellen concluded the Christmas story.

Soon noise and confusion reigned as Johnie gave out presents. In minutes the room was filled with a mess of wrapping paper. The presents weren't important; the love and fellowship were.

Suddenly the room grew silent, and James and Johnie disappeared. Carol took Andy upstairs to put him to bed. Margaret went over to the radio and tuned the dial until she found Christmas music. Matthew loved these quiet moments before the family left for church and the Christmas Eve candle-lighting service. "This is the best Christmas ever," he said aloud. "We're all together." Yet even as he spoke, he wondered if all the same people would be together next Christmas. Life had a way of changing quickly, and sometimes permanently.

Abruptly his reverie was interrupted by the return of his two oldest sons. "We're going over to church early," said Johnie, with James by his side. "We're helping with the service."

James and Johnie made a hasty exit. Matthew couldn't help wondering what was coming.

Beyond the Darkness

Johnie placed his notes on the pulpit. He was more than a little nervous. When Pastor Young asked if he would take over the service, he had agreed. Now he realized the task was bigger than he had thought. What were people going to think of this young Oak Ridge kid leading a service and preaching a sermon?

The organist had arrived. She was arranging her music on the old reed organ. One of these years, Oak Ridge would probably buy a new electric organ, but Johnie wasn't sure that would make the music better. The organist began playing, and James practiced the songs he would sing. A few early arrivals took their seats in the sanctuary.

Johnie decided to escape to the basement for a few moments alone. "Lord," he prayed, "help me get through this. I want to do a good job for You, but also I want to make my family proud of me."

A half hour later, he stood in front of the congregation, cleared his throat, and the confidence came. As he announced the first hymn, Johnie looked out on the congregation. Every seat was filled. He looked above to the balcony, and several people were seated there. Near the front sat Mom and Dad, along with Grandma and Aunt Victoria. Joe and Margaret sat nearer the front with James by their side. For a moment he remembered the dark times he had gone through during the last years. As he looked down to see Dad, he realized that his father had gone through dark times as well, just in a different way. How fortunate he was to have a father and mother who loved him and brought him up the right way.

The service progressed. Several young people read Scripture. The congregation sang several favorite Christmas hymns and carols. The sanctuary literally echoed with the sounds of Christmas.

Next Johnie read the Christmas story from Luke. Then it was time for his sermon. He opened with the traditional prayer and then led into a prayer from a favorite hymn:

> "O Holy Child of Bethlehem, descend to us, we pray.
> Cast out our sin and enter in; be born in us today.
> We hear the Christmas angels, their great glad tidings tell.
> Oh, come to us, abide with us, our Lord Emmanuel!"

Johnie began tentatively. "When Pastor Young asked if I would preach, I said yes. I wanted to give him a chance to be with his mother and father and family. But I didn't realize what a big task lay before me. I'm just a beginner. I haven't done this before. So please bear with me."

Chapter 33

There was a hush over the congregation. He felt all eyes on him, especially those of Mom, Dad, Grandma, and Aunt Victoria.

"We have all journeyed to this Christmas. We have journeyed in many different ways. I'd like to tell you about my journey. It is a very personal one, and there have been dark times. But let me tell you how I have come before Jesus on this Christmas Eve. In many ways our times have been like the times when Christ was born."

When he paused, Johnie knew he had his audience in the palm of his hand. For a moment fear gripped him—the same fear he had felt on the battlefield. But quickly his fear faded and his confidence returned.

"Let us go back to Bethlehem more than nineteen hundred years ago. Those were dark times. The Romans oppressed the people of Israel. They were hoping for the Messiah, but many had lost hope. Just as those years of World War II seemed terribly dark, the days seemed dark to those expecting a savior."

He went on to describe what he hoped was a graphic picture of the times in the land of Israel under Roman rule. Then he continued with his personal story. "Now I'd like to take you back to my journey. In a sense I traveled to the manger during my years of growing up. I played a shepherd or a wise man or even Joseph in the Christmas pageant. I don't know that I realized the true meaning until later. In November before that famous Armistice storm, I'd spent time hunting ducks one morning. Being alone, I had a lot of time to think. It was during a time of confusion and questions in my life. That day I came to the Lord. I began to see myself as a sinner, and I saw Jesus as the answer. I knelt alone in the woods near a pond that autumn morning. That was the hour I really believed.

"But the journey did not end there. I guess I was always a fighter. I probably got into more fights than anyone else in my family. When wrong was done, I wanted to fight to make it right. When the war seemed to go on forever, I knew it was my duty to fight and protect the freedom of Americans. I had to go.

"I saw awful things happen during the war. I saw men whose legs were shot off. I saw others die before my very eyes. War is probably the closest thing to hell that a fellow can experience." At this point deep emotions welled up within Johnie, but he continued. "I was one of the more fortunate ones. I had a gunshot wound in my side. That wound healed, but the wounds and scars within did not. I fell into a deep despair. Some people call it shell shock—and that's not a bad name. I kept reliving all those close calls. I saw men die, men maimed for life. I saw and heard their cries of agony again and again. People around me were walking shadows. I didn't think clearly. I didn't care whether I lived or died.

"Eventually I began to see glimmers of hope. My brother James came to me in the hospital in Norfolk. I knew there was healing and hope out there someplace. I had a job to do, but I didn't know if I had the energy to try. Then I was brought to the veterans' hospital in Minnesota. James kept coming to see me. Mom and Dad made the trip. I still kept seeing all the horrors, but more and more I sensed there was hope.

"Finally the doctors thought it might be a good thing for me to go home. Even there I often walked around as if life were unreal. Those horrors filled my mind—especially at night when I had repeated nightmares . . ." All at once the memories were too much. Tears filled his eyes. "I'm sorry. Even now, the pain is very real."

Johnie wiped his tears and went on. "I began to go for long walks. With spring came a gradual healing. Then one day I walked into this very church. I looked at that stained-glass window that you have seen for so many years. I saw Christ holding that lamb. In that moment I realized I was the lamb Jesus had saved. I was safe in His arms."

Johnie paused. He looked out at his audience and realized there were few dry eyes. His message had reached them. Dad was covering his eyes. Mom and Grandma were wiping their eyes. Even Aunt Victoria was dabbing her eyes with her handkerchief.

He turned and pointed to the large picture in the front of the sanctuary. "That day I looked at this picture of Christ ascending into heaven. There I saw the hope that goes far beyond the present. I saw the hope for all eternity. In that moment I experienced a healing of the mind, body, and spirit."

Johnie turned back to his audience. "Now, let's get back to our journey to Bethlehem. We come back to our beginnings. We come back to our roots. Mary and Joseph returned to their roots many years ago. I have come back home. And now you and I travel again to Bethlehem and the manger. We experience in a new way what Jesus did. He left the splendor of heaven to come to earth to become one of us.

"As I have come to Jesus, I have experienced healing and new life. Let us come to Him and worship Him in a fresh way. Let us see Him not just as a baby but also as our Lord and Savior. Let us come together and worship Him. Let us worship and adore Him, Christ the Lord."

He prayed quietly and then James came forward and began to sing a special song, "Oh, holy night, the stars are brightly shining . . ."

Chapter 33

Johnie thought of the chains that his brother sang about.

Truly He taught us to love one another;
His law is Love and His gospel is Peace;
Chains shall He break, for the slave is our brother,
And in His Name all oppression shall cease.
With hymns of joy in grateful chorus raising,
Let all within us praise His Holy Name.

Silently Johnie breathed a prayer of thanksgiving. His chains of despair and hopelessness had been broken. The terrible oppression of war had ended.

After the service, he walked to the back of the sanctuary. The organist continued playing the strains of "Joy to the World." Neighbors and friends crowded around to shake his hand and compliment him and wish him well. One by one his family came to greet him and shake his hand. Carol hurried to him first—the sister he'd most frequently fought with. "I didn't think you'd ever wind up a preacher," she said. "You didn't do a half bad job." That was a great compliment from her.

Joe and Margaret followed. Joe, usually the quiet one, spoke first. "It's too bad you won't be a real minister in June. Then you could marry us."

"Brother, you did a great job," said Margaret. "You've come a long way."

Grandma came next. He stooped down and gave her a hug. With tears in her eyes she told Johnie, "Your grandfather would be so very proud of you. I believe he's looking down on you with pride. And you bear his name, John Anderson. I love you, my boy." Johnie could say nothing. He simply hugged his grandmother.

Aunt Victoria then grasped his hand. "John Anderson, I'm proud of you. And I'm here to help you any way I can." Overwhelmed by her warmth, Johnie muttered a thank you.

"I'm tired," announced Michael. "I want to go home."

His mother smiled as she hugged her middle son. "Johnie, you will make a fine minister. I can see that already."

Last came Dad. "I'll miss you on the farm, but God obviously has called you. And you are answering His call. That is right."

As the sanctuary emptied, Johnie felt the support of the congregation. It was as if they spoke in unison, "Well done."

Beyond the Darkness

Late that night the two older brothers talked of many things. "You know," said James, "I always thought I might be the minister. People used to tell me that's what I should do. But I feel God is calling me to write and be a teacher."

"I never dreamed I'd do anything but farm," Johnie responded. "I thought I'd be right here the rest of my life. I know now what I must do."

"Johnie, you've always been the fighter and protector. You were ready to fight for me when Jake or others made fun of me and my piano playing or wanting to write. You've been a good brother."

"And you helped me with my sermon. I learned from you how I needed to study."

"As a minister, you'll fight for what's right in a different way. I'll fight for what's right in the classroom."

Johnie reached over and poked his brother. "We Anderson boys are quite a team. We're out to change our world."

Michael awakened. "I don't want to sleep alone." He climbed out of his small single bed and jumped into bed with his older brothers. In minutes the three Anderson boys drifted into a peaceful sleep.

Matthew got out of bed early the next morning. He would let his boys sleep today. They had talked late into the night. After all, he needed to get used to doing the milking alone.

As he put the milk cans into the tank, he saw the first rays of the light of Christmas Day. The sunrise spoke to Matthew of light and hope. The darkness of the past months and years had broken.

A new day dawned.

Chapter 34

June 1947

Matthew never tired of looking at his hills. June was perhaps the most beautiful time of the year. The sun shone bright, turning the lakes a vivid blue. The color of the oaks and other trees was at its richest green this time of year. Heaven and earth seemed to be in perfect tune in early summer. It was a quieter, beautiful season before the full-blown harvest of autumn.

He pounded a few nails into the fence post. If he didn't, the gate would soon come apart. But this simple task also gave Matthew a good excuse to get away for a few minutes and think.

For farmers, late June was a good time for a wedding. The first crop of hay had been cut and put up; aside from cultivating corn, major tasks were complete. Matthew enjoyed this time and loved to walk and check on the fences, but today was different. Margaret would be married this afternoon. He didn't want to play favorites, but he had to admit Margaret was his favorite girl.

"Dad, I knew I'd find you out here." Margaret hurried over and gave him a kiss on the cheek.

"I thought you'd be busy with other things."

"I wanted a few minutes alone with you." She looked down. "I know it's right to marry Joe, but I'm a little scared. Did you ever feel that way when you got married?"

Matthew tenderly took his daughter's hand. "Yes, I was scared to death. I suddenly realized what a great responsibility I had taken on. And I guess I was more shy then than I am now."

"Dad, I think Joe is the closest I can come to marrying a man like you."

"I couldn't ask for a better son-in-law. Actually, he's been like a son already."

"I've dreamed of this day all my life. Now I can't believe the day has come."

Matthew looked down at Margaret. She wore an old housedress, but to him she was the most beautiful girl he'd ever known. He wanted to take her in his arms and protect her forever. "I trust Joe," he assured her. "He will take good care of you."

The hours that followed seemed to go in slow motion—at the same time, they seemed to fly by. Everyone changed clothes and cleaned up, in manner and speed, as only farm families could do. Before long Matthew was in the church basement, waiting for the big event.

Matthew loved people, but all this noise bothered him. He walked through the kitchen and up some steps and out the back way. A few moments alone would help him focus and calm down. He stood outside the church, looking at the familiar hills. In a sense he was losing a daughter. Their relationship would never again be the same.

A familiar voice interrupted his reverie. "There you are. I was hoping to find you before the ceremony."

"Martha! How good that you could come." He gave his sister a strong Anderson hug.

"I have news for you, brother. I'm back home for good. I'm tired of going from daughter to daughter. I need a place to call my own."

"That's great news."

"There's a little house next to Victoria's place. I'm buying it. And if Mother needs some extra care, she can move in with me."

"That might solve a problem." Matthew had noticed his mother was getting frailer. Cooking and keeping house for Joe had been almost more than she could handle. But she was determined to keep going.

Martha turned to go. "I think I better go in. It looks as if the church will be packed. I want my spot near the front."

Chapter 34

"Don't worry. There's a special place for you."

As Martha hurried away, Matthew whispered to himself, "Things have a way of working out. God is in control of our lives." He returned to the church basement, where he found James and Johnie, both groomsmen, in their new suits. Joe was pacing back and forth. The women were in the kitchen preparing the traditional afternoon lunch. Margaret and the girls were in one of those back rooms always used by the bride and bridesmaids.

Matthew walked over to Joe. "Everything will be fine," he assured the young man.

"This is almost as scary as being at war. My stomach feels funny."

Matthew smiled. "It can't be that bad."

"I'm afraid I'm not good enough for Margaret. She's a wonderful girl, and I'm just an ordinary farmer with little education."

"Joe," began Matthew, "I couldn't ask for a finer son-in-law, and I could think of no finer man for Margaret to marry. I've always felt as if I didn't quite measure up either. I didn't even finish eighth grade. Then I started studying and reading more than ever—especially the Bible. Through the years I have read much and learned many things. Now I realize we all have different parts to play."

"Thanks, Dad. I want to give Margaret so much. I love her more than I can say."

"Give her yourself. Tell her that you love her."

"I do, but I'm not good with words."

Matthew thought of the past ten years and all Joe had done. "Joe, you showed your love for our family when you came as a hired man. You have given your love to our family throughout these years. And I have seen how you love Margaret."

"I couldn't have come through the war without you Andersons."

"My daughter fell in love with you years ago. I think she loved you long before you realized you loved her."

"She's more than I deserve."

Matthew became aware of the organ music upstairs. Pastor Young came over and announced it was time for the wedding to begin. The other men left Matthew, walking up the creaking stairway to meet the bride and attendants at the front of the church.

The women emerged from the small room downstairs that had served as a dressing room. First came Larry's wife, Joan. This farm girl had become an important part of the Anderson family.

Beyond the Darkness

Carol followed. Motherhood had changed this daughter. Her hair with its red tint complemented the blue of her bridesmaid dress. This nineteen-year-old had changed from a wild, irresponsible teenager into a mature woman and mother.

Next came Ellen, straightening Margaret's veil. For a moment Matthew saw Margaret as that little girl running to meet him. The little girl merged into the young woman wearing a long, white bridal gown. She was the most beautiful woman Matthew had ever seen. And she was his daughter—his flesh and blood.

The bridal party made its way up the stairs to the rear of the sanctuary. Larry, smiling at Matthew, extended his arm to Ellen. He ushered her up the aisle to the front pew. Matthew noticed the emptiness of the pew on the other side. Joe's parents had not come. Two couples were seated close to the front. He figured those were Joe's older brothers. How sad it was when families neglected their own.

Two ushers, Larry and Joe's cousin, moved forward and rolled out the white carpet. Now everything was ready. The organist began to play the familiar strains of "Largo." Joan moved gracefully in time to the music. Carol followed in equally graceful rhythm. Then Michael marched forward as ring bearer. He seemed to have as much grace as one could expect from an eight-year-old. Matthew felt a moment of panic. He never regarded himself as graceful. And now here he was with the bride, very much the center of attention.

The music of Lohengrin's "Bridal Chorus" filled the church. The eyes of all in the congregation were on Margaret and Matthew. He trembled within. Everything seemed perfect, except Matthew felt terribly awkward as they moved down the aisle. When they finally reached the front of the church, for a moment Matthew wanted to hold back. He didn't want to give his daughter to another man. But when he looked at Joe and saw the intense love reflected in his eyes, Matthew knew Joe was the right man for Margaret. Margaret turned to her father, smiled, and moved forward eagerly to take her place beside the man who soon would be her husband.

James stepped forward and sang the familiar words:

"O Perfect Love, all human thought transcending,
Lowly we kneel in prayer before Thy throne,
That theirs may be the love which knows no ending,
Whom Thou forevermore dost join in one."

Chapter 34

Matthew listened intently to the words. He thought of the change and uncertainty in the days ahead. The familiar words took on new meaning.

Grant them the joy which brightens earthly sorrow,
Grant them the peace which calms all earthly strife,
And to life's day the glorious unknown morrow
That dawns upon eternal love and life.

Pastor Young began to speak the solemn words of the marriage ceremony. "Dearly beloved! Marriage is a holy estate instituted by God Himself for the preservation of the human family . . ."

Matthew's mind wandered many places throughout the ceremony. Before his eyes he felt Margaret changing from that sweet little girl playing with dolls to a young woman teaching a room full of children. He felt so full of love that he could not contain it. God's love was spilling into his life and into the lives of all around him.

Ellen had always known this day would come, but somehow it had come faster than she had anticipated. Her little girl would be a wife. Ellen, the realist, knew that the young couple would face problems and sorrows, just as the hymn's words said. Childbirth was not easy. Death and other difficulties interfered with an otherwise happy life.

Ellen thought of the past years and how various events had brought everyone together this day. Johnie, once missing in action and then in deep shell shock for so long, now brought many people to their knees when he preached. And there was that long separation from James, the son who seemed most like his mother. He was now healthy, studying hard, and using his beautiful singing voice here at this occasion. And Carol, who had rebelled, eloped, and brought a child into the world, then became a widow. Now she was making a better life for herself and her son. Yet Ellen still could not get over the feeling that she had failed this daughter.

As the ceremony proceeded, Ellen prayed. "Dear heavenly Father, give my dear daughter Margaret the wisdom and strength to face the years ahead. Joe still has the scars of a difficult childhood and the war.

But Lord, You heal people. You give new strength and hope. Please guide this couple."

James once more stepped forward and began to sing "The Lord's Prayer." As her son sang, Ellen experienced the words of that prayer in a way she never had before.

Finally Pastor Young introduced the new couple, "Mr. and Mrs. Joseph Nelson." Ellen remembered how she felt when she was first addressed as Mrs. Matthew Anderson. The title seemed to raise her to a higher position.

The music of the "Wedding March" filled Oak Ridge Church as Joe and Margaret walked quickly down the aisle. Johnie and Carol, followed by James and Joan, walked quickly down the aisle. Michael, not willing to be outdone, made his exit by running.

Ellen looked up at Matthew. "I can't believe our girl is married."

Matthew whispered back, "She's absolutely beautiful."

Ellen looked at her husband as if for the first time. He was the same Matthew, but suddenly he seemed older. Hair turning gray, thinning just a bit. He didn't seem to stand quite so tall. He still had that thoughtful look in his eyes, and his whole manner showed kindness and gentleness. *But*, she thought, *my hair is almost all gray. And I don't move as fast as I used to either.* "We're getting old," she said to him and chuckled.

The reception line began to form at the back of the church. The bride and groom stood first, then Matthew and Ellen, followed by the rest of the family. Ellen knew how Matthew loved people, but big crowds bothered him. He placed his hand over his heart, which worried her.

The sound of Ed's booming voice announced that he and Mary had managed to arrive in time. Ellen thought of the many times their families had been together through the years. Now California separated them by thousands of miles. Ellen was so grateful they had made the trip for this important occasion.

Mary quietly gave Margaret a hug and congratulated Joe. Mary looked much thinner and rather pale. The past years must have been hard ones for her. Ed had put on weight, Ellen could tell.

"We have something special for the bride and groom," announced Ed. "We'll tell you later."

Ellen wondered what that would be. Ed could be gruff and tough, but he also was kind and generous.

"Couldn't the kids come?" asked Ellen.

Chapter 34

"They wanted to." Mary sighed and looked away. "Beth and Irene both have jobs, and they couldn't get away. Jake is in the navy, and we don't hear from him very much."

"We miss them."

The reception line seemed to go on and on. Finally the last guests came through with their congratulations and best wishes. What followed was a typical country church wedding lunch. The women of Oak Ridge provided one of their hearty meals—made up of sandwiches, several hotdishes, Jell-O, and other salads, followed by a fancy wedding cake.

The church basement echoed with talk and fellowship of family and community and friends. People were in no hurry to leave. But soon the late afternoon shadows told farmers it was time to return home to do chores. The basement emptied except for family members, some friends, and a few people still working in the kitchen.

Joe and Margaret's car had been appropriately decorated with tin cans and other assorted papers and writing. Ed moved close to Margaret and Joe. "We have something special for you: our wedding gift. Here are the keys to our California home. You can stay there as long as you like. And I'll stay here for two weeks and take care of your chores."

Margaret smiled as tears came to her eyes. "Oh, Uncle Ed, that is so special. We'll get to see a different world. I've always dreamed of seeing our great country."

"Thank you." Joe extended his hand. "You're doing too much for us."

"Not at all, it's for my special niece and her new husband."

Ellen and Matthew said good-bye to their daughter and son-in-law, and Margaret and Joe drove away.

Ellen wiped a tear from her eye. "They'll be so far away."

Matthew reminded her, "Margaret will be close by in just a few weeks."

She turned to her husband, "I guess this ends one chapter in our lives. And we're beginning a new chapter right now."

Four Anderson men stood outside the church, talking quietly. For Matthew and the others it was a time for reflection. He thought of the way women were more likely to give way to their emotions. James was the one to turn the conversation to a reflective mode. "We've seen a lot of change. I can't believe all that has happened and the way people have changed."

"I'm probably the prime example." Larry picked up a piece of grass and began to chew on it. "Look at the way I was before I went to jail. I was out to do anything to make money. I was smoking and drinking and leading a wild life."

"I didn't like you much back then," admitted Johnie.

"I pretty much thought only of myself. I was cruel to people. I can't believe how I pushed around my wife. I can't believe she stuck with me."

Matthew remembered those days. "Joan loved you very much. She believed you could change."

"I think Grandma and the rest of you liked Joan more than you liked me. At least she was more likable," Larry replied.

"Johnie and I were teenagers—rather preoccupied with our own lives," James said, then looked away briefly. "I had some dark times—dark moments of doubt."

"That's hard to believe," responded Larry. "I thought you were the one who always did things right. You walked the straight and narrow."

"I went through a time when I was losing my faith. Johnie was missing in action, and I was afraid he might be dead. I became more aware of all the bloodshed of war. I wondered how a loving God could permit these atrocities. I was angry at God."

"What happened?" asked his brother.

"It was one of those days when I was angry at everyone. I think we can transfer our anger at God to people. I'd had an accident and cut myself rather badly. I know now I was being a first-rate jerk. An army nurse was cleaning the wound and putting on the bandage. She didn't respond to my anger and impatience. Instead she did her job. When she finished she smiled at me and simply said, `God loves you.' I couldn't retaliate in anger. I saw her sweetness and realized God's love was out there."

"It's interesting," said Johnie, "how small, seemingly insignificant actions can make such a big difference."

"That was a turning point. I walked over to St. Paul's Cathedral and heard the stories of how people had guarded that spot day and night. If people could risk their lives to put out small fires and stand guard at a cathedral, there must be more to God's love than I had realized."

Chapter 34

"God works in mysterious ways," stated Matthew. "You never know how He will reveal Himself."

"More than ever, I wanted to do something to help make the world a better place," James continued. "I wanted to write. I wanted to teach—to help young people make good decisions." He finished, and things got quiet again.

"I guess I'm next." Johnie said, as he stuck his hands in his pocket and looked down. "I'm the last one you'd expect to be a minister. I loved the outdoors. I didn't particularly like studying and school. But I did feel close to God when I spent time outdoors."

James reached over and put his arm on his brother's shoulder. "We've seen big changes in you."

"I guess what I had was shell shock. I never felt anyone could experience such depression or despair. Frankly, I didn't want to go on living. I would have welcomed death at any time. But then that spring morning when I saw life bursting forth, God seemed to speak audibly. I went to the church. I saw those stained-glass windows, and Christ became real. I knew I had a mission. I had to offer people the answer."

Matthew looked toward the hills and then at his sons and nephew. "I've seen more change than any of you. When I had my brush with death almost ten years ago, it was then I realized Christ was alive and very real. I came back home with a new purpose in my life. Christ is alive and He is at work in people's lives."

The four men continued to share for some time. *It's strange*, Matthew thought, *how at times like this, people are more inclined to share intimate details of life.* This was a time the four men would long remember.

From the church, Ellen called, "Would you guys check on Michael and Lowell? It's hard telling what they'll get into."

Matthew reached down and took out his pocket watch. The hour told him milking time was at hand. *It's strange*, thought Matthew, *how children and cows bring people back to the basics of life.*

Chapter 35

September 1947

"Tomorrow we'll be alone, except for Michael." Ellen poured Matthew a cup of morning coffee. "It will seem empty around here."

"I guess that's life, isn't it? Change is everywhere."

Ellen sighed, "We wouldn't want it any other way."

"Why did James take off so early this morning? I thought he wasn't leaving until early evening."

"Your mother wanted him to write something for her. She said something about wanting to leave a blessing for her children and grandchildren."

Matthew remembered the last day of Pa's life as he spoke. "Pa did something like that during his final hour. He called each of us to him. He said a few words and blessed each one of us."

"I remember. Like the Old Testament patriarchs. What a wonderful legacy to leave your children."

The couple sat silently for a few moments, then Matthew remarked, "Things are turning out well for our children." He thought of Margaret and the wedding, of Joe and the farm. "Joe will do well running the home farm. And it's going to help that Margaret teaches at the school nearby. Maybe it's a blessing that there's such a shortage of rural teachers."

"It's going to be a challenge for her. There's a lot of work to running a house and teaching a roomful of children."

"I'll miss Carol and little Andy. It was fun to have them around this summer."

Ellen held up the plate with the last cookie, offering it to her husband. "We can be proud that Carol got that job at the courthouse. She'll be able to take care of herself and Andy, and won't need help from the Grants. Then they can't interfere."

"I never dreamed things would turn out so well for her."

"Where's Johnie?"

Matthew now knew and understood Johnie and what he would do before leaving again. "I'm sure he's taking a walk through the hills, probably saying good-bye to his familiar places before he goes back to school."

Ellen stood up. "Matthew, why don't we take a walk in the garden. I want to show you those new gladiolas. Some different colors. They're beautiful."

Matthew followed Ellen outside and appreciated again the beauty of their garden flowers. He looked down at his wife. "I'm a lucky man."

She stooped down to pick a dark red gladiola. "God has been good to us."

With pen in hand James sat at the kitchen table across from Grandma. The little house contained many memories. As a boy he had often run into this kitchen. Grandma always had cookies or cake or other goodies. And they'd had many long talks over the years.

Grandma's hands trembled as she brought out some notes. "I want to say everything just right. That's why I asked for you."

"I'm sure you could say everything well, but I'll do my best."

"My eyes aren't so good anymore. That's why my writing is big. It's a little bit messy, too." She spread out her notes.

James glanced at Grandma's writing. "Where do you want me to start?"

"I want to bless and give my love and best wishes to my children and grandchildren. I also want to recognize those who have passed away.

Chapter 35

Your grandfather was a wonderful man and gave much to his family and community. I want to say something about that."

James looked at the notes she'd written about Grandpa, then suggested, "Why don't you tell me in your own words what is important?"

During the next hours, James listened and wrote as his grandmother talked. The result was a family blessing and story that would be passed down for generations.

"I, Elizabeth Anderson, now in my seventy-ninth year, wish to speak to my children and grandchildren. You have a great heritage of family and faith. I hope you will keep in mind who you are as you live through the difficult years ahead. Life is never simple. Life is filled with change. I can attest to that.

"I'm not ignoring my great-grandchildren. However, many of you have not yet been born. As I contemplate the future, I realize more and more of you will arrive on the scene. Perhaps I shall see only a few more of you in my lifetime. I pray that you also will carry on the family heritage and the faith.

"First, I want to pay tribute to my husband, John Anderson. I can see how the Good Lord brought us together more than sixty years ago. The Lord guided us in so many ways—ways not evident at the time. I don't know exactly when the change took place. John and I had always gone to church. We had been baptized and confirmed and then married in the church. Yet at one point in our lives, we realized our own weakness and sinfulness. Many things seemed to be falling apart. It was then that Christ truly became a part of our lives.

"John was a man of strength and faith, a rock in the community and home. I wish I could put into words the man he was. May you see in him a wonderful example of God's love and strength.

"Martha, my firstborn, you truly care for people. Your husband was an honorable man, and I know that you miss him. I cannot tell you how much it means to me that you are willing to take me into your new home. I'm forgetful, and I fall and can't do so much anymore. The Lord has a special promise for those who honor their parents—and all of you children have honored me. I bless you as a daughter who shows love in a multitude of everyday ways.

"Rachel, Jane, and Corrine, you have followed in your mother Martha's ways. You have given me ten great-grandchildren. Corrine, I know you the best. Your three girls became special to me. I have missed seeing you since you've been away. Your three beautiful daughters are never far from my thoughts.

"Victoria, as a teacher, you have blessed thousands of young people. You have not given birth to children, but you have instilled knowledge and discipline in many. Your students will be an influence for generations to come. And you have taken a special interest and concern for Matthew's children. Your nieces and nephews and your students will bless you as children would bless their parents.

"Paul John, I miss you and feel a keen loss. My firstborn son, you were probably the brightest and best looking of all my children. Yet I am saddened the way you went astray. I hope that somehow during those last moments of your life, you came to the Lord in repentance. More than anything, I want to meet you in heaven.

"Rita, you are still my daughter-in-law. I must say to you that material things are not what are most important. You have wealth and position, but I hope you will find true happiness wherever you are. True happiness is found only with the Lord. And, Noreen, my granddaughter, I don't know where you are or what you are doing. Your separation from the family saddens me. I hope that somehow you will come back to your family.

"Larry, I cannot tell you how happy and proud of you I am. You started on the wrong path, but I see how the Lord has transformed your life. You are a new person. You are carrying on the family name and the heritage of faith.

"Dear sweet Lucille, you came on the scene four years after Paul John. You were the frail and quiet one, while P.J. was forceful and always into something. Your life brought a peace and gentleness that is hard to describe. I always wonder why God took you when you were but twenty-five. Why did he give you a weak heart? But that heart was filled with love, and you enriched the lives of everyone around you. I thank God for your memory and legacy.

"Matthew, you have always been near me. You and Ellen took me in when I desperately needed help. You were always next door or a phone call away. I can never thank you enough for being this kind of son. You have a depth of faith and sensitivity and wisdom that few people have. I believe you are imparting this to your children as well. Ellen, you are more like a daughter than daughter-in-law. You have given your wisdom and strength and learning to Matthew. Matthew somehow felt he didn't measure up to his brother and sisters and other people. To me, he more

Chapter 35

than measured up. With God's guidance, you helped him go far beyond any earlier limitations.

"James, you possess a deep faith and a writing talent. You will tell our family stories and preserve what is important. Your teaching and writing will help make this a better world.

"John, you will carry on the faith and values of your grandfather, your namesake. As a minister of the gospel, you will bring many to the Lord. I'm proud of you. If the Lord gives me a long life, I'd like nothing better than to see you as a minister. I want you to preach at my funeral.

"Margaret, like your mother, you are a teacher and will be a mother. You will carry on the family way of your parents and grandparents. And Joe is as much an Anderson as any Anderson family member.

"Carol, I thank the Lord for the way you have come back to your family and faith. I am proud of way you are working at the courthouse and making a life for yourself and your son.

"Michael, you are not so little anymore. You are my youngest grandchild, and you have the personality of John or Johnie. I pray that you will follow in that strength and way.

"Mary, my youngest, you came at a turbulent time in my life. So much was out of control at that time. I am sorry that during your early years I wasn't the kind of mother I should have been. Even so, you developed a sweetness, though you also had much of Victoria's forcefulness. You have weathered the storm of TB and come out of it a stronger woman. Ed, you are indeed a strong one; yet you have a warm heart beneath that tough exterior. I must say how much it meant to me to have you close by all those years. I miss you now that you live in California, yet I pray that you will prosper and find happiness.

"Beth, or Elizabeth, my namesake, I know that you will make a fine teacher. I pray for you as you begin your first teaching job this fall. Jake, don't ever forget the family you come from. We need strong men in the military. Irene, I realize you are following in the footsteps of your older sister. I remember each of you as children. Please remember you are in the prayers of your grandmother. May you carry forward the faith, strength, and determination of your parents.

"I don't know exactly how to close my thoughts. I pray that somehow the love of Christ my Savior will flow through me. I love you all so dearly, and I want God's best for each of you. God is good, and God loves you. I bless you all now with my love, but more importantly with God's love."

Beyond the Darkness

James put down his pen and read aloud to his grandmother what he had written. He looked into her face and said, "Your thoughts are beautiful. Your children, grandchildren, and great-grandchildren will rise up to call you blessed."

"Thank you, James. You wrote down my thoughts just right." She looked up at the clock. "And now it's time for me to make dinner."

James watched as Grandma brought out some meatballs, potatoes, and peas to warm up. She was a frail version of the woman he had known as a child; her steps were slower and less certain. Yet her eyes had a brightness that age had not dimmed. He wanted these moments to last forever in his mind and in his writing.

Matthew sat quietly on the front porch that evening. He put down the *Daily Journal* and looked east toward the hills. He couldn't help thinking of what lay beyond those hills for the people he loved. The darkness of the past years had vanished; hope and light replaced the hard times.

"You miss the kids, don't you?" asked Ellen as she sat down next to her husband.

"Ever since James was small, I knew he would leave for the city. But it was hard to see Johnie go. I always thought he would be the one to take over the farm. I knew the girls would leave to start their own families. I'm thankful we still have Michael with us."

"We've had our chance to be part of their lives—to love them, to help mold their characters."

Matthew thought a moment. "I owe so much to you."

"God meant for families to have a father and mother. We both have our roles. And I could not ask for a more wonderful husband and father."

Matthew reached over and clasped Ellen's hands. "I love you."

A gentle breeze blew across the front lawn. Shadows deepened. The soothing calm of an autumn evening brought peace to Matthew and Ellen.

Epilogue

A cold breeze scattered the dry oak leaves across the driveway that late September evening. After checking the cattle, Matthew walked toward home. He loved the solitude of an evening walk.

His mind returned to a cold December evening when the first tragedies of war shattered the peacefulness of the Oak Ridge community. Miraculously, all the men from the Oak Ridge area had returned home. The petitions of those women prayer warriors had been answered.

As Matthew looked at the darkness around him, he remembered the words, "Go out into the darkness and put your hand into the hand of God. That shall be to you better than light and safer than any known way."

He looked above as the stars became visible, one by one. A verse from the Bible filled his mind: "The heavens declare the glory of God; and the firmament showeth his handiwork." Matthew surveyed the heavens and then looked out at the darkness around. He turned from the darkness and looked toward his home, where a bright yellow light beckoned. The creation around caused him to think of the creation story from Genesis. God had looked out on that creation and said, "It is good. It is very good."

The light of the moon began to diminish the darkness. Matthew looked at his field, recently plowed, and Ellen's garden with flowers still blooming. He thought of Ellen and their children. They all would face darkness and challenges in the future, but God was there.

Beyond the Darkness

"Dear Lord," he said aloud, "You have saved me and given me a good life. You are alive in all creation. And You are working in my life and in the lives of those I love."

He looked above and around, and finally at the moonlight glistening across the lawn.

To order additional copies of this book call:
1-877-421-READ (7323)
or please visit our Web site at
www.pleasantwordbooks.com

If you enjoyed this quality custom-published book,
drop by our Web site for more books and information.

www.winepressgroup.com
"Your partner in custom publishing."

NORMANDALE COMMUNITY COLLEGE
LIBRARY
9700 FRANCE AVENUE SOUTH
BLOOMINGTON, MN 55431-4399